D0871322

HOME

for

ERRING

and

OUTCAST

GIRLS

ALSO BY JULIE KIBLER:

Calling Me Home

HOME

for

ERRING

and

OUTCAST
GIRLS

·≫[A Novel]≪·

JULIE KIBLER

WITHDRAWN

 CROWN
NEW YORK

Copyright © 2019 by Julie Kibler

All rights reserved.
Published in the United States by Crown, an imprint of Random House, a division of Penguin Random House LLC, New York.
crownpublishing.com

CROWN and the Crown colophon are registered trademarks of Penguin Random House LLC.

Library of Congress Cataloging-in-Publication Data is available upon request.

ISBN 978-0-451-49933-2
Ebook ISBN 978-0-451-49935-6

Printed in the United States of America

Jacket design by Alane Gianetti
Jacket photograph by Ildiko Neer/Arcangel
Jacket texture by Yurlick/Shutterstock

10 9 8 7 6 5 4 3 2 1

First Edition

For Heather, Kelly, Emilie, Kristen, Jacinda, and Katherine,
all daughters of my heart, whether home to stay or just passing through,

and in memory of
my cousin, Ann Lacy Ellison, reader extraordinaire, whose family has
loved many generations of erring and outcast girls.

"They fell down and there was none to help."

PSALM 107:12

Berachah Industrial Home
ARLINGTON, TEXAS
JULY 25, 1933

Even when Mattie's great big dreams had troubled Lizzie, she'd envied her something fierce, for Lizzie came from nightmares, too fearful to dream. But if the Lord gave, and the Lord took away, how did he choose? The choosing he'd done between them, she didn't envy, or even understand.

Their own choices were hard enough.

Still, it was plain that Mattie had found what she needed. In her own way, she'd made good. And even if Lizzie stumbled now and again, she'd come to be her most improbable self in this place. She feared the day she'd need to leave. Soon, she reckoned. They couldn't keep the Home going much longer—an unexpected shame.

But things changed. Girls had more choices now. Maybe more chances.

The Homecoming picture wouldn't be the same this year. Yesterday, Lizzie had gazed at that one in the parlor again—the first-year girls, all in matching white dresses, their hair silky like ribbon, scraped up into pretty buns. They were the picture of innocence.

Well. They were something anyway.

It had taken an act of the Almighty to get them before that camera, and this year, another. The girls were nearly thirty years older now, but when they were Home to see their sisters, no matter where they'd been or what they'd witnessed, they wore their finest dresses and smiled.

Lizzie's tears nearly choked her to think of the last few weeks. How had Mattie stood it as long as she had? Why hadn't she called? She'd promised she would.

They would have said, "Come Home." They'd said it to nearly any girl who entered the place—any time, any reason, arms open wide.

She hoped it wasn't pride that kept Mattie away. . . .

But now was Lizzie's time to make good. Docie was tapping at her door and whispering through the crack. Brother JT wanted them in their places on the lawn.

Lizzie didn't know how she'd do what she'd said she would, even with the promise between them. But she'd do anything for Mattie. Of course she would. Mattie was the sister of her heart and soul, a mirror that reflected everything Lizzie wanted but could not ever choose.

And Lizzie would see Mattie soon enough.

Didn't she always?

PART ONE

CATE

Arlington, Texas
AUGUST 2017

I crawl out of a hotel bed while it's still dark to meet the movers at my new house near the university. My furniture and boxes, enough to fill a few rooms—but not enough to weigh me down—were the last loaded into the huge van that pulled up to my old place. First in, first out.

They place things where I want them and assemble my dining table and bed in thirty minutes. The house isn't much bigger than my apartment was, and with an extra bedroom and a garage, my belongings hardly dent the space. The van rumbles off to meet the next wanderers, and I take my first real breath since I gave strangers access to my possessions.

My running shoes are near the top of my suitcase. I ditch my flip-flops and tie the laces quickly. The first thing most people do when they complete a move is unpack the bedsheets or locate the coffee-maker. Not me. What convinces me I can start over again is reminding myself that when the time comes, I'll still know how to run.

I drop my key in my pocket and stretch only a moment before beginning a slow jog along a circle drive that borders the neighborhood of midcentury homes, with mine at the back. The air is thick with the heady scent of flowers, and lush, dense grass covers lawns instead of the usual pale stubble of late summer. After crisscrossing the country a few times, I worried that returning to Texas in August would be depressing. Everyone has a different theory about the record-breaking rain this year. I'm just happy to see color. The morning humidity, though, has me dripping before I even pick up my pace, and breathing takes extra effort.

At the edge of the neighborhood, I pause. A park is visible from my new backyard. It's the last quiet weekend of the year. Soon, it will teem with students playing intramurals, studying, or socializing, instead of the solitude I seek this morning. It's a good day to explore.

The park is small, and thick with trees. Only a few paved paths connect the busy roads and a parking lot, and it takes no time to run the length each way. On my second circuit, I cut through a playing field near the back edge to see how vulnerable my yard is. The campus police patrol the park and nearby neighborhoods, but now that I see how secluded the area is, I'm relieved my wood fence is in good repair. Fortunately, an even taller industrial fence makes it nearly impossible to access it from the field. My windows and yard aren't visible at all.

I slow my pace, cool down as much as the humidity allows, then walk, taking a long draw on my water bottle.

The sun is at the treetops now, and the sound of traffic is increasing, but still muffled by huge oaks. I walk toward the far corner of the park, curious what lies beyond in the dusky woods. I'm surprised to find another grassy area surrounded by a simple chain-link fence. It's a small cemetery, memorial stones scattered here and there—an odd discovery in this modern-day park. Perhaps early settlers buried their dead here, and the city graciously fenced the space instead of incorporating it into the park.

A historical marker catches my eye near the gate. I struggle to read it in the early-morning light. *Site of Berachah Home and Cemetery . . .*

> The Berachah Rescue Society was organized at Waco in 1894 by the Rev. J. T. Upchurch (b. 1870) for the protection of homeless girls and unwed mothers. Nine years later, he opened the Berachah Industrial Home at this site. Ten buildings were located here, including a print shop for publication of *The Purity Journal*. The cemetery, which contains more than eighty graves, was first used in 1904 . . .

Eighty graves? It hardly looks big enough. Before I can finish reading the plaque, though, my gaze is drawn to movement inside the fence. A young woman lies flat in the grass, raven hair splayed against the green. She gazes straight up beneath a tall, jagged tree near the edge of the graveyard. Gray and leafless, the tree appears to be dead—for years—perhaps struck by lightning. It's split nearly straight down the middle.

I don't want to startle her, but I worry, in spite of an intense desire to leave well enough alone. Is she ill? Injured? Or just resting?

Suddenly, though, she stretches to stand, retrieves an overstuffed bag, and exits the cemetery without a word or even a glance in my direction. I shiver as she disappears beyond the dark canopy of trees.

I'm not superstitious. I don't believe any place or person is haunted by anything but the past. But suddenly, that old saying about a ghost walking over a grave crosses my mind.

And suddenly, I can't wait to get home.

LIZZIE BATES

Tyler, Texas
FALL 1904

The two ladies dressed all in white hovered over where Lizzie and Docie lay huddled in a fetid pile of rags, and she thought it was angels come, finally, to take them away up to heaven. Her heart quickened. She'd figured on the Lord forgetting her and her girl—or maybe just turning his back.

Keys clinked as the jail keeper unlocked his steel cage, shoved into a corner of the room, with rusting shelves for bunks in each half. They were alone in it but for a man sleeping off drink on the other side. The angels bent inside to whisper over her and Docie. Now she feared they'd take her girl but leave her to die alone and suffer eternal hell. She wouldn't have blamed the Lord for thinking to do it that way, for Docie was surely not liable for her mother's sins. Even if Lizzie was not worthy, her Docie was innocence itself, though her tiny body was riddled with the same sick. The child slept at her teat whenever they were together, but Lizzie couldn't bear to think what might have befallen Docie when she couldn't watch her every minute of the day and night. Either way, Lizzie was to blame. She had let her down so many ways.

No more. She wouldn't let anyone, heavenly or not, snatch her girl without a struggle. She sat as high as the metal above her head allowed and wrapped her arms around Docie. The little girl flirted with waking, but her exhaustion was plain, and she slumped against her mother, cheeks fever red and dark lashes scarcely visible against the purple smudges beneath her eyes. Docie could not fight; it was up to her mother to see that they remained together.

But the angel ladies didn't move to take Docie. They only stooped to look, speaking hushed words Lizzie couldn't plainly make out. The swirling in her head and burning in her throat made it too hard to ask their intentions. Perhaps she had not moved to gather Docie closer after all. Perhaps she had simply wished it. Or, perhaps Docie was already close, as she should be.

Lizzie caught scraps of what they said, and the jailer's voice rose as he described their history and condition. How they both suffered from a foul disease. How Lizzie had earned her keep out at the county farm lately, cooking for the Negro inmates. How the farm superintendent had taken her into his own shack to live in sin, feeding her heroin to subdue her, and then passed her to the chain gang boss when he tired of her. How she'd taken sick, and it crippled her so badly she couldn't stand. And finally, how they'd sent her and Docie to the jail, no regard for whether they lived or died.

Her skin crawled. Damn the farm boss. While many around her had been hooked on dope for years, she'd managed to keep off it until he'd sensed her desperation. Then she took it gladly.

But she hadn't needed subduing, not like a wild animal.

She'd needed to forget.

Lizzie had lived hand-to-mouth as long as the jailer had known of her, a decade or more, drifting in and out of town, lately only with her girl, but for years with her people—a no-good cracker and his half-Injun wife. Docie, a wispy towhead with skin so milky the blue showed through, had piercing, near-black eyes from Choctaw still running in those veins, same as her ma and granny.

Lizzie marveled at all the jailer knew from his tenure of locking her up when she had nowhere else to go. One thing they were all sure of: She and Docie weren't long for this world. One or both would slip away soon, with or without angels to guide them. To hear him say it plain was a comfort. She was weary of fighting for a place for her and Docie on this earth.

The women gasped at the jail keeper's speech. Had they come only to eye her condition? Society ladies who wanted to witness the scum at the bottom to comfort themselves? Then they could return to their pillowy houses to preach the perils of drink and heroin and impurity. She shrugged. If she could be a warning, she reckoned her life had some sliver of purpose after all.

She cowered when one lady inched closer to kneel near the pile of shredded bedding.

"You poor dear. We're from the King's Daughters. The jailer's wife asked if we'd take you and your little one to a place we know—a wonderful new home for young women where you could find healing and comfort, Lord willing."

Now Lizzie grinned. Maybe, instead, the lady was a haint! Who'd suggest such a thing?

But the woman stretched her ungloved hand to touch Lizzie's shoulder, and Lizzie felt it, warm and firm, and next, the back of Docie's head, unafraid of the pus-filled sores on their skin or what clouded Lizzie's vision until it was near impossible to make out the woman's features.

Tears cut a path through the crusted grime on her cheeks. She nodded, then fell into a stupor, blissfully free of nightmares.

Her next awareness was of struggling in a darkened room, of sweating and screeching and scratching her skin until it bled.

Vomiting until her throat burned raw.

Hissing and kicking at demons who played at being humans who claimed to be for her, when she knew they wanted to pierce her with knives and prod every secret place of her body.

Throwing herself off the cliff where she slept and then grasping and tearing at the bed until they took it away, leaving her to kick at the floor and walls with fingers and toes that wept blood until they were so scabbed they couldn't.

She wanted her Docie. She wanted her dope. She got neither.

It went on and on, with no difference between morning or night, between one day or another, until finally, she sank into a dark hole, absent the energy or desire to reject what kept her alive, for good or evil. She had nothing left. Nothing . . .

Then, slowly, she became aware of a soft surface beneath her shoulders and hips as she drifted—nearly so soft as the shape of Docie's still-feverish body, finally pressed against Lizzie's side.

Later, more awake, she saw she was raised high again, above the floor of a dimly lit room, and she reckoned she lay in a bed with springs and a ticked mattress—to her recollection, the first real bed she'd ever slept on in all of her nineteen years. She'd generally passed her nights on pallets over dirt floors—at best, a rope cot, and once, the back of a wagon after birthing Docie. Often, in fact, she had no more than the ground itself, inside or out. Beds were for better folk. Beneath her now, this real one felt strangely unstable, jigging up and down and back and forth at the slightest movement, so she kept still, afraid she'd roll off one side or knock her girl off the other. She hadn't the strength to catch either of them.

As the fog cleared her brain, she registered a woman pressing crockery filled with rich broth or cool water to her blistered lips, or cleaning her face and hands with a cloth warmed in a basin next to the bed. At another point, she woke in a panic to realize Docie was gone again, and she screamed hoarsely until someone rushed to carry her daughter to her from a small, nearby cot.

She struggled to recall how they'd gotten there. Had they walked? She was short, but thick, and even in her poorly state she would not be easily carried. How many nights had they passed in this place? She couldn't even guess.

The next time she woke, they got her and Docie up, first settling Docie in a small chair with a rail at her waist, then back to the bed to help Lizzie shift her legs, one by one and dragging like logs from under the bedclothes until her feet rested on the floor. She'd never felt a floor finished so smooth. She rubbed her toes against it, eyeing the fineness of everything. The small room was papered in cabbage roses, and drapes softened the tall windows. The bedclothes were snowy, except where they were rumpled and grimy from their skin. A fancy-stitched coverlet draped the foot of the shiny bedstead. If she hadn't been gripping the edge of the bed, lightheaded from being flat for days, she'd have pinched her arms to check she wasn't dreaming.

The woman peered close, silver spectacles perched on her nose, hair thin at the part, and too young for so much gray. "How do you feel, dear?"

Breathing no longer felt so harsh or stole her voice, so Lizzie opened her mouth, though she doubted sensible words would come. "Feel right fine." It was garbled, as if her mouth were stuffed with stones. She'd never been quick, but this was worse. It was also not quite true.

"Can you stand?" The woman grasped her hands. Lizzie's limbs quivered like scrawny branches in a storm, and she stood a spell until her legs steadied. She took cautious steps as the woman led her to a sturdy chair by the hearth. Embers glowed from a fire set that morning when the early winter sun rose, its rays too weak to take the chill off the room. She was used to the cold, having never lived where wood was plentiful for cooking—much less for waking. The extravagance plain puzzled her. She could see it for her child, maybe. But for her too?

Docie opened her mouth like a baby bird as another woman, young and rosy-cheeked, scooped mush in with a child-sized spoon. She dabbed Docie's face with a towel, no concern for dirtying the bright cloth, and clapped her hands as Docie swallowed. "Look at you, hungry girl!"

Lizzie's face burned with shame. Those playful words spoke truth. They'd verged on starving for most of her girl's life. Food was even harder to come by than wood, which they could sometimes gather for free where it fell dead from the trees. Food was earned another way— trading what was never used up. *Used up* was how she felt.

The bespectacled woman placed a tray before her with steaming porridge, toasted bread, and warm milk. "Can you eat? You're improved this morning. We thought we'd lost you two nights back. God is good!"

Lizzie eased pieces of milk-soaked toast down her throat—until her innards cramped. She feared she might not make the pot. The woman led her quickly to help her squat.

"You'll struggle a while to keep a meal in you. Disease and coming off heroin is hard on the bowels. It'll take time." The woman spoke so matter-of-fact, even dressed fine like a genteel lady. In the worst places, folks were ashamed to admit to their business, doing it in secret as if they hadn't.

This was all too easy. Perhaps she *had* died. Or maybe, it occurred to her, she'd been taken by one of the good whorehouses, with their rumored luxuries and comforts. But she was too worn for that. . . .

"Miss," she croaked, tucked under her warm covers again. "What's this place? We can't pay. And I don't know when I'll be—"

The woman interrupted. "For the time being, you needn't worry about anything but reclaiming your health. You'll be plenty busy later. I'm Susie Singletary, and you may call me Sister Susie. This is the Berachah Industrial Home for the Redemption of Erring Girls. Do you remember agreeing to come when you and your daughter were in the Tyler jail? Perhaps not. You were nearly delirious. But we're thrilled you've joined us."

Lizzie vaguely recalled saying she'd go with those ladies in white, but not that foreign-sounding word. And what was meant by *erring* and *industrial*? By *redemption*, most of all?

They'd surely confused her and Docie for another lady and child. They could not mean to waste such pure goodness on the likes of a girl who paid for food and shelter on her back, letting men have their way nearly longer than she could recall. She knew her place.

Nothing was hers to keep.

Lizzie's one wish, though, going on four years, was something different for her daughter. If they turned Lizzie back out in the streets, they'd likely care for Docie better than she ever could.

But then she gazed at Docie, playing pat-a-cake with the younger woman and giggling. Lizzie tried to imagine leaving her here, and her stomach cramped again, just with the pain of thinking it. As if Docie read her mind, she threw her head round and wailed, reaching with spindly arms. "Mama! Mama!"

No. She'd never leave her. Never again. She couldn't mess up this chance.

But still, her heart pounded. "When I get better, you going to make me leave? I won't let you keep her," she said, jerking her head toward Docie. "She's mine. You can't have her." She sat up again, as if to go to Docie, though she was still so weak, she gasped for breath.

"Goodness, no," the woman exclaimed, looking at Lizzie with surprise—nearly disbelief. "We won't take her from you. We don't do that here. God gave you this child. Even if the circumstances weren't ideal, you're the best mother for her."

Lizzie gaped. She'd never been called the best at anything, and surely not at mothering. "You swear to God? Because we'll leave now if you've a mind to take her away. She ain't going with anybody but me." She tried to swing a leg over the side of the bed on her own strength.

"I won't swear," Sister Susie said. "The Lord doesn't want us to. But I *do* promise."

Could she trust this woman? Trusting wasn't safe. But what else was she to do, when she could hardly get herself out of the bed, even with her claims. Slowly, Lizzie nodded. "All right, then. I'm Elizabeth Bates . . . Lizzie. Howdy do. This here's Docia May, but I call her Docie."

Sister Susie smiled warmly, chuckling, and reached to shake Lizzie's outstretched hand.

When she thought to ask for her snuff, the woman said they didn't allow it. Long before the dope, Lizzie had taken a whole jar of the fine tobacco a week, finding ways even if she couldn't pay. Some days, the little pick-me-up from spooning a pinch behind her lip was what kept her going. All her life, she'd seen her ma take her snuff as regular as coffee. Every woman she knew used it, and she'd never imagined folks might frown on it.

After coming off the dope during the worst of her illness, she wanted to believe she could make do without either now, but her skin itched constantly, as if ants bit her. Even when sidetracked, she craved a pinch of snuff at the least. But she thought better of asking again.

Eventually, she and Docie ventured to the wide porch that ran clear around the house on the second level, same as on the first. The children grinned up at them, eager to play, but Docie hardly knew what to make of the creatures running and playing at a distance. She couldn't do much beyond stare from her mother's lap anyway. The last of the sickness made her eyes burn and blur, and walking was hard from lying in bed for days. Fussy or sluggish by turn, she wanted little more than her mother. Lizzie wanted her close, too, though her own bones ached as she carried Docie to a settee on the porch.

Along with the middle-aged matron, Sister Susie, who cared for her and Docie the most, she'd learned several young women lived in the house, some with infants or children. Brother JT Upchurch, the preacher man who'd built the Home a year ago, lived near the grounds and was in and out of his first-floor study, sometimes accompanied by his wife or the secretary who wrote the newsletter. Sister Susie had shown Lizzie one, and she'd paged through, though she couldn't read the words. Her mother had only taught her counting coins for small goods or train fare, and even then, she mostly held out a hand with her coins on it, trusting the merchant to take his due without cheating her—or trusting a john to place his there, the same.

Sister Susie had said she and Docie could attend Bible reading and prayers when they could no longer pass on their sickness, but she reckoned the other girls would poke fun at her for being stupid, no different from her own people when she'd attempted things and failed so soundly. She'd always hoped Docie would learn her letters. Now maybe she'd have the chance.

Each girl rotated through the Home's industries, learning a skill until she could perform it well, increasing her chances for making a living without having to resort to indecent acts to feed, clothe, and house herself and any children she had. Some took to specific skills and kept at them. One girl had worked for a large printing outfit before, and after birthing her baby in the Home, she helped Mr. Ferry, who printed things on a donated press. Mabel typeset page upon page with few errors. The girls took pride in their work, Sister Susie said, in spite of humbling circumstances.

But what if they couldn't find Lizzie a skill to earn her keep? The first and only thing she'd prided herself on was soothing Docie, holding her and rocking her gently. Even so, she hadn't always done a good job mothering. It haunted her. Who'd trust her with another woman's child if they knew what she'd done?

There seemed no hurry to put her to work, though. She'd keep quiet while they got their health back and care for Docie properly now. They'd see what she could do. She held on to Sister Susie's words, repeating them every morning before she even left the bed—

"I am the best mother for Docie."

Everything she did, from here on out, was all for Docie's sake.

CATE

Arlington, Texas
2017

After I've been at my new job a few weeks, Laurel Medina walks through the doors to University Collections and stands there like a lost child. I feel as if I know her—her eyes, her hair, and maybe even how she winds a long dark strand of it around her finger while her other hand taps a nervous rhythm against her backpack strap—but I'm positive we've never met.

I'm the person, though, who recognizes faces I saw ten years ago in a grocery store—only a slight exaggeration—and familiar voices haunt me. Easily recalling faces and voices is a gift when it's convenient, and a curse when I want to be anonymous.

I like being anonymous. It makes life easier—and more complicated all at once.

"Laurel?" I say, emerging from where I'm half hidden behind a rolling shelf, reviewing her résumé. She nods and smiles nervously, all while her guarded brown eyes seem to note every detail. She's dressed in worn but clean skinny jeans, and I spy tape wrapped around one of the temples of her glasses.

I remember being a poor college student.

"I'm Cate Sutton, the assistant librarian." I reach to shake her hand, and she accepts it tentatively. "Have a seat." I point toward a round table and sit at an angle to her, carefully tucking my full skirt beneath me. I feel exposed here, in full view of a sunny atrium where meetings are held or students study, just beyond our glass entrance doors. But it's the best place for an interview. I can keep an eye on the front desk as I chat with work-study candidates.

I explain what we do, though in truth, I'm still wrapping my brain around it myself. My previous positions were general reference, in public libraries or junior colleges, but I've always wanted to work with archives. This is an exciting change—so exciting I've bought a house in spite of my usual reservations.

University Collections is on the top floor, set apart from general foot traffic and unlike anywhere else in the main library. Dark paneling. Dim lights. Spotless surfaces, absent the organic aromas that permeate the rest of the building—coffee, sandwiches, sweat. And usually silent except for keyboard clicks from the front desk and a subtle hum when the doors open and close. The austerity can be unnerving unless you're accustomed to it. I'm not surprised students are baffled when they enter. They find us by accident—or more often, seeking something a professor insists can only be found here instead of on the Internet. We're a museum of sorts, filled with rare and even one-of-a-kind treasures the university has accumulated, many related to its own history, and others purchased or acquired through donations—often when people die. Donations are hit-and-miss. Sometimes we can't use things. We pass them on or dispose of them appropriately.

But sometimes, I've learned, our acquisitions change lives.

I ask Laurel if it's her first year in college. She gives a noncommittal shrug. "I took college-level classes in high school, but I'm technically a freshman."

"What's your major?"

"I'm . . . not sure yet," she says, as though she feels guilty—maybe even stupid.

I rush to reassure her. I know what it's like to be new at something. "It's okay. You'll figure it out. What are you enjoying so far?"

Laurel tilts her head to study the ceiling. "My archaeology class is interesting, but I'm not sure I could make a career out of it and eat too."

She's clever. But she's not off the hook. "I have a master's in library science, but my bachelor's degree is history. Don't judge so-called useless degrees too quickly. If you're passionate about something, you can nearly always make it pay. I'm not rich, but I love what I do and have what I need."

After I finish my speech, I suspect my soapbox is parked a little too close. I mentally back up. "What do you like about archaeology?"

She hesitates. I wonder if she even knows. But suddenly she talks. "Maybe that it's about the past? That there isn't anything you can do about it. It feels . . . finished. Does that sound weird?" Her cheeks flush, and she looks down, allowing her bangs to hide her eyes.

"No. That sounds a lot like history, actually. The funny thing is, both history and archaeology have a great capacity for change—if new information comes to light, it can transform what we know about what or why things happened."

Laurel stills, as if she can't decide whether the concept is good or bad, and her mind goes elsewhere. But then she shakes herself so slightly I almost miss it.

"That's why archives are important." I point to our surroundings. "We save things that might otherwise disappear. Sometimes, something small and forgotten is exactly what we need to see a bigger picture. By the way, the job's yours if you want it."

Laurel's eyes narrow at my quick offer. She's a little zipped up, and more than a little unsure of herself. But I like her. And I can't help feeling, still, as if I already know her. As if I already trust her.

After only a few shifts, my instincts prove correct. Laurel takes a strong interest in what we do. Her initiative and curiosity are miles beyond those of the other students we've hired, who mostly want paychecks—and preferably, jobs where they can text or scroll social media between duties.

Still, I haven't shown Laurel the Berachah Home Collection or even mentioned it. One day, though, after I've placed one of the boxes back on the cart to be returned to the stacks, she asks, "How do you pronounce this?" She points to the label on the small carton. The entire collection would fit inside a carry-on suitcase. Maybe even in Laurel's backpack, considering how much she manages to cram inside the thing.

I shrug. "However you like, really. Nobody seems to agree. But I tend to think of our former president. *Barack-uh.*"

She doesn't laugh, even when I do. "What is the . . . Berachah Home?"

I hesitate. My boss showed me the collection after I asked her about the cemetery. I've taken oddly personal ownership of it. I almost want to keep the collection to myself, as though if I share, my pleasure in exploring the ledgers and the journals and the photographs might be ruined. But Laurel's curious and careful expression hints that maybe, just maybe, she'll appreciate the subject—and the materials—the same way I have.

It's a slow day. Her regular tasks are finished, and she's hardly had a chance to dig around in the collections since we hired her. The Berachah Home is not a terrible place to start. I can already answer nearly any question she has.

Except the ones that keep me searching incessantly, beyond the collection itself . . .

"Come with me," I say, wheeling the cart around a glass-fronted display case that currently houses a set of black-and-white photos of professional wrestlers. I seat her in the dimly lit area beyond the partition.

I take a deep breath. "The Berachah Industrial Home was a religious home for women and girls who'd been thrown out for getting pregnant before they were married, or who were on the streets for other reasons—prostitution, drug addiction, and so on. They were considered 'fallen women.'" I make finger quotes around the words. "The couple who started the Home thought they deserved second chances. The pregnant ones had to agree to remain there, along with their babies, for at least one year, which was unusual back then. Usually, homes for unwed mothers made them give their babies up. This one was pretty revolutionary for its time—though some now would disagree with their motives."

I open a box from the collection, remove a folder with typed pages, and point to the simple index at the front that lists what the boxes contain. "Here's the finder. This collection is small, but deep. It could take weeks, months even, to wrap your mind around everything it contains once you get started. So much good stuff."

Now I struggle to contain my enthusiasm. I tell myself to slow down. To pace myself. "Go ahead and explore. If you'll note any obvious inconsistencies between the documents and the finder—dates and so on—or things that aren't filed where they're supposed to be, we can keep you on the clock." I half wink. Research universities develop a ton of knowledge through their students. I'm not worried about whether it's in the budget.

"Open one box at a time, and when you get to the photos, you'll need to wear gloves." I point to a pristine pair I've placed on the table. They remind me of the ones I wore for handbell choir back in high school, made of pure, white cotton to keep grime and oily skin from marring the shining surfaces. These make me oddly nostalgic, or sad, depending on the day.

Laurel seems intimidated now. *Good*, I think. As long as she isn't completely afraid to dig in, she'll take care. Reverence is critical when working with archival objects.

But I'm not ready to leave her alone with this just yet, and our other student is working the desk. "I'll be tackling paperwork over here in case you have any questions."

Laurel hesitates, and I point to the finder again. "Start there. Then open box one."

She begins to read. Two hours later, she's still there, immersed in one of the journals. I point out it's past her quitting time, and she asks if she can stay. There's no reason to send her away. The collections are available to anyone, anytime. But it's a little unnerving that she's fallen in as hard as I did when I opened these boxes only a few weeks ago.

By the time we close at five thirty, Laurel seems numb. Or far away. It's hard to tell the difference. Her backpack drags at her shoulders as she waits for the elevator, and once again, she's that lost girl who came in the day of her interview.

I sigh. Letting her look at the Berachah collection could have been a mistake.

As I gather my things to leave, I can't stop thinking about the girls from the Berachah Home either. It's Friday, and my weekend is a blank slate. I have nowhere to be and nowhere to go. It's been weeks since I felt the urge to run, but I keep cross-trainers in my car for emergencies, and they're handy for other things now and then. So I stop by my car and change out of my work shoes with their absurdly high heels—absurd, but oh, how I love them; they make me feel powerful and in control. Then I cross the busy main street to the tree-filled park at the edge of campus, trudging across the arched wooden bridge I now know becomes treacherous if it's the least bit damp, then up the barely noticeable dirt path strewn with leaves and the uneven steps created by the exposed roots of century-old trees, farther and farther away from rushing traffic and exhaust.

The nearer I get to my destination, the more the present world fades, and relief floods my body as I inhale the scent of earth, leaves, quiet peace, easing the tension I hide like a spool of thread frayed somewhere in the middle. Here, if the thread snaps, the witnesses are silent and full of grace.

Even after that somewhat spooky first visit to the cemetery, I've returned again and again, often like this, after a long day at work. Today, freshly mowed grass softly carpets the ground, inside and outside the fence. Its bittersweet aroma lingers. Thanks to photos in the collection, I can now picture the structures that embraced the graveyard a century ago. A white, two-story building with wraparound porches that housed the first girls. A newer, larger dormitory constructed of beige brick, and a homey white cottage for the workers. A windmill. A water tower. Small buildings for various industries—the printing office, the laundry. The white frame tabernacle with a peaked roof that held a thousand or more for community rallies and Camp Meetings. Tucked away, the old barn. And closest to the graves, between the fence and the creek that trickles mere yards beyond, a tiny stone chapel with an arched doorway, a place for solitary prayer. Though hints of the foundation remain, this last existing structure was finally demolished in the 1990s because beer cans and graffiti turned it into an eyesore and, likely, a liability. I'm sad I missed it.

The Berachah Home has quickly become my main research interest. Most of our archives are Texas-themed, with many specific to our
area—in this case, right under our nose. The university purchased the
property in the 1960s, and in the eighties, the founders' descendants
donated the bulk of the memorabilia.

It's not my job to become an expert on one collection among so
many, but that hasn't stopped me from trying. I've sifted through gingerly, sorting, noting, and charting on a growing stack of paper—a
figurative archaeological dig, as Laurel might realize by this point in
her semester. But there are questions I can't answer yet. They keep
me awake, often, deep into the night. Censuses and genealogies and
archived newspaper websites offer clues, but much is unanswered. I've
wished desperately I could take the collection home, but it's against
the rules. If I could immerse myself all weekend, I would. Maybe I'd
discover details I've missed—more pieces to this puzzle. Having only
fragments of time to learn everything frustrates me.

I want to know what happened to my girls.

That's how I think of them already—*my* girls. My favorites, if it's
possible to have favorites among the dead. Two women I've come to
regard as having souls that mirrored each other in spite of vastly different beginnings—and likely, their endings too. Two women I've
come to adore as if I've known them forever, though I've never met
them and by now, they've both been gone for decades.

I enter the simple gate, pass the now-familiar historical marker,
a memorial to the founder, and the few other sculpted memorials
or headstones, so weather-beaten their inscriptions are difficult to
decipher—except now, after poring over the records, I can.

In Memory of Susie Singletary . . . The beloved matron for so many
years.

Pearl Simmons, Missionary for Berachah, Buried in India . . . And a
prostitute before she found the Home.

Dorothy Myrtle Carter, Safe with God forever . . . *Erected by the
Make-Good Club* . . .

The phrase *Make-Good Club* practically jumped off the page the day I came across it in one of the *Purity Journals*—the newsletters published nearly every month the Home was in existence. Dorothy Carter started the club to help the girls stay accountable for their actions after they were rescued by the Home. *There*, I thought. One small mystery neatly solved.

Well, not so neatly once I learned the rest: When Dorothy died, she left a little girl behind.

I walk the rows of graves, weaving my way from beginning to end. I pronounce each name as I pass, pausing to study every stone, the majority no bigger than a shoebox lid, flat against the ground. One of the first marks the grave of the founder's sister. Annie and JT had been poor and desperate, too, growing up with a widowed mother in Waco. After JT and his wife moved to Arlington, Annie carried on the work in Waco, but they brought her here for burial.

Carline . . . Elsie . . . Homer . . .

After several visits, I think I know what each visible headstone reads, but sometimes, I'm surprised. Some names, I recognize now from the *Journals*. Others I don't. I wonder why they're here, how they died. Mostly, to whom they belonged. One, especially, stops me a bit longer every single time. I can tell the stone read *Beatrice* originally, but something—the weather? Or something human?—has flattened certain letters until the stone appears, at first glance, to read *Be True*. Be true to what? To whom?

Another has no legible letters at all. But someone was buried there.

Interspersed between the named ones are some I can hardly stand to read aloud: *Infant no. 17 . . . Infant no. 8 . . . Twins no. 6 . . .* Painful reminders that many of the graves, if not most, are for children. Babies.

Finally, I approach a memorial in the corner, near the massive stump of what once must have been the majestic guardian of the cemetery. Other trees grow inside the fence, including several coppiced oaks with double or triple trunks, but this stump is closest to the graves.

Lined and gnarled, he's a wise old guy who, before he was cut down, overlooked the only memorial here that hints at the support of a partner—one man, besides the founder, who was honorable enough to claim an eternal tie in this sacred space to one of the thousands of ruined women who passed through the Home's gates, broken and weary; deserted or addicted; carrying a child, the scars of one, or the promise of one that never came to be.

I kneel and lean against the comforting old stump, especially thankful now that I changed shoes, and gaze at the rose granite memorial. This one fascinates me most. It stands out, being substantial and one of the newest in the enclosure—if nearly a century old could be considered new. The inscription is fascinating. Heartbreaking. What it represents feels nearly tangible, almost personal, more than the simple names on the others, even with the mysteries embedded in their surfaces. I need to know what happened to this woman. She has taken hold of my heart.

I shake myself. I'm dwelling too much. Again. When my therapist discontinued our sessions several months ago, right before I accepted my new job and prepared to move, she said it was time I dealt with real people and real situations—instead of the dead people I learn about at work, who can't hurt me, who can't break my heart without my permission.

I felt unconvinced then, and I'm unconvinced now. Even though I saw her once a week for a year, she still didn't grasp my internal state, how I barely keep things together sometimes.

How I don't like to get involved.

Except that's a flat-out lie. I love to get involved. I long for and crave involvement.

And it always backfires.

I don't know. Maybe it *has* been long enough now since I stumbled blindly into a relationship without tools to handle the inevitable twists and turns flung at its fragile bond.

Maybe I'm fixed.

The words on the memorial recede into the dusk beneath the ancient trees that surround the cemetery like quiet sentries. And like the words, my optimism retreats too. My eyes fill with the sadness that overflows my heart. The truth is I feel more alone as each day fades into night.

But then I glance toward the fence, where a small figure leans against the chain links, chin on the rail, an overstuffed backpack on the ground beside her. Even at a distance, I know Laurel, my student worker, and now I understand why I recognized her before, as well as her urgency and fascination with the boxes.

She was the girl lying in the grass beneath the jagged tree when I found the cemetery.

That tree isn't comforting—not like my peaceful companion. Its slightly feminine austerity seems a dark reminder of the girls who didn't "make good"—those who couldn't live with the rules and ran away, sometimes straight into the arms of death; or those in need who never found the Home; or, worst of all, those turned away, even in their desperation.

My silent tears are drying on my cheeks, and I long to wipe away their salty sting. But I don't. I don't move at all. It seems inappropriate for Laurel to find me in this vulnerable state.

The tears surprise me every time. I like to pretend they're a response to this small, fenced space. But they wouldn't fall so freely without a personal catalyst beyond them. I often visit the cemetery when I'm bursting with the longing for something I can't have.

Home.

It's possible to long for home, even when you don't have one. I'm an expert.

Situations that require intimacy of any kind, however, topple the careful balance I've worked so hard to create. I accepted it years ago. And despite my therapist's confidence, it remains painfully obvious when I attempt to engage on anything more than a surface level.

I'm a grown woman. I'm a professional. I manage my life well.

But I'm broken. People sense it, and when they do, they walk away. Me? I run.

MATTIE B. CORDER

Fort Worth, Texas
DECEMBER 1904

A month after Mattie Corder's twenty-third birthday, she settled her debt on the room she and Cap had called home for four weeks. She gazed at the stained ceiling while a stranger who stank of tobacco spittle where it had trickled through his whiskers poked and pulled, grunted and groaned, and finally collapsed against her chest. No different than being with Charley, she told herself. If she didn't watch, she could bear it.

But that wasn't so, she knew, not even with her eyes closed tight. Nothing about this compared with what she'd done nearly three years earlier, at the cost of her first job and her home. Despite what her sisters or anyone thought, Charley's touch had seemed sacred. But neither true love nor Mattie's turning up pregnant had kept him from chasing a rumor that money flowed like honey from the molybdenum mines in Colorado—or inspired him to send a single letter since.

Last month, she'd lost another job because pride and impulse got in the way of common sense. Today, after many inquiries at businesses who assessed her situation—an unwed woman with a small child to tend and no family to help—she'd asked her neighbor down the hall, who came and went at odd hours, bringing men back to her room, how she might earn a little money. The girl set her up, clearly pleased for a little break and a cut of the fee.

Now Mattie lay resorting to the most desperate measures a woman could take. She'd spent her final pay packet on two weeks in this dark, overheated room too close to the scarlet district for respectability, and this would pay the balance.

She'd leave the man's thin stack of folded bills untouched until the landlady knocked for her rent, and if she could help it, she wouldn't spend another night here. The hot, damp air was poison to Cap's lungs. Her boy needed a real doctor, not charlatans who took money just to hem and haw. Cap hadn't improved with time, as they'd suggested and she'd dared to hope. She was desperate now, and while love for him had made her stronger than she'd ever imagined, love would not remedy this.

A rattling gasp from the bureau interrupted her thoughts, and Mattie braced herself for a cry. The man still lay against her, fondling her breasts as if they were pears at the market. He turned his head only briefly. Perhaps he believed the sound of labored breathing came through thin walls from similar activity.

Her neighbor had warned her to keep Cap out of sight. "Johns ain't the patient kind, hear. They won't want no whiny kid interrupting." The woman had tilted her head toward the bureau that crowded the tiny room, toward the deep drawer nearly the size of Mattie's trunk, then reminded Mattie to clean herself later with a solution she left on the washstand, if Mattie "wanted to live long." She'd hurried away.

Mattie had given Cap an extra dose of the syrup the last doctor dispensed. She'd worried it was too much but couldn't stand for him to observe her shame, even if he was too young to know the difference. She'd spooned the bitter concoction into his mouth, paused to kiss his forehead, and whispered an apology before slipping him inside, atop their extra clothing. It wasn't so bad—even at two years old, he was tiny, so frail he had room to roll over. She tucked his yellow blanket around him and watched to see if he would stir, then closed the drawer, all but the last few inches. She'd waited for his wail, but a sharp knock at the door had come instead.

Her neighbor had said when the man finished to let him stay in her bed a quarter hour, but her nerves jittered over Cap. He seemed settled to sleep again, but she pushed at the man gently now, restraining her desire to shove him off. "Hour's up, sir."

They'd not even exchanged pleasantries when he'd arrived, but just as the woman promised, he'd not been rough. He pulled on his boots and buttoned his trousers, neglecting to wipe away the seed that ran down his thigh, then pushed hair from his eyes, shoved his hat over his brow, and left.

Mattie tugged open the drawer. Cap still slept. But she'd just begun to cleanse herself when he gasped again, louder, then coughed in the way that terrified her. She sprang up and yanked at her drawers, tying them as she hurried to the bureau. At the sight of Cap's face, she gasped too. She pulled him from the drawer and pounded on his back until he spit up phlegm and his cough settled, all that ever seemed to help, and then she threw on her dress and retrieved her string purse, shoving the money inside. She hesitated, then put one dollar back.

She rushed from their room with Cap wrapped in her shawl and clinging to his favorite blanket—yellow muslin on one side, printed flannel on the back, quilted with knots, and edged in white eyelet tattered from use. It had been her sister Iola's solitary token of support the day she threw Mattie out. Mattie hadn't been particularly enthusiastic to keep it, but Cap adored it now.

The air seemed thicker than ever. Coal smoke from trains and nearby factories mixed with heavy wood smoke. The sky was dark, even for a gloomy December day. There were fires every day in this part of Fort Worth, where wooden buildings had gone up unregulated during the turn-of-the-century boom.

Where the doctor had given Cap the elixir, two blocks away, a *Closed* sign hung behind the door glass, and even when she rapped hard, only the porch's rattling floorboards answered.

She sank to the steps as Cap coughed harder. The infirmary was another half mile, where they'd simply turn her away. The doctors there claimed there was nothing new to be done, even if she showed the money in her purse—they knew Cap's history well. They'd say to wait out the fever, bathe him with ice if she could get it, and rub alcohol on his chest. The aspirin tablets they recommended only made his belly ache worse.

A pamphlet tacked on a pole next to the fence fluttered in the breeze. She focused on the cover's suddenly familiar image. The last time she'd tried the infirmary, a mute cleaning woman had stopped her after watching Mattie plead with the nurse. She'd balanced her mop in her bucket, then withdrew a pamphlet from her waist pocket and tried to press it into Mattie's hand. Her stocky body overwhelmed Mattie—and Mattie wasn't short. Mattie glanced at the cover and shook her head. "They'll take him from me. I can care for my son. He's just sick."

The woman had not uttered a sound, but only shook her head.

Mattie twisted away from her sorrowful gaze. But then she had turned back, for only a moment. "You really think they'd help him?" The woman touched her heart and pressed her fingers against her cheeks. Then pointed up, her eyes raised along with her fingers.

"God? *God* would help us?" Mattie scoffed. The woman nodded. She moved closer and put one arm around Mattie and smoothed the other hand down Mattie's cheek and down Cap's sparse hair. Mattie stood there for a moment, unnerved at the touch, but also strangely comforted. *Oh, Mama*, she had thought . . .

But then she'd pushed away. She'd accepted the comfort, but not the pamphlet. She would never take that chance. Cap was hers. And God was for other people.

Mattie slowed her breathing now, remembering. Cap coughed more as time passed. In fact, she tried to keep from coughing herself, and failed. Was it the smoke, or was she getting sick too? She was generally healthy, but Cap caught everything.

And now she wondered, if she had to choose today, between clinging to her son and giving him up—if it meant he could get well—would she let him go? The keening that emerged from deep in her throat at the thought hardly startled Cap. But she held him away just enough to brush a stray lock from his forehead so she could study the face she knew better than she knew her own. The face she loved more than any other.

She'd do anything for him.

She pushed up from the steps, clinging harder to Cap, and tugged the pamphlet from the nail that held it. She returned to the steps and sat again, her hand shaking. If she hadn't, the words printed inside, beneath a photograph of a man and woman dressed in good clothing, would have caused Mattie to fall to her knees:

THE BERACHAH HOME FOR ERRING GIRLS
WE DO NOT GIVE BABIES AWAY.

And now she remembered the woman's shaking head. If only she'd accepted the tract, buried it deep in her purse to retrieve the day before in her desperation. Instead, in her stubbornness, she'd done worse. Her bitterness and pride had stopped her—and even more, the woman's unspoken, but clear words. After all, God hadn't taken notice when sickness killed her mother, organ by organ.

Why would he care about Cap?

But Cap was running out of chances. He gasped even as she hesitated, another coughing fit thrusting him backward, bringing his distended belly into sharper focus, almost grotesque in its roundness compared to his sticklike arms and legs.

He was dying before her eyes.

Could she trust the words she read? People always wanted something. Nothing was free. And she'd been a fool for sweetly spoken words already. More than one person had convinced her to let them "help," with disastrous results.

This time, though, she had no choice, and the memory of the motherly embrace propelled her. Mattie scanned the pamphlet for directions, then stepped into the street and toward the train station, wishing she'd asked the mute woman's name—though how could she have told it? If they helped Cap at this Berachah Home, she'd have no way to thank her.

The street was eerily quiet, hardly a wagon or carriage to be seen. The boardwalks, usually teeming this time of day, were clear all the way to Lancaster, where the trolleys between Fort Worth and Dallas stopped right in front of the T&P depot. The few people she saw in the distance hurried as fast as or faster than she did. She and Cap both coughed again, and when she reached the end of the block and turned toward downtown, she stopped midstep.

Ahead, the sky was nearly black with smoke. The air was becoming heavier and darker.

And two blocks away, the train depot was engulfed in flames.

A crowd stood between her and the trolley car that could take her and Cap to Arlington. Mattie pushed her way toward two young boys who craned their necks trying to see over taller men. "What's happened?" she said, shaking one boy's shoulder.

"Started up top!" He pointed toward fire hoses shooting massive streams at the building's third story. "They're bringing things out fast as they can—desks and such."

Flames danced high over the structure, which housed the railroad offices and a restaurant on the second floor. How could anyone be brave enough—or stupid enough—to enter a burning building simply to save objects? Were material goods more valuable than lives?

And how could she get to Arlington if the fire delayed the trolley? She glanced at Cap, torn between carrying him far from the smoke immediately and taking him where they might, at least, shelter and pray for the two of them, and at best, find a doctor willing to treat what everyone but her considered a hopeless case.

Not one doctor had determined what ailed Cap, and her persistence seemed to annoy them. Would they have been annoyed had she been married—or had she been rich?

But even the times she could pay, they couldn't say why Cap had stopped growing, why he'd become lighter instead of heavier since she'd stopped feeding him at the breast. He ate everything, yet clawed his belly as if the hunger pangs physically attacked him, and derived little strength from food, scarcely able to lift his playthings. Lately, he'd grown listless, and the frantic crying these last months had nearly driven her to drink the syrup the doctor dispensed when she begged him to do something, anything. It calmed Cap enough that he slept fitfully, a few hours, before he woke again screaming. She'd wondered if a sip might numb her half-crazed mind when he sobbed. But she hadn't summoned the nerve to take what Cap needed more.

At their last visit, the physician listened to his heart and said it beat strong, and asked if he ate well and eliminated regularly. She could scarcely keep his diapers changed, and their odor nearly knocked her flat. The doctor was out of ideas. The boy would simply outgrow his fussy state.

But Mattie knew it was more than just fussing. She knew her instincts as a mother, though young and inexperienced, were good.

And now, she had to fight for what could be Cap's last chance.

She elbowed her way past grown men, ignoring their attempts to hold her back from the depot. "Let me pass!" she cried. "I need the trolley!" When she reached the front of the crowd, a line of fire volunteers blocked the street, the trolley stop across it. "Excuse me," she shouted, moving as close as she could. "When will the tracks reopen?"

One man's answering leer didn't intimidate her. He gestured past the depot. "Still running."

Mattie didn't need a steam train—but if they were running in spite of the fire, maybe the electric cars were too. She shoved past him and ran into the street, toward the corner where a saloon did brisk business day and night—due in no small part to the stop itself.

The crowd roared at her idiocy as a policeman chased her down.

"Madam, you're disrupting the fire crew—and you can't go in that building!"

"I don't want in," Mattie gasped. "I need to get to Arlington!"

He squinted, then shouted over the protest of the crowd. "The Interurban?" Nearly as many gawked at her now as at the flames still eating away the depot roof, though the water was beginning to win. "You'll endanger your child if you try to catch that trolley."

"My child is already in danger. He's sick. I'm taking him for help!"

The policeman removed his bucket hat and mopped his head. "Madam, I don't know what you think you'll find, but no doctor in Arlington will be open by the time you get there."

"I have to. Please, sir. I can't miss the car." She showed the pamphlet. She hadn't wanted to, but today, pride was useless.

The crowd had lost interest, but the policeman looked from her to Cap and then leaned to speak right into her ear. "That's them folks who take girls from our streets to fill them with religion. Same girls come waltzing back more times than not. They like it here. Plenty of business, and no reason for following someone else's rules when you can make your own. Right, darlin'?"

Mattie felt filthier with each word he uttered. He'd probably just as soon push up her skirts himself, in full view of the crowd. She shrank away. "I'm not that kind."

"Aren't you, though? Once you let a man have his way, you belong as much as any. But go ahead. Get the car. And we'll see you next week." He mockingly tipped his hand as he moved to let her pass. "Don't forget your ticket. Conductors won't tolerate spongers—especially from the likes of you."

Mattie didn't give him a backward glance, thankful she'd brought the money. Her maternal instincts might be good, but common sense wasn't usually her strong suit. If she'd had any, she wouldn't be in this predicament. Then again, if she'd had any, she wouldn't have Cap. Sickly or not, she wouldn't trade him for all the sense in the world.

The drugstore next to the saloon had a sign in the window stating they sold Interurban tickets. Purchase in hand, Mattie climbed the narrow, steep steps into the car when it arrived, struggling to lift Cap while clinging to the handrail, nearly collapsing from exertion and the heavy smoke from the fire. She panted as she confirmed the route with the conductor, who said he'd shout out Arlington as they approached, nearly a straight shot halfway between Fort Worth and Dallas. She settled into a seat, thankful for the cushioned chairs in the front of the car. Men rode in the back where hard seats and spittoons contained their tobacco mess, though the section was nearly empty today.

Along the way, there was little to watch besides occasional trains that ran parallel to the Interurban's smaller tracks. The terrain was hilly, but brown. There were few trees and a late November freeze had brought down the leaves. Mostly, the car passed indistinct farms, and the monotony lulled Mattie into a state of cautious dozing, especially as Cap had stopped gasping so constantly once they left the smoke behind. She hoisted him higher as the car slowed and the conductor called for Arlington.

The sleepy station surprised her. In the falling dusk, the town had already closed up shop. Compared to the constant rough-and-tumble of the Fort Worth Half Acre, it appeared nearly deserted, and on a Saturday evening too. Arlington seemed an odd choice for a place that took in women nobody else would.

Homes and businesses lined the street along the tracks. The pamphlet indicated the place was a ten-minute walk south from the station, but south was little more than dusty fields. The wind had picked up, and Mattie regretted leaving her cloak behind. She'd brought nothing but her purse, the light shawl she'd tossed around Cap, and his blanket, which he'd alternated between clinging to and pushing away, even in sleep. She hadn't fussed. Heat radiated from him, and even in the chill of the evening, she was soaked with her own sweat.

Now she saw that one shoe was missing of the good pair she'd worked so hard to purchase from Rosenberg's, inordinately proud to take Cap for his fitting. Her throat swelled. She wondered that she hadn't cried all day. It was only a shoe, but suddenly it represented everything lost. She'd scratched his name onto the soles so they wouldn't be misplaced in the homes where women took in kids while their mothers worked.

But wherever he'd lost it today, nobody would know him.

"Help you with anything, missus?"

Mattie swung around. The lone gentleman from the back of the trolley car held his hat in one hand and a rolled newspaper in the other. Even at twenty-three, she still felt green around men—even after spending the afternoon with one jabbing her indecently. She stared, tongue-tied, no longer the brash woman at the fire.

"You seemed lost. Didn't mean to startle you."

"No, sir," she said quickly. "Just catching my breath."

He nodded but hesitated.

It was growing darker and indeed would be full dark soon. A church bell underscored this—five tolls, with Cap heavier and more lethargic the longer she stood. "Sir, can you tell me, please, how to get to the . . ." She struggled with the name from the pamphlet. "The *Bur-atch-a* . . . Industrial Home? Someone said it wasn't far."

The man backed away, cheeks reddening. "The Berachah?" he said. *Burr-ah-kuh.* He tightened his guarded stance but also craned his neck. "You sure that's where you want?" She nodded and shrugged. He seemed more distressed the longer Mattie said nothing.

"Why, it's just down that road." He gestured toward a dirt track leading south from the station. "Where it curves, keep on, and soon you'll see it on the right. Big white house. Can't miss it. Then again . . ." He pointed up. A metal arch spanned the street and tracks. *Berachah Home, for Mother and Child,* it read, with the shape of a hand pointing south. Now she blushed. He hurried away, as if frightened she'd speak again.

Mattie was accustomed to shame. Doctors often dug for intimate details of Cap's conception, unrelated to his condition. Some suggested an exchange of services once they learned she'd conceived out of wedlock. She'd turned them down flat.

Would things be worse in this town?

Cap emerged from his lethargy to struggle against her hip and clutch his ribs, wailing, as if they poked in upon his swollen belly. She scurried down the darkening road, hoping to prevent attention from the few homes, their windows now glowing with lamplight. The distance between them lengthened until she passed the last, but she was more relieved than nervous. In the increased isolation, Cap's screeches disturbed only empty darkness. And until she arrived at this mysterious place where he could remain in her arms, she preferred not to see another soul.

"Hold on, my love, almost there," she murmured now, with each set of steps, a chant to sustain them both until they found the Berachah Home.

LIZZIE

Arlington, Texas
DECEMBER 1904

The burning exhaustion Lizzie had suffered weeks on, even after the matron declared her sound enough to mix with the others, finally let up. Mornings before sunrise now, she sat with the girls around the stove in the parlor. After the babies were settled in the evenings, while most of the others read or mended by lamplight in the gathering room, Lizzie listened in on singing practice.

She'd never been to church a day in her life. Her people had no use for it, and she'd never heard more than a whore or cowboy singing drunk in an alleyway. Nothing like these melodies written down in a booklet, with the four girls blending the high and low parts so pretty and singing words Lizzie guessed came straight from the Good Book. She wanted to learn the songs but couldn't teach herself from the pages they shared. Gertrude Chase, a dainty girl who tended to boss the others around, said they were practicing for a special program with no time now for teaching.

One evening, though, Lizzie was overcome by their sweet voices. She listened until she couldn't contain her tears, then ran off down the hall to the bedroom she and Docie shared now with others. She fell on her bed sobbing. Dilly, the first girl to live in the home, with the first baby born there, came to see why she wept. Lizzie could hardly speak for crying.

Dilly said she'd teach her the best song. She motioned to Lizzie when she reached the simple chorus. *"I believe Jesus saves . . . And his blood washes whiter than snow . . . I believe Jesus saves . . . And his blood washes whiter than snow."*

Lizzie did her best, but her throat was swollen—not just from months and years of bad sick, going without food or drink, being shoved and hit and sometimes nearly choked by the men who kept her, but also from the questions that whirled in her heart. She struggled to believe that a man, even from the heavens, could do anything for her. Every man she'd ever met had driven her off once he tired of her. But she wanted that peaceful look Dilly had as much as she'd wanted anything.

Dilly asked if she believed the song—that she could be saved from her dark and sinful life. Lizzie wasn't sure, but she nodded anyway. Dilly said Lizzie should pray for it, then returned to the others.

Lizzie didn't know how to pray any more than she knew how to sing, but they all prayed from their knees, so she guessed the Lord heard better from there. She dropped to the floor and sang the chorus in a whisper. It felt how a prayer maybe should. And then, such a weight came off her heart, and even off her physical being, all she could think was how she'd never leave this place. Here, maybe, finally, she could be good.

She ran to find Dilly, her joy overflowing. The girls neither shushed her nor told her she'd wake the babies. Instead, they celebrated with certainty what seemed flimsy and fragile to Lizzie herself. Every hope she'd latched onto before had shattered.

This hope, however, filled Lizzie with cautious peace, more each day. She scarcely wanted to leave the big house. She wanted to savor its safety as long as she could. She turned down appeals to so much as step off the porch. But one December night, dark and quiet as far as sight and sound could reach, she did.

Docie had been restless at bedtime. Lizzie rocked her until she finally slumbered soundly, then settled her in her little cot. Moments later, from their second-story bedroom, Lizzie heard the cries of a young woman, come nearly to the wide steps at the front door. She'd collapsed mere feet away, and she clung to a bundle Lizzie only recognized as human after flying down the stairs and off the porch to where the girl lay on her side, crooning and curled around a child.

Lizzie took them in her arms and helped them in—a choice that rebuilt her heart but also broke it again.

CATE

Arlington, Texas
2017

I pretend I don't see Laurel after she settles herself in her own private corner of the cemetery. She seems okay. Or at least that's the story I tell myself—the one that allows me to leave quickly, without a glance in her direction as I hurry away.

At my house, I peel off my work clothes, then find my oldest, comfiest yoga pants and a soft tank top. Barring fire or flood, I don't intend to emerge all weekend. Digging around online for more information about the girls will take my mind off my crisis of confidence.

What I'm after is a photo of Mattie. I know her last name and enough details that I keep scouring online census records and newspapers, thinking they'll lead me to one.

The library's collection includes many of the monthly *Purity Journals*. The bound publications sent out with news of the Home and rescue work in general contained numerous captioned photos, including ones of Lizzie soon after she arrived, as well as her daughter. I have precise mental images of her and Docie, along with other girls and workers in the Home. I can match several names to faces in the thin, unlabeled stack of photos an Upchurch granddaughter donated, and I've even identified a woman I'm convinced is Lizzie in the 1931 Homecoming shot, nearly thirty years after her arrival.

But Mattie remains a mystery. Photos never accompany any mention of her in the *Journals*. Had she been camera shy? Desired privacy? Or is it coincidence? I want to be able to say, *There's Mattie!* as I can with the others.

In the labeled photos, tragedy and comedy mingle in the depths of Lizzie's dark eyes, which, like Laurel's, give too much away. Not like my silvery-blue irises, which reflect instead of invite. What surprises me most is the accompanying innocence in that deep brown, intact in spite of Lizzie's experiences, contradicting her reflections on a life of horror and heartbreak.

But maybe the dichotomy makes sense. Maybe a youthful outlook kept her sane.

Just as I settle into the corner of my sofa with my tablet and a glass of wine, the rest of the bottle nearby, my phone vibrates. When I did grad school an hour north of here, Angela and I connected over shared music taste during a break in a seminar. Later on, we'd attended a few concerts together. The friendship required so little of me, I'd never had a reason—excuse, frankly—to shut it down. She tries to keep in touch and knows I'm back in DFW, not far from where she lives. I let the call go to voice mail. I want to be alone with my thoughts and feelings. I don't want to cope with anyone else's. Anyone alive, anyway.

I consider ignoring her voice mail too. But something compels me to play the message after all. Ingrained guilt. There's another reason I keep my boundaries out so far: People-pleasing is my superpower—until it's not.

"Cate!" she says. "There's a concert tonight in Oak Cliff—that's Dallas, in case you don't know. What I listened to online was *so* good, and the venue looks amazing. Are you around? It's at seven thirty. I can swing by your new place at six thirty. Call me!"

I contemplate my yoga pants and sigh. It feels like too much energy to change again. Then I remember a striped maxi skirt I bought on a whim recently, thinking it would complement a narrow silk tee I already own. I don't even have a fashion excuse.

So I temporarily banish Lizzie and Mattie and text Angela my address, in spite of a nervous feeling in my gut that escalates as I get ready. I have time for a snack, but I can't eat. As much as I love music, I dread crowds more. A room filled with people can be lonelier than solitude.

Thankfully, Angela has enough enthusiasm for both of us. She arrives twenty minutes late and taps her horn. I'm neither surprised nor offended. She wasn't known for her punctuality in grad school, and I wonder if she manages to arrive on time for her job at her small-town library on the outskirts of Fort Worth.

I climb into her classic Beetle and we roar away, defenseless against my own smile. Angela does everything with a roar. She clambers out in Oak Cliff and hugs me—never my greeting of choice, but Angela grabs a person and hugs hard, leaving nothing to decide. I'm awkward, but appreciative. It's been a long time.

The stately old home, pristinely kept for over a century, is used for cultural gatherings in the gentrifying Dallas neighborhood. On its grand old porch, a woman hovers at a folding table.

"So sorry, we're sold out!" she says.

"We ordered online. Are we on the list? Connelly?" Angela smiles.

The woman frowns. "Oh. We admitted a few extras in place of no-shows and started right on time." She looks at us pointedly. Angela gazes back, equally so. "Unfortunately, there aren't any seats available in the parlor currently, but during the intermission, we'll fill in the aisles. Feel free to stand in the hallway."

Angela gives me the side eye. It's 7:33.

An older man in khakis and a pinpoint oxford descends the ornate central staircase, balancing a few chairs. Most of the other men I see from here are hipsters with volcanic beards or self-conscious waxed mustaches. The man whispers that we can sit near the entrance to the parlor, where we can at least listen, and gingerly places chairs on the parquet floor.

I realize I have no clue who's playing. I've failed to ask Angela and she didn't have paper tickets for me to scrutinize. But once I settle into my chair and start paying attention, I realize I quite like this musician's sound. The solo guitar. A mellow but inviting voice. It's both energetic and soothing, and the strangely familiar tone compels me to lean forward to try to see around the door frame—with no luck. These days, singer-songwriters are a dime a dozen, and though acoustic folk music is my favorite—my parents brought me up on the originals—

the modern stuff is pleasant but usually derivative. Not this. I engage with the lyrics and melody, awed by intricate fingerwork that enhances them.

Between numbers, the musician banters with the audience, telling amusing or poignant stories about song provenance, and then, after nearly an hour, says, "I hope you'll say hello after the show. My music's available online. I've also got these round plastic things for those who like souvenirs."

The youngest people in my line of view crane their necks, as if to see something, but the older folks nod and smile. "Also—download codes for bonus songs, either way." A bottle clinks against the floor. "This venue is perfect. The history . . . the audience members we can't even see . . ." A nearby girl drops the embroidery hoop she's held in her lap the whole time and titters. She wears a short, funky romper and the biggest glasses I've ever seen. I've been pondering whether her embroidery is performance art, and now I see she's literally stitching the word *EMBROIDERY*. Does she take it home after each concert and rip it out so she can start over at the next one?

"I must have startled a ghost." The crowd laughs. "Anyway, I always end with this tune. It's for someone I used to know. She's never in the audience, but I always wish she were."

The room stills, the guitar plays, and I freeze.

I recognize the simple composition even before the lyrics. How can it be? This place, this concert, is two hundred miles and half a lifetime away from the last time I heard the song—not by accident. I'd never expected to hear it again, but confronted with the haunting melody and River's warm, soothing timbre, I can't move.

Moving should be my first instinct—has been for nearly two decades. I should rise from the chair, turn, and run past the elaborate doors of the old house and away as quickly as I can.

But all I can do is sit, and listen, and remember.

Sometimes I look halfway back upon my life, trying to picture the eighteen-year-old me, and think, *I don't remember her at all.* Who was she? Did she think the same way? Act the same way? Or was she so different, not a single person—not even myself—would associate me now with that girl.

In this moment, though, here in this room, where the walls recede and my vision turns fuzzy at the edges, nearly twenty years ago might as well be yesterday.

LIZZIE

Arlington, Texas

DECEMBER 1904

Sister Susie rushed to the parlor where Lizzie had seated the young woman, who clutched at the limp child desperately. Sister Susie took them to the small room next to hers, reserved for those who arrived unexpectedly, like this, or those too sick to mingle. It was the same room where Lizzie and Docie had fought their battle—for hopeless cases, segregated from the general population of the Home unless and until some glimmer of hope emerged after all.

The room was plain, but comfortable, with tall windows looking out on the lawn, a bed made up with snowy linens, and on the wall, a framed print of Jesus with children sitting at his feet. Sister Susie helped the woman change into a nightgown and settled her into the bed.

Lizzie held the child in those moments, over to the side in a little rocking chair, her chin tightening and her hunched shoulders making a shelter around the dying boy as her tears fell on his cheeks and blanket unchecked. Soon, she carried him to his mother, who rocked him and sang to him. But he was already gone. His skin cooled as the fever carried his spirit away.

Sister Susie ordered Lizzie back upstairs after the doctor arrived, but Lizzie listened outside the door, her feet unable to travel the path to her own room after what she'd witnessed. The doctor's voice floated from beneath it in the face of Sister Susie's protests. "She'll be sick from the hysteria if we don't."

In seconds, the wails ceased. No lingering murmurs. No breaths caught. No easing from sobs to occasional hiccups. The girl was out cold. The Home stood firmly against drugs of any kind, but now and then, they did what they had to do. Lizzie said a simple prayer of thanksgiving that they'd given the girl relief—for now. When she woke, her nightmare would begin again, as if it had just happened that minute.

Hot tears dampened the bodice of Lizzie's dress, already scented with grief.

The next morning was silent and gray, and not even the fire's glow could warm the corners of the house. Winter had arrived overnight, too, without warning. Before long, it would depart again, to reappear at whim, or perhaps on a schedule only the winter itself understood. But this morning, frigid air penetrated the tiniest crevices in newly fitted window frames and wooden thresholds that had hardly had time to cure.

Lizzie woke too early, her arms so tight around Docie, her girl complained she was hurting her. When she dared peek around their door at dawn, the others hurried quietly through the hallway, busy with morning tasks. Sister Susie hushed her when Lizzie caught her sleeve. Lizzie wanted to be doing something, anything, to help. "No, dear, let's keep to our routine today. It makes everyone feel better in times like this. You and Docie stay warm in your room."

Lizzie cuddled Docie longer than usual when she dozed, and sat closer than ever to her on the floor while she played with lettered blocks a kind soul brought them. Docie held the blocks as if she hadn't a notion of their use. Lizzie helped her stack them but couldn't name the letters, and she shrugged when Docie pointed.

The young woman rested still, she was sure, or she'd have heard those wails again. Lizzie didn't dare go—until she couldn't stand not to. She settled Docie for a nap and tiptoed downstairs.

The door was ajar, and the young woman gazed blankly at the window, that yellow quilted blanket gathered to her chest. She patted it, as if soothing her boy. Her hair glowed red-gold in the dim light of the overcast morning. The events of the night before couldn't subdue it. But her cheeks were white and her eyes encircled with smudges. She sat straight as a tree, as if the curved rockers beneath her chair weren't even there.

"Miss?" Lizzie said, her voice cracking as the vibration passed her still swollen throat.

The young woman didn't react. When Lizzie took hesitant steps into the room, the girl moved her chin a fraction, but she clenched the blanket harder. Lizzie tugged a needlework-topped stool close to the rocker. She understood grief, more than anyone could guess, and she knew all the girl might need was someone to sit with her, to let her know she was not alone. She had not been alone the night before, and she was not now. Lizzie waited beside her in silence for the next hour or so, until she feared Docie might be stirring. She rose, patted the girl's shoulder, and returned upstairs.

The next three days, she repeated her actions, always finding the girl unmoving, gazing out that same window. After the first day, the yellow blanket was gone.

If Sister Susie was surprised to find Lizzie there one afternoon, she didn't react beyond a small flinch when she entered. "Docie's awake, dear. She's asking for you."

Lizzie flushed. An anguished mother didn't need to hear about someone else's child, not when she grieved so desperately for her own. Sister Susie straightened her shoulders and smiled. "Mattie, I see you've met our Elizabeth. She hasn't been with us much longer than you."

The girl tilted her head to study Lizzie, and Lizzie eyed Sister Susie. Could the matron have forgotten Lizzie was the one who found the girl at the front steps, and the one who summoned Sister Susie when she wouldn't—or couldn't—move? More impossibly, that Lizzie was the one who sat and held her dying child while Sister Susie settled his mother into bed?

But Sister Susie seemed determined to act as if that hadn't

happened at all. Mattie simply turned back to the window. In all three days, the girl hadn't said a word, but Lizzie reckoned if she kept at the sitting, she might eventually—if for nothing else, to tell Lizzie to leave her be.

"I'll get along back upstairs." Lizzie rose, patting Mattie's shoulder, like every day.

She worried Sister Susie would scold her, but at the evening meal, which Lizzie took with the other girls now after their little ones were settled to bed, Lizzie's cheeks burned as Sister Susie praised her compassion in front of the household.

The girl who led the singing glared down her nose. "Isn't it careless for Lizzie to be so close to anyone—especially to those who haven't been around her kind"—she drew out a pause—"of sickness?" Several young women at the two long tables gasped at Gertrude's blunt inquiry, asked as if Lizzie weren't right across the room. Others nodded or shook their heads.

"Oh, Gertrude," Sister Susie said. "Have you learned this from us? To be unkind? To treat girls based on circumstances or perceived value? If so, we've failed at our mission." She paused. "Perhaps it might be tactful to voice such concerns to me privately."

Those who'd backed Gertrude stared at their laps, but Gertrude met Sister Susie's eye. "Please excuse my rudeness," she said, not turning her head until Sister Susie moved on to another topic. Then Gertrude caught Lizzie's eye and glared as if summoning knives from her own.

Lizzie's stomach twisted to think of hurting Mattie more than she'd already been hurt. She shook herself for not thinking of it. She knew better than most, but had forgotten as quickly as anyone.

The next afternoon, though, when Lizzie didn't make her way to Mattie's room, Mattie found Lizzie instead.

MATTIE

Arlington, Texas
DECEMBER 1904

Mattie had not been surprised or angered to learn Lizzie was a mother. After all, Mattie wouldn't have been there herself if not for Cap. She didn't have to see Lizzie's child, and Lizzie never forced conversation, obviously waiting for Mattie to initiate it.

But she did care to know why Lizzie suddenly quit coming. Mattie hadn't even wanted to live after Cap died, but the wordless courage of this girl, who found her, then helped her, then kept showing up, and whose sorrow seemed as deep as Mattie's own, gradually convinced her she had to carry on, with or without him.

If the others were surprised to see the new girl walking the property after staying hidden for days, they didn't let on. They simply nodded their condolences as she passed.

She had no idea where to walk, but by happenstance—or maybe not—she found her new friend near a field shorn to stubble for its winter rest, her knees drawn to her chest atop a cold, flattened boulder, weeping as if she, too, had lost something.

Mattie climbed the rock, though it hurt her hands and hips and knees, already weakened after sitting empty and idle for four days. She welcomed the pain. She settled herself next to Lizzie, then draped her arm around Lizzie's sturdy shoulders.

They cried together in silence.

MEMORANDUM

DATE: December 20, 1904

TO: Mr. Albert Ferry, Printer for the Berachah Rescue Society

CC: Reverend J. T. Upchurch, Founder and Director of the Berachah Industrial Home

FROM: Miss Hallie V. Taylor, Secretary and Treasurer of the Berachah Industrial Home

RE: Next issue of *The Purity Journal*

Inclusions for upcoming issue of *The Purity Journal*

1. Halftones of workers and places at our rescue home, including Sister Maggie Mae Upchurch and Miss Gertrude Chase ministering in the Dallas slums.

2. Halftones of our "Christmas Gems"—babies and children in the Home, with this note: *Sister Maggie Mae purchased a doll for Docie Bates, having learned she'd never had a toy of her own. Docie found it on Sister Susie's desk, not yet wrapped for the tree. She ran to Evening Circle, shouting, "Alpha has got a new toy!" Dilly's boy has no use for a doll, but Docie, at age three, couldn't imagine something so wondrous for herself.*

3. Mabel Jones will relate her experience and tell of snares set for office girls.

4. Details of the recent death of a child in the Home, as well as our first wedding.

5. School report from our instructor, Mrs. Fannie Suddarth.

6. Home receipts for November totaled $428.13.

7. Reminder approved by Brother J. T. Upchurch: *Our family numbers about forty. The expenses are heavy, but the money arrives to meet each obligation. Beloved, if we could express in cold type what is accomplished with the money you send, we're convinced you'd be thrilled with the outcome.*

–HVT

MATTIE

Arlington, Texas
EARLY 1905

After the New Year, once Mattie had time to catch her breath, Lizzie gently prodded her to get right with the Lord too. She said it would give Mattie her hope back. But Mattie was not Lizzie. Hope was behind her now, though she knew she had to keep living, even without it. What else could she do?

Even growing up, she'd been stubborn. Others believed her shy. Her family knew better. At Sunday meetings, Mama sang and shouted, filled with the Holy Spirit. She'd assumed her flock of nine would follow her lead, willingly and joyfully. But Mattie, middle in age—and in the straight-backed wooden pew her family occupied in their tiny Methodist Episcopal church—wouldn't budge, mouth closed, chin tucked, and arms folded tight.

The services often dragged on an hour or two—or three!—beyond the scheduled end, if the spirit moved. Mattie thought she'd lose her marbles before their wagon finally rolled out of the churchyard. She could scarcely wait to get home, where she sprang from the wagon bed, pushing past all the other kids, and raced to brush the mules or fill the troughs—any chore to relieve the tension that built at church until she was twitchy as a shotgun.

It wasn't that she didn't like to sing or shout or wave her hands. To the contrary, it nearly did her in to be still. But she never felt easy with the frenzy. She could never readily accept what didn't make plain sense to her eyes. She needed to roll things around in her mind a spell, and then decide what she would—or wouldn't—believe. It gave her parents and teachers fits, especially Mama, but she couldn't be any other way.

It was no different at the Home. She didn't not believe. She simply struggled to accept that a prescribed formula, spelled out in so many steps, was the one way to heaven. She'd read the Bible, maybe more than most of the girls. To her, the scriptures weren't black-and-white. She saw grays in every verse. Well, except one: *God is love.*

Lately she'd had her doubts about that too.

Mattie could never pretend to be something she was not. Not even hint at it. Not until now.

By the time Brother JT gave the altar call at the end of a Sunday evening service in town, Mattie was nearly frantic from pretending she was whole when inside she ached like a quarry of broken stone. She couldn't contain her need to move. She surprised even herself, barreling down the aisle as if chased by the Devil—at least that was how Sister Maggie Mae Upchurch, Brother JT's wife, described it later. Mattie arrived at his side and, after only the briefest hesitation, exclaimed, "I want to be saved!"

Brother JT enthusiastically pressed her to her knees and prayed over her. She repeated the sinner's prayer, and by then, it was too late for regret. So all the way back to the Home, she sang and shouted at the top of her lungs, just as she'd witnessed her mother and siblings doing countless times. It cleansed her, releasing her pent-up feelings in the loudest cries she'd permitted herself since she'd been under the roof of the Berachah. Oh, it felt good. She couldn't vouch for why the rest did it, but she wondered if she'd been a fool for months—years even—squandering the chance to shed emotion so efficiently.

The sheriff stopped by the next morning to inform them a neighbor had complained about the commotion. Brother JT shook his hand, grinning. The sheriff shook his head and moved on. He was used to the complaints. The community wasn't exactly happy to have the Home just down the road.

As a poor teen growing up in Waco, with a widowed mother who struggled to make ends meet, Brother JT had carried newspapers into the Waco red-light district, where he soon fell into a life of drinking and carousing until he was converted at a church service and called to rescue work. He and Sister Maggie Mae had raised funds independently to open the Home, convinced unwed mothers had as much right to grace and forgiveness as any other sinner. This set the Home apart. Most charitable institutions expected women to quietly hand off their fatherless babies to good Christian couples who couldn't bear their own children. Brother JT's ordaining denomination wanted no part in condoning—indeed fully supporting—the practice of women keeping and raising children conceived out of wedlock. Brother JT had seen the holes their devastating losses left in those mothers' hearts— not to mention, he believed addressing sin in secret did not get at the heart of a matter. The Upchurches extended the same grace to drunks, prostitutes, and opium and heroin addicts. Sister Maggie Mae set out regularly for Hell's Half Acre in Fort Worth or Frog Town in Dallas, frequently accompanied by Gertrude Chase, who already had more responsibilities than any of the other girls. They returned occasionally with a young woman so low, she reeked of her sin. It was harder to entice this type—unless she stumbled in on dying legs. These women left again more often than not, unable to keep the house contract.

Mattie had not confessed to what she'd done only one time, but the girls who fell into the latter group accepted her more readily even so. The new or expecting mothers seemed afraid to even be near her, as if her particular heartache might be catching.

Being a convert made things easier. The Home still often taunted Mattie with reminders she'd sooner forget, but now, at least, instead of watching for her to repent, the Upchurches and some of the girls greeted her with joyful embraces.

When Brother JT approached her about baptism, however, she shook her head. "I was baptized as an infant," she said, though guilt rose in her throat to claim it. She'd never taken Cap to church, much less had him baptized. After he died, she'd asked if they should do it then, but Brother JT had said God didn't hold little ones accountable until they truly knew the difference between right and wrong. He'd welcomed Cap into his paradise with open arms.

Her negligence still bothered her, though—and she wasn't even sure she believed in heaven. She couldn't accept that someone with God's omnipotence allowed children to die. At the very same time, she wondered if her own actions had somehow caused God to turn away when she and Cap needed him most.

"Miss Mattie," Brother JT said, "don't you want to show your inward change to the world through an outward symbol?"

No, she didn't. It rubbed her the wrong way that something as simple as walking the aisle at church was all it took to say she was a brand-new person. She didn't feel so different. She still cried herself to sleep every night until she was nauseated, though she tried to muffle the sound of her sobs. Lizzie Bates often came to Mattie's side, just as she had in the quiet and lonely room downstairs after Cap's death. She patted Mattie's arm and stroked her hair without a word until Mattie managed to doze off.

But Brother JT was a patient man—and not just with Mattie.

One winter day, blustery and bright, she encountered the secretary and treasurer of the Home in the foyer, examining the new issue of *The Purity Journal*. Miss Hallie was a sourpuss, always on the lookout for infractions, much like Gertrude, who'd been there nearly from the first—so long the Upchurches treated Gertrude like a trusted employee too.

Miss Hallie helped Brother JT write and edit the *Journal* each month before Mr. Ferry and Mabel printed it and mailed it to their supporters. She always placed a neat stack on the foyer table for guests or residents who wished to have a copy.

Mattie had avoided the January stack, fearing the latest issue might announce the news she'd rather never encounter in print, but she quietly walked the pretty donated carpet runner now, curious at the woman's absorption. As she drew near, Mattie's breath caught.

The issue featured halftone photographs of the workers, some of the girls, and several babies and children. Miss Hallie smoothed her hand across a portrait of Brother JT, a dreamy smile lifting the corners of her mouth. When her gaze shifted slightly, her lips turned down. Mattie speculated that Miss Hallie was focused on Sister Maggie Mae Upchurch now, seated next to him in the photo. Miss Hallie had not yet married and from the look of her, probably never would. Maybe a decade older than Mattie, Miss Hallie was plain, verging on homely, and certainly not very warm—except in proximity to Brother JT. Then, her cheeks glowed so bright you had to wonder if she was sweet on him. Lots of the girls were, though Mattie herself had no inclination to idolize a married man with four children.

She couldn't help the cough that tumbled from her mouth—a chuckle restrained only halfway. It surprised her, feeling nearly like a betrayal. Her laugh had always landed her in trouble. It had been Charley's favorite thing, and she'd wondered more than once if the gravity of her news when she learned she was expecting, delivered without her usual wit and boisterous laughter, had driven his disappearance. She wasn't much fun by then.

Miss Hallie twisted toward Mattie, flipping pages as if she'd been doing it all along. "It isn't polite to steal up on folks without making your presence known."

"I'm sorry, Miss Hallie. You were so preoccupied, I didn't want to startle you." Mattie barely stifled another laugh, for Miss Hallie had managed to stop on a page where her own likeness gazed straight off it, right at the two of them. The woman harrumphed under her breath.

"That's a pretty picture of you," Mattie said. It was almost true. Miss Hallie's hair, generally frizzier as the day progressed, had remained in place, and her complexion, which tended to angry eruptions worsened by her habit of worrying them with a fingernail, was unusually clear.

But while the photo showed her at her best cosmetically, her lips and eyes seemed more petulant than ever. Perhaps they had been. Perhaps the photographer had pressed the shutter on her portrait mere moments after Brother JT and Sister Maggie May sat for theirs. Witnessing those two in all their wedded glory might have produced a moment of unchecked jealousy.

A commotion startled them both. Brother JT himself pushed

inside the front door in his usual flurry, as if he'd brought the wind with him. For a small man, he had more presence than any Mattie had known. He seemed prepared to mount a passionate soapbox at any time.

He perched his hat on the rack and hurried to look at the photograph. "Why, Miss V, what a fine likeness! Jernigan outdid himself."

Mattie had heard Brother JT address Miss Hallie by her middle initial before, usually with a teasing grin. Miss Hallie used it at every opportunity in writing, as if she wished for a less common name. Appreciation stained her cheeks. "Your portrait is fine as well." She blushed deeply and rushed to correct herself. "Yours and Sister Maggie Mae's, of course."

"Of course," he repeated, with an indulgent smile. Brother JT surely knew Miss Hallie labored to contain her admiration. He had to be used to such displays, but Miss Hallie was clearly mortified. She firmly closed the journal and returned it to the stack.

"Are you ready to go over the financials?" she said.

Brother JT produced a sheaf from his leather case. "Already have. Nicely done." Miss Hallie's face fell. "The association will approve how well our year turned out." As she accepted the report, he rested his hand on hers. "Excellent work this year. I hope you find it fulfilling. Can we ever thank you properly?" He turned toward Mattie. "Miss Mattie, you are glowing today. You must feel better."

She simply smiled.

His hurried words seemed to strike Miss Hallie dumb. As he continued toward his study, she rubbed her hand furiously, as though his touch had scorched it.

Brother JT mentioned baptism twice in February and a third time in March. Finally, Mattie acquiesced. It was a relief, almost as if she had let someone else make the decision for her so she wouldn't have to struggle with it any longer—and she had little energy for struggles.

Alongside her relentless grief, they'd put her to work in the kitchen. It was past time. Kneading bread dough and chopping onions and trimming meat when they were lucky enough to have it gave her aching arms and hands something to do. She was physically exhausted at the end of the day too, and she didn't mind. Often, now, she fell asleep without Lizzie to soothe her.

On the Sunday before Easter, they paraded with palm branches to a section of the creek where water rushed from a wider stream into a shallow pool before forcing its way into narrower crevices beyond. Mattie wore a white robe Dilly had sewn for baptisms, nothing but her shift beneath it. In the quickly warming weather, it was nearly a pleasure to walk outside with a soft breeze fluttering the winged sleeves and the loose hems around her freed wrists and ankles and to sense fresh air at her waist with no corset or stays to restrain it.

But the shock of cold water on her skin brought her to her senses, halfway when she eased into it up to her thighs, and fully when Brother JT pressed her down to kneel after he prayed over her. Under the light touch of his palm, she began to struggle, gasping reflexively and gulping water that was supposed to wash her clean, gazing up at Brother JT, who tilted his head in confusion. He helped her stand again, and she panted with relief.

"What is it, Mattie? Are you not ready to be a daughter of the King?"

Mattie frantically scanned the group of women and the few men on the creek bank until she found Lizzie, whose earlier wide smile had been replaced by a look of panic, as if she'd struggled in the water herself. But Mattie knew Lizzie had gone to her own baptism willingly, as soon as it was warm enough, with no reservations. Mattie had observed quietly at the edge of the group when Lizzie rose from the water with shining eyes and a ringing "Hallelujah!"

Helplessly, Mattie clutched her hands across her chest and belly, feeling exposed now in the drenched and clinging robe. "I thought I was. Now I don't know . . ."

Then, it seemed Lizzie came from nowhere, wading into the water in her heavy dress, not even pausing to remove her shoes. She pushed through, lifting her skirts high enough to reach Mattie's side without any struggle at all.

"I can do it with you," she said.

Brother JT glanced quizzically from Lizzie to Mattie. Mattie knew this was surely not done. She should be ready and willing of her own accord, and there was no obvious reason for Lizzie to be baptized again. But in that moment, it was unclear to anyone whether Mattie was not ready for baptism or simply afraid of the water.

"We have no rule saying you must be fully immersed," Brother JT said. "If you're nervous to go under, there's no need at all. But if you're genuinely not ready . . ."

Mattie looked into Lizzie's eyes again and saw the same strength she'd borrowed for months now. She didn't know how Lizzie had it to give, for she'd begun to tell them all of her horrors before the Home— enough to destroy the hardiest human. Mattie sensed there was even more—maybe more than they'd ever know.

If Lizzie could do this, Mattie could too. She nodded at her friend, who took Mattie's larger, softer hands in her own small, rough ones and held them tight as Brother JT prayed over them both. They knelt together, ducking their heads under, and then rose in unison with water streaming off them, from their sleeves, their shining hair, and their clasped hands.

Now Mattie felt changed.

She had a sister again—one who had saved her instead of abandoning her when she didn't know which way to turn.

After their baptism, Mattie clung to Lizzie in a way she hadn't clung to another woman since her mother died. They were opposite as milk and tea, but complementary just the same. While Mattie kept quiet about her doubts, Lizzie was enthusiastic enough for both of them.

Accepting Docie was harder.

The first time Docie appeared at the edge of Mattie's bed in the dormitory-style bedroom she and Lizzie shared with several other women and babies, Mattie had nearly shoved her away. But she clenched her fists and resisted. Docie couldn't know her pain. And in all likelihood, she was mirroring Lizzie—though she wouldn't have known it was Lizzie doing the comforting.

"Go on now," Mattie told the waif, who tugged Mattie's nightgown sleeve and asked to be held without uttering a word, her dark, enormous eyes begging for comfort Mattie wasn't equipped to give away. She had little enough for herself. "Go back to your bed, child," she hissed, "I'm sleeping."

Docie gripped Mattie's sleeve as if it were rope meant to keep her from floating from safety. "Where's your mama?" Mattie asked, and the girl glanced toward the empty bed. Surely Lizzie had only slipped away to the water closet. "She'll be back. Go on now."

But the child pressed her cheek to Mattie's arm, and though it nearly killed Mattie, she said, "All right. Climb up, but just until your mama comes."

Docie pulled right up into the bed without help, tucking her warmth against Mattie's side as if she'd always known her. Her innocent trust loosed what Mattie had never intended to feel toward any child again. Though her arm shook, she wrapped it tightly around the girl.

When Lizzie returned, she glanced around by the moonlight through the window glass until her gaze lit on Mattie and Docie. She hurried to Mattie's bed in her odd little shuffling walk to fuss at them for frightening her.

"She was alone." Mattie pointed to the now sleeping child. "Can you blame her?"

Lizzie's face fell. "I weren't but a minute. She was sleeping peaceful, and I needed the pot. I were only gone a minute." She reached to take Docie.

Mattie surprised herself again. "Leave her be. If she wakes, I'll bring her to you."

Lizzie hovered.

"Go on now," Mattie said, just as she had to Docie. Lizzie nodded. She glanced back as she went, as if to reassure herself.

Neither slept a wink that night, with Lizzie alert to every tiny sigh or movement, and Mattie to the astonishment of wanting Docie against her heart.

One evening in early summer, when the sun took more time dropping below the horizon than the rest of the year, Lizzie claimed she needed to walk and pray. But by full dark, she hadn't returned. Mattie worried about her wandering alone in a mood, but Lizzie had made her promise not to come after her. In spite of her unease, Mattie waited—although if Lizzie didn't return within the hour, she was going to break that promise.

Docie cried out in her cot, and Mattie hurried to gather the child. Her kicking arms and legs relaxed as Mattie carried her, and her haunted gaze gradually shifted from the look of being trapped inside recurring nightmares. "Aunty Mattie," she sobbed.

"Hush now. I've got you, baby." She pulled Docie's back against her belly, tight to her hip in the narrow bedstead, though the bedroom was already stifling at night. The child's sobs eased until she slept, her breath still catching at times. Mattie wouldn't sleep until Lizzie was safe in bed. She watched the doorway, her eyes burning, until it was only a few hours before dawn.

Finally, just as Mattie was ready to go after her—and maybe to Sister Susie to share her fears—Lizzie tiptoed in, cautiously navigating the evenly spaced beds occupied by sleeping women and the smaller cots beside them, swaying as if she could hardly stay on her feet. Mattie relaxed her eyelids and breathed as if she were sound asleep.

Lizzie hesitated but went to her own bed. She sat to remove her shoes and dress and pulled her nightgown over her head. Mattie was certain she fretted over more than the struggle of whether to bring

Docie back to her bed this time, but eventually, Lizzie dropped to her knees and folded her hands against her coverlet, her head bowed except when she lifted her chin to gaze across the room again. If the rest was routine, Mattie knew that particular prayer was heartfelt. The weight of Lizzie's sigh floated across the space as she settled her stocky body into bed.

Safe or not, Mattie wouldn't let this go. Something didn't sit right about Lizzie's long absence. This was more than a trip to the toilet or a walk around the grounds to pray away a bad mood. Lizzie was on some kind of mission, and by Mattie's estimation, one that wasn't good for her—or for Docie. Otherwise, she'd have told Mattie what she was up to. In the evenings now, they usually huddled together before retiring to their separate beds, chuckling or sighing or complaining quietly as they dissected each day. Gertrude Chase still turned her nose up to see them so friendly. But Lizzie had been distant the last day or so, avoiding Mattie in general. Mattie cringed at unbidden images of Lizzie doing whatever she must to get snuff—or worse. Surely she wasn't so desperate. Her life was good here. Docie was thriving, and Lizzie seemed fine most days.

By now, though, Mattie had seen enough life to know appearances could lie.

They could lie right to your face.

She pulled Docie closer. She was thankful she wouldn't have to disturb Sister Susie tonight, for their sweet matron was already exhausted after days of dealing with May, the most recent dope-addled woman Sister Maggie Mae had brought in. May had thrown the gentle care back in Sister Susie's face, running away as soon as she was half-coherent.

Mattie would confront Lizzie herself, and soon. For now, she squeezed her eyes shut and said her own perpetual prayer: *To forget.*

CATE

Arlington, Texas
2017

River's last song ends, and I bolt. I closet myself in a tiny restroom stall, praying nobody else will need it. Well, *prayer* isn't exactly the word for what I do these days. I have an understanding with God. I won't judge him by the people who claim to represent him if he won't judge me for keeping my distance. But I can't help crying out to something beyond myself when I end up in a situation I think I can't handle alone. I mentally gather the emotions that pour over the edges of what I can contain and hand them up to an invisible being with bigger palms than mine. My therapist suggested this, based on AA—though she thought it would help even more if I allowed another human to play the part of empathetic vessel.

Tonight's the perfect reminder why I don't. History has a way of catching up with you. Something as simple as a voice and a tune can bring everything you've buried right back to the surface.

But I'm not going there again. Ever.

I lean against the wall and try to contain the panic that threatens to overtake me. I press my fingers against my temples and eyelids and breathe in and out. The restroom door creaks open. A voice travels under the door of the stall.

"Cate? Is that you?"

Not answering will make things worse. "Sorry, I started feeling light-headed, but I'm fine now. Enjoy the music. I'll meet you at the car when it's over. Can you hand me your keys?"

"You're sick?" Angela says. "Let's leave, then!"

"I'm fine. I just don't want to stay in the crowd. Promise."

Angela groans. "I don't want you to have to sit in my car alone."

I work to control my breathing. "Oh, please. I'll grab something from a drive-through. By the time I'm back, the concert will be over. I should have eaten earlier is all."

Angela rummages in her purse, and her key clinks against the door frame. "I feel terrible, but I trust you. I'm dying to see this next musician. The first one was so good!"

I close my eyes. Angela needs to stop talking. "Go! Please don't worry."

The door opens a few more times and two women chat while they wait. I cautiously leave the restroom, navigating the wine-sipping crowd in the foyer. A nearby room contains tables laden with hors d'oeuvres and glassware, and my heart punches my ribs to see the back of familiar shoulders clothed in denim. The gestures haven't changed, though the body is that of an adult now—no more skinny teenage arms and legs. I pause, though instinct tells me not to, drawn to those movements, longing to hear River's voice once more.

That would be catastrophic. Not in the way tornadoes or acts of terror are catastrophic. But if our eyes connect, we'll have to talk, and I'll never be able to look River in the eye without telling the truth. And that will be a disaster.

For River. And for me.

I escape through the screen doors, across the porch, and back to Angela's car. I lock myself in, drive around the block, then pull back into the same space, and for the first time in years, allow myself to sob messily. These are not the silent tears that flow in a cemetery. This is unrestrained weeping. This is anguish, rocking my body as violently as if another human is kicking the back of my seat.

On the way back to Arlington, Angela curbs her usual stream of chatter, sensing I'm still not well. When we arrive, I fumble for my house key. The bottom of my purse is a soggy mess of tissues I took from the restroom at the venue.

"Thanks for sticking it out," Angela says. "Oh! I bought CDs." She shrugs. "Nobody besides me listens to them anymore, but the suggested donation was only five bucks—so I grabbed two. It's the least I can do to thank you for soldiering through."

I accept it reluctantly, as if even touching the CD, with River's face haunting me from the cover, is opening myself—and others—to a whole new level of hurt. But I can't refuse Angela's gift. I have no explanation ready. I never intended to talk about this again.

I push the cardboard sleeve into my purse, clutching my keys and eager to cut things short so I can disappear inside the anonymity of my house. "Thanks. I'm sorry I was lousy company. It . . . took me by surprise. I feel terrible."

"Don't feel terrible—you're sick! I feel bad you had to wait—"

I interrupt. "Listen, I have to get inside. I don't think it's anything catching. The first month of school is brutal, and I just waited too long to eat."

"Okay, but I'm calling to check on you tomorrow."

"Don't check on me!"

Her face falls, and I realize I'm being rude. I soften my tone. "Truly, you don't need to worry. I'm turning off my phone, and a good night's sleep will cure this." I climb out of the VW and back away. If I don't, our conversation will circle, apologies flying back and forth until I genuinely lose it again—this time in front of her.

I wave one last time, then let myself into my house, flashing the porch light to let her know I'm safe—just as my parents taught me back when they had an interest in protecting me from the evils of the world. Sometimes I crave their embraces, especially at times like these, when the past invades without warning and threatens to shake my carefully constructed fortress until it crumbles.

But it was my parents who, in the end, became the most surprising enemies of all, who betrayed me, inconceivably and irreparably.

I trudge across the threshold, pausing to kick off my shoes, and sink deep into the sofa I bought on a whim two moves ago. It's the most comfortable, most comforting thing I've experienced that isn't human—and if good sense has anything to do with it, the only thing that will ever embrace me again.

I intend to open my tablet and return to my research on the Berachah girls until my eyes won't stay open. The possibility of discovering something new is still the most welcome distraction I can think of tonight.

Except the CD sleeve draws me instead, mercilessly, as if it's magnetic and I'm the metal it craves. River, in spite of the years elapsed between the last time we were together and when this photo was taken, looks much the same. The reserved, genuine smile. Those golden-brown eyes, so knowing my breath catches halfway down my throat if I gaze too long. Sinewy fingers cradling the fretboard of a guitar, gracing hands that took me places I'd never imagined, whether steering us toward ghost towns to explore a forgotten past, or playing guitar notes so intensely I sometimes laughed and cried at the same time, or touching me, it seemed, to the center of my soul.

I thought I'd exhausted my well of tears alone in Angela's car, but it turns out I have more. They overflow the crater carved in my chest two decades ago, its depth fathomless, no matter how I empty it.

LIZZIE

Arlington, Texas
SUMMER 1905

Docie came scurrying to greet Lizzie when they rose, eyes all lit up like she'd not seen her mama in a dozen years—being all of four. Lizzie felt Mattie eye her from across the room. Mattie stood by her washstand rubbing in store-bought face cream with a cloth, always vain about her skin. They were not to adorn themselves with anything that might subtract from the glory of the Lord, but Mattie managed to get her hands on that cream somehow, and it was doubtful anyone would argue even if they caught her. Her skin was touchy—freckled and easily irritated.

Lizzie never thought on her own skin a minute, but Docie watched Mattie taking care. Even being tall, with a hardy appearance now that she was eating again, and coming from farm folk, Mattie wasn't as strong as Lizzie. Maybe her boy had come by what ailed him naturally. Mattie had mentioned that two brothers and a sister had passed before she was even born.

Docie stopped short when she reached Lizzie. "Mama, you smell like Aunty Dilly. What have you got on you?"

Lizzie flushed hard as she scrambled for an excuse. Dilly kept their clothes spotless in the laundry, and the girls always needled her over smelling like carbolic. Lizzie felt Mattie's gaze again. She fetched her hairpins, then smoothed and twisted her braid before answering Docie. "I took sick during the night, little bug. Had to clean myself and change my gown. Good thing you wasn't in my bed."

Docie's eyes filled. She clung to Mattie when Lizzie wasn't there, but Lizzie didn't doubt Docie loved her best, just as Lizzie had loved her ma best, too, despite all she'd let happen. Her ma had done what she must to survive, and that was how it was for women. Lizzie held to a stringy thread of hope that her ma still loved her. "Docie, honey, run along," she said. "Alpha will worry if you're late for playtime."

Docie's face lit up again. Dilly's boy, Alpha, was only two but looked twice her size, and they were sweet on each other. Docie scrambled away, and Mattie frowned at Lizzie, sidling close. There'd been curious stares from the others as well, but they'd sidestepped in case Lizzie was still of a mind to dispense harsh words.

"Where were you all night?" Mattie whispered.

"Nowhere! I done nothing wrong," Lizzie said. Mattie's brows went high.

Lizzie knew Mattie couldn't fathom her risking Docie's safety with nighttime excursions that broke the house rules. If they found her out, they'd likely pack her back to the jail or the county farm. It was anybody's guess where they'd send Docie. She closed her eyes.

"I didn't ask what you *did*," Mattie corrected. "Look at me. You're like a ditched horse."

"Them old feelings come over me lately is all, Mat. The urges, the ants—I got to walk them off. Before I finally come to bed, I got the shivers and was sick on myself. I hated telling Docie a fib but can't bring myself to explain. She's too little. I'm better now, truly. Leave it be."

Mattie leaned closer, voice low. "You know you can trust me, honey." She looked Lizzie hard in the eye, and Lizzie nearly cracked. She knew she should simply find Sister Susie and confess what she'd done. It was getting too messy.

Before breakfast, they gathered in the parlor to recite verses practiced the day before and share "roses and thorns"—their daily struggles and triumphs. Nobody questioned Lizzie's unusual silence, considering the excuses she'd made. If they only knew how her easy life here troubled her. Her current mission was risky, but she'd pay the rest of her life for what she hadn't confessed when she arrived—could never confess. That long-held secret punished her, but never enough.

The longer morning circle went on today, the harder she prayed they'd dismiss before she burst. But when they did, her innards truly were sick, she was so torn up about the lies she'd told Mattie and Docie. At breakfast, she asked Mattie to guard her plate so it wouldn't get bussed away.

The matron sat in her usual place reading her Bible, finished with her tiny breakfast. Sister Susie had bird bones, and Lizzie guessed she ate only what she needed to keep alive. Maybe she thought staying hungry would prepare her for foreign missions—her biggest dream. Meanwhile, she treated the girls with respect and love, even when they tried her—even when May, the worst so far, had kicked out her window glass before taking off. Sister Susie would have kept right at it had May stayed.

"Sister Susie?" Lizzie said softly, hoping not to startle her. It was nearly the only time you could—when she was deep in the scriptures.

The matron lifted her spectacles. "Good morning, dear. Are you your true redeemed self again today?"

Lizzie felt shame at the woman's gentle look and question. How could she continue her deception? At the same time, she struggled to believe the truth would do anything but punish a needier soul. "Yes, ma'am," she said, "though I'm not right in my gut. You think I could wrap my breakfast for when my belly settles?" Lizzie never left a morsel uneaten, nor let Docie. Passing up a meal was unheard of for her—so of course she'd ask to save it if she felt puny.

"Of course. Have Gertrude put it by. I'll pray you're completely yourself by supper."

Bless her; Sister Susie was the sweetest soul—and the wisest. She didn't let the girls get away with anything, so Lizzie was embarrassed by how easily she'd deceived her. Sister Susie would faithfully bow her head as soon as Lizzie was out of sight. Lizzie nearly spit out the truth again.

It was nearly time for work, though. They had put Lizzie in the nursery once she was healthy, for it turned out she was good with all the babies. Almost as if she had a magic touch—only she knew different. She'd been bad luck before she'd been good luck. But she couldn't talk about magic or luck here. If something wasn't credited to the Lord, the Devil got the blame.

She scurried through the kitchen and out the back door, carrying the breakfast she had no intention of eating herself.

On her return from the battered barn, in a clearing a good walk away from the big house, twigs snapped in the path behind her. She turned her head and stopped short, holding out her hands to slow her friend. She'd always been honest with Mattie, where it counted, until this morning. It had been three days now, and she had to come clean, even if Mattie gave up the friendship Lizzie depended on now.

"Don't touch me, honey," Lizzie said. "I got to wash off."

Mattie sagged against a tree trunk, as if she'd lost the ability to stay upright without it propping her. "Oh, Lizzie, what have you done?"

Lizzie couldn't look at her. Couldn't open her mouth. She'd done something so stupid, she couldn't even tell her best friend.

But then Mattie took a deep breath. "I had relations with a man the day Cap died," she said, spitting out the words as if issuing a challenge.

Now Lizzie pressed her back against a tree. She heard what Mattie said, but she didn't quite trust it. "I know what you're trying to do. I still ain't gonna tell you. It ain't safe for you to know."

"Lizzie . . . honey, I'm not going to judge you. I know it's hard for you to keep on—as hard as it is for me. Maybe for different reasons—"

"No. It ain't that at all. I wouldn't blow my chance—or Docie's—for something as stupid as that. I'm strong now."

"So strong, you won't even leave the grounds?"

Lizzie sighed. "I know what I got to do."

"Then tell me, honey, what could be so bad? You must be imagining some kind of sin that isn't even real."

Lizzie looked at her long and hard.

"I wasn't lying," Mattie said. "I did it. I . . . I had to."

Lizzie knew then that Mattie was telling the truth—and she'd given Lizzie a secret she'd given no one else. Lizzie nodded, then stepped close to Mattie, but not close enough to touch.

"It's May. She came back, and I got her tied up in the barn."

Mattie gasped, and she shook her head, again and again and again.

All that afternoon, Mattie fussed at Lizzie whenever she was near enough. When she brought the little ones' toast and milk up to the nursery and set the tray on the low table, she hissed, "What were you thinking?" Mattie avoided the nursery like it was a terrible beast, leaving this task to Olive or Gertrude, who worked in the kitchen with her. Gertrude was surely curious why Mattie had volunteered today. Lizzie pretended she didn't care to wake the infant she rocked while Bertha cut the toast into small pieces for the toddlers. Mattie left glaring.

When Lizzie took the toddlers out to play, Mattie approached their quilt on the lawn. She kept her distance, loath to touch Lizzie now, though Lizzie had promised she cleaned up thoroughly every time she left May. "What'll you do when they find out? And what about Docie?"

Lizzie could ignore her in the nursery with Bertha nearby. But on the lawn, she tried to make Mattie understand. "Brother JT says there's no such thing as a lost cause. Think if they'd given up on me. Besides, they don't want Docie going without a mama—ain't they always drilling that into us?"

Mattie paced behind Lizzie. Lizzie made funny faces at the babies, and they laughed and clapped their hands and leaned to beg for more. She hid behind her hands to play peep-eye. Not a single thing surprised her—or terrified her—more than this work, caring for the littlest ones alongside Bertha. She cherished it.

"You can't save the whole world, you know," Mattie said.

Lizzie shrugged. "Ain't I supposed to try? The Good Book says it plain."

Mattie knelt in front of Lizzie, tucking her skirt down, though Lizzie caught a glimpse of her ankles. Usually skinny, they were like solid table legs beneath her stockings today. Mattie was taking on too much of pregnant Olive's load in the kitchen; it wasn't good for her. "I have to get back to work," Mattie said, "but I'm a wreck. I'm mixed up in it now. How can I keep my mouth closed with you going behind everyone's backs? How long do you plan to keep it up?"

"Long as it takes." Lizzie spread her fingers just enough to give Leo a peek at her eyes, then popped them wide apart to give him a little scare before scooping him up to hug his neck and blow a raspberry in that sweet spot. "I ain't asking you to lie. It's on me, far as I'm concerned. If you've a mind to tattle, I won't stop you. I won't ask you to do nothing wrong."

She watched Mattie press her elbows into her lap. Mattie's eyes were as blue as Lizzie's were brown, and she towered over Lizzie's stumpy height.

But their hearts beat alike, more than Mattie even knew.

Mattie sighed. "Lizzie, what makes me mad is what I love most about you."

Lizzie went back to her peeking game with the boys. "You got to decide for yourself. All I want is a warning if you think you'll tell."

"I can't lose you." Mattie looked sick, and guilt flew up in Lizzie. But her friend said, "I won't say anything, not yet." She pushed herself back up and brushed a hand along her apron to lay it flat where it had puckered. She glanced behind, then pulled an apple from her dress pocket. From the other, she gave Lizzie a bit of sausage in paper.

Lizzie smelled it before she peeked inside. "What's this?" she said, but knew she'd won Mattie over.

"Don't make me say it. Be sure it goes where it's needed and you don't get caught." She made to go, but on her way, she stooped to kiss Lizzie's forehead, so quick Lizzie scarcely had time to register it. "Your heart is as big as my mother's was. She would have liked you."

Mattie was as real a sister as any. Family had meant nothing but misery for Lizzie before.

Here, she'd found a true one.

. . .

After supper, Brother JT kept them late. "Dear ones, our coffers are nearly empty. We're functioning on a shoestring budget—if we could afford shoestrings, that is."

The girls chuckled. He nearly always cushioned the truth with gentle humor.

"We must operate leanly, taking only what we need, being frugal with soaps, and so on. We want you healthy, happy, and clean, naturally. But we mustn't stray into gluttony. Our Father loves even a glutton, of course, but he thrills at the sight of a disciplined saint. Yes, ladies, you can rightfully consider yourself saints if you're saved and sanctified." His eyes twinkled at the snickers. "It's true. The Good Book says so."

Lizzie wondered how many of the girls pictured the Heavenly Father looking like Brother JT. It was easy. She twisted her dinner napkin in her lap, hoping no one could detect the yeast roll she'd tucked inside after taking two from the basket. But she had no time to worry.

That evening, after her visit to the old barn, Lizzie found Mattie pacing the back porch. It wasn't quite bedtime, the sky still hemmed with orange fringes. Docie played nearby, in Mattie's care after their supper, making pictures with a twig in a dried-up flower bed. The zinnias, puny and thirsty already, drooped like August instead of June.

Lizzie's heart danced into her throat at the sight of the little face beaming with pure pleasure to see her, her eyes no longer hollow from hunger or from pain. Their separations had not always been so brief. Before Berachah, Lizzie had sometimes been forced to leave Docie with her ma and stepfather and his sons to seek work. She'd had little choice, but now she feared it had been her worst mistake.

That last time, when Lizzie retrieved her, Docie's eyes had looked dead, and she was eerily silent. It still liked to kill Lizzie to think about it. She promised herself and Docie then that she'd never leave her again. If the vow had nearly killed them both, death—even in the bowels of a jail—would have been glory over that kind of hell.

The hug Docie gave her tonight was fierce, but just long enough to show her joy. Then she wanted to show Lizzie her pictures, dragging her by pudgy fingers. "Mama, see my pretty flowers? Now the real ones won't be sad. You like them?"

They were the most beautiful Lizzie had ever seen.

Mattie perched in an old chair stripped of stain and missing an arm. Lizzie caught her tension halfway down the porch. She shooed Docie back to the flower bed to make more pretties, then approached cautiously. "Just a few more days, I reckon."

"In a few days, it won't matter," Mattie said. "Gertrude asks too many questions and I'm out of excuses. She knows you're up to something."

Lizzie sighed. Gertrude was head over the kitchen, so Mattie couldn't avoid her, reporting to her as she did. Mattie had attempted every industry anyone set her on. In the printing office, she'd struggled to contain her temper at any inefficiency in their process. In the workshop sewing handkerchiefs and fancy work, her busy thoughts led to too many dropped stitches. Each time she blew it, she was right back in the kitchen. She was quick, but her blasted mouth and sharp mind ruined any opportunity beyond the talent as natural to her as breathing: She could cook like she was born to it. Everyone tucked into Mattie's meals. Mattie had said her made-up recipes had pleased even her picky little sisters at home when her mama took sick, and when she went into service, the family had discovered in no time she cooked better than the wife.

But Lizzie knew Mattie was sick of feeding and cleaning up after other people and sweating over a stove. It took a lot of fire to feed forty souls. And it took more patience than she had to be supervised by Gertrude while doing it.

Gertrude was always in the middle of everyone's business, tattling over some violation of the house rules hardly worth mentioning. Why, she'd even told on Docie before, as if the four-year-old, no bigger than one of the kid goats in the newer barn, could suppress curiosity and noise. Lizzie quietly told Docie to pay Aunty Gertrude no mind.

Gertrude might be more genteel, but if you believed the Good Book, she was as fallen as any of them. Gertrude blamed the world, smoothing over her part in what gave her a baby without a daddy. The Upchurches and Sister Susie seemed blinded by her piety. Lizzie wondered if they had any idea the different face she showed the Home girls.

Lately, Gertrude had been keeping company in the parlor with the young preacher who led their services now and then. She'd hinted they might have a notion to marry. Lizzie knew that chafed at Mattie. She had wanted to marry Charley so badly, but then he'd run off. It seemed unfair that Gertrude should have that so effortlessly when she had a real issue with humility. Lizzie herself wished the man would ask for Gertrude's hand soon—before her britches split right off, for they grew tighter with pride every day. Her trials should have given the woman a humble heart, but she'd become an unbearable, self-anointed saint. *Saint Gertrude.* That was what Mattie called her, sometimes right out loud. It made Lizzie giggle—she couldn't help it.

Lizzie could never begin to think of marrying again. For all she knew, Willis was dead—leastwise, he was to her. But their vows held her to him until she saw proof. During one of their first talks, Brother JT had explained what the Bible said unambiguously about divorce. The never-married girls, wrecked or ruined, had a chance. At least nobody could call Docie a bastard.

The kitchen door clattered, and Saint Gertrude herself emerged with a pail of scraps for the garden. Lizzie thought to volunteer to take them—maybe she could salvage something for May.

"Gossiping again, girls?" Gertrude said.

Mattie's cheeks colored to match her strawberry hair. "Mind your own sins instead of worrying about everyone else—remember, a man doesn't like a busybody."

Lizzie gasped under her breath and shot Mattie a warning frown.

But Gertrude swanned Docie's way. "What're your mama and Aunty Mattie up to, Miss Docie? They whispering things little girls shouldn't hear?"

Docie gazed up at Gertrude, and then at Lizzie. Lizzie smiled helplessly. She'd never ask Docie to lie. But it bothered Lizzie something awful for Gertrude to put a child up to telling tales on her own mother.

Mattie walked hard to where Gertrude stood. "Don't trick a little girl just because you're jealous. Reverend Woods might have *real* second thoughts about courting you."

Gertrude flushed, but she backed away, the pail tight to her chest. "Whatever do you mean? I'm only trying to help my sisters. Mind yourself, Mattie. Someone might think *you're* jealous." She flounced inside, the scrap pail forgotten in her arms. She might be forced to rise from bed to carry the pail out in the dark, or it would smell up the kitchen something awful by morning.

Lizzie had no pity. But she did worry whether, in the deep quiet of the night, Gertrude might hear something that would tip her off to the wild creature in the barn.

MATTIE

Arlington, Texas
SUMMER 1905

After Lizzie took Docie to bed, Mattie stole through the dark to the small clearing between the house and the narrow creek that ran through the property. Besides buildings and newly planted shrubs, the grounds were mainly scrub and dusty dirt, but here, like the front lawn, they'd sown grass seed, and it had flourished. Most of the trees on the property were donated saplings, with only a few live oaks and towering pecans there long before the Home was built. One day, there might be a fine grove, tall and thick enough for good shade and a cool breeze for sleeping instead of the suffocating heat already chasing away spring.

Beside a fledgling blackjack oak, Mattie dropped to her knees and inhaled the dusky aroma of earth, grass, and bark, and then she tried to pray. Tried to feel as if someone—anyone—heard her when she pleaded into the relentless cry of locusts. Their din made the responding silence deafening.

Then she allowed herself to imagine what might have been if she'd had better chances.

Even now, Mattie had bigger plans than Lizzie ever would. This thing with trying to save May—well, her friend could be even more shortsighted than little Docie, content with knowing when their next few meals would come and where they'd lay their heads to sleep, to the exclusion of all else. She was not nearly careful enough.

Mattie appreciated security, but she was already considering where she'd go from here. She'd healed in the welcome of the Home those first months, nothing required of her beyond grieving so hard it made her vomit at times, even when she was so weak from the weight of her pain she could hardly face eating. Any fat she had to spare had melted off her bones, leaving her gaunt and without any energy at all.

That physical dwindling had been better, in ways, than the nightmare leading to her arrival—though she'd bargain with the Devil tonight if it meant seeing her son again. She wished she'd found the Home sooner, but it might not have changed a thing.

After Mattie had been at the Home a few weeks, Sister Susie had thought to ask how she'd found it. She showed her the pamphlet from outside the doctor's office but stopped short of mentioning the cleaning woman at the infirmary. Then, one cold January evening, the girls had gathered around the stove, their toes propped as close as they could get to the cast iron without burning them. "I miss Eunice," Dilly had said, suddenly. "It was odd how she could hear just fine, but not speak—though she could make herself perfectly clear when she needed to. I miss her quiet wisdom." She'd sighed.

Mattie usually tuned out the chatter, but she sat up straight. "When did she leave?"

Dilly had looked cautiously to the others before answering. "Oh, well, she was fine one minute, sick the next. She'd just gone to work in Fort Worth last spring, cleaning at the infirmary—no more than a week or so—and came down with pneumonia. We brought her back, and it only was a matter of days. We were terribly sad, but thankful she died here and not alone with strangers. She's out there in the burying ground." Dilly had nodded beyond the back of the house, and then carried on with her knitting while Mattie swallowed the lump in her throat. Even if she'd discovered the woman's name, she would never have been able to thank her.

It comforted Mattie now, though, knowing that Eunice, with her compassionate and motherly embrace, rested here with Cap. If Mattie could only believe in an afterlife . . .

Had Cap been punished because Mattie strayed from her mother's principles? If so, real faith was out of the question. How could she trust a God who would allow such a thing?

She dreamed now of living anywhere but Texas, where summers were more than she could bear. She had put weight back on and then some, now she was cooking again, but she often went light-headed just climbing the stairs in the heat—another reason to avoid the nursery.

She detested being seen as a weakling.

And she had her heart set on a *real* job—in an office or shop, earning enough to cover a decent room and essentials. She'd settled for her basic school diploma when they'd needed her at home, but did that mean she had to settle for cooking for a living the rest of her life?

She sighed. Her mother's voice, only six years gone, was hard to summon now, but her insight rang clear. "Smart as you are, you think the world should serve you," she'd have said. "That'll bring you nothing but heartache, my girl. Humble yourself. The blessings will follow."

Except her mother didn't know the humility Mattie had endured by now. She missed her something awful but was grateful Mama hadn't witnessed her downfall—either of them. Still, Mattie wouldn't wish away her years with Cap. She'd learned how far her heart could stretch, and that was no small thing. It was everything.

She ran her finger along the place grass didn't grow to trace the letters of his name on the tiny stone marker. *C-A-P.*

Oh, Cap.

The only time she allowed herself to think his name was here, in the quiet space of the burying ground. When her mind obeyed.

She struggled back to her feet—it seemed harder each time she left, when logic said it should be easier—and shook out her skirts. Back inside, the girls readied for bed, brushing each other's hair and sharing stories one minute, bickering over perceived slights the next, just like sisters. Sister Susie hovered in the doorway to remind them that arguing wasn't very Christian (and Saint Gertrude wagged her chin).

Mattie missed her real sisters—all three. Sometimes she wanted to slap these girls for diminishing what she, and so many of them, had lost with one shortsighted choice. Thank God Lizzie made it tolerable, replacing family as best anyone could.

But Lizzie had to come clean soon. Mattie had no intention of losing another sister.

CATE

Grissom, Texas
1998

I was sitting alone in the school cafeteria the day River placed a full lunch tray across from me and slid in without scoping out which groups sat where, without asking or waiting to be asked.

"So, what does anyone actually do around here for entertainment?"

I nearly dropped my book on my half eaten lunch. My best friend, Jess, and I had different schedules, of all years. We were seniors, and lunch was lonely, but I was used to it. The question, the way it was worded, could only have come from someone new, someone who didn't fit the Grissom mold. But that much was obvious. While the rest of us wore boot-cut jeans and T-shirts, River wore work pants sewn tight all the way to the ankle and a pearl snap shirt that could have come straight from someone's granddad's closet—the sleeves rolled multiple times. Nobody else I knew could have pulled it off, but the full effect was, in a word, disarming.

I promptly lost all abilities of intelligent dialogue.

"Sorry." River smiled. "I'll start over. I'm River. And I didn't mean to sound condescending. You're Cate, and you're a native, right? I assume you should be able to tell me what *you* do for fun, anyway."

Native. I half laughed at the description. "Well . . . I'm a library assistant?" I felt my cheeks flame.

I'd arrived late for lunch after the librarian asked me to handle a task that ran past the bell. I hadn't even cared. I loved the library, helping wherever I was needed—not to mention the break from my frustrating peers. Some days, I thought if another smart girl morphed into the village idiot around the football players, or if one more obnoxious boy grabbed his crotch behind a girl's back while his friends howled, I'd walk out the front door and never return. The librarian called me an old soul. I wasn't completely sure what that meant—but if it meant I could hide out in the library, I was on board.

My answer to River, however, with the uptick at the end, as if I wasn't even certain, sounded lame. River didn't abandon the conversation, though, even with that perfectly good excuse. "What about after school? Or weekends?"

"Read? Hang out with friends?" I shrugged, increasingly frustrated by my lack of conviction. "I . . . used to run track. I still like to run when I have time." I shrugged again in apology for my lackluster answers.

"I can see how you'd be too busy," River said bitingly, but added a repentant smile.

The truth was, my church was a big commitment. The biggest. When the doors were unlocked, my family was there. We had keys. My dad had been a deacon since I was two, and my mother had taught Sunday school to every third grader for eighteen years, including me. Sundays and Wednesday nights were standard. Fall meant Christmas music, spring meant fund-raisers, and summer meant camp, mission trip, and Vacation Bible School. Youth group kept us busy and, usually, out of trouble. Being a church kid was practically a full-time job, no time for anything else. No time for track.

But how could I explain all that?

While we—mostly River—talked, other students glanced our way, as if still trying to place the new kid, though the school year was more than half over. Because of the tech boom, unfamiliar faces in our small town northwest of Austin were becoming more commonplace, and it was no longer a given that we'd known every student in our class since before kindergarten. I pointedly ignored the looks. River seemed oblivious, as if not seeing them were the most natural thing in the world. Starting a new school senior year couldn't have been easy. I was intrigued.

The next day, River staked out a seat in the library after pulling a Texas history book from the stacks. Most kids came in only for required reading or sources for research papers. River, having moved from Colorado, cited cluelessness about the state's history beyond the Alamo. It didn't seem so off the rails—especially with what I knew after only one lunch: River's rails went where they wanted to.

I wondered at first if it was genuine interest, or just an excuse to be in the library—maybe near me. I was flattered but slightly uncomfortable with the thought. My classmates didn't need extra reasons to hassle me. I wasn't sure my already dubious reputation as the quiet, conservative church girl who worked in the library could tolerate any more. But when we walked to lunch together, I was suddenly elated to have a companion. I'd been lonelier than I'd realized.

After two weeks of the same—library, lunch, and casual conversation—River found me in the hallway after the Friday dismissal bell, carrying a battered guitar case and a flyer advertising an open mic at a new coffee shop. "There's this thing I'm playing tonight. You can come if you want to."

River hurried off, as if avoiding the possibility I might turn down the invitation. As if generally caring—despite nonchalance toward other students—whether I actually showed up.

So I dragged Jess with me that night, claiming I wanted to check out the new place. I didn't mention the open mic—or River. While Jess ogled community college boys, mostly already paired up with girlfriends, I watched the performers from the vantage point of a dark corner. When River stepped up to sound check, then began playing without further introduction, I leaned forward—not easy in a shabby wing chair with broken springs—caught up in the lyrics of the first stanza:

"Nobody notices you, not the way that I do . . . not the way that I do . . ."

It was a simple song, folky in rhythm and tune. My parents still listened to their old records—John Denver, Simon and Garfunkel, Joan Baez, and more—though they'd never admit it to their church friends. I'd cut my teeth on love ballads and quiet protest songs from the sixties and seventies. I'd pretended to tolerate them for years, but listening to River, I realized my parents had instilled an actual love for folk music in me despite my efforts to reject it.

And performed by a peer, the nostalgic lyrics and melody were mesmerizing.

In the car, on the radio, at youth group parties, at camp, pretty much everywhere, the only music my friends and I listened to was contemporary Christian. It was not so different from the Top 40 everyone else listened to, except instead of obsession and heartbreak, the songs were about unconditional love and Jesus. But I'd had no idea people my age were writing and playing music like River's. I'd been living in a bubble, but there was a separate one I didn't even know existed.

The music transformed River from a quirky, gangly teenager to an adult. An adult I was drawn to in ways I couldn't clearly articulate. It terrified me. River was not someone I was supposed to consider this way. I'd told myself we could be friends, someone to pass time with at school, but certainly nobody I'd ever view as more. Beyond the obvious, River's religious life seemed nonexistent, or at least, not the right brand—or we'd have met in church. Church was the only place to meet someone acceptable for dating. Plus, I'd been crushing hard on a former member of our youth group since well before he'd left for college two years earlier. Now Seth was back as our church's youth intern, and I'd been hoping to connect more meaningfully.

At least that was what I'd told myself until this moment in time, what I'd told my best friend, and even what I'd told my mom when I let her wiggle into my business.

But watching River lean close to the microphone, confiding the deepest of secrets into its depths, I felt something different than I felt when I was around Seth. I struggled to even recognize it for what it was, but I knew I was headed for trouble.

By the next Saturday, when I agreed to spend the afternoon driving to an abandoned train depot in a ghost town, with no second thoughts about whether I should ask my parents' permission, I was already half gone.

We drove nearly a hundred miles west into the Pedernales Valley in the Hill Country. River wanted to see the remains of a once-thriving resort town where, in the early 1900s, city dwellers from San Antonio, Houston, or Austin had taken in the scenery and the cool breezes that flowed through hotel galleries. The depot building was deserted but still standing. Could it, or anything else, reveal what a brief description and a few photos in an old Texas history book couldn't? Why had people gone to the trouble of building a town only to abandon it to the elements? River was full of curiosity but also loved photographing places where time, literally, seemed frozen. I'd always loved history. Most of the books I read were set in the past. Our mutual interest intensified my attraction to River, though I didn't admit that at first.

We almost missed it. But from studying the map and watching the odometer on the dash of River's battered Honda Civic, I knew it had to be coming up soon. "Slow down," I said, peering at low piles of rubble and ruins. Farther afield, scattered farmhouses looked as if they might or might not be occupied.

"Okay, Bossy Pants." River's smile convinced me not to be offended.

"That's Miss Bossy Pants to you. Pull in there." A road perpendicular to the two-lane highway was little more than a rutted path, but wide enough to park. The farther you looked into the distance, the more the path disintegrated, tall weeds growing up in the center fifty yards or so away. Nobody had driven this road for months—maybe years.

While I stretched, River retrieved a thirty-five-millimeter camera from the trunk.

"This is crazy," I said, as we walked toward the one remaining building.

River's responding smile was tight, and I backtracked. "I mean how little is left. What used to be a whole town is just being absorbed back into the dirt. Like scraps in a compost pile."

River's face relaxed again. "You know what compost is? I thought maybe it was just a Colorado thing."

"Before my parents found religion, they were hippies."

River raised an eyebrow. I found it hard to believe too.

"Maybe not like Colorado hippies, but definitely counterculture for around here. They lived in a little commune in Austin from the midseventies until right after I was born. I think it embarrasses them now. My dad had really long hair and—actually, so did my mom. Macramé. Bell-bottoms. The works. They even drove a VW van." I laughed nervously, as if I were telling a made-up story. I struggled to imagine them that way, but I'd seen the photo album on the lowest corner of Mom's bookshelf. "They probably even smoked a little weed back in the day, though they'd never admit it now. I think it was only a phase."

"What are they like now?" River said.

"Well, we have a garden and a compost pile, but you wouldn't know they were the same people. And they would definitely not approve of me taking off like this."

"You didn't tell them?" River seemed genuinely surprised.

I shrugged. "Some things are better left unexplained."

Leaving town without telling my parents would have been an act of rebellion, even if they'd known River. Taking off along a highway winding west from Austin and then an even windier road to abandoned Carr City, however, was an outright violation of trust. In spite of my outward nonchalance, I felt guilty. I'd suggested we meet at the coffee shop's parking lot without explaining that I was basically sneaking away. The shop stayed open late on Saturdays, and we would return before it closed. If my mom saw my car there, she'd assume I was inside studying for AP exams—just as I'd told her that morning.

But River deserved a better explanation. I took a breath. "My parents are the opposite of hippies now. When I was a baby, they went to this huge religious revival in Florida. Now they're as devoted to church as they were to being hippies. They are nothing if not passionate."

I braced myself. I knew where the conversation would go next.

"What about you?" River said. "I mean, are you into church? How often do you go?"

We'd paused near the buildings, and I sighed. This was where things would get sticky. River's eyebrows furrowed more the longer

I hesitated, and that feeling rose in me that so often came with the territory when I had to explain my life to kids who lived differently. It seemed foreign to them—and usually not in a good way.

I definitely hadn't been up front about how I spent my free time. But I'd learned something from my God-fearing parents I absolutely agreed with: Honesty really was the best policy, in every situation. It had been easy to pretend I wasn't deceiving them that morning—I *had* studied in the coffee shop for an hour before I left with River. But it was a lie of omission, just as this had been. Now I regretted it.

"Sunday morning," I said. "Sunday night. Wednesday night. Lots of times between."

I started walking again, and as we arrived at the abandoned train depot and the small building that flanked it, River slowed to lift the camera, focused on the rusted hardware on a door at the side, then pressed the shutter, shifting several times to get the shot at various angles.

"I don't know anything about any of that. I've never even been inside a church. My grandparents used to try to convince my mom to take me, but she refused. I guess around here, people would probably consider us, like . . . heathens? I'd just say agnostic. But that wasn't uncommon in Colorado. No wonder you didn't tell them we were hanging out—I mean, you've probably figured me out at least a little by now."

I had. It was me I was all confused about.

I shrugged. I couldn't deny it, and I wasn't sure I cared. That scared me. In fact, this whole day was beginning to scare me more than I wanted to admit. The funny thing, though, was that when I thought of Seth now, I hardly felt anything.

River lowered the camera and reached to test the doorknob in spite of the obvious black-and-orange *No Trespassing* sign posted on it. The door was not locked, but I hung back.

"You don't have to go in," River said, shrugging indifferently, "but I want to see what's in there and take some pictures."

This happened all the time. When people learned how involved

I was in church, they treated me differently. A bit defensive on one hand, as if they felt continually judged, but slightly patronizing on the other, as if I were some cute, slightly exotic zoo animal in a cage, lacking the freedom to live a real life. It didn't help to explain that for the most part, I actually loved my life, and that my church friends and I would do almost anything for each other. That we had fun together. That my parents never forced me to go, and I'd never used them as an excuse.

I had chosen that life.

But something made me brush aside the caution I usually felt when tempted to do something forbidden—and the guilt at entering this off-limits place.

"I want to see what it's like," I said.

I followed River through a door clinging to hinges barely attached to the frame. Inside, an almost eerie half light poked through several holes in a ceiling that had been solid at some point in the past but seemed now as if it could cave in at any minute.

"Are you scared?" River said.

"I might be."

"We'll be fine. Do you think anyone is going to haul two people like us off to jail?"

I looked at River, then down at myself, and conceded it wasn't likely. I took the hand I was offered and allowed myself be tugged along, deeper into the murky light.

LIZZIE

Arlington, Texas
1905

Lizzie understood Mattie's wishes to make a new life outside the Home more than Mattie could guess, even if she did not relate to it. Mattie *could* find a respectable job, with only herself to support, and a room in a boardinghouse with the protection of a careful landlady.

Lizzie worried about Mattie's health, though, and her smart mouth and her rapid, sometimes reckless decisions, here or anywhere else. Mattie's fury at Gertrude last night had only increased that unease— even if Mattie's determination to help May seemed equal now to Lizzie's. If Mattie had any hesitation left, you'd never know it.

After scripture and prayers the next morning, with little time before they'd expect her in the nursery, Lizzie barreled along the central hall, fast as her clumsy legs would take her, toward Brother JT's study. He'd encouraged her to bring questions for him to comb through, instead of leaving them all tangled in her head. She couldn't examine the scriptures like the others could, and Brother JT was patient and kind when she couldn't find understanding through prayer alone.

Today, though, she reckoned she might stump him.

As she neared the end of the hall, hushed voices drifted around the doorway to the tiny reception area for Brother JT's office. One male. One female. Lizzie slowed. Lizzie had left the dining room ahead of Sister Susie, and Brother JT's wife was rarely at the Home so early. She was generally across the road getting her older kids off to school.

The woman laughed softly, and Lizzie realized it was just Miss

Hallie, who arranged the newsletter each month and helped with the money. She seemed to love her work, but she kept the fallen girls at arm's length. Their talking seemed private, though. Nearly intimate.

Eavesdropping was sinful, yet Lizzie struggled to move her feet. Miss Hallie herself had an essay in *The Purity Journal* that warned of the perils working girls faced. Mattie had read it to her. But Brother JT was a man of high morals and character. Lizzie knew it herself, beyond a doubt. Miss Hallie would never be in any danger with him.

Lizzie exaggerated her uneven gait, allowing her foot to drag heavier than usual against the floorboards. Miss Hallie's laughter cut off abruptly and a chair scraped the office floor, louder than Lizzie's shoe. Lizzie rounded the last step into the office. Miss Hallie and Brother JT stood behind her desk.

Miss Hallie was no more attractive than Lizzie herself, but Lizzie's dark hair and eyes increased the sharpness of her nose and square chin, while Miss Hallie's mousy waves washed out her softer features. Today, though, her cheeks and eyes glowed, nearly pretty in spite of nature's hand. In fact, Lizzie would almost vouch that Miss Hallie was flustered.

Brother JT strode around the desk. At the pulpit, you'd never suspect the Reverend Upchurch was shorter than most men by half a foot, hardly bigger than a boy. He was gentle and sweet-tempered with the girls, but when he preached the Word, he seemed to impart the actual voice of God. He appeared anything but small.

"Good morning, Sister Elizabeth!" he boomed. "To what do we owe this pleasure? Are we running short of diapering cloth? Toys? The budget is dire, but we won't let our little ones suffer—even if I go without a pay slip again this month." Brother JT often refused his modest salary from the funds he raised—he said so frequently in his addresses.

Lizzie twisted her fingers into the edges of her apron. "Some things been puzzling me lately, if you got the time."

Brother JT waved Lizzie into his study. "Come, come! Your curiosity keeps me honest, in my own studies and other ways."

Lizzie felt her cheeks burn, but his smile calmed her. She sank into a springy upholstered chair near his desk, then moved back to the edge. She shouldn't get comfortable. Not today.

Miss Hallie pulled her desk chair just inside the door. She no longer glowed. Lizzie dragged her gaze away from Miss Hallie's glare and swallowed her nerves. She hadn't expected an extra audience that treated her like a bother at best and a threat at worst.

Brother JT didn't seem threatened. He leaned his chin on his clasped hands, bolstering her with his warmth.

"Brother JT, you brung so many here in the worst condition, hardly worth the trouble—"

He interrupted. "Every single soul is worth saving and absolutely worth the trouble."

"But you let a girl go when she were at her worst. Is she not worth it too?"

Brother JT stilled. As always, he carefully weighed his response. He gave every complicated question a thinking reply, not rattled from a list of easy answers. She trusted him as she'd trusted no other man.

Miss Hallie had been silent. Now she drew her shoulders back. "We can't have girls doing whatever they please and jeopardizing our reputation. We have our limits. We help those willing to help themselves."

Lizzie took a big breath. "But sometimes you have to do the thinking if a girl can't do it on her own. Sometimes dope speaks louder than the truth."

"A valid point," Brother JT said. Miss Hallie plucked at her collar, as if her brooch pin suddenly poked her sallow neck. "We often ask ourselves how far to go . . . how forceful we should be. Should we keep a girl against her will? It's not our practice. You must be thinking of May." He paused for an instant, and Lizzie pressed her fingers harder into her apron. She forced herself not to scratch her arms, for they always set to itching again when she felt nervous. "May was the hardest case we've attempted. We didn't think she'd survive the first night. We believed we were providing a final resting place for a girl too far gone."

"I were far gone, too." Lizzie released her apron and grasped the edge of Brother JT's desk. "I shouldn't have lived through what I done."

Brother JT leaned closer and covered Lizzie's hand.

"You had a reason to fight," he said. "An angel needed her mother. One of the best motivators we have is the innocent child that so often accompanies the woman. It gives her a real, tangible reason to make good."

Docie had been her reason; Lizzie knew it. Without her and the grace of God, she'd never have pulled through. But that didn't answer the rest. "If ever' single soul is worth saving," she said, "why wouldn't we fight for those who can't do it for themselves?"

Brother JT sighed. "We make our hardest decisions in the interest of who could be hurt by our stubbornness. May was given more than a fair chance. We were willing to look past the damage to Sister Susie's quarters, but when she threatened physical harm to those caring for her, we let her go. We couldn't force her to stay, not at the risk of the health of our workers, or girls, or heaven forbid, our children."

He searched her face. "Can you understand, Lizzie? You have a generous heart. You want every fallen girl—every human and . . . every creature—to gain the security you've found. The sad truth is, though we can attempt to emulate our savior, we are not God. We can only do so much. I wish as much as you do that we'd been able to help May to a better life. She was so very sick. No telling where she might be now—or if she's even alive."

Lizzie couldn't look him in the eye. "I'd best get back to my babies. They'll wonder what's happened to me."

Brother JT followed her to the door. He patted Lizzie's shoulder. "You're always welcome here. I'm proud you're strong—and courageous enough—to devote your heart and mind to difficult questions. Our Heavenly Father must smile."

Lizzie forced a smile of her own and walked toward the outer door, where Miss Hallie had positioned herself, as if to be sure Lizzie left. Lizzie reckoned Miss Hallie needn't worry about anyone but herself.

On her way out, Lizzie recalled a few months before, when she'd seen a stray dog wandering the property. She'd watched first Gertrude shoo it from where it begged at the kitchen door, and then Sister Susie, who backed away from it on the front porch, commanding it to leave.

The dog had run off down the walk into the dirt road but returned eventually to where Lizzie sat on the steps. She hadn't the heart to yell. The dog followed her all the way beyond the buildings to the farm field, then clambered up next to Lizzie on her favorite sitting rock.

Lizzie had noticed that the dog's belly was full, her teats pink and hanging low. Her heart sank. The dog's patchy hair teemed with fleas, eyes and ears crusty from scratching, but Lizzie knew she was expecting pups—any minute by the looks of her. And she gazed at Lizzie through weepy golden eyes.

Sighing, Lizzie had hopped back off the rock and walked farther with the dog. Several in the Home had campaigned for a house pet but were firmly turned down by Sister Susie. It was no use asking if they could make a place for it, even in one of the outbuildings.

The dog trotted alongside her with swinging belly and panting tongue as Lizzie approached the Berachah Beauty Spot—a little meadow near the southwest property line, so named for the wildflowers that bloomed there each spring. It was usually one of the quietest places on the grounds, away from the clatter of everyday activity. But that day, Lizzie heard an unmistakable sound—Brother JT's gentle, but booming voice.

She and the dog came up over a small rise, and there he stood, before the field of flowers that quivered in the breeze, like a sanctuary full of rapt worshippers nodding with each beat of his sermon. He held up a hand to prevent Lizzie from speaking until he finished. She waited patiently, the dog beside her.

"What have we here?" he said a moment later.

She blushed, embarrassed to be interrupting. He assured her he was simply rehearsing his message for the following Sunday. "It's my favorite place to preach," he said. "The flowers tell me if I've been listening to God or chasing rabbits. Now, who's this?"

"A stray, I reckon. I never seen her and she's covered in fleas—and about to have her some pups."

"Ah. Sister Susie won't have her at all, will she?" He grinned at Lizzie's shrug of mouth. "My wife and Susie would have my head for this, I think, but lead her to that old barn across campus. Surely we can find a few rags to stuff down in a crate, and I'll get my hands on something to feed her until they're ready to move on. You know we can't keep them, don't you, Lizzie? But I'll ask around town to see who's in the market for a puppy."

She'd followed his directions, and by the time he appeared in the barn, the mama dog was pushing the first pup out. They settled her quickly in the wooden crate and watched together as she birthed the first, and then three others. The last one didn't wriggle, not after its mother licked the membrane away or when she pushed the tiny creature with her nose to the far corner of the crate. Lizzie's eyes filled as she carefully removed the runt, feeling how cold he already was.

"I was afraid that might be the case," Brother JT said. "I've seen a few litters of pups in my lifetime. I'll bury it after a while."

She nodded. The other three latched on to the mother's teats and sucked vigorously, with tiny mewling noises.

"I'll check on them, morning and night. Don't you worry, we'll find them homes." Brother JT's eyes twinkled, and Lizzie grinned in spite of her sadness over the dead one. "It'll cost an arm and a leg in meat as long as she's feeding the babies. We'll have to be creative."

Lizzie's neck and ears had burned. She'd brought yet another expense upon an already struggling household of nearly forty. "I can get you some money easy," she said.

The words tumbled out, before she could think to stop them, as if her life hadn't changed at all since coming to the Home. Brother JT swung his head from the litter. She clapped her hands over her mouth, her face aflame.

"No, no . . ." he said. For once, he seemed otherwise speechless.

In her contract, she'd promised to never to be alone with a man. She'd promised to think before acting. And she'd promised to never again offer her body in exchange for money or favors. In less than ten minutes, she'd broken the first two and suggested the third.

She cowered against the crate. "I don't know why I said it. Please don't think I'm bad."

When she dared to look at his eyes, he shook his head. "I'll take responsibility for the dog and puppies. But see, Lizzie, we must be careful. People like you and me, when we see a need, we struggle to manage our hearts."

She'd run back to the house, begging the Lord's forgiveness the entire way. She told herself her extreme desire to help one of God's creatures was the only reason her shameful words surfaced, a knee-jerk reaction.

Several weeks later, the Upchurch children squealed in their yard as their daddy carried a puppy under each arm across the road. The mama dog was gone, and Lizzie assumed she was safe on a farm somewhere, maybe with her third baby. She'd wondered now and then where Brother JT had buried the littlest but trusted he'd taken care of it, just as he'd taken care of the entire situation, quietly and without judgment.

Leaving Miss Hallie's office today, Lizzie said, "Bye now."

Miss Hallie sniffed and nodded, but as Lizzie went down the hall, she sensed those eyes boring a suspicious hole in her back. She didn't blame her. She didn't trust herself some days either.

Brother JT's arguments about May were sensible. But when Lizzie thought of her, tied up in the moldy hayloft in that same old barn where the pups had lived, in the fight of her life, she knew the Home had missed a chance. They had to go further, in spite of everything, and Lizzie had to be the one to prove it.

MEMORANDUM

DATE: June 1, 1905

TO: Mr. Albert Ferry, Printer for the Berachah Rescue Society

CC: Miss Hallie V. Taylor, Secretary and Treasurer of the Berachah Industrial Home

FROM: Reverend J. T. Upchurch, Founder and Director of the Berachah Industrial Home

RE: Statement for next issue of *The Purity Journal*

Please include the following thoughts in next month's issue (bordered box, page three):

Among all the sinners he redeemed, none attracts and holds the attention of a lost world like fallen women. There is something so utterly hopeless in their case that even an attempt to reach them immediately attracts widespread attention.

The work has suffered some on account of enthusiastic workers persuading girls to go to the Home, as if it were Heaven, which, when reached, would settle all other questions.

The most difficult of all the work we do is out at the Home. Every girl admitted there is a problem in need of a solution.

And some are stubborn problems.

—J.T.U., ed.

MATTIE

Arlington, Texas
1905

Mattie had wanted to stop Lizzie from rushing off after breakfast. She knew where she was headed and hoped she'd take care. If she got herself thrown out—and heaven forbid Docie with her—the world would chew her up and spit her out as fast and as far as you could think. She was an angel with the babies but had no skill for anything else but menial labor. Her family had plainly told her if she darkened their doorstep again, they'd kill her.

Lizzie hadn't deserved the hand dealt her the first twenty years of her life.

Mattie's own family hadn't been so evil. She'd disgraced them, after all. It was only fair they'd pushed her away. And she'd pay the rest of her days—in all likelihood, alone. A man who would take on a woman with her history was rare.

Sister Susie caught her arm on her way out of the dining room. "Come by my desk when you have a minute, dear. I have something for you."

Mattie could have gone then, but Lizzie would walk directly past the kitchen after leaving Brother JT's study. She propped the swinging door open with a bootjack.

Gertrude slammed a lid on a pot. "Five minutes until the nursery tray has to go up."

"Olive's feet are swollen, and Lizzie Bates is down the hall. She can take the tray up with her."

Gertrude harrumphed, but Olive's time was nearly on her, and they insisted she keep her feet up when possible. Olive shot a grateful look from where she dried dishes, belly crowded against the drainer.

"What's Lizzie bothering Brother JT about now?" Gertrude said.

Mattie held her tongue—biting hard—until she was able to speak without yelling. "You know Lizzie always has questions about how to truly love one another." She couldn't help dripping sarcasm like honey.

Gertrude ignored it. "Well, we must be mindful of Brother JT's time. Oh! Mattie," she said, pausing to slice bread for the griddle, "someone's been downstairs in the night, snitching food. Would you know anything about that?"

Mattie nearly dropped a plate as she stepped back and forth loading the tray. Gertrude monitored what went in or out as if she paid the food bill herself. "Who would do such a thing without asking?"

"With you and Lizzie loitering on the porch by my kitchen door, you might wonder."

"Oh, Gert. If Docie were still hungry after her supper, you wouldn't begrudge her a bite, would you, even from *your* kitchen?"

"That child eats entirely too much," Gertrude said, shaking out her apron. "Everyone spoils her. And the other little ones don't run wild with the Upchurch children when they visit. She should know her place."

Mattie gaped. "At three years old, she should know that other children are better and can't be her playmates because of who her mother is? *Was*?" She placed extra emphasis on the last word, for they were daily reminded they were new creations, not who they used to be.

"Well, that's not *exactly* what I'm saying."

Mattie couldn't bite her tongue again. "And why would a woman with an illegitimate girl in the nursery keep company with a man of the cloth? Surely *she* should know her place."

Gertrude gasped, and spots rose on her cheeks. "Reverend Woods and I have Brother JT's blessing. I've confessed, I'm forgiven, and the Lord is gracious. How dare you suggest I don't deserve a second chance?"

Mattie gazed at Gertrude, her lips set in a line.

They heard Lizzie's dragging steps in the hall. Gertrude scowled and banged a mug onto the tray, shoving it at Lizzie as Mattie pulled her into the kitchen. "Mattie said you'd take it, seeing as you're already downstairs. You two know too much about what the other is up to."

Lizzie's mouth went slack. Mattie simply shook her head and touched a finger to her lips. Following Lizzie into the hall, she leaned to whisper. "What were you—"

"For heaven's sake, leave Lizzie to her work," Gertrude hollered. "Can't leave the two of you alone. Maybe the Devil has hold of you both again." Lizzie cowered, the weight of the tray dragging at her. "Mattie, we thought you'd experienced a real conversion, but maybe it was all for show. Are you trying to bring Lizzie down with you? Make her think she can do as she pleases? For shame."

Mattie felt mad enough to hit the woman, but Lizzie jumped between them as Gertrude approached. "She ain't done nothing wrong. She encourages me, straight in my ear, when I can't hardly stand being good. She's an angel."

Gertrude pressed her palms against her waistband, looking from one girl to the other, clearly unconvinced. Lizzie wasn't one to make a speech. "I won't remind you again to hurry with that tray. Those poor babies surely think you've abandoned them with no morning milk."

Lizzie cringed. Mattie closed her eyes. Gertrude herself knew how to hit harder than Mattie would ever think to.

Suddenly, Miss Hallie emerged from the shadows, startling all three. "Gracious, Miss Gertrude! Those were stinging words. No need to shame Lizzie. The children are fine."

Had she been listening all along?

Gertrude drew herself up. "Please forgive my thoughtlessness."

Lizzie gave Mattie a sideways glance. Mattie was still furious. "Sister Susie asked me to see her in her office," she said. "And I don't believe the kitchen is the best place for me."

"Nonsense," Miss Hallie said. "Two new girls arrive this afternoon. They'll need feeding."

Mattie stomped back into the kitchen and clattered dishes against the drain board. For all of Miss Hallie's distance keeping, at least the woman wasn't cruel.

But now she'd be watching them like a hawk.

CATE

Arlington, Texas
2017

I allowed myself that one night of unrestricted, unrestrained remembering. I listened to River's CD and then buried it far back in my nightstand drawer. I could throw it away, but something stops me.

Over the next few weeks, I think of River more often than I have in years. Hardly a day has ever gone by without some song, some movie, some tiny scrap of life to remind me. But I've always swept it away. Now, my mind is crowded with all I've never been able to forget, and I cannot clear it out.

By the time the semester settles in, with everyone accustomed to the rhythm and flow of classes, papers, and exams, Thanksgiving break is around the corner.

My experience starting college was overwhelming—exceptionally so, considering what had happened that spring and summer. College was the last thing I wanted to think about then.

I assume most students I meet in the course of my work are facing various pressures, but I've rarely allowed myself to get close enough to know how they're really doing—especially the freshmen. Are they coping with the different expectations college presents? Are they overwhelmed? Homesick? Missing family and friends?

I'd been all that and more, because I'd been cut off from my support system in one fell swoop. Or, more precisely, I cut myself off. But I still missed them.

A week before Thanksgiving break, on a quiet afternoon, Laurel

finishes her routine work and pulls the Berachah collection. I'm reviewing activity logs at the desk, but I can see her. First, she dons the
gloves and sifts through the photos. She looks up at one point, sweeping her long bangs off her forehead and behind an ear.

"Lotta white girls in these pictures," she calls, a smirk on her face.
I've noticed too. In one photo of everyone gathered in the tabernacle, I
had spied a lone black woman at the very back of the auditorium, with
a young black boy a few rows ahead. I've wondered who they were. A
family housekeeper? Her son? And if they were welcomed, why only
them?

Laurel's last name, tawny skin, rich brown eyes, and jet-black hair
would have made her stand out, too, though not quite as much. Would
a Latina girl have been admitted into the Home? It's impossible to
guess. There's one girl with coloring similar to Laurel's in a group
photo, but her ethnicity isn't clear.

"It was the times," I say, sighing, with no other explanation to offer,
though I realize how pitiful it sounds. "In one *Journal*, JT mentioned
a rescue home for black women in St. Louis. Maybe some women
were referred up there. But it's hard to say. And maybe those families
weren't so quick to kick girls to the curb."

"Yeah," she says, resigned to the hypocrisy—the indisputable flaws
of this history we've come to love. We can hope things have changed,
but we both know how much disparity there still is in our world.

Laurel opens one of the ledgers. After a while, she pushes back her
chair and slams it closed. She's never handled anything in the collection carelessly, not even the newest, sturdiest items. She gazes straight
ahead, with a set to her mouth I haven't seen. Without looking my
way, she says, "I need to talk to a teacher about an assignment. Can I
leave early?"

Today is Laurel's longest afternoon shift. She's proven to be a me-
ticulous worker, reliable and responsible to a fault. Her sudden request
surprises me, even though it's a quiet day. "Sure," I say. "Will you be
back?"

"Would you mind if I just took off the rest of today?" She twists her bangs forward again, nearly covering her eyes. It's no wonder her hair often appears oily, though I wonder how often she washes it—much less gets it cut.

I stand and walk close to her. "Are you okay? Anything going on?"

"Nope. I'm fine," she says. Her nervous hands contradict her. Something has shifted, but she's not going to say why. Witnessing someone shut down like this is eerie. Like a mirror I don't want to look into but also can't escape.

"Okay, then," I say. "See you Thursday?"

Laurel shrugs and quickly returns the ledger to the box. I glance at the year on the cover: 1921. "Anything interesting in there?"

Instead of my question breaking the tension, her voice gets an even sharper edge. "Yep. Instead of taking girls in, they were turning them away." She loads the cart and pushes it to the desk, then retrieves her overflowing backpack from the drawer. I watch through the glass doors until she steps into the elevator, then pull the ledger back out of the box.

Laurel is correct; the majority of entries for 1921 pertain to requests for the Home to accept new girls, followed by the matron's reasons for rejection, reiterating their lack of space. The few accepted were pregnant, jilted by sweethearts or deserted by husbands. One entry catches my eye: *Mrs. Mattie Madigan, Oklahoma City, called to see if we will take a young girl who works in a laundry, susceptible to advances of young stepfather. Turned down. Not ruined.*

I've read it before—and had been thrilled to see her name. But the surname is different and Mattie wasn't an unusual first name for that time. I haven't been able to confirm for sure if it's *my* Mattie. Now, though, I'm really worried. Laurel has hinted that she left home before finishing her senior year of high school, staying with friends a few weeks at a time until she graduated. Her abrupt departure today has me especially curious to know why.

I peer closer. Halfway down the page, something has dripped onto the page, but it's not faded, as damage a century old would be. The smear is in process. Still damp. The words, firmly penned years ago, distort before my eyes. I replay the image of Laurel at the table. Liquids aren't allowed anywhere but the break room, and besides, Laurel doesn't break rules.

This teardrop is fresh.

I file the ledger again, then grab my jacket and umbrella from my office. It was pouring when I left for work this morning. Another student worker is manning the desk, so I peek into my boss's office to say I need to run across campus. A good delegator, she rarely questions anything I do. Today, she hardly looks away from her screen.

On a hunch, I walk toward the busy road at the edge of campus. I've worn practical boots for a change, and I'm grateful as I cross the footbridge and wind through the rooted path. It's chilly and misty and gloomy—even more under the canopy of trees. The leaves haven't all fallen, but the ground is strewn with them, and it's muddy and slick. Autumn has finally, forcefully, made an appearance after the green but hot and humid months that began the school year. I've avoided the cemetery since the concert, and the change is startling.

Today, I knew Laurel would be here, for reasons more instinctive than logical. I debate entering. I mostly want to see if she's okay. That she's safe. The realization jars me. I never expected to—never *wanted* to—experience these kind of maternal feelings, but they've crept up and slammed right into me. My relief at seeing her is, undoubtedly, one of the most unsettling emotions I've experienced in years. Of course, this fall is already one for the books.

She stands before the memorial to Reverend Upchurch, and from a distance, I watch her grip the top, firmly, almost as if she's shaking someone by the shoulders, though the stone doesn't budge. Then she steps back, and I can't decipher her words, but she speaks loudly, harshly. She sinks down by the concrete block and her entire body trembles. I can't help myself—I rush through the gate, but carefully, so I won't frighten her.

When she sees me, she flinches, and she hides behind those bangs. "Sorry. I shouldn't have lied, but I had to get out of there."

I shake my head. "You're not in trouble."

Her expression remains defiant. "You know, I like my job. I love looking at the archives—especially the Berachah things. But some of it makes me so sad. And *mad*." Her fists are still clenched.

"Yes," I say.

"An entry in the ledger . . ." Her voice fades, but I wait. "About them not taking a girl Mattie wanted to send?"

"I read it after you left," I say. "I knew something upset you." I note how she says Mattie, just like I do, as if we both know for sure it's *our* Mattie. My obsession is hers, too, now.

She sighs loudly, but then she can't unload quickly enough. "The Upchurches made a big deal about getting girls off the streets and helping them make new lives. Why wouldn't they take one *before* she messed up—before someone messed *her* up? Why wait for the solution to be hard when it might have been easy?" She throws her hands high, fists finally open. "They only wanted to clean up."

I nod. "It bothers me too. Society worked hard to make sure girls weren't doing things they weren't supposed to—but in general, nobody was there to pick them up after they stumbled. So maybe the Home filled a gap nobody else could. Or would."

"It was only one girl. They didn't care about her." She practically shakes, breathing hard.

"I bet they cared," I say, even while unwelcome feelings creep up my neck, forcing me to remember things I don't want to. "Okay. I want to *think* they cared. I really do. They were willing to take girls who had nowhere else to go, ones nobody else would touch. Surely they cared. But maybe their hands were tied."

"I guess." She takes a deeper breath, sighing.

I do too. Once again, my excuses sound half-empty.

Laurel gazes into the middle of the cemetery, where stone after tiny stone marks graves for babies and children who perished while living in an institution. It's hard to call it that, because it feels like the Home was so much more. In reality, it would never have been anyone's first choice. "Do you ever wonder," she says quietly, "whether adults who claim to be doing good really do care? Or are they doing it for other reasons? Maybe just for show. Like, 'Hey, look at us!'"

And now I have gooseflesh. Could Laurel know what happened to me at exactly her age? Because what she says is true. The adults in my life were too busy maintaining the illusion of doing good works. The adults who were supposed to look out for me protected themselves instead—especially one who should have taken the blame but left me to clean up alone. There's no way Laurel could know this. I've never spoken of it to anyone. But there must be a reason she's so tuned in to how I felt.

I'm scared to be blunt, though. I recognize her tendency to run when things get personal. I'm the pro, after all. "You're right," I say, carefully. "Life is unfair. People often worry more about their own reputations than about what happens to those who depend on them. I wish I had a better answer." I run my fingers across flecks of lichen encrusting the rough surface of the Home's dedication stone. They catch at my skin, and suddenly I'm spurred to impulse.

"What are you doing for Thanksgiving? Will you be with family? Friends?"

The simple question shutters Laurel's face again. She shrugs. "Probably. But right now I can't worry about anything but school and getting my work done."

Thanksgiving is nine days away. I plunge on. It seems critical now. "I don't have family around, and I'm not a big holiday person, but I usually try to scrounge up something festive—even if it's a little turkey dinner from a restaurant. If you have no place to go, let me know before school's out. You can even text me that morning."

Eating turkey and dressing alone is not necessarily festive, but I make a mental note to actually order dinner, Laurel or no. I'm not sure what I'm suggesting is allowed. Instructors aren't supposed to fraternize with students, but I'm not an instructor, exactly, and we're more or less co-workers. *I need to not worry about that right now.* "I hope that doesn't seem weird. I just hate thinking of anyone being alone on the holiday." *Like I've been,* I think. For nearly twenty years.

Laurel shakes her head. "I'm sure I'll end up somewhere, but . . . thanks."

She claims she needs to prepare for her night class. We walk back toward campus, where we part, me toward the library, her to who knows where, and I promise myself I'll keep an eye on her over the next week. Someone needs to care about her, and it looks like that's me.

In the process—in the caring—my cold heart may thaw a little. I struggle with the full knowledge that there might be—most certainly will be—pain in the thawing.

LIZZIE

Arlington, Texas
1905

Lizzie walked with more drag in her step than ever. All the years of hard living hindered her now, especially if she was fretting, as if worries weighed her down in some physical kind of way. Soon she'd have to give up this secret to more than just Mattie. When Lizzie arrived at the barn, though, May was waiting quietly, more peaceful than on any of Lizzie's other trips, and Lizzie could almost believe the plan might work.

May had come back Sunday, only a day after her departure, tail tucked, but high on dope again. She'd pleaded on the Home's doorstep, repentant and regretful that she'd wasted her chance to get clean. She couldn't help her actions in her state, she'd said, but they'd turned her away. Their facilities were inadequate to keep a girl who wouldn't—or couldn't—cooperate.

She'd found Lizzie gathering early cotton bolls in the field to make dolls for the little ones and begged her to take her somewhere safe—safe from herself. Somewhere she could get off the dope without hurting anyone. "You'll have to tie me down," she said.

Lizzie had gaped at May. Her heart had felt sick. Even if the worst sinner was worthy of grace, she hadn't expected May to show up in that field, asking her to prove it.

All her life, though, Lizzie had given herself fully when asked, an obedient girl nearly to a fault, for it hurt her more often than not. But between Bible time with the other girls and her talks with Brother

JT, she was learning that the evil she'd thought her fault was forced upon her.

Her real pa had drowned before she was old enough to know him. When Lizzie was six, her ma, weary of trying to make it alone, had married the first man who would take her. He was not the honorable sort, nor his sons. She wondered whether Ma had known better when she walked them both into that den of vipers. Maybe she was used to cruelty. Maybe her people were no different. The first time Lizzie's stepbrother took her, out by the creek, her mother whipped her for tattling. She'd been no more than eight or nine, and so Lizzie assumed that was the way of being a woman. The way they lived, off in the towering pines south of Tyler, there weren't any girlfriends or teachers to tell her different. Lizzie didn't learn what was proper until the Home. Sometimes the change had been hard. Sometimes she'd wanted to run away herself, mostly when she tired of the heavy expectations. But she'd stuck it out. Soon May would be strong enough to stick things out too.

That first day, May had cooperated, of course, for Lizzie wouldn't have carried out her request if not. She'd huddled in the floor of the hayloft while Lizzie brushed away the worst of the moldy straw to make a soft spot to rest her head. She was still there when Lizzie returned with a tattered sheet from the rag bag, a pail for May's business, and a coiled rope she'd pinched from the new barn after lifting her eyes to ask for grace once again.

Lizzie hadn't fed her that night, knowing the runs and vomiting would begin before long, and it would go easier and faster on an empty stomach. May went to the pallet and willingly undressed to her shift, even removing her bloomers, then held her wrists out for Lizzie to tie so she couldn't free herself. She'd cried before Lizzie left, praising her kindness.

And then it was time to wait, for May had been floating in a dope haze, just high enough to forget the hell of withdrawal.

The second night, Lizzie changed the bedsheet, crusted with May's mess. May was like a child begging for a sweet: "Be a love and clean my face. I can't stand the stink of my own sweat and vomit. Just a cool cloth to wipe my forehead and mouth. Please, honey?"

Lizzie had thought to trust May, with nearly two days conquered, but May had lurched and clamped her jaw down tight on Lizzie's fingers. Lizzie knew May felt powerless, like a street dog, a poor, wounded mess of sores and blacked eyes and stink, nothing but rotten teeth to fight with. Why May hadn't bit her when Lizzie fed her, Lizzie couldn't guess. Maybe it was the distance of the spoon—or maybe May wouldn't risk a meal if she wanted free.

"Let go, May," Lizzie had said, her voice steady, projecting her last bit of calm while her brain screamed she was an idiot. Her dumb trust had brought her nearly all the trouble she'd ever seen, so when it tripped her again, she wanted to strike her own face and call herself all the ugly names she'd tried so hard to forget at the Home.

May had pressed her teeth tighter and glared a hole so fierce it drew a shiver from Lizzie.

"Now, May, you don't want to do that. I'm trying to help you overcome what's killing you from the inside out. It's the dope talking. It ain't you."

"Untie me, you little witch," May hissed. The words were muffled, but Lizzie understood. "You're short. Fat. Ugly as a troll. How did any man stand getting you with child?"

She let go just enough so Lizzie could free her fingers. May spat as Lizzie backed away. Lizzie wiped her bare arm with a clean rag from the laundry, grateful it wasn't covered in a sleeve, having pushed hers high before going in the barn. She'd need the carbolic before she returned to the house, but leastways she wouldn't have to launder her dress. Putting one in the wash that appeared perfectly clean would cause a ruckus.

May screeched again. "You can't hold me prisoner. If any of those self-righteous bitches hear me scream, you'll be out on your ass and on the street again. Once a whore, always a whore!"

Lizzie sighed. There was truth to May's taunts. Luckily, this far out from the big house, chances of anyone hearing her were slim. But if anyone happened along nearby, they were done for. "You said no matter what, I was to keep you tied up until you was done with the shakes," she said.

May kicked at the bucket near her feet, filled with her own slop. She shrieked, "I'll shit on the bed, and you can clean that up, too, if you don't let me go!"

Lizzie sighed. May was vile, but her profanity couldn't conceal her generally refined way of talking. She hadn't always been this way. Lizzie would leave the bucket close and hope May used it. She'd clean up her mess whether May toppled it or not. Others had done it for Lizzie, and she prayed she had the stomach now. May hadn't had to go much yet anyway, for she'd been brought to the Home starving, having eaten nothing but grass or sawdust for days—and whatever vermin she might have caught.

Lizzie hurried to finish the chores she'd started. She swept the crumbs of May's supper off the loft's edge to keep varmints out, then propped the broom in a corner. "I'll be back with breakfast, or your dinner if I can't get away."

"Don't bother," May growled. "I'd rather die *here* than in that hell-hole with all you useless whores."

"It ain't a hellhole. If you can bear these next days, you might see yourself clear to a new life. These are good folks who'll care for you like they done for me—if you don't ruin it again."

"So many goddamn rules," May said. "Everything is an abomination. A simple smoke, or heaven *forbid*, the tiniest crumb of bacon." She twisted her lips in a self-righteous frown. *"The LORD GOD says this . . . the LORD GOD says that . . ."* By golly, she did look nearly like Gertrude, and Lizzie barely caught herself from laughing.

Sure, the rules weren't easy. Lizzie had had no notion that being saved could be so exhausting. And this new life was better a thousandfold, but it didn't erase the past. Sometimes Lizzie struggled something awful. Her old nature lied, saying comfort from the bottle or the needle or the tin was better than "putting away earthly things." But it only led one way: to a shallow grave, not even a wooden box to shield her skin and bones from worms.

May's face changed again, and Lizzie saw something new—and

genuine—in her eyes: pain, so much, and the only reason Lizzie kept trying. May couldn't live with that pain forever. She cried out, "My skin is crawling, like ants biting every single inch of me. It burns so I can't stand it. Please, Lizzie, bring me something for it!"

Lizzie tightened her muscles again. "You know they don't keep medicines."

"You can find some!" Tears rolled down May's cheeks now, with real sobs shaking her.

Lizzie sympathized, for she still got that dreadful sensation. When it came, she went off on her own for a spell, so as not to take it out on the others. She was lucky to have that for her excuse to go to May now, but even white lies were a slippery path. If the lying was for good, she wondered, could that maybe make it right with the Lord?

May kicked against the floorboards, and her muffled yelling carried in the wind as Lizzie hurried back to the house. She'd tied rags across May's mouth every time she'd left, hoping the screaming might ring less sharp, but the noise was still something to behold from a woman as bedeviled as May.

That night, Lizzie had prayed as she walked back to the house. Simple prayers were still all she knew. She hoped they were enough. She'd prayed for May, that she'd be able to push through and see the light. She'd prayed for Mattie. If Lizzie's gut told her right, things would get worse for her beloved friend before they got better. And she'd prayed for her Docie, that she'd never in her life need to make the kind of choices the erring girls had. *Please Lord.*

The third day—the day Mattie caught her leaving the barn—Lizzie had climbed the ladder to the loft, braced for May's usual spite. But as she reached the last rung, she'd gasped, thrusting her breakfast crockery down on the planking and screeching May's name. She'd left her on her back earlier, but May had dragged herself around until she practically hung from the post where Lizzie had bound her, face down in the hay, purple from her weight on the rope.

"May! What've you done?" Lizzie dropped to her knees to see if May breathed. Would May being carted off by the undertaker, and her by the police—for murder!—be the price for Lizzie's lies, never mind her intentions?

Wispy breath still warmed May's mouth, but she didn't respond. Lizzie was close to full panic before May's eyes fluttered. She coughed weakly. "Water . . ." Her voice was like gravel.

Lizzie pushed and pulled May to a proper lying-down position, then held the jar to her lips. "Oh, May. I thought you was dead."

"*Wish* I were." May took a long pull, water tracking down her chin and neck. A person would think she was forty, as worn as she looked, though she was surely closer to twenty. Many showed up at the Home looking like hags, but May was maybe the worst they'd seen.

"You feel that bad, you might be near to kicking the habit. Time you stop this nonsense and count yourself lucky to be alive." Lizzie's chest still heaved from fearing May had been dead. She was lucky too. She shivered in the heat to think how it could have gone. She made herself breathe slowly. "You want your breakfast? It ain't much, what with Gertrude breathing over me."

Lizzie's mind wandered while May forced down the cold toast and mush. She was determined to clean May up while she was in a quiet mind. "If I bring soap and a clean nightshirt later, promise not to hurt me?"

"Why do you keep trying?" May's voice, less rough now that she'd taken food and drink, was still aged as an old woman's. "What good'll it do? I'll be back on the streets in a week. I'm not meant for anything better."

Lizzie knew the poison of apathy. But if *she* could change, why couldn't May? "Look. The Lord changed me. He can change you too. You just got to believe it."

"Oh, hon, I just want to be sound enough to get my business in order. I'm a whore—never will be anything else. But I'm a good one." She straightened her shoulders. "A year ago, I was entertaining the most powerful men in town at the finest house in Dallas. If I get clean, they'll take me back."

May was fooling herself. No respectable whorehouse—respectable being relative—would take her. Even prostitutes had a class system. That burned-out horse carriage where Sister Maggie Mae and Gertrude had found her was the lowest rung. If anyone let her back in the cribs, even, it'd be a miracle—and not the holy sort.

"They're not taking you, and you won't survive on the streets. You got to let me help."

But May shook her head. "You know I'm not going to make good."

"I'll be back, likely after dark," Lizzie said. "You hold on. I'm your strength for now. No more twisting yourself to where you might not be breathing for real next time I come."

May had nodded wearily. It was enough. And that evening, while Lizzie bathed her, she was a lamb.

Today, after the confrontation with Gertrude in the hall, Lizzie had waited until after the babies were settled for afternoon naps before she sneaked out. May was docile again. Anyone but Lizzie might have trusted her. Not yet. There'd be more of what she'd been through the last three days, though easier with each round.

May gobbled what Lizzie brought like it was a bear's spring breakfast. It was Mattie's, who'd pushed it on Lizzie that morning, saying she was too hot to eat anyway. It worried Lizzie, but she took it. May couldn't chew or swallow quickly enough. Then she pleaded. "Tell them I'd be grateful for one more chance. I'm in my right mind now."

Lizzie shook her head. "You ain't ready yet."

May sighed through her nose. "I've never been better, not for years. The thought of another chance with you girls thrills me. I hope Sister Susie can find it in her heart to forgive the broken window. I'm ready to see what the Lord has in store."

Lizzie reared back and laughed at May's talk, obviously for show. "Oh, honey. You got to take my word for it, like I gave mine that I'd keep you safe from yourself."

May's shoulders drooped.

"You talk like you're from good people," Lizzie said. "You got a mama somewhere?"

May drew in on herself. Genuine tears wet her cheeks. She must have been a handsome young lady once, with bright hair and eyes like light in a wood. "She'd no more admit I was her daughter now than when she turned me out." She scoffed. "Even if my tutor hadn't been married, my mother thought we were above him. And when I showed up carrying his child, his wife sized me up as though I weren't the first—and wouldn't be the last—gullible girl to knock. She asked if he had business with me, and when he shook his head, the door hit my face."

Lizzie sighed. The story of the ages.

"A woman gave me a room in exchange for work, but first she gave me something for my trouble and time to rest from the cramps and bleeding . . ." Her voice faded. "Then I was in her debt. She said I needn't stay longer than it took to repay her. But you change once you give yourself away for money." May shrugged.

It was the longest speech she'd made, but no different from many Lizzie had heard in the months she'd been at the Home. It was always the man who took what he wanted, and always the woman who lost everything.

Back at the house, the nursery was dim, with the babies still napping and Bertha with her feet up, catching a rest too. Her labor would begin any time. Lizzie had the urge to look in on Docie.

She'd be down the hall in the big playroom by now, eating her snack with Alpha and the older children, already awake from their rest time. Mr. Gus, the old Negro who fixed things for them, had cut a little window high in the playroom door and filled it with glass so the mothers could peek without riling the children. Lizzie was nearly too short to reach it. She rose as high as she could and almost fell through the door, which hadn't been properly latched.

The scene was chaos. Alpha had tipped his juice cup, and juice had spread everywhere on the floor. Jewel was mopping him and the floorboards with the same rag while the rest ran a wild circle around them. Her helper was nowhere to be seen—a relatively new girl who was always threatening to leave.

Lizzie settled the kids in a corner with a wooden train, while Jewel finished cleaning up and then collapsed in her chair. "Bless your heart, I thought you'd never come. Irma's gone off to who knows where." She sighed. Then looked up. "Where's Docie?"

Lizzie stilled. "I was about to ask you."

Jewel shook her head. "I sent her down the hall to find you."

Lizzie fled from the room. Docie wasn't in the water closet. She could go by herself now, but she always seemed to wait until Lizzie could take her. She clumped downstairs, more alarmed. Docie wouldn't go down alone, she didn't think, but Lizzie hurried to rooms that would be accessible to a child not quite four years old. The kitchen was empty, filled only with the aroma of their roasting dinner while Mattie and Gertrude worked outside in the kitchen garden. Olive had been sent to bed after lunch, her late-term swelling likely worsened by the tension in the kitchen. Lizzie hoped her labor would go quick and easy, during the day, with nobody wandering the house or property at odd times.

She ran to the front of the house now and threw open the front door. Where to begin—the fields? The creek? Heaven forbid, the old barn—or the road! They rarely had motor traffic in front of the Home, but it wasn't hard to imagine Docie trampled beneath the feet of a horse and carriage, the driver pushing to see how fast he could go.

Lizzie's leg throbbed, and she limped to peer one way and then the other. The road was silent, no floating dust to signify a vehicle had been by lately. As she turned away to go check the new barn, where the kids liked to visit Mr. Gus's mules, she heard a shout.

"Lizzie, I need you immediately!" Sister Maggie Mae Upchurch hollered and waved from her home across the road. Lizzie nearly stumbled, running as fast as she could. Maybe Docie *had* been hurt, and they'd been looking for Lizzie while she was off in the barn. Her face burned with fear and shame. But when she arrived at the porch, Sister Maggie Mae looked appalled, not frightened.

"What's happened? Is it Docie?" Lizzie said, relieved but still dreading the answer.

Sister Maggie Mae gestured for her to follow. She marched inside and upstairs to a hall lined with her children's bedroom doors. From an open one, Lizzie heard the giggles of girls. She saw Miss Ruth and Miss Alla Mae, two of the Upchurch daughters, first. They were seven and ten, already in school, and couldn't have been home long.

"Girls, tell Mrs. Lizzie what you told me." Sister Maggie Mae pursed her lips and paced the floor. The girls hung their heads. Docie *was* in the room. She raced to clutch Lizzie's skirt, hiding her eyes from Sister Maggie Mae. Their youngest, a boy Docie's age, grinned from the bed.

"Girls?" Sister Maggie Mae gave them a look.

Alla Mae didn't budge, but Ruth sniffled.

"Ruth, honey?" Lizzie said. "What's happened?"

Ruth spoke to the floorboards, so soft Lizzie strained to hear. "We saw Docie on the big porch on our way home from school. We waved and she came running." The Upchurch children weren't allowed to set foot on the property without one of their parents. "She wanted to come play, and we forgot to ask permission."

Lizzie relaxed. She wasn't angry. She was simply relieved.

"And then what?" Sister Maggie Mae said, for apparently that wasn't all.

"We played house. We made Docie the mama and Willie the daddy." Ruth whispered it.

"When I found them, your daughter and my little boy were in the bed," Sister Maggie Mae said. "They were under the covers . . . kissing!"

Lizzie half wanted to laugh. Kids played house, didn't they? She'd done it when she was little. But then she thought of the time her stepbrother said they'd play house down by the creek, and she almost gagged. And she could see how it looked.

"Of course I'm not angry with *her* . . ." Sister Maggie Mae sighed now that she'd expressed her dismay. "Girls, what were you thinking?"

Alla Mae spoke up now, and Lizzie saw a spark in her eyes. "We didn't say to. She *wanted* to kiss him," she whispered, pointing at Docie.

Panic flashed in Sister Maggie Mae's eyes, but Lizzie knew a lie when she saw one, even from a ten-year-old child. She wouldn't argue with an Upchurch, however, no matter how young.

On their way home, she held Docie close, inhaling the scent of her hair and sweaty neck, more aware than ever that her past had placed a curse on her daughter. People would always look at Docie the way Sister Maggie Mae had after Alla Mae made her accusation.

"Honey," she said. "I know you love your friends." She wouldn't shame Docie.

"Mama!" Docie said. "They said I should get in the bed with Willie and kiss him on the mouth! Aren't they funny?" She giggled. Lizzie fought anger. They were only children . . .

But lives had been ruined before by those who didn't know any better.

"Where were you, Mama? I looked everywhere."

"I'm here now," Lizzie said. "But never leave the big house on your own again. Promise?" Lizzie gripped her tight as she carried her upstairs. She kept Docie in the nursery to finish the day.

If she hadn't been in the old barn that afternoon, it would never have happened. She couldn't do this any longer. It was time to turn May loose.

CATE

Grissom, Texas
1998

River dropped me off after we returned from Carr City, and I went inside the coffee shop, as if starting and ending the day with the truth could make up for what I'd neglected to tell my parents about the in-between.

I sat alone with a frappe and my thoughts, but when I walked to my car, I saw a note under one of my windshield wipers. My mom or dad never checked up on me when I went somewhere to study or just hang out. They trusted me completely. I panicked, afraid something had happened and they'd had no way to contact me.

But the note was from Jess.

Your mom said you'd be here. Where ARE you?
Call me ASAP! BIG news!!

My conscience twinged. I hoped Jess hadn't called my house again after she left the note. Instead of going straight home to field questions on the kitchen phone, though, I went by her house. I had a good idea what she wanted to tell me.

Prom was approaching quickly. Our church had no strict rule against dancing, unlike some other conservative denominations. We were expected to use common sense, and of course, to *"leave room for Jesus!"* Our youth group leader encouraged us to stick with youth group members for school dances to avoid uncomfortable—or risky—situations. "The Devil you know . . ." he'd say with a wink at the boys.

Neither Jess nor I had been holding our breath for dates, though, and I'd felt no more than half-wistful regret. Even if I had an acceptable date, I'd be miserable at prom. Any natural grace I'd possessed as a child had fled after one summer of astounding growth. At the end of seventh grade, I'd barely topped five feet. When eighth grade began, people I hadn't seen all summer gaped. I hardly recognized myself, and certainly not my new long limbs. In high school, the track and cross-country coaches salivated and recruited me on the spot. After I leveled out at five feet nearly ten inches, however, it seemed every remark about my height was followed by a hurried, "But you have such a pretty face!"—leaving me with the unsettling sense I was not quite feminine enough now that I was so tall.

At prom, while everyone else on the dance floor swayed like gazelles, I would flail like a newborn giraffe, and during slow dances, the whole world would notice visible sweat stains under my arms and my hands in all the wrong places—at least that was how it would feel.

Most importantly, though, my afternoon with River had convinced me I didn't care about prom at all. Jess did, however, and I didn't have to ruin her excitement. Without a single shy or awkward bone, she'd dance the night away. She wouldn't care how she looked or who watched. That, I envied. I'd be thrilled if she had her dream date for prom—and not terribly sad if I didn't. Our mothers had suggested going in a group of girls, but I suspected change was in the air for Jess. She'd been talking to one of the other seniors in youth group lately— very cute, but very busy with sports and a million other things. He'd never given dating the time of day, but Jess had hoped their recent flirting might translate into a prom invitation if she could focus his attention properly.

I pulled up to her house and she spotted me from the window. She raced down the sidewalk. "Guess what?"

I pretended ignorance.

"Jordan asked me to prom!" she shrieked.

I clapped. "Of course he did!"

"But wait, there's more." I tried not to laugh, picturing her selling something on late-night television. "It's a two-for-one."

I felt my eyebrows merge. "He's taking both of us?" I nearly snorted. I wouldn't be a third wheel for prom, thanks and no thanks.

"No! That would be weird. But we happen to know that someone else will be inviting you very, very soon."

I fended off a scowl but couldn't help gaping. Fielding a potentially unwelcome invitation sounded horrible—not to mention, all the other seniors in youth group had already paired off or had just asked Jess.

"You'll never guess who," Jess said.

"No kidding. Please, put me out of my misery already!"

"I can't. But you'll be okay with it. Everyone is going to be super jealous."

"Hmm," I said. By *everyone*, I assumed she meant the girls at school. None of the girls in youth group would care. We were usually happy for each other when nice things happened.

"You'll know soon enough. But you better get home. Your mom was worried when I called two times."

My head swung up.

"Relax—I didn't tell her you weren't at the coffee shop. I just said I needed to talk to you again." She patted the hand I rested on the door frame—the same one River had tugged me by. It felt conspicuously changed. Could she tell? "By the way," Jess said, as if she could read my mind, "where were you all afternoon?"

I fumbled for an answer. "I was just . . . not really in the mood to study, but didn't want to freak my mom out. She's on my case about AP tests right now. I went for a walk." I kept my eyes down so Jess wouldn't read me. I hadn't felt like studying, and I had taken a long walk. I didn't say I'd been doing it two hours away and hadn't been alone.

I was afraid to tell Jess about River.

In ways, it made no sense. Jess was my best friend, but she didn't have a jealous streak. She'd been the kid who invited the whole class to her birthday parties even without her mother suggesting it—exactly why she wanted me to have a prom date.

But this new friendship, this new thing I couldn't even describe yet, had me wanting to keep it to myself for a while, at least until I'd figured it out. River wasn't like any friend Jess or I had had before, and I wanted to define it before anyone else tried to. I sensed, however, that things were about to get complicated—as if they weren't already.

Jess shooed me home. "Call me," she said.

My mother assailed me at the front door. "Hello, Miss Popular. The phone's been ringing off the wall."

I rolled my eyes. I was not popular by anyone's definition, and definitely not based on two calls, but at least she wasn't suspicious. Jess and I practically had a second sense about where to find each other. We'd been friends since cradle roll, sharing crackers and juice during children's church, then Bible drill and mission clubs, and for the last six years, youth group—though now, we preferred Dr Pepper and Doritos.

"Did you talk to Jess?" Mom said.

"Mm-hmm," I said, lugging my backpack toward my room.

She followed. "She seemed excited."

"Mm-hmm," I repeated. "Prom date."

I hoped she'd let it go, but my mother was nearly as maternal about Jess as she was about me. I was an only child, and she latched on to the other kids we knew.

"What? Tell!"

"Jordan. No surprise."

"Oh, *really*. I didn't know they liked each other. When did that happen?"

I sighed. This was why I didn't talk to her about crushes, mine or anyone else's. If you said one word, she slapped the marriage contract on the table. "They're just friends, Mom."

"Just wondered." Her mouth drooped. It was so easy to upset her these days, and I wondered if she was struggling with me growing up. But she rebounded fast. "Anyway, that sounds fun. Guess who else called? Seth Baxter."

And like that, it was clear. As clear as mud.

Seth? Why on earth would he ask me to *my* prom? And why now, of all times? He'd gone away to a private Christian college for a year, but now he attended community college nearby while he worked as an intern at church. We'd all been surprised to see him back home, but he'd wanted to be a youth minister for years and said he needed hands-on experience. He worked with the middle schoolers because of his age—technically, he was still one of us. Seth's family had been at the church for centuries, or so it seemed. *Baxter* was on every dedication plaque in the building.

He'd had one fairly long relationship during high school with another girl from church, then flirted with me for about five minutes after they broke up. I'd been flattered, but I'd also known he was on the rebound and leaving for college. I knew what happened to younger girls when their boyfriends went off to college. It never ended well. But he'd been my first big crush. In fact, my only big crush. I'd nurtured it, even after he'd gone to college—and I'd been thrilled when he came back. But after today, I knew implicitly that my crush on Seth was different from how I felt about River. And even more important, how I felt when I was *with* River.

"I always thought Seth was nice. He's pretty easy on the eyes too," Mom said.

I nearly laughed. "Mom, you're not allowed to say 'easy on the eyes,' especially about someone my age." At this moment, I really needed her to stay in her role and keep her distance.

She winked. "I'm just saying he's not a terrible option."

"Please. Don't."

I slammed her into meek silence with only two words. As I approached adulthood, I'd realized the way to keep my parents out of my business was to make them painfully aware they were middle-aged and, thus, clueless. Not having siblings to spread their focus made it worse. When I left home, Mom would struggle. I felt sympathetic sometimes. But not today.

"At any rate, he called." Her voice drifted off. Mom's feelings were hurt. I regretted being rude, though it was the only thing that worked.

"Thanks," I said, smiling more gently. "He probably wants help. The middle school group is always short on female volunteers. Can't say I blame anyone . . ."

"His number's on your desk."

"Cool." I knew it by heart—from all the years I'd hoped to see it show up on caller ID.

"The cordless is in its cradle," she called as I continued down the hall.

I sighed again. "Thanks, Mom." I was happy she'd found the phone, because it was likely charged now and I wouldn't have to call from the kitchen, but that meant she'd pawed through my laundry.

"I was just getting towels!" Mom yelled.

I rarely emptied pockets until right before I washed things. I was afraid that inside one was the flyer about the open mic, with a little message scrawled in the corner. I hadn't noticed it until after River walked away that day.

"Please come! I'm writing a new song. It might be about you."

It had seemed a little weird, considering we hardly knew each other—but River didn't seem weird. My mind went to the song now. The one I suspected was about me. The lyrics and tune had lodged in my brain, a little earworm that popped up often. I'd wanted to ask River about it, but I was too self-conscious. I'd carried the flyer in my pocket for days.

If Mom had seen the note, things *would* get weird, but surely she'd have asked. My laundry was in a neat pile on the floor, not scattered wherever I dropped it as I frantically scavenged for school clothes. I was no longer the bright-eyed freshman who carefully planned outfits at night, hoping I'd catch someone's eye at school—someone I had a crush on, like Seth, or the popular girls, who might then invite me to sit at their lunch table. I was a senior now. I just needed to be covered.

I didn't hurry to return Seth's call. I wondered if Jordan and Jess had put him up to it. I remembered seeing Jordan and Seth at the last basketball game of the season. I hated sports—except for running, which wasn't even in the same category as far as I was concerned. I dreaded watching games so much, I only went when Jess begged. That night, I'd said hello to Seth, but as soon as Jess started chatting with Jordan, Seth headed off to a different section. It was part of his job to go where the middle school kids hung out, and in Grissom, that meant basketball games—but I'd chased him so long, being left in his wake was nothing new.

My fingers dialed slowly. He picked up immediately. "Cate! How's it going?"

Ugh. I'd forgotten caller ID worked the other way too. "Oh, hi!" Suddenly, the hand that held the phone shook, and I heard it even in my voice. My nervousness confused me.

We talked about colleges I was considering. His classes. The internship. "So," I finally said, "did you need help with the middle school girls?" He needed to get to the point.

"Actually, I hadn't even thought about that. You'd be great! But . . . no, something else."

"Okay?"

"Jordan mentioned he asked Jess to prom today. I assume she said yes?"

"She did." *Ugh ugh.*

"He thought I should see if you wanted me to take you."

I sat, unsure how to respond. It wasn't an outright question.

"So . . . would you like that? It might be fun."

"Can I think about it?" I said, but after an awkward silence, I felt bad. It had taken at least a little nerve to call, even if Seth was technically doing me a favor—even if I didn't want a favor.

"I thought Jess might have mentioned it."

"Not exactly."

"I mean, assuming you didn't already get asked. Maybe you—"

"No, I didn't," I interrupted. "I just need to give it a little thought. You know me. I think too much."

Seth's answering laugh was forced. I found myself wanting to re-assure him. My reaction was bewildering, even to me. I'd liked him for so many years, it was surreal to realize I hadn't thought of him in days. But something unexpected was happening with River. Some-thing real. And prom with River was out of the question. I couldn't imagine it, not even casually.

Now, going with someone else seemed like a distraction.

I didn't want a distraction.

I wanted River.

I was more honest with myself in that moment than I'd been all day. All month. Even if River wasn't the kind of person my parents or friends would approve of me seeing—ever—I wanted it. My certainty took me by surprise.

"Welp. No big deal," Seth said. "Let me know. I'm happy to go. I always had a huge crush on you, you know."

I hadn't known. Because he hadn't had a crush on me. Not at all. I wondered why he felt he needed to pretend.

At dinner, Mom couldn't help digging. I could tell she'd men-tioned the call to Dad because his eyes smiled when she brought it up. He wasn't surprised, just not as obvious.

"He volunteered to take me to prom." I made it clear it was a mercy date, hoping Mom would hold off on wedding deposits.

"Oh, honey!" Mom said. "I always hoped the two of you might get together."

"I didn't say yes yet. Is it even allowed?" I looked at Dad. I wasn't sure Seth was permitted to date anyone still in high school. Dad was the one tuned in to all the church policies—if there was one for this.

He considered. "Well, he's not working with the high schoolers, and you were already friends. It's probably fine. I could run it by the personnel committee—"

"Oh, let's not get the PC involved," Mom said. "They'd probably want to draft a whole new handbook." She gazed at me, eyes excruciat-ingly bright. "Honey! Say yes!"

I swirled my spaghetti around on my plate. She knew I was wavering.

"He's a really nice guy, and his priorities are in order. Go! You can't miss prom."

Dad had already pushed his plate away and unfolded the newspaper on his placemat to scan headlines. He didn't really care. But Mom was so fervent, I felt guilty for upsetting her earlier, and worse for lying. Her life had revolved around me for nearly eighteen years. If I didn't go, she'd never get to scratch the prom itch moms probably felt. Helping me prepare for prom was definitely on her checklist.

I had to go, and I could do worse. I'd waited for Seth to notice me— *really* notice me—forever. Now he had. "I'll call him back," I said.

Mom jumped up and hugged me. I thought she might cry. "We can dress shop next weekend! And talk to Jeanne about your hairstyle." She eyed my ponytail.

I face-palmed. "Let's not get carried away, Mom."

Still, she beamed. I couldn't ruin her moment.

I apologized to Seth, saying it took time for me to adjust to surprises, but his invitation was a surprise I was pleased to accept. In a small way, I was, after seeing my mom's pleasure.

I dug River's flyer from the laundry pile. I studied the words again, then folded it carefully and put it in my desk drawer, beneath a stack of journals. I'd never been one to write about myself, so whenever I received a journal as a gift I added it to the unused pile. Now, though, I carried the topmost one to bed. Before I slept, I wrote what I was scared to speak aloud—to my mom, to Jess, and especially to River, who'd caused my feelings to emerge so unexpectedly.

I'd always assumed something of this nature would occur gradually, with a warning it was on the way. But like every single Texas summer, when it hit, I was blindsided.

I slipped the journal under my pillow and drifted off, remembering the afternoon. How once our eyes adjusted to the dim glow inside the deserted depot, we'd stood still, River clasping my hand, both of us astonished. Someone, maybe a century earlier, had painted murals on the walls, framed top and bottom by intricately carved wainscoting now scratched and coated with dust. The murals depicted forgotten life in Carr City. Though dusty and slightly faded, their detail was exquisite, living and breathing scenes in a palette as rich as a cornucopia's. The workmen. The maids. The mothers and fathers, children and dogs. A summer hotel with airy balconies and a paddle wheel churning a rushing stream.

And while the floor was littered with trash, and the woodwork nearly ruined, the art was virtually untouched, as though any who witnessed the stunning record of a time gone by had revered it instead of scarring it with graffiti or sharp objects.

After we caught our first breath, we walked, hand-in-hand, studying the panels. River refused to use the camera flash on what had been preserved so well for so long, and only captured a few more shots outside once we emerged, blinking as our eyes readjusted to the modern world and the bright afternoon sunlight.

We'd driven back to our real lives in companionable silence, acoustic music in the CD player. I felt, for the first time in a long time, stirred. As if we had shared something holy.

I could hardly explain it. There'd been no Bible reading or preaching. But what we'd seen had shown me something bigger—something greater even than the God we'd crammed into a box of our choosing, at a church that told us how and when and what we would worship and believe. That humans could create this thing of beauty in such a common and temporary space, and then honor an unspoken agreement to preserve it, maybe for a hundred years, helped me believe in divine intervention more than anything in that box.

It made me question more than that too. It made me question why River, who seemed more suited to my personality and temperament than anyone my parents and youth minister deemed appropriate, and who had helped me see this bigger picture, was off-limits.

MATTIE

Arlington, Texas
1905

Mattie finally found a moment to see Sister Susie near suppertime. The shock of the visit sent her outside, behind the house. When she thought she'd pulled herself together enough to go to the dining room, she spied Miss Hallie marching toward the house, disgust twisting her face.

Mattie knew instinctively she'd found May. She wanted to simply sink to the ground and cry like a child. It was all too much for one day. She'd had worse days, though, by a long shot, and if she wanted to keep Lizzie and Docie safe, she had to be strong. She stood in the woman's way to slow her. "Good heavens, Miss Hallie, have you seen the Devil himself?"

"If not the Devil, something equally evil. There is"—Miss Hallie sputtered, as if her own words might choke her—"an unclothed woman in the loft of the old barn. That woman who broke Sister Susie's door glass. She didn't say how she came to be there, but I have my suspicions."

May would not hesitate to give Lizzie up eventually. And Mattie knew what Lizzie couldn't see—that despite Lizzie's rough past, returning to the real world now would destroy her.

She locked her knees. "I can explain." Miss Hallie's answering gasp could have stopped a thief, but it was no match for Mattie's loyalty.

Mattie had left Sister Susie not ten minutes earlier, and the woman came quickly upon seeing Miss Hallie's horror-stricken face. They gathered in Brother JT's study, where Mattie stood before the three and substituted herself for Lizzie in the story. Her cheeks flooded easily with tears once she faced her jury. "I knew it was a risk," she claimed, "but I couldn't let her leave, not after everything I've learned here. The Lord placed her before me, to care for her." She focused on her shoes. If they didn't throw her out for breaking the rules, God might strike her dead for lying.

Brother JT tugged at his coat buttons, his doubt obvious. "It's difficult to understand why you'd flout our authority so blatantly, and this brings to mind another conversation I had this morning, with—"

"Lizzie had nothing to do with it!" Now Mattie went from sobbing to shaking. *Why* had she spoken Lizzie's name?

Miss Hallie scoffed. "Good heavens, to think I defended her today! Gertrude was cruel, but I *knew* something was askew."

Mattie cringed. Now there'd be more lies, but Lizzie couldn't be implicated. "You know she goes walking after dinner when she needs to, Sister Susie." The woman nodded cautiously. "She caught me in the barn."

"Caught you? How long, exactly, has she known?" Miss Hallie's voice rose on each word. Brother JT hushed her.

"She struggled with it horribly. She wanted to tell. I—I said I'd blame her if she did and say she was lying. I deserve to be expelled, but not Lizzie!" Mattie collapsed on the hard floor and buried her face in her skirt. Her insides heaved and the undigested sausage she'd intended for May, but gobbled earlier when anxiety had pushed her to it, rose in her esophagus. She feared she might vomit, right there on the polished floorboards. What if they didn't believe her?

But Brother JT tilted her chin up and looked into her eyes, as if searching for the whole truth, even if he didn't make her speak it. "Get up, Mattie," he said. "How is May now?"

Mattie struggled to her feet, hoping her stomach would cooperate. Lizzie hadn't updated her today. "She's . . . better. Eating, drinking, and all but done with the sweats. She wants back in." Mattie's uncertainty increased her anguish. "I knew it was near time, but . . . I was afraid. I've done a terrible thing. I've taken advantage of everything you've sacrificed for us."

"You've risked our reputation, indeed," Brother JT said. "As if it weren't precarious already. But what if someone discovered we keep half-clothed drug addicts in the barn?"

Mattie stared. Behind his stern expression was a hint of amusement. If she wasn't mistaken, he was *laughing* inside. Finally, her stomach began to calm.

"We will retrieve May from the barn and bring her inside. Sister Susie, we'll isolate her again, naturally, until she's no longer a danger to others. Perhaps it won't take long."

"She broke her contract," Miss Hallie said. "Do our rules mean nothing?"

"Miss Taylor, surely you agree rules must be adjusted for circumstances at times. What Lizzie said this morning was true. What would we teach about grace—with a capital *G*—if we turned May away now, especially when she's half well?"

Comprehension dawned in Miss Hallie's expression, though still fused with judgment.

"Sister Susie?" Brother JT said. "Shall we bring our lost sheep home?"

The one who'd suffered the brunt of May's temper nodded. Mattie breathed a sigh of amazement. She might have given Gertrude the nickname, but Susie Singletary was the real saint in this place.

"Now, Mattie, you meant well," Brother JT said, "but deception isn't without consequence. Sister Susie will need a right hand with May."

Mattie nearly laughed—not from amusement, but from marveling at the chaos this day had brought. Worse, it wasn't over yet. And helping with May certainly wasn't how she'd planned to get away from the kitchen, but it was better than packing a suitcase—or worse, watching Lizzie do it.

When they returned to the barn to fetch her, however, May was already gone.

LIZZIE

Arlington, Texas
1905

Something crackled on the path behind Lizzie. She pulled May's supper pail close and the flounce of her skirt around it. She stepped soft and listened hard but heard nothing else. A green acorn had probably hit the dirt. At the barn doors, she looked about to be sure.

With May able to carry on mostly sensible conversation now, maybe Brother JT would give her another try. Lizzie prayed as she climbed the ladder. Since she'd found May facedown in the hay, she'd held her breath each time she went up. Tonight, when her head cleared the floorboards, her gut twisted like a hand turned it deep inside.

May was gone.

Lizzie recalled the noise on the path. Had May escaped, then watched Lizzie's approach? She scrambled up and tossed the loft, like the vice squad in the dives, even shoving back the straw to be sure May hadn't burrowed until she was invisible. Finally, she dropped onto her haunches. It was silly to keep at it. Everything was gone. Even the rope. If May had taken it with her, it might mean . . .

Lizzie couldn't go there.

She pressed fists to her cheekbones, using pure might to keep from crying out. She wanted to shout May's name, ask why she'd given up when she was so close. She sobbed, from disappointment and maybe dented pride—even if only Mattie ever knew.

Along her return, she discarded May's supper on the slop pile, asking forgiveness as she buried it in the stink, in full view of the house.

She gazed at the windows lit from within by oil lamps. The sweet scene had brought her peace and joy for months, but tonight it was mixed with sour. Her failure weighed her down more than expected, even knowing May's chances had been slim.

Since Lizzie had been at the Home, she'd been sorry to see others go, rejecting help and friendship. How could the workers carry on, knowing more would leave than stay? She couldn't stand it, and she'd tried to save only one.

When May had come begging, Lizzie should have turned her away. But she'd believed if the good Lord could rescue her and Docie, he could rescue anyone.

Now she knew better.

MATTIE

Arlington, Texas
1905

It was nearly impossible to fake repentance in the face of May's disappearance, and between scrubbing what Lizzie had used for May and returning the items to where Mattie hoped they belonged, there'd been no chance to warn her friend about May's abrupt departure—or Mattie's lies. Lizzie would be beside herself.

It was well after suppertime by the time Mattie hurried to the dormitory, where three of the childless women surrounded Docie, playing with her hair and tickling her bare toes. She squealed to see Mattie, who gave her a quick hug and said she'd return soon. "I haven't seen you all day!" Docie said, her lip trembling. "Where's my mama?"

"I'm going after her. Find your gown and get ready for bed." Mattie waited at the door until she heard Docie's giggles again, then headed downstairs. She struggled to summon the energy to search—she felt physically beat up, sick still—but she hadn't much choice.

Lizzie wasn't in the old barn, or anywhere along the path. Mattie plodded each inch in the humidity that crept in every evening as darkness approached, nearly worse than the dry heat of day. The other outbuildings were empty. Everyone else was inside by now, and the workers who didn't live on the property had gone home. Mattie envisioned Lizzie's hysteria at discovering May was missing. Had she run away herself, ashamed of her self-imposed failure?

No. Docie would be gone too.

Mattie paced until she remembered that gloomy day, months earlier, when Lizzie hadn't come to visit her grieving new friend, when she'd stayed away out of fear she might hurt Mattie worse—the day Mattie realized how much she'd come to rely on Lizzie and sought her out instead, finding her alone on the boulder in the field, where they'd held each other and wept.

Lizzie wouldn't look at her tonight. Mattie climbed onto the rock, as she'd done that other time, and put her arm around Lizzie's thick shoulders. Nascent cotton bolls peeked from the stalks in the soil the girls had tilled.

"She's gone." Even after Lizzie spoke, she didn't turn her head. "Why'd she do it? I worked so hard to help her. Where do you reckon she is? Do you think God cares at all?"

Mattie couldn't answer the last question any more than she could seven months ago. Instead, she pulled Lizzie's chin toward her, much as Brother JT had done with her earlier, and told her what she knew for sure. Lizzie's jaw went slack in Mattie's hand. She eyed Mattie as if she'd flat-out lied. She wept again, over her guilt at Mattie taking the blame, and at Brother JT's grace—even if May hadn't stayed long enough to accept it. Miss Hallie had admitted she'd untied May the moment she'd discovered her, and May had obviously run away just as soon as Miss Hallie left.

When Lizzie calmed, Mattie pulled an envelope from her pocket. She hated to worry Lizzie even more, but she needed her wisdom, for Lizzie had more even than Mattie had believed. Lizzie knew what was right—even when others couldn't see it. If they'd simply let May back in when she'd asked, maybe she'd still be here now, recuperating in the house instead of headed toward sure death.

"What's that?" Lizzie said.

That afternoon, after working with Gertrude in cold silence, Mattie had finally made it to Sister Susie's desk in the small parlor where she conducted the Home's domestic business. Noting Mattie, she'd pushed her paperwork aside and reached for an opened envelope with several postmarks. "A letter came for you, dear."

Mattie had stilled. Not a soul knew she was here except her oldest sister. After her baptism, Sister Susie had encouraged her to write her family, to share what had transpired since they'd asked her to leave home. She'd resisted. Finally, though, she'd sent a note, giving only the Home's name and address and saying she was well—without mentioning Cap. If they hadn't wanted to know her child when she needed them, they didn't deserve to know he was gone. She hadn't expected an answer. None had come in the months since.

Sister Susie had pushed the letter toward Mattie. "As you know, we read all mail to ensure that every girl is honoring her contract."

It was addressed to Mattie in an unfamiliar hand, though Mattie's old address at home was crossed through. Below it, in her sister Iola's distinct hand, was *FORWARD* and the address of the Home.

The name of the original sender cut her like a knife.

Mattie had left the parlor, determined to read it alone, when and where she could manage her emotions privately. She'd been headed toward the burying grounds when Miss Hallie had come storming around the bend in the path, and she'd hidden it away unread. The letter had dragged her pocket down since, almost as if it kicked at her, crying for attention.

Now Mattie inhaled long and hard before breathing out the name she'd excised from her vocabulary three years earlier. She'd waited months, giving up only when she admitted her condition to her sister—long enough to know there'd be no support of any kind from the man who'd given her all he ever would: her Cap.

"It's from Charley," she said. "Cap's daddy."

LIZZIE

Arlington, Texas
1905

It was a shiny idea, Mattie going off to Colorado to join Charley, as he'd suggested, where the mining towns promised excitement. But when Mattie read his letter to Lizzie, Lizzie said, "All he wants is a warm body in his bed. Maybe a cook. He's asking 'cause he's lonely. Don't forget what he done." She pointed out his lack of remorse and his failure to make even a single mention of the child—as if it hadn't occurred to him Mattie would bring Cap along, if she could.

Mattie had nodded, though Lizzie still detected the tiniest glimmer in her eyes, as if excitement didn't sound awful at the moment. She could hardly blame her. Mattie had to pretend she was penitent over the fiasco with May, while Lizzie had to pretend her warnings were justified. If they hadn't been so tuned to each other, it would have been impossible.

Each time Lizzie caught Mattie pining, she took her aside and reminded her, "Charley's just a good-time guy, honey. You don't want him."

After a time, though, she began to suspect it was more than just that. Mattie was moving so slowly, as if she walked in a trance—nearly like she had after Cap died. The weather was partially to blame. After a record cold winter followed by a spring of violent storms, the summer heat bore down on them now, relentless, nearly like birthing pains. She knew Mattie didn't tolerate high temperatures well, and now she worried the heat was making her sick.

Tempers grew short in the Home, and the girls found the smallest reasons to flare up at one another. One afternoon, a young woman who'd been settling in nicely flew off the handle at another for accusing her of stealing. She packed her trunk and shoved it to the landing, where it fell open and the stolen items tumbled down with it to reveal the truth of the matter.

Sister Susie had her hands full, between refereeing such squabbles and calming the nerves of those approaching childbirth. Bertha's baby boy had arrived in the wake of May leaving, and Lizzie was overwhelmed in the nursery without her while she recuperated. Olive's girl soon followed suit, and Mattie ended each day steely-eyed under Gertrude's judgment, worse than ever after Gertrude convinced Sister Maggie Mae to tell her what had happened with May, only to hold it over Mattie's head if she so much as sneezed in the wrong direction.

As August approached, everyone began praying for rain in earnest. Their fairly insignificant crops at the Home were failing, while area farms were taking on the look of devastation that said it would be a skinny winter if they didn't see rain—and lots of it—soon.

It appeared their prayers might be answered as the miserable month reached its end, when storm clouds gathered and the wind chased away the heat. But the unexpected north wind brought gritty dirt instead of rain, sweeping it up from dry fields and dumping it willy-nilly, including over the Home, where it forced its way through the smallest crevices, even after all the window sashes were lowered and clamped shut.

The others huddled in the interior hallway upstairs, away from windows and chimneys, attempting to avoid the worst of the dust, but when Mattie didn't appear, Lizzie went after her. She finally located her alone in the kitchen, gasping for breath, her mouth and nose covered with a damp rag, already orangey brown from the floating dirt. Mattie coughed harder with each new gust that rattled the window glass, and sank closer to the floor, grasping her belly, as if even it struggled for breath.

"Mattie, we're all in the hall upstairs. What are you doing here? Come with me until the wind and dirt settles."

Mattie turned terrified eyes on Lizzie. She shook her head behind the rag and retreated deeper into her squatting position against the wall. "I can't." She coughed until she choked.

Lizzie stared at her, baffled. "This dust is going to kill you. Can't you hear yourself?"

Mattie just looked away and held the rag tighter to her face, a new series of coughs shaking her from shoulders to toes. When she had a respite, Lizzie grasped her arm and began to pull her up, but Mattie shoved it off. "Leave me alone," she cried. "I can't go up there! It's so closed in and dark, I'll lose my mind. Lizzie, I don't feel well . . . and the rain is coming in here, just a little. I can stay here."

She grasped her belly again, and Lizzie gazed at her. "There's no rain, Mattie. It's dry as bone out there, and the dust ain't stopping for a while."

"It is raining. I felt it coming inside. It wet my skirts. I tore a piece to cover my face . . ."

Lizzie noticed then the window was open a crack, and she hurried to close it completely, but nothing except dry wood covered the sill. "Mattie, you ain't making sense. There's no rain. You wet the rag at the sink, didn't you, honey?"

Mattie slumped the rest of the way to the floor, spreading her legs wide in front of her to point to where she'd torn fabric from the hem of her white petticoat. Indeed, it was damp at the edges, and now Lizzie saw it wasn't pink from the dirt, but from liquid that pooled at Mattie's feet. The backside of her skirt was soaked.

"Is it your time of month?" she whispered to Mattie, shuddering at the thought of Mattie using her female fluids to dampen her face.

"It was the rain, Lizzie. I saw it and felt it with my own eyes. Do you think I'm lying?"

Lizzie knelt carefully in front of her. She thought back over the months since Mattie had arrived. She'd lost so much weight after Cap died, wasting away from refusing to eat at first, sometimes from feeling so sick with grief she struggled to get, or keep, anything down. Gradually—especially after they'd put her to work in the kitchen— she'd put it back on, and in the last few months, Lizzie had even poked fun at her, saying she was getting plump, but mostly she was relieved Mattie seemed happier and had her appetite back. In the last few weeks, though, she'd stopped eating again, along with her lethargy, and though Lizzie had chalked it up to the heat, she'd worried. She hadn't thought about Mattie's menses at all, however. Each young woman in the Home cut her own supply of rags and washed and dried them privately, no mention or display. Lizzie's bleeding came like clockwork now that she was healthy, a part of life she assumed Mattie also attended to without any fuss.

"When's the last time you had your monthlies?" she said.

"It . . . stopped after Cap died. I lost so much weight, I reckoned my body didn't have the capacity for it." Mattie shrugged. "I've bled since then, though not so heavy. But I'm back on track now. Last week, it came like it used to . . . nearly. I had to use the rags."

"Mattie," Lizzie said carefully, "that water you used, it ain't from rain. There's no rain outside, darlin'."

Mattie looked at her skirt, at the torn place along the hem. A look of horror crossed her face. "Is it . . . do you think I've started again? Oh, Lizzie, I think I might be sick—" She leaned to the side and retched, covering her mouth. It was nothing but air, for the storm had come before supper.

"It's fine, honey. You didn't realize. But I've been worried about you since—well, ever since that letter come from Charley. And with May and all. You just ain't been right. Does your head hurt?"

"No . . . but it feels like it's somewhere else, up high above me sometimes. I've been having pain in my stomach though. Everything I eat makes me nauseated and dizzy, but also like I'm starving to death. What's wrong with me, Lizzie? I'm so worried that whatever was wrong with Cap has got me too." She clutched Lizzie's arm now, her eyes going dark. Then suddenly, she doubled over, drawing her knees as high as she could, and leaned between them. The noise that came from her mouth then could only be described as keening, going on and on until she went slack again without warning. She gazed at Lizzie, shaking with the terror the pain had drawn from her.

"Lizzie . . . am I *dying*?"

Lizzie scooted as close as she could and pressed her hand against Mattie's side, waiting a few seconds to see if Mattie would cringe, and then moved it closer, feeling Mattie's abdomen through the layers of cloth. Mattie's corset was laced tightly at the top, but hardly at all near the bottom, with the stays pressed out toward her hips. Lizzie tugged carefully until a wider area was palpable beneath Mattie's skirts. She pressed her hand against it, waiting.

Eventually she spoke. "No, honey, you ain't dying."

Mattie looked relieved, but then another pain gripped her, and she bent again, able to lean farther this time without the confines of her corset. She reached to grasp Lizzie's hand where it still pressed her belly, and held it in an almost viselike grip. Lizzie's fingertips turned white as she stroked Mattie's back with her other hand until Mattie relaxed the hold.

"Then *what is wrong with me*?" Mattie cried.

"Honey, don't you know?" Lizzie whispered, taking Mattie's hand in both of hers now.

"What is it? Tell me." Mattie leaned toward her, deep lines etching her forehead.

Lizzie shook her head. She was convinced Mattie was unaware of the reason for her pain, and for the contractions that convulsed her body in the midst of the dust floating thickly in the air around them. "It's a baby, honey. There's a baby in you."

Mattie's chin jerked down and she stared at the tear in her skirt, and at her heaving belly. "No," she said. "There can't . . . That can't be." She looked back at Lizzie, fear and confusion plain now in her eyes.

"Remember what you told me? That you had relations with a man the day that . . . the day you came here?" Lizzie couldn't bring Cap into the conversation. It was obvious anyway.

"But last time, it was months before . . . months before I got . . ."

"Maybe Charley was careful," Lizzie said. *Not careful enough*, she thought. "There's things that help some."

Mattie went silent, as if recounting her days with Charley,

comparing them with the time in Fort Worth. "No," she said again, shaking her head again and again. "I'd know, Lizzie. I'm not stupid. I'd know."

Lizzie thought so too. But now she considered the months since Mattie came, the pattern of weight lost, and then gained, and recently lost again, Mattie's violent nausea for weeks after Cap's death, her inability to deal with the oppressive heat, her waning appetite and lethargy . . .

And then Lizzie thought herself stupid—again. How could *she* have missed it? How could *anyone* have missed it? She counted quickly on her fingers. Eight months, nearly to the day, since Mattie had arrived.

"Mattie, you're having a baby," she said, gently as she could, and stroked Mattie's arm, just as another wave of cramps hit her friend.

"No. *Noooo!*" Mattie screamed now, sobbing with the intensity of the pain Lizzie remembered well, and then dissolving into quiet whimpers as it abated. When it had, she sat back against the wall, a resolute set to her chin. After her breathing evened out, she looked straight at Lizzie. "If there's a baby in me, I never want to see it."

She turned her head toward the kitchen door and stayed eerily silent through her next contraction, which Lizzie recognized only by the visible tightening of her muscles. Somehow, she even stifled the coughs the dust wanted to incite in her heaving chest.

It reminded Lizzie of things she'd rather forget. The chalky taste of clay nearly choked her too. But she was there with Mattie.

There to stay.

CATE

Arlington, Texas
1998

Seth caught me after church Sunday to ask if I could help him at middle school youth group that Wednesday. He taught them the first hour, and they joined with the senior high group for refreshments and games the next. Usually another adult was present, but that week's volunteer had canceled last minute. Seth said he'd worked hard on the study and hated to postpone if they had to combine with the high schoolers all evening.

I agreed reluctantly, because I'd clearly told him I'd be happy to help. These days, what came out of my mouth didn't always match the sentiments in my head. I arrived early at his request, and he put me to work placing question sheets in the empty chairs.

"I need to run through a few songs I've been working on for tonight," he said.

I watched him pull his guitar from the case, remembering when our youth director had let him play for the senior high group. Even as a starry-eyed freshman, I'd known music wasn't his gift, but I'd tried to overlook that. He'd been interested in youth ministry even then, and churches were always pleased when paid staff could lead music too.

When he began strumming, I could tell he'd improved—some. But he still played chords laboriously, with tiny pauses between them while his sturdy fingers, more suited to sports, struggled to press between the frets. At least he knew the right chords these days. Before, we'd all smiled encouragingly and kept singing even when the chord was clearly out of tune. Seth's voice was passable, but nothing about it stood out—except that he still tried too hard. The volume, for what was meant to be a quiet song, was excruciating. He didn't say anything when he finished playing until I looked up to find him waiting patiently for my reaction.

"What do you think?"

"Wow. You've been working hard." It was the best I could muster.

He shrugged. "I love music. Sometimes I feel like it's a wasted gift. If I weren't going into youth ministry, I'd definitely give music everything I've got. You want to hear a song I actually wrote? It's not a worship song—just warning you."

What could I say? I smiled and bit my lips together as I waited, mentally crossing my fingers it wasn't a love song. If he hoped to impress me, a love song would have the opposite effect. We were both lucky, though. Seth had always loved alternative Christian music—ska, mostly—and he pounded out a decent copycat tune, which made better use of his enthusiasm.

It was nothing like River's music, of course, and while I was able to nod and tell him it was a good one when he finished, all I could think of was River at the coffee shop, and the song that "might have been" for me. The one that wrapped me up in bliss.

I felt sorry for Seth.

Eventually the middle school kids wandered in. They listened to Seth's teaching and answered the questions on the sheets of paper. As he played the songs he'd worked on so hard, the boys mostly sighed and scratched at their growing Adam's apples, some actually moving their lips, though no audible words emerged. The girls sang, several with eyes closed, worshipful expressions on their faces—already so innocent and naïve to me, only four or five years younger. Two couldn't take their eyes off Seth. I remembered that feeling, watching him adoringly, daring to dream he'd notice my new haircut or the plaid shorts that showed off my long legs, or how eagerly I volunteered to read in Sunday school and showed up for everything. Seth was well out of their age range, but it was hard not to crush on a good-looking older guy—especially one who'd already committed to the ministry. He seemed mature compared to the scrawny boys in the room, and even to the ones in the high school group.

I wanted to take them aside and tell them, *Don't waste your time mooning over something that can never happen. Look around at these nice boys here—they'll grow up one day soon. Just have fun!* But I knew it would be a waste of breath.

At the end of the evening, Seth volunteered to give me a ride home. I'd come with my mom, who attended prayer meeting like she brushed her teeth—without fail—and I told him I was good. But Mom overheard me in the hallway. "I have flower committee, sweetie. You go on home and study."

I half wondered if they'd planned it. And I didn't need to study. I'd completed my homework as soon as I got home from school so I could talk to River that night. In the past, Jess and I would have compared notes about the day or youth group over the phone while we finished our math problems or English questions, but now I loved to stretch out on my floor or bed while River and I talked. It required more than the scattered chatter Jess and I happily shared on speakerphone. It required my full attention. I gave it willingly.

But pressing the point would have been rude. So I shrugged and followed Seth. After a few steps, he dropped behind and put a hand at the small of my back. I tried to contain my shiver at the unexpected touch.

One of the eighth-grade girls watched us, and when our eyes met, she rolled hers and turned abruptly away. I guessed she'd wanted to tag along as he walked to his car, stealing a last few delectable minutes in his company under the pretext of asking another question about what he'd taught that night. I knew all the tricks.

At the last minute, Seth called, "Night, Becca. See ya Wednesday!" Her shoulders went back and her face glowed with the thrill of his notice. He chuckled as he unlocked the passenger door. "These girls need to be careful. They're too mature for their own good, like you were . . ."

He winked and my face flamed. I was suddenly torn—in several directions. I'd spent so much time in the past dwelling on Seth to the exclusion of anyone else, I wondered now if I was wasting an opportunity by being standoffish. He was blatantly flirting with me, and I could so easily return the attention. I remembered the shivers that ran up and down my arms if we so much as brushed each other in youth group—and the perplexing shiver of a moment ago.

And then I recalled the quivering ache that ran up and down *all* of me when I lay in my darkened bedroom and listened to River's hushed voice, sharing ideas and dreams that seemed not only plausible, but vital, and River's attentive silence as I did the same.

It also occurred to me that Seth hadn't said he needed to be careful too. These girls were just kids, hardly capable of managing their out-of-control hormones and feelings. That responsibility lay with him. I almost said something but held back. He might have been clueless when I fell over myself to get his attention in middle school and early high school.

But he was an adult now. He wasn't stupid. He knew.

It wasn't my job to remind him.

MATTIE

Arlington, Texas
1905

Mattie fought through each contraction, scarcely able to fathom her condition and what was happening now. How could she have been so ignorant? How could she have missed the signs?

Had she? Now she second-guessed in the quiet spaces between the pains. She'd always been irregular but should have questioned the way her bleeding came at random, never for more than a day or two, and never heavy until the last week. The constant nausea early on, and again lately. Her swollen ankles.

Lizzie was right. It seemed impossible.

But she'd never wanted another baby. Not after Cap.

She couldn't bear the thought of having to comfort her child again as it cried, as it looked at her with terror. As if she should be able to protect it from anything.

She loved Docie now, more than she'd ever expected to, and the babies in the nursery were sweet. They were gone before you knew it, most of the time. After the Home's required one-year stay was up, their mamas took them off to new lives, with everyone crossing their fingers the young mothers would make it and not return defeated—or worse.

But she would never kiss the silk on the top of her own infant's head again. She would never grow attached to a creature who smelled like her milk, smiled like her mother, and cried with the echoing timbre of her history. It would kill her if she failed her own child again.

For it was her failure that had killed Cap. Something in her blood, at the very least. Her mother had lost babies over time, maybe with ailments that mirrored Cap's, and Iola had lost one before the girls. Some weren't meant to live. One who didn't was too many. But at least they'd had partners to walk them through the fire.

At the worst, she'd made mistakes bringing him into the world. She hadn't been fit to raise a child, and God, or whatever being had control of these things, had known it. She'd been too stubborn to give up Cap—the only choice her sister had offered. Iola would have taken him and raised him as her own if Mattie had kept her pregnancy secret. But Mattie had refused.

In the long run, he would have died anyway. She was sure of it.

Another pain gripped her, and she couldn't help looking down at herself. This was another baptism, but by fire—so red and sharp and hot that when she cried out for relief, she nearly believed again.

Lizzie startled from her own reverie—Mattie had asked her not to get Sister Susie, and she'd sighed and said she had to think on it. She sprang from the floor now. "Mattie—oh my! There's so much blood!"

Indeed, when Mattie looked closer, what had looked like fire gushed from her insides now. The contraction passed and she glanced up, smiling weakly. "It's . . . okay . . . don't worry, honey. I'm fine now . . . just a little . . . blood. Nothing to . . . fret about . . ." Another pain came, almost on the tail of the one that pushed out the blood, and she squeezed Lizzie's hand. But suddenly, Lizzie seemed far away. No matter how she tried, she couldn't hold on . . .

Maybe it was okay. Maybe it was time to let go.

LIZZIE

Arlington, Texas
1905

Mattie's eyes went glassy, and Lizzie knew she was in real danger when flecks of dirt began clinging to their dry surfaces without her blinking—as if the gushing blood hadn't been warning enough. She wouldn't leave her as long as she grasped Lizzie's hand tight, but when Mattie let go and slumped sideways, she knew she was losing her.

The wind still howled outside, and not a soul had ventured downstairs. Earlier, Lizzie had whispered to Sister Susie that she was going after Mattie, and not to worry—they'd hole up somewhere until after the dust storm if necessary.

Dilly helped with the laboring women before they sent for the doctor, sitting with them as they faced their early pains, then made them comfortable as the doctor prepared to deliver, providing any assistance he needed. She was nearly a real midwife by now.

Lizzie grasped Mattie's hand again and shook her a bit. "Mattie, honey, I'm going for help. You got to hang in here until I'm back. You gonna be okay?"

Mattie groaned and focused on Lizzie again weakly. She blinked the dust from her eyes, which Lizzie thought a good sign, but then another contraction stole her strength. "Don't . . ."

"I have to, Mattie. You got to make it through this. I'm afraid, honey."

But Mattie held her hand tighter. "Don't . . . tell. Give . . . baby . . ." She took a deep breath to push out the last word at the end of the contraction. ". . . away."

Lizzie was stunned. Mattie had said she never wanted to see it, but she'd figured it was just her grief talking. Once she'd seen the baby—if she managed get through this birth—she'd surely fall in love. But there was no time to argue.

"Okay, honey," Lizzie said. "I hear you. I'm going for Dilly now."

She clumped up the stairs and the gathered group in the hallway jumped at the clatter of the door banging open and closed. Lizzie forced a smile as she scanned for Dilly. Sister Susie approached with a look of concern. "Where's Mattie?"

"In the kitchen," Lizzie said. "She's ate something that made her sick and wants Dilly."

Sister Susie furrowed her brow. "Now? Shall I see to her?"

"No, she said Dilly would know what to do—if she can stand the dirt. You stay with the girls and kids, or they'll all be vexed."

Docie spied Lizzie and came running down the hall. "Mama! I was scared! Where were you? Look how brown my stockings are!" She pulled up her skirt to show the gritty mess.

Lizzie leaned to whisper in her ear. "I have to go back to Aunty Mat, darlin'. She ain't feeling good. Will you keep Alpha company while Aunty Dilly and I help? Can you be a big girl and do that for Mama? But don't tell anyone she's sickly. We don't want them worrying."

Docie nodded, her eyes huge. She whispered back, "I can, Mama! I'll make you so proud, you'll see. But Mama, you be careful, and tell Aunty Mat I love her!"

Lizzie kissed Docie's cheek and hurried to pull Dilly downstairs with her.

In the kitchen, Dilly gasped to see the blood pooling between Mattie's legs. She turned to Lizzie in horror. "What . . . Oh, Lizzie, what's happened?"

"Nothing we ain't seen here before." She had to keep Dilly calm. "Baby coming."

Dilly gasped again, and Mattie moaned. Lizzie was relieved to see she still breathed, even if she hardly seemed alert to Dilly's presence. "I'm worried, though," she said. "That blood all came at once, and she's faint. She nearly passed out on me before I come for you."

Dilly was already down on the floorboards, tugging up Mattie's skirts until she could see clearly. She felt Mattie's abdomen, and as she pressed, more blood poured onto the drying pool.

"We must get Dr. McNeil here without delay. I've only seen this once before, and it was just a matter of time . . ." She shook her head. Now Lizzie remembered the talk of a young woman who'd not survived her labor, not long after the Home opened. They'd lost her and the baby too. "I think the placenta—the afterbirth—is too low or unattached. She's hemorrhaging. Go quickly and tell Brother JT or Sister Maggie Mae to call Dr. McNeil." Dilly's face said there was no time to humor any emotion.

Lizzie ran from the house and across the road, the swirling dust striking her like thousands of tiny needles, and she prayed a simple prayer, again and again. "Save them . . . save them . . . save them . . ."

She pounded on the Upchurches' front door, and Brother JT answered after nearly a minute. He saw her covered in dirt from head to toe and pulled her inside.

"Miss Elizabeth, what on earth—"

"Ain't no time," she said. "Call the doc. We got an emergency across the street. Woman in labor and bleeding bad."

Brother JT tilted his head. She recognized his confusion. The only girls close to birth had just passed that milestone—Olive and Bertha were safe in the upper hall with their infants. The next girl wasn't due for three months.

"Please, just call the doc, and bring him to the kitchen." She rattled back through the door and took off, terrified Mattie would be dead by the time she returned. She had to give her Docie's message. She'd forgotten in the midst of Dilly's quick instructions. She shouted a last statement over her shoulder. "Tell him to hurry—I'm afraid she might not make it!"

Brother JT nodded, his face white. He closed the door when she reached the other side of the road after struggling this time directly against the wind and dirt, which had yet to let up at all.

Dilly had rolled Mattie onto her side on a nest of white towels and bed sheets. She paused frequently to check her pulse and give her momentary comfort between putting water on to boil—covered to keep the dirt at bay, as if it were possible. She'd laid out a pair of kitchen shears and a knife, and fetched a small case Sister Susie kept near her desk filled with basic medical supplies—gauze and smelling salts, needle and thread for stitching up cuts, and a bottle of vodka, still sealed. She held it, as if trying to decide whether it would do Mattie any good.

Mattie was screaming practically every minute now, and Lizzie was thankful the howling wind might disguise it upstairs. The children would be terrified to hear screaming, and the younger women too—especially those in their early months of pregnancy if they knew what was happening. It was better if the noise continued. Lizzie intended to tell anyone who came to the door that Mattie had taken a bad fall and they were cleaning her and stitching her up. There was no need for anyone to know she was with child yet.

Brother JT entered the kitchen ahead of the doctor's arrival, averting his eyes from the corner where Mattie lay. Dilly quickly informed him of her situation, and though his eyes went wide, he nodded. "Dr. McNeil said he'd be here as soon as he could get his horse saddled. He wasn't even going to try to bring the carriage once I told him what Lizzie said. It would take too long. The man needs one of those motorcars . . . though I wonder if it would even run with all the dirt flying. We must pray the storm ends soon."

Soon, the doctor clattered through the kitchen door. Brother JT beckoned Lizzie to join him in the opposite corner, where he knelt with his arms on a chair near the table the women used for peeling vegetables or shelling peas. Lizzie only left Mattie's side briefly. "I'm staying with her. I promised. And I'm praying every minute."

Brother JT nodded and put his head down. Lizzie wondered if it was more than asking the Lord for a miracle. His face was pale, and he looked as if he himself might faint any minute.

Lizzie couldn't worry about a touch of squeamishness.

"Honey," she said, once she'd scurried back to Mattie's side, "Docie said she loves you."

Mattie's screams had decreased to low moans again, as if she'd run out of energy for anything more, and she gazed at Lizzie. "I love her . . . I do love her . . ."

Lizzie tore her gaze away for a moment and looked hard at the ceiling. Mattie needed strength, not tears. If she blubbered, Dr. McNeil would likely shoo her away.

The doctor confirmed Dilly's suspicions. "The placenta has detached and it's down in her cervix—a very dangerous concern." Dilly nodded, her face blanching.

"What will we do?" Lizzie said.

He sighed. "We'll have to take it by caesarean."

Dilly was surely not surprised at the news, but still she sat down hard in the chair she'd pulled nearby. "Can she survive it?"

He shrugged. "We'll do our best." He took a few steps toward Brother JT. "Reverend, you understand I must put the mother's survival above the infant's?"

Lizzie's heart sank at the question. Though he'd directly addressed Brother JT, it seemed this should be Mattie's choice. Mattie was hardly present, mentally, but she was still alive.

Brother JT nodded. "You'll do your best for the baby too?"

The doctor shrugged again. "It's hard to say what condition it's in, with the blood loss—maybe for weeks. The baby is likely very small. How far along is the pregnancy?"

Brother JT looked at Lizzie accusingly.

She shook her head. "I didn't know. *She* didn't know. She thought she was sick."

Brother JT's jaw slackened. He turned to the doctor, his eyebrows raised.

"Happens more often than you'd think," Dr. McNeil said. "A

classic denial of pregnancy. More reasons for it than not, sometimes."
He turned to Dilly. "I'll need your help—have you the stomach for it?"

She nodded.

"Let's get that baby out."

With liberal doses of the vodka poured on Mattie's abdomen to cleanse it and possibly numb the pain from the cutting—though likely less pain than she'd already suffered—and more down her throat to calm her anxiety, Doctor McNeil performed surgery right there on the kitchen floor. He lifted a tiny, limp creature into the air. He cut the cord, which was skinny and flaccid, and placed the infant in a towel Dilly had warmed in the oven.

"Give her to . . ." He pointed at Lizzie, who cowered at first. He hadn't made any pronouncement on the condition of the child. "We have more work to do here," he said. "We'll have to take the uterus if she's to live. Please see to the baby."

Lizzie closed her eyes and took a breath. Could she hold this baby, too, if it was dying?

She wasn't sure.

"Elizabeth!" Brother JT shouted from the corner. "Take it!" And Lizzie scrambled to her feet, and to her senses. Of course someone needed to hold the baby, dead or alive, until they knew what to do with it.

"Rub her limbs, her buttocks," Dr. McNeil said. "Clear the mucus and blood from her mouth. Then put her inside your dress if needed. She must stay warm if there's to be any hope."

The storm had abated some, and with it, the temperature had dropped, even with the stove burning to warm the towels.

Her. It was a girl. Mattie had a baby girl.

Lizzie pictured Docie in her mind, as a pink, squalling infant, eager for life and for her mother's milk. She accepted this tiny bundle, though it lay listless in her arms, eyes half open and vacant, skin blue beneath the white coating that still clung like wool fat.

She'd seen that blue too many times. There wasn't time to waste.

She hurried with her to the rocker they'd brought in for Olive when the young woman could hardly bear the weight of her own baby—the same one Lizzie had used to hold Cap; the same one Mattie had used after—and she took another towel from Brother JT to drape over her head, until all she could see was the baby girl, and all the baby girl could see, if she was able, was Lizzie.

Mattie would never know the difference, as sedated as she was now by drink and her endless pain. For now, Lizzie was the best mother the little girl had.

Lizzie began to rub her arms and legs and belly and back. She wiped inside the slack mouth with her smallest finger and thumb, sweeping stringy mucus from it until it seemed clear, and she kept massaging the tiny, still body, and she talked to her.

In the background, Dr. McNeil instructed Dilly on what to hold or what to hand him, or where to push or pull. She waited for Mattie's voice but heard little over theirs and her own, pleading with *this* child to live.

Eventually the rockers of her chair stilled. She gazed down at the tiny, wrinkled face. The little girl screwed up her chin, her eyes squeezed down toward her nose, and she let out the smallest mewl, no more than a kitten, and then she opened her eyes wide and gazed at Lizzie.

"You hungry, darlin'?" Lizzie said through her tears, as she brought the baby's cheek to her nose and inhaled. And, "That's it . . . that's it . . ." as the baby's faint cry turned into a clamoring shriek.

To Lizzie, it sounded like pure joy. It sounded like life.

MATTIE

Arlington, Texas
1905

Mattie woke slowly, to the sound of metal clattering against metal, to voices, most she recognized, one she didn't, and to the warmth of something wriggling in the crook of her arm.

Lizzie knelt at her side, and her eyes pleaded for Mattie to accept what she'd placed on soft towels next to her, between Mattie's ribs and her elbow.

Mattie looked down. She saw it.

The face, the grasping lips and hands and pedaling feet.

The shining cap of hair on its head.

She froze. And then she screamed. "Get it away!" She pushed at the infant, and Lizzie caught it before she'd rolled it clear off the towels.

"Mattie, honey, this sweet little girl wants her mama. She needs to eat." Lizzie clasped the infant tightly now, then leaned to return her to Mattie—now to her exposed breast.

"No!" Mattie shouted, slapping at Lizzie's arm as Lizzie's eyes widened and she moved the baby to safety. "Take it! I told you! Take it away!" She screamed and twisted, tearing at the places where the doctor had sewn her back together after cutting her open to remove so much from her belly. "I'm not its mother. Take it!" She paused and looked straight at Lizzie and said with a questioning sob, "Lizzie? Please?"

She twisted away again when she knew Lizzie heard her.

The doctor had rushed back to Mattie's side and now he tried to hold her still, to keep her from ripping her wounds open again. "Dilly, my bag!" He didn't bother to ask Brother JT's permission. He sprinkled clear liquid from a bottle onto a cloth and placed it over Mattie's nose.

She remembered watching Lizzie, huddled protectively over the small bundle, Brother JT's arm draping her shoulder.

And Lizzie sobbing as they left through the back door, going into the now-hushed world, where sunlight glimmered through the haze of a million dust particles still hovering in the aftermath of the spent storm.

MEMORANDUM

DATE: November 18, 1905

TO: Mr. Albert Ferry, Printer for the Berachah Rescue Society

CC: Miss Hallie V. Taylor, Secretary and Treasurer of the Berachah Industrial Home

FROM: Reverend J. T. Upchurch, Founder and Director of the Berachah Industrial Home

RE: Items for next issue of *The Purity Journal*

Boxed halftone photograph for front page, with this explanation:

This is a photograph of a woman Wife and I encountered while in Louisiana. Diseased and drug-addicted individuals like her sleep under old bridges and wharves and eat rotten produce and spoiled food from trash barrels at night, as the police keep them away from the streets by day. A woman from similar circumstances recovered and was brightly converted in our Home. She lives now in Dallas with her new husband. For this type, we've created the Refuge from an old barn on the property, with four nice rooms and two baths. We still need linens, tableware, etc. Any surplus will be used in the Home, for it is always in short supply.

For Home Notes section:

One of our girls, Alma, has returned from Brother and Sister Jernigan's home in Greenville, where she was helping out with Sister Jonny's sick mother. Mattie Corder has gone in her place.

Several months ago, a foundling was left on the back porch of our property caretakers, Mr. and Mrs. Hyde. After waiting a good amount of time, and following our many prayers that the mother might step forward, they've decided to keep her, for they are unable to bear children of their own. She is a robust child with green eyes and a shock of fair hair. They feel blessed by the Lord and have named her Ruth, honoring history's most famous adoption. We are sorrowful that the child's birth mother was unable to care for her, given our Home's mission, but trust that God remains gracious.

The Home itself continues to overflow, and Sister Susie Singletary reminds us that new girls "knock for admittance" continually. We're praying for a bigger building, the Holy Ghost funds, and the Holy Ghost right-of-way no matter what we undertake to do.

·◦⟩[PART TWO]⟨◦·

You scorn the poor outcast as she passes by,

Forgetting that there is an "All-seeing Eye";

But when the truth search-light shall find you at last,

Beware, lest it find you below the outcast.

—FROM "That's Why She's Sinking Today,"
AUTHOR UNKNOWN

CATE

Arlington, Texas
2017

A box of microfilm from the Berachah collection has been missing—copies of the *Journal*s from 1915 to 1930. It's bothered me since the first time I looked at the finder and couldn't find the corresponding box of film. Late in the day, the Monday before Thanksgiving, I finally locate it, filed under the wrong name in the microfilm drawers. Instead of *B* for *Berachah*, like the rest of the collection, it's under *P* for *Purity Journal*. Now it seems obvious.

It's like I've discovered a whole new world—fifteen more years with my girls. By the time Laurel comes into work Tuesday, I've been in front of the reader for hours, eyes glued to the screen as I scroll, thankful I'm caught up on paperwork and have no other pressing duties.

I've watched for signs that Laurel is dreading the upcoming holiday, but to broach the topic again, I show her a piece in the microfilm about the Home's 1915 Thanksgiving celebration. The secretary has abruptly changed the spelling of her name from Hallie. Now she's Hallye V. Taylor. Laurel and I puzzle over that, but not for long. There's so much more.

Friends of the Home had donated boxes of "goodies," and the girls prepared a huge meal for guests. The article mentions fifteen-year-old Docie carrying the American flag into their morning worship service.

Laurel smiles as she finishes reading, but I sense tension behind the smile.

"That would have been a fun day," I say. "It makes me think of big family holidays. My family was small, so we never really had those Hollywood-style celebrations. What about yours?"

I regret it as soon as I say it, but Laurel only shrugs. She has circles under her eyes and I notice she's wearing the same shirt she wore Friday. Also the day I found her in the cemetery. It occurs to me suddenly that she rotates the same few, over and over. I wonder if she's purchased a single article of clothing since she left home.

Wednesday's a campus holiday, so I stop beating around the bush. "Did you decide about Thanksgiving? I hate to think of you sitting alone in the dorm all weekend."

Dorms used to close for holidays. I had to scramble for places to stay. But our student body is incredibly diverse and the dorms remain open these days. Some students don't celebrate, and many don't go home the whole time they're in school because of international visa requirements—especially with constant uncertainty over immigration policy. I'm sure many receive invitations from friends, but kicking students out of their homes, sometimes for weeks on end, is an unnecessary hardship. Laurel has a place to sleep, but I'm sad she won't enjoy a traditional meal. She's become important to me. I care.

All I get from her is another shrug. I grab one of the little pencils and scraps of recycled paper we leave on the tables for notes and write my address and cell number. "Come around two on Thursday, and we'll have turkey and dressing. Or whatever you like. Do you even like turkey?"

She sighs deeply. "Fiiiiiiine," she says, with a growling tone, drawing the word out as long as the sigh. "You are so bossy. And I freaking like turkey."

Unspoken gratitude flits behind her smile.

Thursday, the doorbell rings right on time. Laurel looks worried, as if my invitation were bogus or I've forgotten. I welcome her enthusiastically.

She carries her backpack, full of sources for a project due Monday, she says. I shake my head. Due dates right after long holidays are the bane of a librarian's existence. Of course students shouldn't wait until the last minute—but they're going to. They frequently show up in a panic, desperate to locate items for papers or projects before heading out of town. What are we going to do? Turn them away?

Suddenly, I wonder if Laurel is just humoring me with her presence. Lately, I feel a little ancient. I'm not even forty, and I look young for my age—being tall and slim has become an unanticipated advantage. But I remember eighteen. People in their late thirties were really old.

I still feel like a kid in more ways than I'd like to admit—and simultaneously decrepit. Aging isn't for wimps. I think of my mother for a quick second, then put that image away.

Holidays are bad like that—not for wimps either.

"It smells so good," Laurel says, her face now undeniably eager.

I relax, wondering how long it's been since she had a home-cooked meal—home-cooked being relative. Once she admitted she liked traditional fare, I ordered from a local farm-to-table restaurant. They guarantee their dinners won't taste previously frozen, as if they came from the grocery store deli.

The only thing I've truly made from scratch is a pumpkin pie, cooling on the counter now. It does smell good. My stomach growls in agreement, and Laurel laughs.

"The rolls get ten minutes at three fifty," I say.

"Is anyone else coming?"

"Just us!" I scurry around the corner to the kitchen to slide the rolls into the oven. "I save all my real partying for the cemetery."

"Weird," she says.

I shrug.

The meal is so delicious I groan. Then take seconds. When we can't eat any more, we crash in my living room. "Stay and work on your project," I encourage Laurel. "No reason to hurry away."

I channel surf, finally settling on *The Sound of Music* as it grows dark outside. I catch myself humming along, even singing a little under my breath.

"I used to watch this with my mom," Laurel says.

My face flushes hot. "Me too."

We both sigh. Heavy sighs.

The movie ends with Laurel asleep on the sofa under a throw blanket, curled into a small ball in the corner. I knew my sofa was magic. I hate to wake her. When a commercial blares, though, she springs up, startled. She obviously doesn't quite remember where she is and stares through glassy eyes until the cobwebs clear.

"You okay?"

She nods. "For a minute, I thought I was at home. It . . . scared me." She huddles again under the throw. "I should get going."

Before I consider the wisdom, I say, "I have a guest room and an extra bathroom. Why don't you just stay here?"

"You sure? I don't want to impose," she says, but with a yearning that tells me she wants to stay.

"Of course!"

We watch another movie, and then I give her a new toothbrush and clean bath towels. She claims she doesn't need them, but I push them into her arms anyway. I get her settled in the guest room, which I furnished recently in a fit of domesticity.

That night, I listen to the sound of my house with someone else in it. There's never been another human asleep in the other bedroom while I've lived here, or anywhere in my house after the movers left, for that matter. Or anywhere I've lived for many, many years. The decorated guest room is simply evidence of my weakness for pretty things. Laurel is the first to see or use any of it.

Somehow the silence is deeper and more comforting than when I'm alone. I'm surprised to find I don't mind this kind of silence at all.

MATTIE

Arlington, Texas
1910

In the half decade since Mattie's arrival at the Home, she'd left briefly three times—after her first summer, to help Sister Jernigan in Greenville for a few months, and twice later, to fill in for cooks at the newer rescue homes in Pilot Point and Texarkana. They'd begged Mattie to stay, but she figured if she was cooking for fallen girls, she might as well run a kitchen where she had friends—family by now.

But by now, she was tired of the dark memories that chased her endlessly here, like a dog after its tail—not to mention, Mattie had begun to worry she was taking up needed space.

When Brother JT said they had girls sleeping in the Home's hallways, there was no accompanying wink. One wide end of the upper balcony had been converted into a sleeping porch, but in bad weather, they moved the beds inside, wherever they'd fit—including the central hall. It was, in Brother JT's words, a good problem. After a long haul, their reputation was solid, and the more the public knew about the Home, the more girls arrived. Civil servants and neighbors wrote regarding young women who'd fallen for promises of marriage, were on the verge of homelessness, or were already on the streets. Sister Maggie Mae's excursions into the vice districts had dwindled, but she remained passionate about reaching girls in the lowest places. The Refuge, created from the old barn with funds Brother JT had raised after May had run off the second time, helped them recover or come off opium or heroin safely, separate from the others. Brother JT said each time the workers gathered to make admittance decisions, it was a meeting of sighs. They had to meet the standards of their particular mission, but too often they felt they were condemning girls to life on the street—or worse, death.

Saint Gertrude and her preacher lived far off in Denver now, running their own rescue home, and sent word of a new baby nearly every year. Mattie set her jaw with each announcement, while Miss Hallie appeared close to tears. Mattie knew now that she and Miss Hallie weren't so different—both old maids who had wanted nothing more than husbands and families.

They'd all made their choices.

Miss Hallie still carried a torch for the wrong man. Mattie had the best of her there. On the slim chance she ever married, she'd find a strong, handsome man, tall enough to make her feel feminine again, and one hundred percent available.

Miss Hallie took Brother JT's teasing too seriously. When he ribbed her over a typographical error, she pouted. Then he gave her puppy-dog eyes, as if he owed her when he was clearly just keeping the peace. Mattie wondered how Sister Maggie Mae tolerated their mutual silliness.

At the 1909 Rescue Rally in Fort Worth, Sister Susie and Sister Maggie Mae had flanked Brother JT on one end of the crowded pew, with Mattie and Miss Hallie on the other. Sister Maggie Mae's brown-striped shirtwaist matched her chestnut hair, which she'd pulled up in smart buns on either side. She was as youthful and pretty as the day Mattie entered the Home. The girls marveled that she could pull it off, between helping Brother JT and bearing him five children in fifteen years. The rest of the Home girls sat a row ahead, ready to sing in identical white dresses. Tiny pleats decorated their bosoms, with puffed sleeves on their shoulders. You'd never have known they were rescued girls, as respectable in appearance as any church choir.

Brother JT had tapped Miss Hallie's arm with his rolled-up program, then leaned so Mattie could hear. "Can you believe how many folks came out for a rescue rally in Cowtown?"

Fort Worth was where civilization met the Wild West. Pinstriped bankers walked the boardwalks beside cattle drivers with dung still clinging to their spurs. The city was a popular watering hole, with a scarlet district that rivaled any. Brother JT believed the rampant drunkenness and debauchery was what put so many women on the streets. Supply followed demand, he claimed. He wanted the district shut down. Mattie marveled that she'd ever lived there.

Brother JT's proximity in the public venue had flustered Miss Hallie. "You continue to underestimate your calling," she'd said, finally.

"You flatter me, Miss V." He smiled, and even Mattie heard Miss Hallie's ragged breath. The woman straightened her back and gathered her skirt close, smoothing it alongside her leg so it no longer grazed the fabric of Brother JT's trousers. Even so, Mattie imagined that the secretary still sensed his warmth across the brief space, as if they touched anyway.

As the chairman had introduced the speaker, Miss Hallie waved her program gently near her face. A fine sweat beaded her upper lip and the cleft of her chin, and she ran her fingers across them. Mattie couldn't force her attention away. When Miss Hallie's arm and skirt relaxed again, Mattie glanced covertly at Brother JT. His right hand rested on Sister Maggie Mae's, atop her own skirted thigh, but he made no effort to shift away from Miss Hallie. His eyelids drifted until he appeared deep in prayer, but Mattie was certain his leg trembled.

Mattie rarely made it through a service without the others wanting to physically lay hands on her for fidgeting, but that night, Mattie herself had hardly stirred, intrigued at this interaction.

Some things at the Home had changed. Some never did.

Each May, the Home girls bustled to clean every surface until it shone, baked and boiled and roasted whatever would keep, and spread their freshly laundered Sunday dresses on the lawn to bleach brighter in the sun, then starched them until they could nearly stand upright. In conjunction with the Home's anniversary and Homecoming celebration, hordes arrived by car or train, carrying camp gear and supplies for the annual Camp Meeting on the grounds.

"We're believing for the largest crowd ever to gather in the state of

Texas for an event of this kind," Brother JT had said in a recent service at the Home, "where the lost souls of the cities can find saving and sanctifying power—whether they be women like yourselves, nothing to give but hearts, or everyday folks with deep pockets to help our work."

He'd convinced the Interurban railway to discount the ride from the cities out to the Home and enlisted Bud Robinson as their speaker again this year. Uncle Bud was everyone's favorite. He wasn't smooth or polished, and he spoke with a lisp and stuttered so often it took him twice as long to say what anyone else could in half the time. But he was so honest, you forgot his rough edges, and before long, his stutter, and then, instead of irritating, the lisp soothed.

Mattie enjoyed Camp Meeting—one of her favorite times at the Home, when former residents often returned. She always feared the Hydes might return, too, however, and scarcely breathed until they sent their fondest regrets once again, claiming the trip was too far to make from their new home out west—even if many others made the same journey. Mattie expected they felt much the same as she did, seeing as how Brother JT had tried so hard with her, for weeks on end, and then said she could change her mind, no matter how much time passed.

She would never change her mind, but how could the Hydes be as sure? It was better for everyone involved that she never saw the child again.

Lizzie, on the other hand, loved Camp Meeting because she didn't have to set a foot off the property. She still hardly wanted to leave the campus, always volunteering to watch the little ones while their mothers sang or played for events elsewhere. Mattie worried that Lizzie would never leave and wondered if she needed to nudge her in a new direction. Otherwise, she'd be as dependent on the Home in a decade as she was today, and what if something happened? What if, heaven forbid, the Home ever closed?

In the first service of this year's Camp Meeting, Mattie's heart suddenly raced when Uncle Bud called for volunteers to accompany his evangelistic band to Oklahoma City to start a new church. The city had sprung up nearly overnight during the 1889 Land Run, when five thousand settlers raced in. By the time Oklahoma became a state in 1907, the city had over sixty thousand. He'd brought photographs clipped from the Oklahoma City papers that showed bustling streets, tall buildings, and fancy hotels. Uncle Bud needed folks to pitch the meeting tent and carry flyers—and one good cook to keep the workers fed.

Fort Worth held memories Mattie never cared to revisit. Dallas felt too established and too uppity. But Oklahoma City? It seemed like a place where a person could reinvent herself.

If she volunteered, she'd see new things. Smell new smells. And just maybe, a man with a similar interest in the mission work might take pity on a former fallen girl and see his way clear to marrying her. Charley had broken her heart—or so she'd thought until she knew how a true broken heart hurt—but she'd loved having the affection of a man. Wanting that seemed safer now that there was no more danger of babies coming, but it would never happen inside the confines of the Home.

During Uncle Bud's final altar call, as the crowd readied to disperse for another year, with many already gone home, Mattie headed straight down the aisle like she had more than five years earlier, only this time she exclaimed, "God wants me for your cook," and fell into Uncle Bud's waiting embrace. She added quickly, "I'll go to Oklahoma."

He squeezed her hands, then turned her to face the remaining crowd, filled with faces she loved. Uncle Bud asked them to lay hands to bless her call. Her tears flowed, less from the call and more from realizing she was going to miss them all terribly.

Lizzie forced her way to the front, where she grabbed Mattie's hand and gazed up at her, her face twisted with competing emotions—most apparent, shock. And was that hurt?

Mattie had never mentioned she'd been thinking of leaving with Uncle Bud. Lizzie would be anxious, and she'd have reason to be. Mattie regretted not warning her. Lizzie would worry as she had constantly, ever since . . . Well, and she'd make Mattie admit she wasn't interested in the ministry alone. The conversation would be touchy.

Mattie was torn, too—mostly because she'd have to say goodbye, for now, to Lizzie, and to Docie, who was growing into a pretty young girl, smart and good at her sums, and you couldn't keep her in books. Docie no longer sneaked in with Mattie, but she trailed her at bedtime, asking about worldly things she wasn't supposed to care about—but that she knew Mattie liked too. Mattie kept it simple but believed even if Lizzie never left, Docie would need to find her own way outside the Home one day. Without disgrace hanging over her like the fallen girls, she might chase dreams of her own.

Mattie kept her smile on her face and lowered her eyelashes as Uncle Bud prayed over her. If the people crowding her seemed more moved by her call than she did, it wasn't anything new. She'd never been propelled by emotional excess. She was propelled by the need to make new memories to cover the old—and by an adventure she couldn't wait to begin.

LIZZIE

Arlington, Texas
1910

When she dared to peek, Lizzie watched Mattie's face, for the prayers went on and on. She knew Mattie's mind wasn't entirely on them, but that didn't surprise her one bit. Mattie's mind always wandered, and today was no different. Mattie had been looking for a way out of the Home forever, especially once her heart had a chance to mend some, and then her body too.

Well, now she'd get it. She'd go away, as Lizzie had expected.

And Lizzie would be left alone.

"Where's my girl?" Mattie exclaimed as the crowd finally loosened around them, but Docie had already run off to play chase with the visiting children until their parents took them home. She was oblivious to what Mattie's decision meant, and Lizzie wouldn't spoil her fun.

At Camp Meeting, the children didn't whisper behind Docie's back like the girls at the Arlington school she attended still did, often sending her home crying. Lizzie loved watching her run and play carefree this one weekend a year. This year, Docie had carried the Bible for the pledges, while the middle Upchurch children had carried the American and Christian flags. She'd stood at the front, upright and proud while the crowd recited the pledge to God's Holy Word, and Lizzie's heart had nearly filled to bursting.

Lizzie shrugged away from Mattie and pointed out Docie and her friends. They'd captured a smaller boy, and he screeched inside their ring until Miss Hallie showed up to shut down their boisterous behavior. Lizzie half regretted pointing, for Mattie saw Miss Hallie's mouth open and swooped over there.

"Docie, come give Aunty Mat a hug, darlin'. It won't be long until I can't do it every day." Docie dropped the other girls' hands, and the little boy escaped. Miss Hallie continued to look askance, but it was too late to read the riot act once the others ran away.

Docie threw her arms around Mattie and sobbed on her shoulder. Lizzie couldn't decide whether to be happy with Mattie for saving the kids from Miss Hallie, or cross because she'd made Docie cry again, here of all places. It didn't take much to set her off. It wasn't always that she was upset. She was just fragile, every way. And she'd share anything with anyone. Her exuberance was the best reason for fencing her in here at the Home for a good long time. She clung to Mattie now, and Mattie patted her. "Don't cry, honey. I'll visit every chance I get, and you and your mama will come see me too!"

Lizzie simply shook her head and tried to stanch her own tears. She'd ventured up that way once, long ago, one too many times. And she'd never let Docie go alone—leastways not until she couldn't keep her from it. Mattie caught Lizzie wiping her eyes, and said that for all they knew, she wouldn't even like Oklahoma City.

Lizzie knew better. So many girls who'd left had promised they'd visit, but the Homecoming group was always slim. Mattie would likely never come this way again. Moreover, without all the painful memories to chase her around like ghosts, Mattie would thrive.

As for the city, Mattie would adore it. And what would Lizzie do without her?

MATTIE

Arlington, Texas
1910

Uncle Bud wanted to move on to Oklahoma nearly immediately, so by late Monday morning, Mattie was packed. She'd arrived with nearly nothing, and what she'd accumulated over five years took no time to tuck into a trunk left by a runaway girl. Her dresses and undergarments. Her "secret" face cream everyone knew about. Her Bible and a few other books she'd received as gifts.

The garments Cap had been wearing the day he died.

They'd been carefully laundered and returned to her. They'd buried him in a little suit handed down from one of the Upchurch boys, but she'd given up his blanket.

It belonged with him.

She'd wrapped his tiny shirt and pants—and his remaining shoe—in tissue, and now she transferred them from the bottom of her dresser drawer to the bottom of her trunk, laying her own garments on top. She'd know his things were there, but she wouldn't have to see them.

She had an hour left before Uncle Bud's entourage would depart. With the trunk fastened and waiting at the foot of her bed for someone to help her drag it downstairs when it was time, she looked around the room she'd shared with Lizzie and Docie and a revolving cast of Home girls and children for the last five years. She brushed away a tear that came from nowhere.

Families in Oklahoma City had offered beds to the visiting

evangelists, and those who stayed would eventually find permanent quarters. If she stayed after the band moved on, perhaps she'd even have her own room. That would be a first.

But she'd miss this . . .

The morning call to rise, certain girls meeting the day as if they couldn't wait, while others hid under covers for a last moment of rest—then rushed to make morning prayers. She'd been in both camps.

The evenings, when lamplight or firelight warmed the room, beckoning the girls to settle quietly, babies tucked around them in donated cradles or bassinets—or close to their sides if they preferred—and the older kids in cots, sleeping soundly after their milk and stories and prayers. A few girls, like Mattie, alone, tormented or comforted in turn by those sweet little faces.

And the between times, when any shallow excuse to fetch something from the dormitory would do, maybe a letter to post or a pin for unruly hair. Mattie was certain every girl, over the years—maybe even Saint Gertrude, who'd rarely wasted a moment—had slipped up here for a moment of peace, away from the hubbub of the Home.

Something about the bedroom in the middle of the day, when motes floated in sunlight over their neat white coverlets and the muted noise of the household gave way to the rustling of leaves and the sigh of a breeze grazing the curtain, made her feel entirely at home.

She would miss all of it more than she'd realized.

The door opened, and she shook her nostalgia away. Lizzie had come, finally, and now Mattie would need to be strong enough to make the break for both of them.

Lizzie was worried. They were all worried.

Brother JT had invited Mattie to his study after breakfast. Seated across from her at his desk, he'd questioned her stamina for an environment so different from the Home. In roughshod Oklahoma, she'd work harder than ever, cooking plain meals—not the indulgent recipes they'd often allowed her here. She'd had more freedom in the Home than she wanted to admit.

He'd said, "Oklahoma City is a crude place, especially where they're building the mission. Are you strong enough? And are you confident in your faith?"

Had she ever felt confident in her faith? Certainly not the way he did, or Lizzie did. Mattie had more questions and doubts at nearly thirty years old than she'd had as a child—and at age twenty-three too.

How could she not?

But she was confident that working through the questions—even if it left her with a trust still cloaked in uncertainty—had helped her regain her footing. And if it could work for fallen girls like her, perhaps it could work for others: Families who sold everything to claim a scrap of land in a new state. Men who drifted in and out with the railroads, laying track or shoveling coal, longing for community in spite of—or maybe because of—their perpetual movement. And maybe most of all, other women who needed new beginnings.

"Yes," she'd said to Brother JT. As for being strong enough, how could anyone ever know? She'd been strong enough to pull through tragedy, not once, but more times than anyone should have to, and she was still standing, wasn't she? She let her one-word answer stand alone too.

Brother JT had blessed her and sent her away. Miss Hallie hovered in the hallway, as always, and Mattie forced a smile and a handshake on her way back upstairs to pack. "You always mean well, Miss Hallie," she'd said. "It must have been hard giving up a regular life to help with us girls. You'd probably like to be married, with children of your own. Thank you."

Miss Hallie had tilted her head back and forth in a way that said she was taken aback. Finally, she said, "Well. I'm entirely content to be in service to the Lord here. My work is my life, and the Upchurches have made me family. I can't imagine any other, but to each her own. I do hope you'll be cautious. So many will take advantage of naïve young women."

"That's true anywhere, but I can stand up for myself now. You be careful too."

Miss Hallie stepped back, and her eyes looked like a grown dog's caught sneaking into the kibble, but her lips stayed pursed. Mattie thought that must surely be exhausting.

But as Mattie had continued toward the stairs, Miss Hallie called, "Take care, Mattie."

Mattie looked back to see her lip quivering.

Now Mattie turned to Lizzie. She embraced her, then pulled her downstairs and away, to the secluded grove that had grown so much since they'd arrived. They circled the burial ground, arm in arm. They walked past the little headstone sunk into the ground and Mattie slowed. Could she truly leave without looking back?

"I want letters," Lizzie said. Mattie looked at her sideways. "Docie's learning her reading and writing fast. She'll read them to me. Someone will."

"I can't tell you everything in letters."

Lizzie swung her head up. "Mattie, don't you go forgetting all you learned." Her eyes went darker, more exposed than ever. "I'm awful afraid for you. I ain't sure it's the right thing."

Mattie had half thought to avoid this talk, knowing it would dampen her enthusiasm, but it was inevitable. Lizzie had to understand. It was impossible for her to stay—harder each year.

"I won't forget what I've learned," she said. "But I can't write everything we'd laugh over in letters, not when others will read them. Especially not Docie. She'd be horrified. You know I'll find plenty to laugh over. I'll save certain things for when I visit."

She watched Lizzie struggle to contain her grin. They did love to carry on in private. No telling how often they'd stifled giggles when someone read aloud one of Miss Hallie's sanctimonious pieces in *The Purity Journal*. Mattie knew Lizzie felt guilty for it, but Mattie always reminded her that if they didn't laugh at life sometimes, they'd keel over from keeping so straight their joints froze.

Lizzie's grin faded now, and her mouth tightened again. The past— *both* of theirs—still tormented her. Not so often these days, but Mattie regretted causing her any worry at all. "Oh, honey," she said. "I'll be good. I promise I will. I have to be. And I won't throw myself at any ol' fellow that happens along. Don't you think I've learned my lessons?"

But Lizzie's leg kept dragging as they continued to walk the path Mattie had worn nearly by herself inside the circle of oak trees, and they were quiet for a time, remembering how hard those lessons were. They never spoke of them aloud.

Mattie had one more thing to say, however. "You must promise me something too. If anything ever happens to me . . ." Her voice faded. She gazed across the clearing, swallowing hard.

"Hush, now," Lizzie said. "You got your whole life ahead. And if you need it, you can come back home."

"I know," Mattie said. But she bent her head and pulled Lizzie along, sharing what she'd thought about as long as she'd known her, the till-now-unspoken hope she'd nursed more than any other hope.

Lizzie nodded, and though she protested even the idea of it, inside and out, she promised she'd do what Mattie asked. She owed her that and more.

CATE

Grissom, Texas
1998

Nothing could match that first day in Carr City, but over the next several weeks, River and I continued to drive to abandoned places within a few hours of home. Most of the buildings we explored were gutted, hardly passable after years of abuse by vandals, animals, or the weather. Sometimes we struck a small vein of gold, but what I craved most was our time together.

I'd invented a Saturday study group at the home of a classmate so I wouldn't have to fake being at the coffee shop anymore, and then, as AP exams approached, I studied half the night to make up for time lost on the weekends. I felt confident. If anything, I felt nearly euphoric, as if I had endless energy. My ability to retain tiny details—names, dates, and places; obscure terms and theorems—blew me away. If falling for someone felt like this, it was proof a person actually could live on love.

I grudgingly insisted on a weekday for prom shopping with my mom. She was shocked to see that my usual dress size hung off me. I wasn't surprised. My clothes had grown looser since I'd met River, as if, along with my reduced need for sleep, I didn't need to eat either. For once, I was not only model tall, but nearly model thin.

Mom tugged at the dress after zipping me into it, frowning. "Honey, are you eating?"

"*Mom*," I said. "I just forget sometimes. I needed to lose a few pounds anyway. I look good, don't I?" One perk of shopping with your mother was that you could be obnoxiously arrogant and she just laughed. The other was her credit card.

But she tilted her head after zipping me into the next size down. I did look beautiful—even I could see how my eyes gleamed, and my skin had a new glow. Saturday afternoons outside had something to do with it. Because I burned or stayed exactly as pale when I tried to tan on purpose, I'd always preferred to remain pasty while my friends tanned for hours. This spring, however, gradual exposure to the sun had lifted my complexion to the slightest golden tone, and my arms looked healthy and strong.

"I hope you're not dieting," Mom said. "You look great, but don't go overboard."

"I won't," I promised, though I had little control over my appetite these days, and would not give up my time with River.

We bought the dress, matching shoes, and accessories, and booked a hair appointment—makeup, too, because Mom was on a roll. By the time prom started, I wouldn't recognize myself. But she was happy. Jess was too. She and Jordan and Seth and I were all going together.

Telling River I was going with Seth was last on *my* checklist—but most important—and prom was two weeks and a few days away. River never assumed we'd spend time together, but we had a routine. Each week, at some point during my library assistant period, River paged through the *Encyclopedia of Texas* and pointed out a former landmark or town.

"This one?"

I'd interrupt whatever I was doing to look. "Perfect!" I'd exclaim, or now and then, I'd say, "That's the best you can do?" with a sarcastic shrug. River liked a challenge.

We'd begun talking late at night, after my parents had gone to bed. They were used to the murmur behind my closed door. As long as I kept up my grades, they didn't care if I was on the phone. Jess didn't notice me calling less; she was always talking to Jordan. She'd hoped for a prom date, but it seemed she'd gained a boyfriend as well.

That Saturday, two weeks before prom, River decided to surprise me, not giving up the details even when I begged. We left as early as I could manage without worrying my mom and drove more than three hours west. AP exams were approaching quickly, so Mom didn't even blink when I rushed out the door at eight a.m.

River never pressed for more on why I didn't want my parents to know about our excursions. By the same virtue, I didn't ask many questions. River's parents were a vague image for me, though I'd learned the basics. They'd always moved a lot. Both were software engineers, and like most of the new people in town, they'd wanted to be near the high-tech sector of Austin but with better schools and less traffic. I was surprised two engineers had managed to birth a musically inclined history and photography freak, not to mention a quiet rebel with little appreciation for order—unless the order made random sense to River. Not engineer-y at all.

I was grateful not to be stereotyped either. But for the very first time, when we pulled up to River's mystery destination, I balked.

The Hotel Zagosa was different from the other places—mostly ghost towns or abandoned buildings in the country. It was in the middle of a functioning small town, with cheap chain motels on the outskirts and a clearly living population. Trying to sneak into an old building where someone was likely to see us made me nervous, but River assured me we'd be fine. If anyone tried to stop us, we'd leave, and if we got caught inside, we'd claim ignorance—River still had a Colorado driver's license and plates.

Besides, it was Saturday afternoon. Once we found the abandoned hotel, the small-town traffic was nearly nonexistent. Nearby businesses were closed for the weekend, and nobody was outside the few adjacent homes. Still, after we drove around the block, I shook my head.

I eyed the façade of the Spanish colonial-style building, its windows mostly boarded on the first level and broken on the second and third. Here and there were gaps nearly big enough to slip through, but *No Trespassing* signs glared from every side of the stucco building.

River parked near a few other cars in a nearby lot. We walked toward the front of the old hotel, craning our necks. It didn't hurt to just look, I figured. Terracotta tiles covered the overhangs, amazingly unblemished considering a historical marker dated the building to 1893. The marker was the only reason it hadn't been demolished. Overly optimistic history buffs probably hoped a wealthy investor would happen along, but from the looks of the town, that seemed unlikely.

A balcony spanned the upper level across the front, shading the entry area except where arches allowed sunlight to illuminate the boarded and bolted doors. Not a single vehicle had passed so far, and we hurried beneath the balcony's cover. The few uncovered windows in front contained filthy glass. River shined the flashlight against one cloudy pane. We peeked through and saw nothing. Then River pointed to the building's corner, where a tall chain-link fence that went all the way around the backside of the building was bent enough to create an opening just wide enough to negotiate.

"I know what you're thinking," I said, "and it's dumb." I had stopped worrying about voicing my true opinions well before that day.

"We haven't seen a single person since we got here," River said. "I bet people go in all the time."

"I'm not people."

"You don't have to. I won't judge."

I also knew by now that was true. River glanced toward the street, then pulled back the fence to pass through more easily. "Just yell if you see anyone, okay?"

I stood there only long enough to decide waiting was scarier than going in.

All my life, it seemed I'd followed rules carefully while everyone else bent them. I wouldn't be judged by River, but I would have disappointed myself. So I ran between the buildings and rounded the corner. "Wait!"

River stopped climbing inside where a board had been loosened— probably by the same person who'd made the opening in the fence— and chuckled. "Hi, people!"

I rolled my eyes.

Inside, I plugged my nose. This was nothing like the old depot. There were no pretty pictures on the walls. People had used this building indiscriminately. Empty condom wrappers—and the used

condoms—along with broken glass, smashed cans, and plastic sy-
ringes littered the floor. The walls were covered in graffiti, not to
mention pentagrams and other symbols teens had likely painted to
convince friends that satanic cults gathered here to offer blood sac-
rifices. Even assuming they were faked, the sight of them gave me
chicken skin and a queasy stomach.

We peeked up a staircase too dilapidated to even try.

"I think I'm done," I said.

River nodded easily. "Disgusting. We should stick with less obvious places. I'm sorry for dragging you all the way out here."

I shrugged. "You know, sometimes I have the sense that history is
worth exploring. Other times, I'm just repulsed by humanity."

"You're telling me . . ."

We started back toward the opening, but as we neared it, we heard
rattling. River's eyes widened in the flashlight's gleam. We grabbed
hands, for the first time since the depot, and we huddled together, frantically seeking another escape. My heart felt as if it would thud right
through my skin, and I wanted to cry. River switched off the flashlight.

"Zagosa Police," a deep voice called. "Do not make any sudden
moves." He sounded weary, as if tired of busting people and hoping he
wouldn't see something he didn't want to see—teens doing the nasty
on the nasty floor, or a junkie shooting up. We stood still, as he'd
ordered—and also because we were terrified—though we dropped
our hands to our sides. After the officer maneuvered his stocky body
through the opening, he shined a light much brighter than ours, then
shook his head. "What are you kids doing? Can't you see the signs?"
He was obviously annoyed but seemed almost relieved to find fully
clothed teenagers.

"Just taking a look," River said. "Sorry, sir. We shouldn't have ignored them."

The officer sighed. "You from around here?" We shook our heads.
"Didn't think so. Got a call about Colorado plates. Figured hippies
thought they'd located free lodging, though why anyone would want
to stay in this shi—excuse me, *pit*, I have no idea. That your car in the
lot next door?"

"Yes, sir."

I'd never heard River say *sir*—or *ma'am*. I was used to it, having grown up in small-town Texas, but it sounded weird to me, even so.

"ID?"

"In the car," River said, and I nodded my agreement.

"Next time, carry it. Someone catches you inside a place like this, not as sweet as me—maybe slits your throat and leaves you for dead— it's good to have something for easy identification."

I shivered, and we both nodded again.

"Gonna let you off with a warning. It'd take more time to book you than it's worth. But I'll shoot straight—if I ever find you in my precinct doing something like this again, I *will* take you to jail. I don't care who you are or how nice you're dressed. It's illegal to trespass."

I released my long-held breath. "Yes, sir," we both said. We followed him to the opening, and he held the board while we passed through and trailed us all the way to River's car.

We drove to the edge of town in silence before we pulled over at a gas station, where River finally glanced at me guiltily, and I burst into hysterical laughter. I don't think either of us was taking it lightly, but laughter was all that could release the tension that had wound through our bodies the minute we entered the hotel, and only increased when the officer arrived.

Finally, we spoke at once.

"Holy mother of—"

"Holy crap!"

We dissolved again, grabbing our sides where they hurt from laughing so hard.

"Okay," River said. "You were definitely right on this one. We'll stick to the smaller stuff. Can you picture us trying to rob a bank?"

We laughed off and on all the way back, reliving the moment again and again, but as we neared home, I asked River to take a detour. I had to say something about prom. We carried gas station drinks into a park I knew, to a picnic area hidden in the trees. I sat on top of the table. River clambered up by me. "Why are you suddenly so *serious*?"

I sighed. "I'm going to prom."

"Okay?"

"I thought you should know."

River gave me a small, curious smile, and I felt almost stupid for bringing it up. We hadn't talked about our relationship in terms of . . . well, anything. Were the feelings mine alone?

"I have a gig that night. The only reason I really care is I hoped you could come. I didn't take you for the prom type, but *maybe* . . ."

"Stop," I said. River laughed. "Someone asked, and my mom seemed heartbroken that I might say no. She's into it. I'd much rather see your show."

"No big deal. But . . . who's someone?"

My heart quickened. "Just a guy from church. You wouldn't know him."

River looked off toward nowhere.

I knew I should say more, but I didn't want to talk about Seth. I wanted to talk about River and me—*with* River. Instead, though, I thought of all of the sleepovers where Jess and I had talked for hours, her about Jordan, me about Seth. How our names sounded with their last names. How far we'd go if we ended up going out. After a retreat about God's plan for sexuality, the how-far part was still fuzzy. Jess had always speculated bluntly while I cringed.

I'd spent countless hours daydreaming about a person who had rarely given me the time of day before, but met every qualification I thought mattered, while River, whom I'd never needed to chase, was right here, right in front of me, and completely off-limits.

So this *was* a big deal. To me, it was.

We sat silent. Eventually, I reached to wind my fingers through River's. The gesture seemed clear to me. More so than tugging each other along into murky places, or clinging to each other in terror. It was deliberate. Intentional.

But was it clear?

In case there was any question, I picked up River's hand and kissed our clasped fingers.

LIZZIE

Arlington, Texas
1910

The days were long with Mattie gone. Lizzie wandered aimlessly in the evenings after getting Docie to bed, moving quietly from group to group, but never settling, like a ghost of herself. Before, she'd have been happily huddled somewhere with Mattie. She tried to be an example to the newer girls, but they often regarded her with silent mistrust. She was the "old" one now—at all of twenty-five—and they likely worried she'd tell on them if they made any wrong moves. She didn't have the heart to convince them she was as prone to stumbling as they were.

Soon after Mattie's departure, Lizzie volunteered for the Refuge, thinking maybe it was time for a change for her as well. The work was grueling, and Lizzie struggled to keep emotion from ruling her head—not to mention, her replacement in the nursery proved helpless. The flighty young woman ordered changes that made the babies cross and uncomfortable, so Brother JT and Sister Susie thought Lizzie should return. They put Lizzie in charge this time, answering only to Birdie Cagle, a girl who, like so many, had been jilted after becoming pregnant. Smart, quick, and responsible, she'd been at the Home several years now and headed the children's department in general. Birdie gave Lizzie room, and now the babies were sweet angels again. Everyone commented what a fine job Lizzie was doing, with three others to help. She loved all her babies, but the Home was a different place now. Lizzie missed Mattie so much it hurt to even think about her some days.

Before Mattie left for Oklahoma, the two of them had usually spent Sunday afternoons walking and talking, enjoying the quiet after long, busy weeks. Now Lizzie dreaded the loneliness. After Sunday services, most of the girls memorized scripture, learned music, or flocked to Sister Maggie Mae's literary society, called by Greek letters Lizzie couldn't even pronounce. They talked about books or put on little plays—sometimes for worship services and Camp Meeting. Though Sister Maggie Mae claimed Lizzie was welcome, she'd always felt outside the circle. That word, *literary*, meant things she'd never be. Better not to be reminded.

One summer Sunday after service and dinner, she settled Docie inside with one of her precious chapter books. Docie had tried yet again to show Lizzie how numbers and names broke up the pages and words, but everything stubbornly turned upside down and scrambled in her brain, like always. Once Docie was deep in her book, Lizzie wandered outside.

There used to be a path worn through the brush to the Refuge, but they'd cleared everything between it and the printing office to give a clear view. Even now, Sister Susie wrestled inside with a girl who'd come from San Antonio to get off the dope.

Seeing the building always made her think of May. Lizzie had been so sure her determination could save her, but she'd finally learned. In the aftermath of the chaotic dust storm, Lizzie had confessed everything about that situation to Brother JT, sitting in his parlor between him and Sister Maggie Mae, holding the baby Mattie had rejected, nearly hysterical herself with sorrow and guilt. She'd admitted she'd worried something was off with Mattie but kept quiet about it. And then she'd told how she'd been the one to bring May to the barn.

Brother JT had said Mattie could stay, even if she continued to refuse the baby. It was, in his opinion, one of the times they'd have to bend the rules. It was a special circumstance.

When he gently praised Lizzie for coming clean, and reminded her how proud they were of her determination and compassion, she'd handed the baby to Sister Maggie Mae and knelt right then and there, giving her life over to helping fallen girls see the light.

Now, though, she reckoned that meant taking care of their babies while someone else did the hardest work. She was no good at the other.

Lizzie turned away from the Refuge, walking until she stopped to heft herself onto the big stone that overlooked the fields. She felt close to Mattie there.

One of Lizzie's newest helpers in the nursery, Ivy Bernard, had arrived shortly after Mattie's departure, and she knew Lizzie missed Mattie something fierce. Her history wasn't clear yet, but her companionship made up some for Mattie's absence. At times, though, her hanging on got to be too much, especially when Lizzie needed to be alone. She'd probably hurt the girl's feelings earlier today when Ivy had asked if Lizzie wanted company.

Lizzie had said, "No, thank you, dear."

Ivy's face had darkened. "You're tired of me."

Lizzie laughed. "Hush! I just need room for thinking. I get weary of baby talk all week and need to recall how to think like a grown woman again. You come find me in a while."

Recently, with the help of a new girl, Lizzie had dictated a letter to Mattie, telling her about Ivy, how relieved she was to have someone to talk with now and then—especially one who understood some of her struggles. She didn't tell her what Ivy had told Lizzie in secret: Like Lizzie, she could hardly read or write. Lizzie had said it hadn't mattered to anyone at the Home that she still struggled with both. Even if they intended to send girls on their way at the end of a year, with training that would earn them a decent living, they wouldn't put Ivy out. After all, Lizzie was here nearly six years now. They said the girls had a home for life if needed, and they meant it. Uneducated girls like Lizzie and Ivy had little choice but the street or jobs that didn't pay enough to keep them off it. Good homes weren't likely to hire them for cleaning or caring for little ones once they found out their histories. They'd lost the privilege of protection.

Listening to Mattie's reply, Lizzie had quickly realized Mattie resented her new friendship. But she wouldn't give it up. Lizzie couldn't understand why Mattie would begrudge her the pleasure of another good friend now. It wasn't as if God gave each human only one. Lizzie would joyfully include Mattie in their new little circle if she came for Homecoming—but now she worried Mattie would claim Ivy was trying to break them up. Lizzie wouldn't have the patience for it. Mattie had yammered about finding a way out of the Home for years. She'd found it, and she'd gone away, as Lizzie had expected. And now Lizzie would not be alone after all.

Lizzie turned her head at footfalls on the path. She beckoned and shifted to make room. She wouldn't mind sitting with Ivy now. Ivy climbed up hesitantly, but Lizzie insisted she take her fair share of the rock.

The rock made a fine place to set lunch pails while they sowed seeds in the spring and harvested crops in the fall. Nearly everyone helped with the harvest—corn for eating, and cotton, weighed and sold at the gin. The girls kept a portion of what the Home earned from it so they could purchase letter paper, postage, or personal items from the general store or druggist in town. Lizzie rarely needed anything but the occasional undershirt or pair of stockings for herself or little things for Docie, so she'd saved nearly all of her money in a knotted handkerchief in the corner of her drawer.

Lizzie pointed out to Ivy the first heads of corn forming on the stalks in the field. After a wet spring, they'd wondered if they'd ever show. But it had warmed up finally, and good.

Ivy interrupted her small talk. "Do you ever miss your husband? Or your family?"

Lizzie hadn't thought of Willis in months, though her marriage was common knowledge around the Home. He'd left her not two months after their wedding at the courthouse in Sulphur, and every time he'd shown his face afterward had been for nothing good.

"Like I'd miss a flock of birds roosting on my head," Lizzie said. "This is my family now." She gestured toward the big house, just visible over the treetops. "Guess I'm like Ruth in the Good Book." As soon as she said it, a great lump rose in her throat. That couple who took Mattie's baby had moved far away less than a few months after it came. She guessed they were worried Mattie would change her mind, but Mattie had never even said her name, not even to Lizzie.

Ivy tugged at a lock that had escaped from her bun. She struggled with something else. "What is it?" Lizzie said, once she'd regained her voice. "You know most of *my* secrets."

That was true. Once they'd put her story in the *Journal*, she'd felt clean and free, even if folks wanted to judge what she'd done. She worried for Docie, with everyone knowing, but Lizzie had needed to confess for the world to see. It was the only way to stop the guilt. She'd held back a few things that concerned only her girl—that would be Docie's to tell, if she ever remembered.

And of course, there was the one other thing she couldn't make herself say out loud.

But the Lord knew.

Ivy's next question came fast and low. "Do you ever miss a man's touch?"

Lizzie forced herself not to shudder. She'd seen how Brother JT kissed Sister Maggie Mae's cheek when he thought nobody watched. It was sweet, but nothing she yearned for. "Men never had no need for me beyond planting pain in my womb," she said. "No such thing as a gentle touch."

Willis had romanced her the month they met, her only fourteen. He was a good looker and knew it. At a barn dance, he'd led her around the floor, then pushed her down in the grass behind the place before she knew which end was up. Why he'd listened to her mother's threats and carried Lizzie to the courthouse was anyone's guess.

He did what he wanted. So maybe he'd had some kind of affection for her.

She'd been tangled in her thoughts again and had stopped paying attention to Ivy. She looked down. Ivy's hand covered hers on top of the stone. Lizzie glanced up. The girl's eyes were like a doe's, shiny, right before the shot ripped through its heart.

Lizzie's breath caught. She and Mattie had held hands more times than she could count, swinging them as they walked, or skipped arm in arm as they shared their delight over something. They hugged on each other in their dark times, just as sisters would. It was perfectly natural, what she and Mattie had done.

This was different.

Ivy said, "I never craved a man's touch. Not ever." Her fingers crept between Lizzie's now, and with her other hand, she stroked the tender inside of Lizzie's wrist.

It tickled, but Lizzie stayed still, so as not to spook her. She felt comfort from the hands on hers, to be sure, but this was more than simple affection. Mattie was right after all. Ivy's sticking so close was maybe more than just longing for friendship.

In the cribs—tiny, filthy shacks where she'd made money at the worst times—she'd seen two women together, usually to entertain a man who could pay. And at times, a proper woman with money had asked in the dark for another. Lizzie had always been taught it was more wicked than anything else, what with the preachers and scriptures calling it an abomination—maybe worse than Lizzie's sins.

Except she had little room to judge, and she knew it. Ivy was fragile. Lizzie didn't want to send her running.

Lizzie carefully placed her other hand atop Ivy's to stop her. "No, honey," she said. "Even if I wanted a man's touch, I couldn't have it. I'm married. And this?" She shook her head gently.

Ivy wrenched herself away. "I'm sorry!" she said. "I didn't mean it. Please don't tell." She strained both toward Lizzie and away from her at the same time, as if she couldn't bear to stay but was afraid to leave.

"You're my friend," Lizzie said. "What you were thinking—it's a secret to keep. I don't think you should tell anyone else. They might be less forgiving."

It was kinder to be gentle.

Tears threatened Ivy's eyes, and she held herself tight. "I thought . . ." She shook herself. "I'm just plain wicked—going straight to hell!" She ran off, way across the field, trampling the new cotton.

Lizzie had seen enough in her years at the Home to know each person carried her own burdens, none alike. Every girl here—Lizzie included—had had the world thrust on her, no choice but to submit to the ugliness women had suffered for all ages.

But Ivy's struggle seemed different. She was a sweet and innocent young woman—no matter Mattie's jealousy. And while Lizzie believed what she'd been told—that it was wrong for two men or two women to lie together—she couldn't help but wonder what made Ivy that way.

Surely she wouldn't choose it. Why would anyone choose something so hard?

Ivy avoided her for days, saying only what she must, taking the babies off to play instead of setting them on the floor between them, rocking a little one to sleep in a quiet corner.

She just needed time.

Finally, when the other girls were in an all-day meeting, where the community came in to sing and pray and study the Good Book with them, Lizzie got up the nerve to talk to her.

Ivy didn't take kindly to it. "I don't know what came over me and would thank you not to throw it back in my face."

Lizzie gaped. She'd only said she loved her and was worried about Ivy's relationship with the Lord. But now she said, "What happened before you came? You're not expecting, and you've been so quiet about it."

"I gave my confession," Ivy said. "Brother JT said it was nobody's business but mine to share with who I wanted."

The Upchurches were big on the girls confessing. Some took longer than others, and some gave more of the particulars. Ivy had never said more than that she'd been ruined by a married man. That was common enough, but maybe there was more than Ivy had let on.

She wouldn't push her. In time, Ivy would trust her, just as Mattie had.

Lizzie was good at two things, in addition to keeping babies happy:

She could keep a promise. And she could keep a secret.

MATTIE

Oklahoma City
1910

Every corner of Oklahoma City was under construction, it seemed, with stores and offices and hotels rising on the flat plains faster than she'd thought possible—one day, an empty lot, the next, the frame in place, then before you knew it, an *Open* sign hanging in the window. Buildings with multiple stories went up so quickly, it was a wonder they were safe. Skirts were shorter and hats bigger—and waists, too, or at least it looked like it given the more relaxed corsets. The place was exciting, but the hustle and bustle overwhelmed her sometimes, especially after life at the Home.

When she was homesick, she wrote it away in a letter to Lizzie.

> *By the time we get back to our rooms, my feet are falling off, and my eyes are nearly as tired from looking. I never knew there were so many shades of brick and paint, or that hundreds, maybe thousands, could want hotel rooms on a single night. And the food, Lizzie! Oh my! I carry paper to make notes about what I see in the restaurant windows, on the sample carts and menus . . . there are too many choices, but I want to learn about all of them. I've always thought I was sick of cooking, but you know what? I'd like to run a restaurant one day. All my complaining about it being my only talent—I had no idea what a person could do. Sure wish you were here! I miss you so much, and I can hardly stand to sleep without my goodnight hug and kiss from Docie.*

Lizzie's transcribed responses were flat, reporting about Docie's year-end exams, and how she and Ivy had done this and done that and . . . it never ended. Something bothered Mattie about Ivy, and it wasn't simple jealousy. Mattie understood Lizzie's need to replace her, but she bristled at the quick depth of their intimacy. At the top of her letter, though, Lizzie had carefully penned, so Mattie wouldn't miss it, *We miss you, too,* with a heart and flowers from Docie.

Mattie's homesickness faded. If Lizzie stayed, at least she was content. But Docie would become restless eventually. When that happened, Mattie would convince Lizzie to let Docie visit, and she'd show her the real world. She'd keep her safe. She knew the dangers.

In the meantime, Mattie had more than enough to keep her busy. Preparations for Uncle Bud's crusade lasted more than a week. The men cleared brush beside a dilapidated building in the city's worst section, then raised a tent while the women distributed notices from house to house and business to business, and handed them out to packing plant workers, who streamed past their corner in the morning on their way to slaughter livestock and back in the evening, covered in blood and stink. Mattie struggled not to gag. The packers would do nearly anything for liquor or women, and their crude comments humiliated her. These were not the kind of men she'd intended to meet. She hadn't come for this. But she reminded herself she was no saint. She'd gone low too. She breathed through her mouth while smiling politely.

The first meeting pulled in fifty souls with more each night once word spread. Many walked the aisle, and several pledged to attend future meetings and help build a church.

Before Uncle Bud left, two weeks later, he praised Mattie's cooking and invited her to go farther west with the band. She thought it over but decided to stay. Packing plants aside, she hoped to support herself eventually, and she thought she could do it here. Traveling with Uncle Bud, she'd be in a loop, never truly settled.

Another woman decided to stay on as well. Sister Welch had some means, and she rented adjoining rooms for herself and Mattie near a drugstore that had offered its basement for a Sunday school. Two local women joined their efforts. The three together were the liveliest church women Mattie had ever known—even more than her mother—always shouting in the services, and skipping and clapping up and down the aisles during the singing and the altar calls. Mattie got the giggles as their hats and hairpins flew. Aside from their boisterous enthusiasm, she felt unequal to their faith. She wasn't stupid, but as they prayed and quoted scripture, it seemed they spoke a tongue she had no desire to learn. She craved real conversation. She missed her talks with Lizzie, and even Brother JT's frank advice. She'd have been lost without the women's guidance, but their fervent piety was sometimes more than she could take.

Worse, at the Home, there'd never been more than the matron and her assistant caring for all the girls; Mattie now had three personal chaperones. Sister Welch was the oldest—and consequently, the nosiest—dissecting Mattie's every move. Mattie began to feel under lock and key, more than ever before. She wondered if Brother JT had given Uncle Bud a warning, and whether Uncle Bud, in turn, had advised Sister Welch to be on guard for any slip in Mattie's mental state. If anything, Mattie figured it more likely she'd go crazy over their extreme vigilance.

It had been five years since she'd lost her mind, so to speak. They'd all, even Lizzie, assumed she'd had a nervous breakdown when she chose the way she did, but she'd known what she had to do—once she'd understood what was happening to her body. Even the doctor had said she hadn't been the first in all of history to miss the signs . . .

She was lucky they hadn't had her committed to an asylum.

But they had nothing to worry about here. She simply longed to explore, alone. Women walked on their own downtown—she'd seen them herself.

Three weeks in, after the Sunday school class dismissed, Mattie grew sleepy and numb to the prayers the sisters said together before returning to their homes. As best she could tell from the scriptures, the Good Lord had intended Sunday for rest, but it was the busiest day of the week for churchgoers. June was growing uncomfortably hot, and while the basement was cooler than the store above, her corset pinched. She wasn't sure she'd last another hour— and it wasn't unreasonable to assume they might carry on that long.

Sister Welch caught her yawning. "Mattie, dear, are we keeping you from something more important?"

Mattie sat up straighter. "I'm sorry. I'm just . . ." She hesitated a mere second before the fib emerged. "Perhaps I'm coming down with a summer cold, especially going from the heat outside to this basement. No telling what all these folks bring in with them."

"Oh dear," Sister Welch said. "I hate to keep on if you're not well."

A convenient tickle struck Mattie's throat, and she coughed behind her hand. "Why don't I go on home?" Their rooms were minutes away, and on Sundays the railway men and packers slept off Saturday night carousing. Respectable folks ruled the streets today.

Sister Jones had lived in the city several years. "Mattie's been a real help the last few weeks, and she's so responsible. I'm sure she can make her way back without any to-do."

Sister Welch studied Mattie. "All right, then. Go on. I'll be along in less than an hour."

Mattie purposely drew heavy breaths climbing the stairs to the druggist's shop.

The store was closed, but the manager sat at his desk, high up over the floor. He always waited to see the ladies out when they finished. His weary wife corralled five or six youngsters at the services, and Mattie suspected he appreciated an extra hour of peace. He hurried down to unlock the door. "Hotter than a frying pan out there. Where're you headed?"

Mattie repeated her story.

"Care for an escort?" he said. "Folks in these parts can be up to no good."

She assured him it was not necessary, but he watched as she went the first block. Having a man take care was nice, she supposed. Surely unmarried ones like him existed—somewhere.

She turned the usual direction, then looked over her shoulder. Instead of making the next left, she continued toward downtown. If she was conspicuous alone, you'd never know it. Nobody paid her any mind. She relaxed, glancing through windows and at various street activities—a surprising number for a Sunday.

When they'd first arrived, Uncle Bud had arranged a walking tour for the group, pointing out respectable businesses alongside saloons, houses of ill repute, and vaudeville theaters. New hotels had multiplied like dandelions near the end of downtown. She'd gawked through the window of one before being pushed along by the group. Her eyes and brain felt stretched, gazing at men and women in expensive clothing who dined on lavishly prepared feasts.

She wanted to see more restaurants, but as Mattie neared the area today, she sensed someone trailing her. Folks had walked behind her the whole time, of course, but she'd heard the same footfalls now for several blocks. She slowed to peer in the reflection of a store window.

Behind her, a man slowed as well, taking his hat in his hands mere steps away. She turned, prepared to send him on his way. But it was just Mr. Percy from the drugstore. Her cheeks flushed hot to be caught in her lie.

Mr. Percy tilted his head, with a smile that set her on edge. "Miss Corder, are you lost?"

"I took a wrong turn, I'm afraid. My sense of direction isn't what I thought. But I must have needed fresh air. I feel better already."

He nodded but stood his ground. She squirmed under his scrutiny. "Perhaps you'd point me toward home now," she said.

Finally he spoke. "I decided to see that you arrived safely, but I didn't want to startle you. Of course, maybe you truly meant to go this way . . ." He shrugged indifferently, but his eyes clearly spoke his thoughts as he gazed suggestively, looking her up and down.

Mattie searched her memory, trying to recall whether he'd heard her testimony during the crusade, but she knew there was likely mention of her time at the Home among the church planners. She was the only one from the rescue homes, after all. Her former reputation had not mattered in the Home, but here, a man might think her loose simply because she'd been an unwed mother. She spoke sharply now, forcing Mr. Percy's gaze back up. "Sir, are you questioning my intentions?"

"Now, ma'am, why would I do that? I simply wondered if—"

"Wondered what?" Mattie interrupted, glaring. She knew what.

"If, perhaps, you were seeking male company." He grasped her arm, grinning lasciviously again.

Mattie drew herself up and shook his arm away. She stood nearly as tall as any man she'd met, and Mr. Percy hovered only slightly taller. "You are mistaken."

"Things I've heard might make me believe otherwise," he said. "But I'll see you to your lodging, and naturally, I'll see my way to forgetting you took a wrong turn. If you change your mind, though . . . I know a convenient place."

Mattie gasped as he reached to run his finger under her chin. Further rebuttal was futile. He saw her only one way—in spite of the talk he talked in meetings. She backed away and fled. She didn't need any escort, and especially not one who'd taunt her with her past. She glanced behind as she half ran for the building where she lodged with Sister Welch. She threw the lock, then backed against the door until she was certain no noise came from the stairwell.

She put herself to bed in her small room next to Sister Welch's. Shivering under the covers, she knew now to avoid close quarters with Mr. Percy. She'd have to take more care than ever—the true drawback to leaving the safety of the Home.

But she'd hold strong against any such foolishness. She hadn't risen this far only to fall again.

CATE

Arlington, Texas
2017

The morning after Thanksgiving, I sleep late, as if the presence of another human causes me to sleep deeper than I have in years. Maybe I've been on constant alert without even realizing it.

The temperature outside dropped overnight. I pull on yoga pants and a sweatshirt and emerge from my room, stopping to switch on the heat for the first time. In the kitchen I start the kettle boiling but suddenly wonder if Laurel drinks coffee. I prefer tea, hot, strong, and straight-up sweet. Coffee makes me retch.

Little noises come from the dining room and I peek through the opening over the bar. Laurel sits at the table, straightening papers and stacking her books.

"Good morning," I say. "You're an early bird. I'm not this morning. Or any morning, actually." But I wonder now if living by myself for so long has even affected my morning energy. Then again, I was always a night owl. "Finish your studying?"

Laurel nods. "Yup. I can relax for a few days now. Thanks for letting me stay. I'd still be procrastinating if I wasn't here." She sniffs. "Oh my gosh, I love that smell."

I know what she means immediately. Not the water boiling on the stove. The scent of dust burning off the heating coils. I love it too. It smells like winter.

"Hungry?"

Her cheeks redden. "I'm always hungry. I might have already had leftovers." She raises her hands weakly with a meek smile. "I hope you don't mind."

I laugh. It makes me happy, and some other strange emotion. "I'd never eat all that myself. Do you want hot tea? I don't have coffee."

"Okay." She smiles curiously, and I wager she's never had it. I add splashes of milk and generous amounts of sugar to both mugs, then carry them to the table. Laurel sniffs the pale mixture, then sips with the spoon I brought her. "I like it." She shrugs. "I usually have warm Dr Pepper for breakfast."

No surprise. Dr Pepper is a Texas institution, a reasonable substitute for any morning beverage or, really, any meal in a pinch. But warm?

"What will you do the rest of today?" I ask.

Laurel leans back to study the light fixture. "Probably just get a head start on reading. Maybe binge-watch something if my computer cooperates."

"I'm going on a quest," I say. "I've been waiting for a day I don't have any other responsibilities—no cleaning, no car maintenance or catch-up work. I'm going to wander around Arlington and Fort Worth and scout out places the girls might have been."

She knows what girls I'm talking about. Her eyes light up. "That sounds intriguing!"

I chuckle at her choice of words. "You can come."

I'd figured after a full day of company, I'd be so overwhelmed I'd want to be alone, but I'm not. And I don't. And I hope Laurel doesn't think it's strange I've invited her. If I'm correct, she'll worry more about whether it's strange to accept. We're two people hungrier for company than we even realized.

"Okay," she says. "I want to pay for something today, though. You spent so much on Thanksgiving food."

I could refuse her offer, but I sense Laurel doesn't want to owe a debt just because someone made a bigger investment.

"You don't have to," I say, "but that would be nice."

When I'm showered and ready to go—and Laurel uses the towels, too, in spite of her protests the night before—we climb into my car.

"Should we stop by your dorm? Drop your backpack or grab a coat?"

"I'm good," she says.

Suddenly I feel self-conscious. My jeans are nearly new, and over a black pullover, I've twisted two scarves together at my neck. My lined tweed coat is in the backseat in case I get cold, and my boots are one of six pairs I own. Laurel is in one of the three shirts she wears on repeat, and her jeans are torn at the knee—not as a fashion statement. The warmest thing I've seen her wear is the hoodie around her waist.

In Arlington, the majority of historic buildings are gone. The city neglected preservation for too long, like so many others. Progress was all about modern entertainment at the edges—sports arenas, malls, and amusement parks. In the last decade or so, however, the planners have taken great care with what remains, and a nice little downtown area now boasts a gorgeous concert pavilion in near proximity to a number of renovated industrial buildings, several with lofts up and interesting shops and restaurants down. We can only picture in our minds, however, the Home buildings and Upchurch house near campus and the Interurban depot off Main Street.

Soon, we head west on what was part of the first transcontinental road in the country—called, depending on the decade, Texas Highway 1, US-80, the Bankhead Highway, and even the Broadway of America. The road still runs near the railroad tracks. We could take the interstate, but seeing where folks would have driven and where the Interurban cars ran between Arlington and Fort Worth when the girls were alive is more interesting. When the Home first opened, there wasn't much more than a dirt road between Dallas and Fort Worth.

In downtown Fort Worth, the old train stations have been repurposed as housing, event spaces, and classrooms for university extensions. A restored Interurban car is on display outside the current Intermodal Transportation Center. I don't know where Mattie was before the Home, but I've imagined she rode a car like this one, which stopped across the street from the original T&P station. She might have walked these very streets.

We walk and I tell Laurel what I've learned about the area from studying the archives—and through my own curiosity. We're in the middle of what was Hell's Half Acre, where outlaws roamed for years and where women lived when they turned to prostitution. The buildings, many of which are original, were crowded with saloons, dance halls, and bawdy houses.

Fort Worth is proud of its history, but at that time, the area wasn't safe or advisable for respectable women, even in broad daylight. Times have changed. We still wouldn't walk here alone in the dark, but in daylight, it's about as safe as anywhere downtown.

"Butch Cassidy and the Sundance Kid frequented the Half Acre," I tell Laurel. "The only known professional photo of the Hole in the Wall Gang was taken in downtown Fort Worth in 1901." I'm not sure she has any idea who I'm talking about. She nods politely, and I make a mental note to find the old Robert Redford movie online.

Laurel shyly shares that she's never walked around downtown, despite having lived in Arlington her whole life. She remembers attending the holiday parade once.

"What have you been doing, girl?" I say, half joking. I wonder if she might open up more soon. I'm not one to talk—but I like history and I've spent a lot of time exploring it alone.

"Not much of anything," she says.

We continue up Main toward Sundance Square, with the courthouse in view on the other side. A few years ago, they demolished an ugly 1950s addition that hid much of the original exterior. Now it looks generally like it would have in the early 1900s. "Isn't it crazy to think that Mattie and Lizzie might have stood right here, looking at these buildings?" I say.

We know the Upchurches took at least some of the girls to the old Methodist church nearby, where they sang and talked about their pasts. Mattie and Lizzie had surely been here at some point.

Down the bricked street, in the fading afternoon light, the regal old courthouse is flanked by buildings already lit for the holidays. A clock tower glows at the top. "It's so pretty," Laurel says. "Probably prettier than it would have seemed back then with everything going on."

She gets it. She feels the way I do. Wistful, in a way. Nostalgic for another time. But aware things were likely worse. We've glamorized the story of the girls to a point. I hate to think of what they went through to get to a better place—and even then they were still barely scraping by. The journals are full of pleas for food, linens, and clothing. Laurel and I may have histories that prevent us from personal peace, but we have modern, comfortable beds, plenty to eat, and so much more. Compared to the Home girls, we're rich.

It doesn't help the heartache.

Suddenly, I know I have to ask her what happened. I don't know how she'll react, but I feel as though I have no choice. Right here. Right now. If she doesn't want to talk, fine. If she does, and I don't take the risk, I could be sorry later.

"Laurel, what happened to your family?"

She goes quiet. Then says she's cold. But when we're settled at a sidewalk cafe on Sundance Square, our hands hugging mugs of cocoa still too hot to drink, she talks.

"My mom got pregnant and my father wasn't in the picture. I don't even know who he is. She waited tables. We managed. I had what I needed. My little brother came along, same story. We moved constantly. She couldn't pay the rent. We got kicked out. Sometimes we stayed with my grandparents, but they didn't like her choices. It was always a fight. My brother and I dreamed about my mom finding someone and getting married so we could have a stepdad and be more settled, but the guys she found in bars were scum. She never let them meet us."

She sips her cocoa, cooled down now, and becomes tentative with her words, as if speaking them aloud makes her less sure of the story. It's a familiar feeling.

"She met someone online and everything moved fast. One weekend, we went to Six Flags, like a family with a dad on trial." She scoffs.

"I had a weird vibe from him, but she was totally sucked in. He had a good job, a good car. And she was so happy . . ." She gazes onto the plaza, where families wait to see Santa, fathers with kids on their shoulders or holding their hands. "He kept saying, 'You're so cute,' and running his fingers down my hair." She shivers, still haunted by the ghost of that unwelcome touch.

After a quiet moment, I ask, "Did your mom notice?"

"I think she was just relieved someone wanted her, who could take care of her—and us—after doing it alone so long. I have a hard time judging her for that."

Laurel judges her for something, though. I know by her tone. And I dread what I'm about to hear, even though I've invited this. "But . . . ?" I say.

"I wonder what might have happened if I'd been brave enough to say something to her then . . . but I doubt she would have listened." Laurel looks up at me, her eyes naked in their grief. "Cate? You know Lizzie's story in that one journal? Where her mother didn't do anything when her stepbrother molested her? How she actually *punished* her? And then her stepdad did it too?"

My stomach aches. I'd suspected ordinary teen angst. But this? I hate this.

"Don't worry," Laurel says. "He didn't get a chance to do anything. I didn't let him."

I'm relieved, but there's more to her story. Maybe it's the worst part.

"So I woke up with him in my room one night, sitting on the edge of my bed. He said I was so pretty, and he'd realized he wanted me, not my mother. I felt sick. And scared. I said I'd scream if he didn't leave." She pauses. "The next day, I told my mom . . . but she didn't believe me." Her voice breaks with the weight of it. "She *blamed* me." Laurel goes terribly silent. Her shoulders shake, as though she fights to keep sobs from emerging and they fight to break out.

Finally she says, "I've never told anyone that. It's embarrassing."

I place my hand over hers, hoping she won't be startled or angry, but I can't leave her alone with misplaced guilt. "You have nothing to be embarrassed about." I know she's not speaking of her tears. "That wasn't your fault. A grown man knows better. And your mom . . ."

I shake my head, nervous about laying this blame: a mother who knew and did nothing.

But it happens.

"She told me to get out. I was freaking seventeen!" Laurel's words are gasps now, as if they're physically painful. "She said I'd always been needy, always wanting more than my brother—from everyone. And that I'd probably done it on purpose, trying to steal him from her."

My face gets hot and prickly. *How could a mother say that to her own child?* I rage at this woman I've never met, as if this is my own history. How could she take another side when she'd promised, by virtue of giving birth, to guard her child's well-being above anyone else's?

How could she live with herself? How could any mother live with herself . . .

We've seen, together, the multitude of ways parents failed their children, in the archive's journals, in the ledgers, in that lonely Bera-chah cemetery, but hearing it from the mouth of another heartbroken girl makes it new all over again.

Each story is unique. Each story is devastating.

And I know it firsthand. My parents failed me too.

On the way back to Arlington, Laurel tells me she stayed with vari-ous friends until graduation, and how she's still trying to declare in-dependent status for financial aid. I nod. I understand the difficulty of the process. Her academic scholarships cover tuition, fees, and books—but only if she can keep her grades high enough. It's a lot of pressure.

I pull into my driveway. It's been a fun couple of days, even with this emotional ending. We've both enjoyed the company, nearly like a normal holiday for the first time in a while.

Laurel thanks me for Thanksgiving dinner, for letting her stay and hang out—and for listening without judging. All she ever told her friends was that she and her mom had a falling-out. She worried that if their parents knew, they'd believe she was more trouble than they were willing to take on. Her brother is the only family member she's spoken to since her mom threw her out. He'll graduate in a year and plans to enlist. She hopes they can have a real relationship again—but not while he's at home. She never told him either.

Laurel hesitates before she leaves my car. "Cate? What happened to *your* family?"

My insides knot. She's kept her secret more than a year. She has no idea how hard it is to talk about what you've bottled up for nearly twenty. I gaze toward my front door. For two decades, a glowing porch light has been the only thing to greet me when I go in from the dark.

Finally I say, "Oh, honey, it's late. It's a long story."

"I don't mind. You listened to me."

I sigh. It seems like a simple transaction to her. I'm just not sure I can do it. "Look. What happened is so far in the past, I hardly think about it anymore. Bringing it up again isn't healthy for me. I've moved on."

Laurel looks at me with disbelief. Her heat rolls across the car in waves, even on this cold November night. And before I can do anything to temper her fury, she grabs the door handle and nearly leaps from the car. Before she turns to go, though, she stops and leans inside. "I actually get that," she says, "but it seems a little hypocritical. I mean, *you* asked *me* to tell you—"

I interrupt. "Wait—!" I never wanted her to feel coerced. That word scares me, and I've tried hard not to push her.

But she speaks over my protest. "Nobody trusts an eighteen-year-old on her own. They believe whatever happened must be my fault—just like my mom did. But I thought you were different. I thought you trusted me." Her look sears me. "You're just like everyone else."

She slams the door and I'm alone again, stung by her anger.

She's right, though. I'm a hypocrite. Worse, I know exactly how she feels. And now, I'm forced to admit I've been telling a lie a long time. When I tell myself that people leave me, that there's something about me that makes them walk away, it's not exactly true. I always—always—run first, before they have the chance. And though I haven't physically run, not this time, I've pushed Laurel away, right when she needed the reciprocity of trust.

LIZZIE

Arlington, Texas
1910

Miss Hallie had raised a ruckus about Mattie going off to OKC, but in the next breath she disappeared herself. She'd agreed last minute to accompany Brother JT and some of the girls on a campaign. Over three days, the girls would sing and testify in small-town churches.

Sister Maggie Mae had been geared up to go with her husband when Miss Ruth Upchurch, now thirteen, reminded them of her piano recital on the weekend. Ruth had nearly fallen into a tantrum when she realized her mother might miss it.

Sister Maggie Mae always tried to ensure that her children never felt overlooked in favor of "the girls." She suggested Miss Hallie go in her place. Miss Hallie had attended enough rallies and knew the procedures. Birdie Cagle, the music leader, could act as backup chaperone. They trusted Birdie implicitly.

If Brother JT worried about traveling with that many single women, he didn't show it. The vice districts were booming, and fundraising was more critical than ever. He never took a break. He was so engrossed in the matter of fallen women, Lizzie wondered if he sometimes forgot the unwavering one under his nose. Sister Maggie Mae was just as devoted to the cause, but Lizzie reckoned it was hard to share.

The long-time Home girls had all observed the mounting tension between the couple. Minnie, who had cooked and cleaned in the Upchurch home since their youngest daughter's birth, whispered to

Lizzie that she'd seen Sister Maggie Mae look right through Brother JT recently when he returned from a monthlong journey out west. Instead of immediately embracing his wife, he'd gone straight for his slippers and a sweater. In the hallway later, Brother JT halfheartedly pecked Sister Maggie Mae's dutifully offered cheek.

Sister Maggie Mae nearly singlehandedly ran a household of five children while Brother JT spent most of his hours elsewhere, focused on other women and their children. Being housekeeper, head tutor, and disciplinarian while her husband pursued his higher calling must have been exhausting. Lizzie wondered why they kept having kids. There were things now to curb that—something to consider when you'd married a man with two passions—though she doubted Sister Maggie Mae had much say over her relationship with JT, at least in the romantic sense. Maybe romance was overrated. Lizzie wouldn't know.

Brother JT returned from the journey without Miss Hallie, but with renewed devotion toward his wife. There was the official story, but Lizzie had overheard Birdie telling Sister Susie another.

On their journey, Brother JT had been seated across the aisle and up a row from Birdie and Miss Hallie on the train. While writing in his leather notebook, he'd reached to rub his neck. Miss Hallie tensed in the seat beside Birdie, then physically leaned, as if she wanted to stretch across the aisle to aid him. Her face reddened when she noticed Birdie watching. She closed her eyes and leaned against the headrest.

"Are you all right?" Birdie said.

"Oh . . . yes. Why do you ask?"

Birdie shrugged. "You're flushed, and the grippe's going around again."

"This car is simply stuffy. Perhaps I'll take some air."

Birdie averted her eyes and opened her Bible to prepare for the service that evening as Miss Hallie rushed to the space between their car and the next and clasped the railing. The train rocked along, and Birdie's eyes drooped closed, but when she opened them again, Brother JT stood on the platform too. She sat higher to watch. Brother JT harped on the girls about being alone with men. He wouldn't even counsel one in his office without another woman nearby. Perhaps the platform, in view of the car, didn't seem private.

Their conversation, however, certainly was.

He smiled, obviously teasing Miss Hallie. Miss Hallie bristled at humor from anyone else, but all she did now was grin. Birdie followed Miss Hallie's gaze to where Brother JT's hair caught the afternoon light snaking between the cars and gleamed like a handful of gold and silver coins. Birdie jumped up and hurried to the door, yanking it open to join the two at the railing.

"It is hot in that car," she said. "No wonder you were flushed, Miss Hallie."

Miss Hallie turned. She seemed half-surprised, half-annoyed.

"You were saying?" Brother JT's tone indicated he'd repeated himself.

"Next month's article," Miss Hallie stammered. "It's on . . . temptation." As the word escaped her mouth, she blanched.

Brother JT simply seemed puzzled. "I don't recall discussing it, but that's a perennial topic. You feel qualified to undertake a full essay?"

Miss Hallie blundered on. "Well, yes, seeing as we are all tempted, being human. Naturally, I'd consult the commentaries. Perhaps"— she paused—"your own thoughts might help. Have you not dealt with temptation yourself?"

Brother JT's eyes suddenly went guarded, but Miss Hallie threw off restraint and carried on breathlessly. "We are not gods, even with our callings. We are, first, men and women."

Birdie's jaw fell.

Miss Hallie stepped toward the door of the car, and Brother JT lurched to hold it for her. He didn't follow the women in. Birdie imagined that Miss Hallie's artless words required deciphering. But Miss Hallie didn't appear to regret them, not when Birdie squeezed past her to reclaim her own seat, and not later, when Miss Hallie lugged her own suitcase from the overhead rail and held her nose higher than ever.

Miss Hallie didn't continue on when the group departed Hamlin.

A member of that church joined them for the remainder of the journey without explaining why Miss Hallie remained in the tiny West Texas town.

When they returned to the Home, Sister Maggie Mae announced that Miss Hallie had accepted a position at Hamlin's small Holiness University. They'd needed her so desperately, she'd immediately sent for her things.

CATE

Grissom, Texas
1998

The Monday after my ill-fated exploration of the Hotel Zagosa with River, I came home from school to a freshly made bed. "I washed and changed your sheets," my mom called as my backpack sagged against my door frame. "You have so much to do right now. I thought it might help."

"Thanks, Mom," I answered casually—while my heart did a flip. Had she discovered my journal as she tucked in the clean sheet? Washing my sheets wasn't unusual, but she always left it up to me to remake the bed. I replayed her voice in my head, trying to ascertain her mood.

I'd continued to process my feelings on paper. There were a lot. I left most of the details intentionally vague, never even writing River's name. I didn't want anyone accidentally reading about or prematurely judging our relationship—not when I was unsure where it was headed myself. But I needed to put the feelings somewhere. And after things had taken a physical turn that weekend, I'd written in greater detail and then hidden the journal. Even without names and places, these were things you wouldn't want a mother to read.

Soon, I'd have to be honest with my parents, but I wasn't ready. At dinner, I studied Mom's face and her attitude toward me. She seemed her usual self, if somewhat tired and distant. She didn't bring up prom at all. I almost congratulated her. Instead, I relaxed. She always wore her feelings on her sleeve. If she'd read the journal, she would never have been so calm—upset or elated, depending on her assumptions, but not calm.

The previous Saturday afternoon at the park, sitting on the picnic table with our hands entwined after I told River about prom with Seth, we'd fallen silent, me stroking my other thumb along a tiny tattooed sun on River's wrist bone, both of us leaning more into each other as the silence deepened.

Out of the blue, River asked, "Why did you quit track, really?"

Startled, and not quite ready to leave the quiet moment, I'd shrugged. "Not enough time."

"Because of church?"

I thought about it reluctantly. The simple answer was yes. "I wasn't that good anyway."

"I don't believe you."

My head snapped up. "You don't?" I said, though I already wanted to change the subject. I wasn't particularly proud now of the real reason I'd quit.

"No. I don't."

River's facial expression was new to me—not ridicule, though. The opposite.

It said, *I believe in you.*

"Fine." I jumped off the table and leaned forward "Race me."

River laughed, but clambered down to copy my stance. "On your mark . . ."

"Get set . . ."

"Go!" we shouted in unison, and off we went, leaving our drink cups behind on the picnic table, no better than the vandals in the old hotel. That was the last thing on my mind.

River didn't catch me for twenty yards or so, not until I slowed slightly to catch my breath—and maybe for other reasons. "Where's the finish line?" I said, panting, though I hadn't even broken a sweat.

River slowed too, and suddenly leaned to grab my ankle, pulling me down into the grass.

"Right here! I win!"

"You cheated," I said, laughing as we rolled into a heap, with more body parts connecting than just our hands or shoulders now. River was skinny, but no athlete, and I continued to laugh as our chests rose and fell together—mine beneath, heaving from adrenaline, River's above, from true exertion. Eventually, my laughter faded, and though I kept my mouth carefully closed, the sound of air flowing through my nose grew so loud, I worried River might think I was afraid.

I wasn't afraid. I was terrified. But not afraid.

River leaned closer, bringing our foreheads together too, and then our noses, making it clear now that I wasn't the only one who struggled to silence my longing. I closed my eyes, unable to focus, dizzy from our proximity. Almost too much. We stayed there until River gently pushed back again, rolling away until we both lay on our backs, gazing at a patch of bright sky through the trees. Wispy clouds threaded the blue, but they had no chance of darkening this sky, or this day. It might have been the best day I'd ever had.

"Hey," River said, eventually.

"Hey."

"Now will you tell me why you quit running? For real?"

"I never said I quit running," I said. "I quit track."

"Still. Why?"

"It's hard to explain."

"I'm fairly intelligent."

"Yes, you are." I took a deep breath. To me, my reason for quitting didn't seem strange; however, I knew that from the outside looking in, it wouldn't make sense. But River hadn't given me reason to be leery of telling the truth so far.

"Our youth minister always says we shouldn't miss church for other things—especially not for sports. It's about priorities. God is more important than anything else."

River had rolled onto an elbow. "Okay. I get it, I guess. Except church isn't exactly God, right? Church is church. God is God. What am I missing?"

That actually made sense. I didn't have an answer.

"Sorry," River said, and I shrugged.

"I guess church attendance is equated with serving God, to make things simple. So when I started track in high school, practice always made me late to youth group. And when we had meets on Wednesdays, I didn't get back in time at all. But the final straw . . ." I paused, because suddenly, I saw it in a new light.

"Was?"

"I was running varsity as a freshman, beating upperclassmen at meets . . ."

"Uh-huh . . . because you aren't any good at running."

I pushed against a skinny elbow enough to knock River off balance.

"We had this invitational meet—by runner, not by team. It was to pick kids for a summer training camp, where they'd stay on a college campus, compete with other good runners, and get trained by college coaches scouting for their teams."

"And they picked you?"

I sighed.

"Seriously?" River said. "That's amazing. I bet everyone was so excited and proud."

I nodded. "It was an honor to get picked for the camp. But by then, my youth minister had been giving me flack, and . . . some of the kids. They thought my priorities were mixed up. Anyway, I couldn't go to the camp. It was the same week as mission trip."

River sat up and stared at me in true disbelief now. "You didn't go?"

"Nope. I quit."

"You quit something you were amazing at because you had a—wait, what's a mission trip? Did you, like, go to Africa?"

I laughed, though it hurt a little. "No, silly. We went to another town in Texas and built handicap ramps for disabled people for a week. It was fun."

River's eyes were closed by then. I was sure it was to keep from spouting obscenities or other seemingly inappropriate expressions of incredulity. I wouldn't have minded. I felt incredulous now too.

"Let me get this straight. Your parents made you build ramps instead of going to a running camp with the best coaches and runners in the state?"

"No," I said. "They've never forced me to do anything at church. That's not their style. I just . . . I wanted to go on the mission trip. It's the highlight of our summer—an entire week with your best friends, doing crazy stuff, not just free labor. Music, swimming, food fights. It's a blast." I felt the need to keep explaining, though River nodded.

"Okay. I can see that, I guess, but that happens every year, right? Wasn't the camp, like, the opportunity of a lifetime? What if you did so well you earned all kinds of scholarships and every coach was fighting over you?"

"I don't think I was *that* good," I said. "I made a choice. I chose the mission trip. And it was easier to quit track than deal with my coach's disappointment. So I . . . walked away."

River's head moved in a very slow shake, and I felt nearly nauseated watching. "That was what you really wanted?"

My nod took so long, I'm sure we both doubted it.

If what I'd told River was bad enough, the whole truth was worse. After I was invited to the camp, Jess bragged about me in Sunday school, and I'd lowered my face, embarrassed by the attention. I hadn't decided whether to go yet, and my parents had left it up to me—they knew my priorities were fine. I'd never been rebellious.

But Seth hunted me down between Sunday school and church. "The track thing is cool, Cate. But you're not going, right?" he'd said. "You're not skipping mission trip for some running camp." His lip curled as he said it, and I felt his derision, but I forced myself to ignore it.

"I haven't told them one way or the other yet," I said. I'd heard a rumor Seth and Miranda were on the rocks—that they would definitely be breaking up before summer. We'd both be on that mission trip if I went, and he'd finally be available.

"I'd think about it hard," he said. "You know what Brad's always saying, and Pastor Lance. Church is our first priority. We're supposed to be set apart."

My stomach twisted at his words. He was right. He was older, wiser, already talking about going into the ministry after college. My personal calling, even as a fifteen-year-old high school girl, was supposed to be the most important thing in my life. If it wasn't, well, what would God think of my commitment? Of me? And what would Seth think?

"Of course I'm not going," I said. "Are you crazy?"

His smile lit up my face again, even if doubt lingered in my heart. I'd needed to be set straight, and I was glad it was by Seth. Maybe he'd want to go out when he and Miranda split.

Monday, I handed in my uniforms. I explained I had to miss too much church for track. My coach tried to talk me out of it, saying I could keep running for the team even if I didn't go to the camp, but I was firm.

"I don't know anymore if it's what I really wanted," I said now. River had waited patiently through my silence, and waited longer as I saw that conversation in a whole new light. Seth hadn't broken up with Miranda for another year, and hadn't even spoken to me much on the mission trip. Not on purpose, I was sure, but because he really hadn't thought about me like that. He'd just been exerting the authority he thought he should as a student leader.

I'd thrown away a chance at what might have been something big. Not for God. For a *boy*. I'd been trying to impress Seth.

River's voice snapped me back to the present. "I think you really wanted to go, but people were pressuring you. Wrongly."

My face went hot. Because I knew, deep inside, for the first time maybe, that what I'd tried to believe was the right choice probably hadn't been. When I'd quit, I'd given up the opportunity to do what I loved nearly more than anything. Not more than God, but definitely more than building ramps in hotter-than-hell Texas summers. I ran like I had wings on my feet—and if I was good at it, if God had given me that talent, would he have wanted me to waste it?

Now I'd never run track in college. I could walk on, maybe, if I was lucky, but I doubted I'd have the time. I'd have to work to pay what my academic scholarships wouldn't cover and my parents couldn't afford. At any rate, I'd been dreaming of running a library since I cataloged my books at age six. I'd have *loved* competing, though. Now I never would.

But I could still run. River had reminded me.

I jumped up again. "Race you to the car."

"You're on," River said. "But this time, run like you goddamn mean it."

·◦] PART THREE [◦·

"*Despair in matters temporal and material is often terribly crushing and saddening, but when it comes to the heart of a fallen girl, it is fearfully enhanced, not alone by the consciousness that she has lost her good name, and that she has no one to look to for help, but far beyond this in the depths of her being, she feels her condition takes on the awfulness of the loss of her soul as she realizes she is bankrupt before two worlds.*

No one who has not been in her case can fathom the unspeakable depths of her grief, or taste the bitterness of her cup of self-lashing torment; albeit she is filled with the bitterest contempt and fiercest anger, at the monster who has wrought her ruin."

—ANNIE T. ARMOUR, "None to Help,"
HERALD OF HOLINESS, MARCH 13, 1913

MEMORANDUM

DATE: July 10, 1916

TO: Mr. Albert Ferry, Printer for the Berachah Rescue Society

CC: Reverend J. T. Upchurch, Director of the Berachah Industrial Home

FROM: Miss Hallye V. Taylor, Secretary and Treasurer of the Berachah Industrial Home

RE: Three items for next issue of *The Purity Journal*

Dangerous Occupations for Women:

Trained Nurses: Exhaustion and stress create desire for drugs and alcohol easily obtained.

Domestic: Vicious or loose women work alongside her, or her employer may take advantage.

Factory Hand: Subject to the same environment as the domestic.

Waitress: Customers consider her fair game, yet she cannot reject advances for fear of offense.

Stenographer: Perilous field, especially for newly educated girls, ignorant of men.

—Summary of report by Charles P. Neill, U.S. Commissioner of Labor

TWO COWS NEEDED

Two good cows could be used in Berachah. Who might consecrate one, and who, the other, for our cause and sanctified mission?

How many bank ledgers will gaze us in the eyes when we appear before the Greatest Judge, and how many professing followers will face the outcast girls and hear this: "Ye did it not unto one of the least of these."

Shall our Home be closed? Shall our Mothers and Babies be cast out once more, and left to perish on the commons? They Await Your Reply.

—HVT

LIZZIE

Arlington, Texas
1916

Change and unrest overseas eventually made their way to Berachah's little corner of Texas. War seemed nearly inevitable, though they appreciated President Wilson's efforts to keep them out of it. Sister Susie had finally been granted a mission to India, to care for girls who needed help as much or more. The girls saw her off with both joy and sadness. Two years later, she contracted malaria and never recovered. Her fellow missionaries would write them at length about her lengthy illness later, but the night of her death, they sent a simple, devastating telegram: *SINGLETARY DEAD.*

Nobody at the Home could bear to think of their dear former matron suffering. They held their own tearful memorial service and placed a stone in her honor in the burying ground.

The Upchurches allowed another preacher couple to take over the running of Berachah for a time so they could spend more time crusading. But it was as if a bad spirit slowly took over too. The usual joy-in-trials attitude dissipated, and even the children became insolent from breathing the poisoned air. People with grudges against the Upchurches spread false stories, and when he took back control, Brother JT was forced to place a notice in the *Journal* to quell them. What had been a flood of nasty notes from disgruntled donors finally slowed to a rare drip, but everything had left Lizzie feeling scarred, once again, even after the situation improved.

After five years away, Miss Hallie had returned too. It hadn't been terrible without her sour face hanging over them at every turn, but it wasn't terrible to have her back, either. She spelled her name differently upon her return, as if to say she'd turned over a new leaf. The girls who remembered her rolled their eyes at every *Hallye V. Taylor* they read.

But Miss *Hallye* did seem changed, like her name.

She wasn't so stiff-necked as before, though still frazzled at times, and she worked as hard as anyone. She spent more time with the girls and even seemed to enjoy it, even if they still kept her at arm's length. Her prickly reputation had been handed down like a family heirloom.

That wasn't the only change. Miss Hallye, having become thoroughly modern, ordered a textbook on women's health and venereal diseases. Their old-fashioned line of treatment—prayer and faith alone—wasn't completely successful. She spoke up in a staff meeting after studying the book, saying that God had given men—and women—brains, and quite often the tools to fix things. It was a disservice to their residents to ignore the latest treatments.

Sister Maggie Mae and Mrs. Nettie, the matron who'd replaced Sister Susie, waved her off, as if she had no standing—and worse, not enough faith. But while Lizzie squirmed to hear Miss Hallye speak so frankly, she appreciated her honesty and diligence. It might have saved her and Docie much heartache if people had been blunt about what was right and wrong and what could kill you before they'd ever set foot in the Home. They'd suffer some of the effects forever.

Lizzie had begun to doubt whether she and Docie would both survive the girl's growing up intact. The fifteen-year-old swung from happy to sad to angry and back in the space of a minute, enough to make a person dizzy.

Ivy knew what to expect from girls Docie's age. She talked Lizzie out of burying the young lady alive more than once. Lizzie's own wildness had surely given her mother fits, though understanding that now didn't change anything.

While she and Ivy fed the babies their midday meal one Friday, she asked Miss Ruby—the new children's home matron hired when their numbers increased to where they needed an additional paid worker for consistency—to read the first letter she'd had from Mattie in months. Sometimes Docie read them, but these days, Lizzie was careful. Mattie didn't go into much, knowing Lizzie was at the mercy of volunteers, but she seemed restless. Lizzie kept waiting for her to say she'd gone and done something foolish.

Mattie had gone quieter around the time of the tenth anniversary of the Home. She'd never come back to visit, and in spite of Lizzie's pleas, she'd even refused to attend the special Homecoming celebration, which they'd planned and prepared for extravagantly. Lizzie figured Mattie worried about seeing the Hydes and their adopted daughter, but personal discontentment became obvious in her words, too, though she claimed she was just going through a spell. She wrote that she badly wanted to cook for a fancy hotel, but nobody would train a woman—much less one with a murky past. She had no choice but to keep at church work. Sister Welch still fed her and clothed her and kept a roof over her head.

Mattie still poked fun at Lizzie's friendship with Ivy too, though she'd never met her. It annoyed Lizzie, but she ignored the digs. She wanted letters for catching up, not fussing over silliness. For several years now, Lizzie hadn't mentioned Ivy in any of her dictated replies.

As Miss Ruby read this letter, Lizzie was thrilled to learn Mattie had a new job and living quarters, imagining how elated Mattie must have been to escape old Sister Welch. But then she set in on Ivy. This day's letter went farther than usual. Lizzie was sure Mattie hadn't meant anything by what she wrote—*How's your little girlfriend, Ivy?*—for Lizzie had never told a soul what had happened. But Ivy's hand stilled from flying Duncan's spoon into his mouth with a buzz— they couldn't get him to eat otherwise. He tilted his head back and screeched when the pretend flying machine stopped midair. "Mohhh bite!" he shouted, and wailed.

Ivy shoveled carrots into his mouth and slammed down the spoon. She glared at Lizzie and stalked out, leaving Duncan sputtering and Lizzie with a stone in her throat.

Miss Ruby finished Ivy's job. "Goodness. I didn't even read the part where Mattie asked if she was 'still clingy, like her name.' What was your friend thinking?"

Lizzie's face was surely red, it burned so hot. "Mattie's jealous I'm friends with Ivy." She couldn't tell Miss Ruby the whole truth.

"But Ivy seemed upset with *you*. Will she be all right, do you think?"

"I hope," Lizzie said. Ivy was likely thinking all kinds of untrue things. Lizzie remembered Ivy's frantic fear after she'd tried to hold Lizzie's hand.

"They've eaten what they will. I'll stay so you can find her once they're down for naps."

Lizzie prayed the babies would go down easily. Thirty minutes later, all but one slept soundly. Miss Ruby sent her on. "Settle things. I'll need you both in time for their walk."

Every afternoon, Lizzie and Ivy piled the toddlers into a contraption Mr. Gus had fashioned, like eggs in a basket, and wheeled them around the grounds. The kids adored it, but it took two workers—one to pull, and one to keep babies from toppling out when they went over bumps or to carry the fussers.

Lizzie tiptoed from the nursery. Ivy's dormitory was quiet and dim, with everyone busy this time of day. The common room was empty but for a sick girl reading. Lizzie pictured where she'd go if she needed to hide. The only quiet space today was the laundry. By Friday, the Home clothes were clean, and nobody in town wanted deliveries on the weekend, so the laundry girls usually helped in the fields or with stacking and cutting in the printing office.

Lizzie walked the rows of donated machines and emergency purchases. Heavy breathing came from behind a bulky old wringer in the corner—a reliable workhouse they affectionately called Woodrow after their beloved president. They only used Woodrow when a more modern machine broke down or they had extra work.

"Ivy?" she called into the dim corner. Sniffling was her only answer. She called out again.

"Go away."

"Miss Ruby wants us back soon. You got to come out, even if you won't listen."

Ivy sprang up, eyes swollen and wild. "You told," she cried. "You said you never would. All this time, I thought you were my friend, and you told behind my back—someone I don't even know!"

"I didn't," Lizzie said. "Mattie's letter . . . she don't mean it that way." Her words tangled, but she had to make Ivy understand. "It's your business to share or not. Mattie's just jealous I have a friend. She's lonely."

"*She's* your girlfriend!" Ivy yelled. "If I had one, it wouldn't be you. You're homely and dumber than a stump. I'd pick better."

Lizzie gasped. For Ivy to call out her insecurities, even in anger, stung. "I said what I come to say—an apology and an explanation. Mattie's words meant nothing. And just so you know? She never called anyone stupid or ugly, even in all her teasing."

On her way back to the house, her leg thickened up again. She was furious with Mattie—she'd been rude even if she didn't know the full effect—and she'd cost Lizzie her one good friend at the Home. She kept walking, right past the house. She heard running steps behind her and cursed the leg that slowed her down right when she needed to speed up.

"Lizzie, wait!"

She didn't want to, but Ivy caught up and grabbed her arm. Then she dropped it as if it were hot. Lizzie sighed. She had never shamed Ivy for touching her that day at the rock.

"I . . . I need to tell you," Ivy said. "Everything. I'm sorry I said those things. You're beautiful and wise and—oh, Lizzie, I can't lose you." She clasped her own face, as if to contain her weeping.

Lizzie knew she'd give her a chance. She led her down the path she and Mattie had walked so often, toward the clearing nobody bothered unless they needed peace and quiet—or unless they were holding a funeral. They stood, heads together under a tree.

Ivy had always claimed a married man caused her ruin. He was married, indeed—her own father, who found her in an embrace with a neighbor girl. He *learned her proper what men and women did in bed—not girls together*—then threw her out. In Waco's scarlet district, she resorted to whoring until she learned of the Home from Brother JT's sister, Mrs. Annie.

Ivy had never told anyone else her two darkest shames. Lizzie knew one of those for herself, though hearing that someone's real father could commit such a deed hurt her even more.

She swore her confidence again. Then Lizzie wrapped the girl in her arms. It was neither uncomfortable nor unnatural. The girls had no mothers to comfort them here—for their real mothers were dead in life or in spirit.

In times like these, they had no choice but to mother each other.

CATE

Grissom, Texas
1998

AP exams came and went, and finishing was a relief. Beyond prom and finals, the year was nearly over. Time dragged — unless I was with River. Then it rushed like a downhill train.

We didn't see each other the week of prom except at lunch or when River got a library pass during my assistant period, but we talked late into each night, me frequently rubbing in how soundly I won our second race, but also about things that kept me awake sometimes long after we disconnected.

Saturday, I struggled to awake, even by eleven, when my mom burst into my room and tickled me. "Morning, sunshine," she said. "It's prom day!"

I groaned and covered my head with a pillow. The phone slammed into my cheek. We'd talked until three a.m., when I couldn't keep my eyes open any longer.

"Better get your beauty sleep to impress Seth," River had said, holding back a laugh.

"Shut up," I'd said. "*You* better get sleep, too. So your music doesn't suck."

"Night . . ."

"Night . . ."

I'd listened to the lullaby of our fused breathing until the phone clicked on the other end, then fell asleep with the receiver pressed to my ear, as if River's spirit slept inside it.

"Your appointment's at two, and you still need to shower!" Mom said now.

"I knowww. Go away . . ."

She was bulletproof today, so excited, nothing I said fazed her.

I wished I could say the same about my own attitude.

The idea of going to prom with Jess, Jordan, and Seth should not have bothered me. They were friends I'd known forever—Jess was my *best* friend!—and it was one of the last times we'd all be together before college. But I could hardly stomach the thought of so many hours of being made up like a doll, wearing an uncomfortable dress, and trying to talk to a guy I was over when I'd rather be with River. I had to force myself out of bed.

By the time we left the salon, my hair was pulled so tight I cried real tears. My eye makeup ran, and Mom had to redo it after she loosened the pins in my hair. Seth arrived with a tiny box under his arm. The white rose wrist corsage perfectly complemented my aqua dress, which was simple, with double spaghetti straps that crisscrossed in the back, and matching ballet flats. At the store, I'd salivated over strappy silver sandals with three-inch heels. I'd wanted to not care, but I knew I'd feel clumsier than ever in them. My mom thought the flats looked better—and she thought Seth would be more comfortable if I wasn't six feet tall. He had at least four inches on me. I rolled my eyes, but she was paying.

My parents followed us to Jess's house to snap photos of the four of us, then the couples, then Jess and me alone. My face hurt from forced smiles, but Mom looked as if she'd died and gone to prom heaven. Finally, we set off for downtown Austin and the hotel ballroom where prom was being held.

Jess and I both wore form-fitting dresses, so we picked at our food, which was mediocre anyway. When the DJ started playing dance music, nobody budged. Our unfamiliar attire changed the dynamic. Finally, the drill team girls dragged their dates onto the dance floor, breaking the tension—for everyone but me. I figured Seth would want to dance right away, but even Jordan and Jess were content to sit through a few more songs.

I told Seth I wasn't a good dancer but finally followed him to the floor, where a disco ball spun flecks of light on all the sequins and costume jewels. To most of the kids, it probably felt like a fairy tale. I was a little sad it didn't for me. Once upon a time, it might have.

Jess rested her head on Jordan's shoulder, eyes closed, during a slow song. She looked so happy, I was happy for her. But my stomach knotted as the music changed. The crowd went nuts at the first measures of our class song, Creed's "Higher." Rumors that Creed was a Christian band had made the song wildly popular even for the youth group kids. But Creed's music wasn't for goofing off, like Smash Mouth, or romantic, like Green Day. The song managed to be both too fast and too slow for either.

The other kids kept moving. I panicked. "What's wrong?" Seth said, when I froze.

"I have no idea what to do. I actually hate dancing."

He looked amused, and slightly baffled. "Whatever you like!"

"That's the problem," I said, shrugging. "I'm the least spontaneous person on earth."

Not quite true, I reminded myself. I had trespassed a century-old dive of a hotel a mere two weeks earlier. And I had grabbed River's hand first.

"Here," Seth said. "Put your arms around my neck and we'll pretend it's a slow dance. Nobody will notice." He put his hands at my waist, and we simply swayed. He was right. Nobody paid attention to us except Jess, who threw me a thumbs-up. They weren't slow dancing. Jordan was, in fact, playing air guitar while she laughed helplessly, dancing all alone. I longed for her freedom.

Recalling Seth's pressure on me to quit track had brought up all sorts of anxieties, but so far this evening, it seemed he'd lost some of his old arrogance. Maybe he'd had a few challenges of his own since then.

He tightened his hands on my waist throughout the song. When the music ended, I dropped mine. Dance over. I could sit. He held on. "This one's easy too." I didn't argue, but I began counting measures in my head. The sad thing was, I actually loved the Aerosmith ballad, but now it felt endless. Seth wiped his palms down the fabric of his trousers, one at a time. I wondered if he was sweating too, or if it was all me. He placed them higher on my rib cage, and his thumbs massaged me where the dress met my skin. I straightened my back. His hand dropped back to the fabric, and he smiled.

Oops, sorry, he mouthed. Just loud enough, he said, "I wish I'd taken you to my prom."

I laughed self-consciously. I would have killed to go with him as a sophomore, but he'd gone with his girlfriend. "What about Miranda?"

He shrugged. "We were going through the motions. Ending senior year without drama."

"Hmm," I said.

He twitched his shoulders. "We're here now. I waited a long time for this." His thumb slid up again. I wondered if he thought that because he had rewritten history, I'd relax.

The song ended, and I dragged Jess to the fancy hotel restroom with a private stall big enough for both of us. "Seth is confusing me. I never thought he liked me, but now he's acting like he has for a long time. And he's getting a little handsy. It's messing with my head."

Jess seemed surprised. "Really?"

I wasn't sure which part she was responding to, but suddenly I felt guilty for bringing her down when she was having so much fun. "It's okay," I said. "But I can't take much more."

"Why are you suddenly so flipped out?" Jess said. "You've wanted him forever." Suddenly, though, she leaned close and lowered her voice, as if the solid walls could hear. "Also. I'm not going home tonight."

"What?" I said. Seth dropped from my mind faster than I'd have thought possible.

"Don't worry, I'm not *doing* anything. We're just staying out all night. Here's the thing—I told my mom I was staying at your house. I hope you don't mind."

She hoped I didn't mind? I stared. She'd been the goody two-shoes of our class for thirteen years. But then I remembered I'd been lying to her for two months—if only by omission—whereas she was being honest.

"Where are you going?"

"I don't know. Just around Austin. Jordan has it all planned out."

Jordan wouldn't get them into any trouble, but it still bothered me.

The dance wound down. People trickled out, and Seth went for his car. We'd agreed to meet him in ten minutes, but intro notes to Savage Garden's "I Knew I Loved You" came over the sound system and even I shrieked—the most excited I'd been all night. When we heard it, Jess and I always danced like crazy alone in my house or hers. It was sweet, innocent, and didn't offend anyone. I didn't even protest when she dragged me back onto the floor, along with nearly everyone else.

And suddenly, I felt freer than I had in forever—except when I was with River. I let go, swaying and spinning with the rhythm, sometimes with Jess—because for this song, nobody cared who danced with whom. It was a fantastic free-for-all. Gazing up at the spinning ball and falling into the lyrics, I disappeared into my own fantasy of a future that felt like it could work out after all.

In the past, listening to the song, I'd pictured Seth, or even Jess, caught up in the joy of having a friendship that had lasted our whole lives. But now, it was River I saw—of course it was—and just for that moment, I went with it.

As the music faded, I opened my eyes to discover I was the only one of our group left on the dance floor. Jess and Jordan waited near the exit with Seth, who gazed at me, his eyes confused. Hurt. I stilled, my body flushing from the ankles up, my face surely deep red, my heart exposed to the world, even if my friends had no clue what—or who—had inspired my abandon.

Seth walked out ahead of us, his shoulders stiff. I hurried to catch up, even though I wanted to stay inside my euphoria without judgment. I nudged his arm. He glanced back, stone-faced. "Thanks for taking me," I said. "I had fun when I wasn't being an idiot."

He visibly shook off his gloom and smiled, though uncertainty remained behind. "Sure. It was my pleasure. Just wish it had been our second prom."

I swallowed the rest of my pride and said, "Me too!" Back then, I'd wished it.

I didn't argue when Jordan invited us to join their all-nighter. I was certain they'd had it planned all along—and I didn't want to offend Seth again by refusing.

"I have to call my parents," I said. Seth pulled a bulky cellular phone from his console. None of the kids I knew had them. They were too expensive. "I can use a pay phone. That'll cost too much."

"I have a budget," Seth said, and I realized he probably had the phone for emergencies when he was out with the youth group.

"Not for this."

He shrugged. "I get thirty minutes every month. I never use them. Nobody cares."

Telling my mom I didn't want to leave Jess alone swayed her. "I know you're having a great time, but I won't sleep until you're home," she said. She didn't name a curfew. My parents trusted me more than Jess's trusted her.

The boys had jeans and T-shirts, and Jess had stashed extra clothing in the car—a casual sundress for her, and a jean skirt and top for me. "You left them last time you slept over," she said, and I realized how long it had been—and that this portion of the evening had definitely been planned by everyone but me. I laughed and shook my head.

We changed at a gas station, then drove to an all-ages venue that closed at midnight. The doorman marked Xs on the backs of our hands after viewing our IDs. We claimed a table to sip soft drinks and listen to the music. One musician finished his set, and we chatted while the next one set up. Suddenly, Jess exclaimed, "That's your friend from school. River, right?"

My head swung. On the low stage, River tapped a foot switch and attached a capo, then leaned toward the mic. "Check-check. Check-one-two."

"Yeah," I mumbled, my mouth suddenly full of rocks. River hadn't mentioned the specifics about the gig. There hadn't been any reason once I said I was going to prom. But lots of local bands and solo musicians played here. It made sense, but I still felt sideswiped.

When River began to sing, Jess and Jordan were duly impressed. Seth fidgeted. I knew he loved Christian ska bands, and for a time, I'd become a walking encyclopedia of lyrics by the Supertones, dc Talk, and especially Five Iron Frenzy. It was another way I'd been a chameleon for his attention. I admitted it to myself now—I hated ska.

I couldn't help gazing at River. By now, it seemed every song was meant for me. Then I looked over and found Seth frowning. It made no sense. Jess had called River my friend. I'd tried to keep my face neutral. I was Seth's date, after all. Jess and Jordan cuddled in the corner of the booth, oblivious to anyone else. River's music had that effect.

After the set, I excused myself to the restroom. Jess didn't even notice.

River was in the same hallway, near the green room. "You found me! I didn't want to bother you, but I at least wanted to thank you for coming."

I realized it appeared we were there intentionally. I couldn't respond. River grabbed my elbow and pulled me into the green room, lips quickly—accidentally?—grazing my cheek. I froze as others looked up from conversations. "Come on, sit with me for a minute. I don't know a single person in here. Oh, but wait—do you need to get back? I'm so happy to see you, I'm, like, throwing up joy."

I relaxed and laughed at River's enthusiasm. "They won't miss me yet. Jess and Jordan are all over each other."

"And Seth?"

"He's . . . he's fine," I said. Then I sighed. "This night can't end soon enough."

River squeezed my shoulder and took my hand. The others paid no attention at all, but holding hands in public was brand-new, and awkward—especially with my date in the building.

"Is this okay?" River leaned close and gazed into my eyes.

I nodded and shivered, but not like when Seth had stroked my skin earlier. River's free hand rubbed my arm where it rested against our touching legs, and I tracked the sun tattoo with my gaze. I'd have given anything to ditch everyone else in that moment. I could hardly face going back. I wanted to stay, like this. I knew it now, even within my apprehension.

I wanted River.

"Better get back," River said, though, when I went so quiet, and tugged me up from the sofa. The others smiled, and studied us with interest now, but I no longer felt uncomfortable. We were just another couple they didn't know from anyone. It felt good.

As I headed for the hallway, River held on to my hand with a gentle clasp—a braided fingers clasp. A *don't let go* clasp.

So I didn't. We leaned against a wall, shoulders exactly the same height. I'd always imagined someone tall enough to look up to, but River was just tall enough. Everything fit. Our hands. The curves of our bodies separated by less than a breath. Our thoughts.

After a moment, I sighed. River smiled, half amused, half regretful, then turned and kissed me, lips barely on mine, just long enough to say every single thing. Our first real kiss—no accident—and despite everything, it was perfect.

Perfect.

I hardly convinced my feet to leave, or my fingers to let go.

Back at the table, Jess gazed at me. "Hey, you. Where'd you go?"

A hand pressed the small of my back. "*There* you are. Should we get out of here?"

As we left, Seth studied me with a touch of something that puzzled me. Maybe, it alarmed me. That seemed silly, so I shook it off.

MATTIE

Oklahoma City
1916

On Labor Day, the hotel manager promised Mattie could take off early if she finished her rooms quickly. Everyone would be watching the parade—if they weren't marching. Their guests were working-class, and this was their day too. Mattie rushed through making beds, sweeping, and shining tubs and sinks, then changed from her maid's uniform. She didn't want to miss the start of the parade. It would be her first since moving away from Sister Welch, who had not been interested in parades, unions, or much of anything beyond the church.

A few blocks from the hotel, spectators were seven or eight rows deep on the downtown parade route—a mile by half a mile. Mattie elbowed to where she could see well enough. Thank goodness the heat had broken, if only temporarily, with the expected high only in the upper seventies. All summer she'd sweltered under the weight of her wool work uniforms. Perspiration left embarrassing stains that dried white against the black fabric, and she was only allowed two, laundered weekly, so she spent evenings scrubbing the one she'd worn that day, then hanging it to dry. She'd been thrilled for a cool enough day to wear a gabardine suit she'd purchased from Kerr's after she received her first pay packet. The forest-green fabric set off her eyes. She felt pretty. Even so, with the crowd pressing in and the midmorning sun beating down on her hat, she wished she'd worn her cotton day dress, though it was mended many times over. Others eyed her as she waved her fan vigorously at her cheeks and neck.

The police musicians' band led off, and then each union marched by, every division headed by another band. The unions had concealed their costumes for weeks, hoping to take the prize. After the third division appeared, Mattie leaned against a light pole and waved her fan faster. She was simply too warm. Finally, she pushed her way back through the crowd, ignoring annoyed onlookers. "Sorry! Excuse me!" She finally reached the wall of a building, where a cop walked, swinging a club back and forth to create a walking aisle.

She'd stupidly skipped breakfast to work quickly. By the time she neared the hotel, she was nauseated. On a whim, she followed the aroma of refreshments inside a moving pictures theater half a block away. "Pardon me, miss," the ticket agent called. "Have to buy a ticket if you're coming in."

She nodded, undeterred. She needed food in her stomach. She'd never been able to go without a solid meal more than a few hours during the day, and sometimes she woke so hungry, she thought she'd keel over before she could eat. As a result, she'd only plumped up two times in her life, and that hadn't lasted. People teased her for staying skinny. The truth was, she liked being slim—except it made no sense she got so hot.

She handed over two nickels, and the agent pushed her ticket under the grille. A refreshments vendor carried a box suspended at his waist, overflowing with cones of popcorn and peanuts. "One each, please," she said, pulling more coins out, then balanced the paper cones, unsure how to maneuver without spilling.

An usher called, "Lights out in two minutes, madam. Better claim your seat."

She'd never been inside a moving pictures theater. She shrugged and went in. It was dark, cool, and nearly deserted. Everyone else was enjoying the weather and parade and other entertainments of the day. She quickly found a seat. Balancing the snacks on her lap made them easy to eat, and she crammed handfuls into her mouth, the combination of sweet and salty bringing her back to herself. She'd catch her breath, then return to her room to rest.

A fellow in coattails sat in front of a good-sized organ near the front. He arranged music on the stand and then began to play as the lights dimmed and words came up on a white cloth screen, listing the director, the producer, the actors. She'd heard of Charlie Chaplin. The other maids and the hotel patrons went on and on about him. She'd thought of going at times—just once—to see what the fuss was about, but her conscience had always stopped her.

Mattie had worked hard and toed every line for six years in OKC. When the hotel on the other end of the block from the drugstore offered her a housekeeping position, she'd assumed Sister Welch would be proud. She was aghast. "Mattie, what a terrible idea! It's not a good area for single women, even if you weren't surrounded by transient men in the hotel."

"We're single women. We've lived in this area more than five years," Mattie had said. Most of the guests were lodgers anyway, not transients.

Sister Welch's lips puckered. "I won't be able to keep an eye on you."

Mattie promised to attend Sunday school and services. Now she dreaded them, and the church building was too close for comfort. At thirty-four, she felt as if she was experiencing life as an adult for the first time in years. The Home and the ministry could keep a woman sheltered forever if you let them, and what had come before now seemed as if it had happened to a different woman altogether. She kept those memories at a safe distance.

She'd heard it preached often the last few years that moving pictures were sinful. She didn't know *why*, exactly—just that they'd put her soul in peril. From the moment the lights went down, however, and the organ began to play and the short man with a funny mustache, dressed like a tramp, flickered onto the cloth screen, she was entranced. By the time the half-hour show ended, and the organist drew out the final chord, she understood the ban. Alcohol and morphine might turn some into drunks and fiends over time, but she was hooked on this miraculous entertainment in one stunning experience.

The lonely tramp in *The Vagabond* busked for change playing the violin, harassed or ignored by most who passed. One day, though, he played for a lonely gypsy girl. He drove off the man who beat her and worked her like a slave, then slept outside her caravan to protect her. Eventually, he discovered she was a rich town girl, kidnapped by the gypsies.

The story was melodramatic, and Mr. Chaplin's antics over the top. A baseball windup with his bow. Pretending a stick was a fishing rod right before bopping a man on the head. Pulling a checkered shirt from his pocket to make a bathing towel for the girl, and later, a table-cloth. Mattie hadn't laughed so hard in years. She'd been lonely for good company. In spite of her frustration there, she missed the Home. They'd had good times, mostly.

When Mr. Chaplin sacrificed everything, but the woman still fell for a more sophisticated suitor, Mattie wept. As they rode into the sunset, the girl suddenly recalled the tramp's kindness. She didn't for-sake her gentleman, though; she simply invited her rescuer along—the worst kind of burn. Mattie hoped the girl would see the light, maybe on the other side of the sunset.

Mattie's notion of moving pictures had been vague—people drink-ing alcohol, perhaps smoking cigars. Worse, having unmarried rela-tions. What she'd seen instead was exactly what the church preached: a compassionate soul caring for one who was down and out.

When the next feature began to roll, Mattie left. If *The Vagabond* wasn't typical, she didn't want to know. Not today. In a way, she was the gypsy girl, longing to be rescued again—this time, by someone who could make her laugh and cry grateful tears too. Her eyes were open, but if she could visualize her own happy ending vicariously through the sweet story, she would.

Unlike the girl in the movie, however, she'd go with the right guy.

LIZZIE

Arlington, Texas
1917

Lizzie had wrestled all evening with the dark energy she hadn't sensed in years. Fidgety and twitchy, she headed out for a walk. Docie had rushed to read her a note from Mattie, impatient to visit with the middle Upchurch girl, who would leave for her first year of college the next day. Docie worshipped Miss Ruth, especially since Mattie had gone away, and ran to her for every little thing. At nearly twenty, the young woman seemed glamorous to Docie's sixteen. She'd given her piano lessons and tutored her in school, and now Docie even fixed her hair the same way—with Miss Ruth's assistance, naturally.

Lizzie loved the Upchurches, but sometimes she envied the attention they showered on Docie—or more, the attention Docie returned, as if she were a real part of their family. Some days Lizzie felt useless. Docie no longer ran for Lizzie's hugs and kisses when she had a bruised shin or feeling. Lizzie was no longer her favored giver of advice. Docie hinted that Lizzie shouldn't tell her what to do, considering her history. Lizzie flip-flopped between shame and anger at her own child.

Docie worked hard at what she wanted, but Lizzie wondered what she'd do once she finished her schooling. It worried her something fierce, Docie being so impressionable. Her sass hid innocence as pure as the day they'd arrived. Folks might take advantage. But she'd have to grow up some on her own. Miss Ruth was the kind of influence Docie needed, with a strong foundation from the Home to guide her too, so Lizzie was grudgingly grateful.

Mattie's letter had been as rushed as Docie's reading. Lizzie reckoned Mattie wasn't telling everything. In the last year or so, her letters were less specific, and more *howdy* and *see you soon,* though she never did. Lizzie longed to see Mattie's face.

She sighed. Calling on the telephone was a fortune, and things were tighter than ever in the Home since they'd entered the war. Docie lectured everyone on saving every last cent for the cause—same as she heard at school. Sometimes Lizzie couldn't help but plug her ears when Docie preached on Liberty Bonds.

When Lizzie couldn't talk to either of her favorite girls, she substituted this: a walk and a worry about them. At the end of the path between the big house and the tabernacle, she paused. It was still warm, even with the sun gone down, for the grass and dirt baked all day in the late September heat. She turned toward the burying ground. The trees had grown tall around it over fourteen years, and the grass was thick and green over the plots, making for cooler steps.

Just in view, though, she ground to a halt. One moment she saw someone walking catty-corner across the cemetery, and the next, nothing but branches swaying in a breeze. If someone was paying respects, she wouldn't interrupt. Two girls had lost babies lately, and the long-timers were still so torn up about Sister Susie dying, they often visited her memorial to grieve. Lizzie reckoned her eyes had played a trick. She carried on, walking the edges, careful not to step over the graves. Brother JT said superstition was of the Devil, but some things she couldn't get past.

She fixed her mind on a quiet prayer, for Mattie and Docie—and for her own attitude. But when she neared where she'd spotted the figure, she heard a low keening. She followed it toward a girl huddled over a headstone, too dark to identify. She was on her knees, and there was clinking and scraping, metal against the stone. The sharp sound raised the hair on Lizzie's arms.

She peered closer. In one hand, the girl held something thin and pointed, and in the other, something heavier. She hit at the stone marker with both. Lizzie considered running for Mrs. Nettie. Maybe the girl had recently buried a baby and was determined to get at it.

Suddenly, though, the clouds cleared, revealing the moon. The girl raised her head. It was not a girl after all. It was Miss Hallye, kneeling with a chisel in one hand, a hammer in the other.

Lizzie knew that headstone now. It had Miss Hallye's own name on it, spelled the old way. Several years back, they'd been told, a girl had come and gone overnight, staying long enough to bear a stillborn child. Many of the stones for newborns were engraved with only "Infant" and a number. But the girl had seen Miss Hallie's name in the *Journal* and wanted it for her child. She wouldn't give up the lifeless bundle until they promised. None besides the doctor and matron had met the girl, and though the situation was pitiful, there'd been private laughs at Miss Hallye's expense. Nobody in her right mind would name a helpless infant after such a fussbudget.

Lizzie wished now she'd returned to the house when her gut said to. Mrs. Nettie would know what to do.

"Who's there?" Miss Hallye called, squinting in the moonlight, straining to make out Lizzie's face. "Who's spying? Go away . . . Don't . . ." She collapsed, then curled like a child around the stone, holding the tools close to her chest.

"It's just me, Lizzie, Miss Hallye. What's got into you?"

"Leave me alone!" Miss Hallye cried. "Don't come closer or I'll— I'll—" She thrust the chisel away, and Lizzie shielded herself in case Miss Hallye let loose, but she didn't back away.

Miss Hallye had been hacking at the letters on the stone. Likely, none were legible now. It was a crumbled mess, with dust at the edges and on the surrounding grass.

"You don't want to hurt me, Miss Hallye. Should I go for Mrs. Nettie? Or Sister Maggie Mae? You all right?" Lizzie treaded carefully, giving her the space to get ahold of herself.

Miss Hallye pulled up again and wrapped her arms around her knees, letting chisel and hammer thud to the ground. "It was always taunting me. I know you girls whisper when you think I don't notice. But I see you. Judging me, ridiculing me . . . I wanted it gone!"

Miss Hallye's distress seemed enormous compared to an insignificant stone, but Lizzie gently called, "Miss Hallye, we only laugh to think why a poor girl who never laid eyes on you would give her baby your name. I'm sorry. It ain't right. I'll tell them not to—"

"No!" Miss Hallye nearly screamed, and Lizzie jumped with the force of it. "Not a word. It's gone now. Are you listening?"

Lizzie hesitated. Common sense said she should run and get Mrs. Nettie anyway. But she could see how humiliated Miss Hallye seemed about the stone. Lizzie understood humiliation. But she wasn't convinced that was all. Her mind skipped back across the years, over conversations with Mattie about Miss Hallye's crush on Brother JT, so obvious, as if she didn't realize they all saw it.

The stone had been placed while Miss Hallye worked in West Texas, quietly in a corner, no ceremony to mark its arrival. Suddenly it hit Lizzie. Did Miss Hallye worry that the girls believed it stood for an infant not only named for her but maybe even belonging to her?

She stared at the woman, always the picture of propriety, even with her obvious infatuation, her cheeks coloring when Brother JT was close, gazing with doting eyes when not. But if any of the girls so much as touched his sleeve, she bristled to remind them that ladies did not touch men who were not husbands or brothers or fathers.

Miss Hallye seemed to have forgotten Lizzie now, and she rocked, whispering to herself. Or was she whispering to the child buried beneath that stone? She abruptly stopped and stared wild-eyed at Lizzie. The air felt chilled now, even in the warmth of the night.

"Yes. Go get them," Miss Hallye said, her words measured. "Tell them my shame, here in the dark, trying to hide from God and all of you. No better than any woman. All you girls are free to tell the places you've been, your awful deeds, the ruined lives. Encouraged to start over clean, while I . . . always must pretend that I never fell for anything. Or anyone." She dropped her voice nearly to a whisper. "If I told what I know, who would be on the streets? Who has worked faithfully, year after year, without any real reward? I'd ruin too much with my truth."

Suddenly, Miss Hallye threw herself toward Lizzie, and Lizzie jumped back. Anyone hearing her insinuations—especially if they recalled the adoring eyes and blushing smiles—would grasp the stakes. If her rambling hints were true, it wasn't just Miss Hallye's life and livelihood at stake. It was Lizzie's, Docie's, and that of each woman and child in the house.

"Miss Hallye," she said, firmly, "let's get you cleaned up, and then you need to go on home. You been working too hard, and you ain't thinking clearly. What you need is a good night's sleep."

Miss Hallye's eyes nearly burned a hole through Lizzie, but eventually, her shoulders curved. She allowed Lizzie to help her rise and walk to the laundry, where they scrubbed dirt and dust from her nails and brushed her skirt where she'd rubbed her hands and kneeled in the grass. Then Lizzie lit a lantern and walked Miss Hallye to the workers' cottage. Across the road, lamplight from the windows of the Upchurch home gleamed in the dark. Miss Hallye's breath caught at times.

"If you talk to anyone, better be Brother JT himself," Lizzie said, as she turned Miss Hallye toward the cottage. "Don't bother Sister Maggie Mae. She don't need to hear it. All this is our secret, for all time."

Miss Hallye walked inside without a word, as if Lizzie weren't even there now, but Lizzie reckoned her advice was unnecessary.

At Miss Alla Mae Upchurch's bridal shower two weeks ago, across the street at their home, Miss Hallye had sat beside Lizzie, and as it ended, she'd said, "We should help Maggie and Nettie with the crystal and china in the kitchen."

The other two women had headed toward the back of the house moments earlier, but as Lizzie and Miss Hallye eased through the guests and down the hallway, voices floated softly from behind the half-closed door to the master bedroom. "I can't believe Alla Mae's marrying," Sister Maggie Mae said. "Only yesterday I was wheeling her little rollie chair. She's grown up so fast—though we've wondered if she'd find someone. But Frank's a good one."

"He is that," Mrs. Nettie said. "I should have been so lucky." They all knew Mrs. Nettie's husband had run off with another woman—her own sister. That was what landed her at the Home as matron.

Miss Hallye shrugged and began to carry on to the kitchen, but then she froze at Sister Maggie Mae's next words. "Could you believe Alla Mae's face when she opened Hallye's gift?"

The women chuckled, though muffled, as if by hands.

Miss Hallye stiffened. Inside the box she'd wrapped so carefully, along with a shiny ladle from Alla Mae's registry, she'd tucked a copy of the most recent *Journal*, which contained some of her own thoughts on marriage. The girls had giggled when Alla Mae held it up to see. Lizzie knew she should pull Miss Hallye along now, but her own feet were like wet bales of cotton.

"She autographed her articles," Sister Maggie Mae said, snorting.

Mrs. Nettie erupted. "She didn't! Oh, my. You know, when I read them, I was honestly puzzled. Why would she think to write about marriage? Bless her heart."

"She'll never marry. We'd hoped sending her off to Hamlin all those years ago would help, that she'd find some nice man who would appreciate her—shall we say—*unusual* personality. At the very least, we had to get her away from here . . ."

"Away?"

"Oh, Nettie. I shouldn't say this, but it was obvious to everyone. She'd been sweet on JT since the day she latched onto the ministry. At first, we thought nothing of it, but after six years, we had to do something before she embarrassed herself—or us. It was a disaster in the making. Thank heavens JT listened. Then, at Annual Conference last year, she seemed like a new person. She's very good at bookkeeping, and ours were a mess. I wasn't sure, but so far . . ."

Lizzie sensed Sister Maggie Mae's shrug.

Mrs. Nettie was silent. "Goodness. I had no idea," she said, finally.

Miss Hallye had doubled over and rushed toward the bathroom, her shoe crashing into the bedroom door as she went, flinging it wide open. The murmur cut off, and silence flowed into the hallway like ice water. Miss Hallye shut herself inside the bathroom, not emerging or even answering when Lizzie tapped gently on the door and called her name after Sister Maggie Mae and Mrs. Nettie skirted Lizzie in the hallway with forced smiles.

When Miss Hallye had finally entered the kitchen, she'd smiled, her voice carefully modulated. "Wonderful shower. Well done! Alla Mae is loved. Thank you for inviting me."

After an awkward pause, Sister Maggie Mae had replied. "Of course! Alla Mae will use your gifts with pleasure."

Maybe they'd anticipated hysteria, but Miss Hallye had more class than anyone could have imagined. "The pleasure is mine," she'd replied, hardly glancing at Mrs. Nettie, whose hands were entwined in a dish towel, before she exited the back door.

Miss Hallye had never mentioned the event. Lizzie had assumed Sister Maggie Mae and Mrs. Nettie were left to deal with their own consciences.

Now Miss Hallye was safely inside the workers' cottage after her bizarre, yet not entirely mysterious outburst. These days, Lizzie was hard-pressed to blame her for her prickliness.

Come morning, Miss Hallye's desk chair was vacant. But Brother JT stood near it, gazing out the window while running his hand across its smooth wooden back. He didn't see Lizzie pass—or he ignored her. The next morning, the girls gathered before breakfast to read aloud from the new *Journal*.

> *Miss Hallye is on sabbatical at her sister's farm. Her hair has turned white from stress, and her nerves are shattered. We trust she'll return soon, with recovered health and spirit.*

Lizzie hushed the girls' snickers, and they obeyed with surprise. Lizzie's heart pushed up to crowd her throat. Like any girl who left here, Miss Hallye could always come back.

She pondered over the next several days how the Home had accepted her with no judgment. Others had sacrificed so much for the girls. What had Lizzie given up? Nothing. Instead of giving, she took, every single day. Her sweet babies in the nursery were easy, more pleasure than work. Even Mattie, with her fancy dreams, had labored for the church in Oklahoma City for nearly six years. She deserved that new job if anyone did.

In early days, Lizzie had stood up for the girls like May, who hadn't a hope otherwise. The Refuge had been created for them. And she'd helped carry Mattie through her worst times—and even understood her choices more as time passed. But now, suddenly, Lizzie's determination to stay safe in the Home felt cowardly.

It was her time to get on fire again.

She thought of the letter on her desk. She'd ignored it for a month after Mrs. Nettie read it to her. Lizzie hadn't believed Mrs. Nettie when she said who'd sent it. She couldn't imagine how her mother had found her. The words were gruff as ever, but her mother claimed she and Pa were slow moving now, and it was hard to do for themselves. The boys were gone, and they lived alone down a remote road in Hill County. Lizzie being a strong Christian woman now—or so she'd heard—they needed her.

The tone made Lizzie breathe hard, like it used to, as if everything they'd done to her and all the trouble she'd run away from—and toward—was her fault. Brother JT had helped her see the truth: They'd not been a family at all. Folks with the Devil inside had thrust sin on a child.

The letter ate at her after Miss Hallye left for Arkansas. It took some convincing for Brother JT to agree that going back was the right thing. He worried she'd hear those sin-nature voices again, calling her into darkness, and off she'd go, believing she deserved no better.

He feared that Lizzie would just give up.

But she wouldn't, not ever. She had something to get back for. Her girl would need her, no matter what. She'd never leave her defenseless, not the way her ma had left her. And she knew this too: If her people didn't hear the good news from her, they wouldn't hear it from anybody.

CATE

Grissom, Texas
1998

"Wake up, sleepyheads! Next stop, Mount Bonnell!" Jess gave us our marching orders as we climbed into Seth's car. She'd also mentioned Kerbey Lane for breakfast after sunrise—a place that served pancakes as big as your face along with the crack of dawn. I wanted to scream at the thought of staying awake another five or six hours. After the concert, we'd bowled two games at a scroungy alley and were already sagging. Except for Jess. Her eyes still gleamed.

My feet ached. My brain ached. My *heart* ached. But I wouldn't let her down.

The park near the base of Mount Bonnell was officially closed from ten p.m. until five a.m., but we parked the car on a dark residential street and walked in, carrying blankets and sweatshirts from Seth's trunk. Jess had thought of everything.

We spread the blankets in a rare clearing in the forested grounds, too deep for a security patrol to spot us easily. I pulled on Seth's sweatshirt, keeping my arms inside, cold now that we'd finally stopped moving. Eventually, I reclined and drifted off to the sound of the other three murmuring in the background as they identified the few visible constellations.

I woke to silence, except for a whisper of breath. I'd dreamed, briefly, of River stroking my arms, my ears, my lips . . . My bearings shifted until I realized Seth leaned across me, his breath tickling my ear. I shrugged his face away.

He smiled indulgently. "You looked sweet lying there asleep." He reached and took the sleeves of his sweatshirt and playfully tied them together. "There. You needed a bow."

I laughed. "You're weird. And I seriously never thought you liked me that way."

"What do you mean?" He wriggled away and put his hands behind his head.

I shrugged. "I liked you for years and you hardly noticed me."

"I noticed you." He sighed. "You were too young."

"Two years?" It wasn't a lot, and not enough to explain away his insistence.

"Yeah," he said, as if stalling. I waited. He shrugged. "Pastor Randy took me aside for flirting with one of the eighth graders, so I was being cautious."

I pushed up on my elbows, looked him in the eye. "While you were with Miranda?"

"More or less." I sensed his flush, even in the dark.

"It seems like there was a lot of more or less there," I said.

"Exactly." He and Miranda had had a publicly intense relationship, lots of drama and jealousy on her behalf. Now it made more sense, and it made me thankful he *hadn't* given me the time of day.

"How did Pastor Randy even know?"

He stared at his shoes. "Her parents griped. He called me in and made me promise not to hang out with her. I wasn't supposed to even *look* at the younger girls. They were embarrassed, I think. They left the church."

Now I wondered why her parents had cared so much. Simple flirting seemed like no big deal. I wondered at his definition of flirting. And this sounded like a little more than being "taken aside." Mostly, I wondered why, if Pastor Randy and at least one set of parents had been concerned, Seth was allowed to work with the younger girls now. Did anyone else even know?

But grace was a huge part of our church's theology.

Worse things had likely happened.

I heard a lot living in my house, where my dad and mom sometimes conversed quietly about private church business when they didn't think I was listening. One wife had been counseled to stay with her husband, even after he'd cheated on her multiple times. They thought she should forgive him as long as he asked for forgiveness—seventy times seven. Another was counseled to stay with a husband who had anger issues—but he hadn't hit her. Not yet, anyway.

It made me mad, listening to them. And my mom shook her head and kept her mouth shut. The elders and pastor made those calls, not the women. It was what the Bible directed—at least the books written by Paul, which I'd been reading again lately through brand-new eyes.

I could blame River for that.

Now it seemed as if Paul, through his writings, had created nearly all the "rules" we lived by. It bothered me. Who was Paul to do that? Why had the priests who decided which writings would go in the Bible think Paul knew all the answers? I'd always thought Christianity was about Jesus—about doing what *he* said and following *his* example. Every time I compared his "red-letter" words with Paul's writings, I became more frustrated. We were taught that the Bible was the inerrant and final word of God, but there sure was a lot of contradiction. We seemed to pick and choose what was relevant. With so many contradictions, I guess we had to.

Seth had been watching me carefully while my mind went off on this tangent, and now he reached to run a finger from the soft spot behind my ear down to my collarbone. I shivered, and I guess he thought that meant I liked it. So he ran the finger back up and around my earlobe and along the cartilage. I pushed my hand at him from inside the sweatshirt. "Stop."

He tilted his head and looked at me, squinting with a small smile. "Why? Shouldn't we see where this could go? You're old enough, and I'm available now."

I sighed loudly, feeling guilty now that I'd accepted his invitation to prom. He was so sure I would be as ready as he apparently was to jump right into something. "Look," I said—it was past time to be blunt—"I have to be honest. I like someone else."

"I know," he said. "I saw you."

The mood shifted rapidly, and another shiver slipped up my spine. I'd brushed off his annoyance earlier at the club, telling myself he'd been impatient to leave. Now I knew better. "Okay. But whatever you saw has nothing to do with us. I truly don't like you that way."

"Well," he said. "I wonder if you'd like this." He leaned, but I turned my head, and his lips landed on my cheek. His razor stubble tickled my skin, and I struggled not to laugh, both at the tickle and at his expression.

"Sorry, but no," I said. "I don't think you heard me, though. You're a little too late."

He frowned, and sudden anger flashed across his face. I regretted my flippant statement, but before I could react, he twisted and clutched my arms, still tied inside his sweatshirt. He pressed his mouth to mine, digging his tongue inside until I feared I might vomit. His teeth scraped mine. I wriggled, and he held me harder, as if that meant I was into it.

"Do you like it now?" he said, when he finally paused and I managed a full breath.

"No. I *really* don't like that. Seriously. Stop."

I could hardly think. And now, he wasn't just annoying me. He was scaring me.

Any comparison of this gross experience to River's kiss was impossible. The two kisses shouldn't even be the same word. One was a pleasure, the other an insult. And it made me highly aware of the differences between Seth and me. Even with my height, he was taller and stronger. His size should have made me feel protected . . . secure . . . safe. But it didn't.

I'd been preoccupied before, thinking about his past, mine, River, comparing everything. Now my focus was completely on Seth. I considered suggesting a walk with Jess and Jordan to defuse the mood, but it occurred to me then that Jess and Jordan weren't even in sight. They'd been on a nearby blanket when I fell asleep. I'd assumed they were sleeping too.

Seth, still pressed against me, saw me peer into the distance. "Jess and Jordan went for a *walk*." He put finger quotes around the word. "They said they'd see us at sunrise. I'm sure they're having a great time." He wiggled his eyebrows. "Come on, just let me kiss you again. You can't know whether you like something unless you really try it."

"I just tried it," I said. "And really, I don't. Look, can't we just hang out? Let's talk about what you're doing at church. How are you liking the internship?" I hoped he'd figure out, as I lay there motionless—relaxing to the highest degree I could, given the situation—that I was not playing hard-to-get. That I was just not at all interested.

And then he'd give up.

But he didn't. He leaned harder, heavier, and I began to struggle. My arms were trapped and useless inside the sweatshirt, though I tried to push at him from inside it. "Seth, come on!" I said, but he moved higher and pressed his chest against my mouth so I could hardly breathe, much less cry out. I felt crushed and suffocated by his weight, but I couldn't budge him, couldn't shout, no matter how I tried.

Eventually, though, the pain silences me, as forcefully as a knife at my throat—it seems like forever, though it can't be more than a minute or two, the hands that squeeze and pinch my breasts and pull at my skirt, the thrusting and shoving against me, and in me, the jolts that pierce and sear like blue flame—and then he shudders and rolls away.

"Holy cow," he groans. "I did *not* expect that at all."

I'm speechless. I'm . . . wordless.

"We shouldn't have done that," he says.

I can only stare. At my bare legs, bent and shaking. At the ground. At nothing.

And then suddenly, unbelievably, he begins to gasp, and silent tears stream down his cheeks. The salty scent of everything curdles in my stomach. I try not to vomit, though I gag.

"I can't believe you let us do that," he says, his voice rising. "*Why* did you? I thought you were different, not like other girls . . .'"

I pull my knees close now, and they shake worse with the effort.

Let us? Did I? Was that what I did? What he did? I'd tried to be rational, to stop him before it got out of hand. I should have cried out earlier, louder, when I still could. Had I said no, specifically, out loud? I did in my mind, again and again as he pushed into me and I fought against him. He'd been crushing my windpipe; I couldn't make any noise at all.

But did that mean I'd let us?

And what did he mean, *different from other girls*?

"Are you on the pill?" he says, panic emerging on his face now.

I gape at him, unable to answer, unable to even shake my head.

Why would I be?

He buries his head in his hands, his elbows on his knees. He runs his fingers through his hair. He twists little strands, pulls them out. Holds his hands before him and watches them fall.

"You'll be fine," he says. He nods, hard. "You'll be fine."

Except everyone knows what happened to the girl who gave herself to a boy one time . . .

I see myself, at fourteen. In a new white dress, I walked the church aisle with my mom and dad. Along with my friends, I pledged to remain pure until marriage. Our parents promised their support and placed rings on our fingers. I never removed mine, not even to shower.

I twist the ring around my finger now. Am I supposed to take it off? Put it in my pocket?

Seth had been there, his own ring already shining on his finger, shining on his finger today. "We need to pray," he says suddenly, his eyes screaming for my response, examining me.

Moment by moment, the emotions emanating from him vacillate. I say nothing.

He grabs the sleeves of the sweatshirt I still wear—his sweatshirt—and I shrink further inside the stretchy fabric, though he still clings to the cuffs. He bows his head. I continue to gaze at him in disbelief.

"Father God," he prays, "we come before you with humility, imploring . . . *begging* your forgiveness. Forgive us this temptation, for desiring the apple you commanded us to leave on the branch, for listening to the serpent's lies. We gave in . . . We're so *weak*, Lord, so depraved, I don't know how you can love us, but you do . . . Thank you, Jesus. Thank you . . ."

Even in the midst of his endless prayer, delivered in church-ese, I understand him clearly.

He holds both of us responsible for what he did to me. He holds both of us responsible for what he did to me without my permission. Mostly, he holds *me* responsible for all of it.

I'm Eve.

He's certain I believe it too.

Finally, when the sky is graying, he stops praying. "We better go," he says. "Jess will freak out if we don't show up in time for the sunrise." He unties my sleeves and then folds the blanket. My arms can slide into the sleeves of the sweatshirt properly now, though my hands don't reach the cuffs, and I wrap them around my chest. If I weren't cold, I'd tear it off and leave it here on the dewy grass.

Seth walks behind me as we find the car to leave the blanket. He's silent except for random cursing under his breath. I can't tell who or what he's cursing. Himself? Me? As Jess and Jordan come around the path, their blanket wrapped around both of them, Seth mutters, "Excuse my language." I gape. I can't help it. He's sorry about his *language? That's all?*

We climb the steps to the terrace at the top of Mount Bonnell. Not really a mountain. Just a ridge with Austin's skyline visible to the east and the river to the west, extravagant homes along its banks. I struggle with the steps, my insides and outsides sticky and sore. Seth presses his hand against the small of my back, and I physically flinch. He drops behind. Not far enough.

The sun is rising over downtown when we arrive at the top.

Jess basks. She glows. Her eyes, her mouth, her entire being is joyful. I haven't seen her ring in a while.

While the others face east, Seth with hands crammed in his pockets, Jess and Jordan marveling at the fierce and delicate strands of pink and red and orange and blue that thread the sky and around downtown and through the water far away, I face west and fling my purity ring beyond the stacked stone wall and listen for tiny clinks as it tumbles down the hill. I close my eyes to imagine the splash as it hits water not yet touched by the sun, and concentric circles that increase until they're too far apart to discern.

Jess is asleep before we reach the interstate, breakfast forgotten. She doesn't stir as I quietly open and close the car door at my house. Seth emerges to accompany me, but I ward him off with my arm. He glances at Jordan through the glass. "I won't tell," he says, his voice steady, steely. We both know what it was, that voice reminds me, and the blame lies squarely with me.

I ignore him. As I turn the front door knob, I can't help looking toward the car, still idling at the curb. In the street, Seth leans against his car door, his arms folded on the roof, his chin on one fisted hand. His eyes burn like coal, begging. Judging.

I slip inside my house. My mom quietly snores on the family room sofa. I turn off the porch light and tiptoe past her. Soon, she peeks inside my room, then pads down the hallway to hers. I lock my bedroom door, and I lock my bathroom door, and I stand under needles of hot water for what feels like hours, until it runs cold and I'm shivering again.

Then, I sleep.

LIZZIE

Tyler, Texas
1917

Other than a few tears when Lizzie explained what she meant to do in Tyler, Docie took it well. "You'll be back for Christmas, right?" she said. "And for my school program?"

"I wouldn't miss it for the world," Lizzie said. "I'll be gone a month, six weeks at the most. I'd miss you too much to stay longer."

Docie had nodded that way nearly grown girls did, more concerned with friends and school than whether her mother was around. She'd learned how to behave like a proper young lady watching Miss Ruth, though Miss Ruth had gone off to college and would likely return with her M.R.S. if things went the usual way.

Docie had more mothers than a girl needed. Ivy had promised once she finished growing, she'd turn back to human again, and she'd been exactly right. Docie's emotions didn't bounce up and down and all over the place so much now. Lizzie would never have left anyone else to deal with that. Besides, Mrs. Nettie had promised to keep a close eye. She'd promised that if Docie so much as mentioned a certain boy, she was to tie her up—ha!—and send for Lizzie.

Docie had taken a shine to young Mr. Wilbur Upchurch, a right handsome boy. They'd been friendly all through the years, especially after the Upchurch girls had pushed them into playing house that time, so she wasn't surprised. Docie's eyes lit up to see him.

Lizzie knew the look. She'd seen it on those who fancied themselves in love.

Lizzie's own heart should have gone soft watching her daughter in her first big crush. But something was off about Mr. Wilbur. He was obstinate inside and out. Once, Lizzie caught him sneaking a smoke behind the printing office, his insolent look daring Lizzie to tattle. Then, last month she'd sat near him in a service and caught a whiff of something strong when he'd opened his mouth to sing. Brother JT and Sister Maggie Mae were so busy ministering and traveling, she wondered if they had any notion what he was up to.

All Lizzie had yearned for in her wretched youth was constancy and calm. The same made Docie itch. Lizzie feared she'd want things that mightn't be good for her, and people too. The part of her that craved excitement, just like her Aunty Mat had, worried Lizzie to pieces. Mostly, she hoped Docie wouldn't throw herself at the boy. She feared Mr. Wilbur would catch her, happily, and then throw her away in the long run, like Mattie's Charley—and every man Lizzie ever knew, at least before the Home.

Getting off the train at the Tyler depot was eerie. Late October was usually bright and sunny, but once the heat broke—along with Miss Hallye's nerves—the autumn had gone gloomy. Clouds painted Tyler even grimier than she remembered. Main Street was cluttered with horses and carts, and motorcars kicked up the dirt. The train engine noisily belched smoke as it took on more passengers.

Mrs. Nettie had sent a letter ahead, but Lizzie's nerves knotted to wonder if anyone would meet her. If her journey commenced with neglect, she'd know the outcome too.

Lizzie hadn't seen her mother in thirteen years—nearly all of Docie's life. But her ma waved her down from the street, and Lizzie knew her at once. She reckoned the faces of kin etched the brain as sharp as the notion of how they'd treated you.

She picked up her borrowed satchel full of serviceable dresses plus a nice one for Sundays, along with sturdy boots and stockings. Hard work lay ahead—the least would be what her mother asked. Her step-father hardly tipped his hat as Lizzie shoved her bag into the wagon bed and hauled herself up to a board nailed across the sides behind the spring seat. Her mother looked her up and down, taking in her luggage, her dress, her hat, and her good coat—which Sister Maggie Mae had insisted on giving her for the journey.

"Ain't we Miss Fancy now," Ma said.

Lizzie waited for a more affectionate greeting, but Ma directed Arch to pull out, and they headed away from town. Lizzie had already determined she would not call him Pa again. He'd never deserved it.

She watched the road, noting what they passed. Brother JT had said to hightail it back to the depot if things weren't what she hoped—or if she had no one to take her there whenever she departed. Their place was near where they'd lived before, in a little community just below Tyler with a store, a gin, and a sawmill. Along with planting what land surrounded the interchangeable rent shacks, Arch had taken jobs in the lumber as long as she could remember, other than when they'd tried for land in Oklahoma. They'd come right back when their number wasn't pulled.

Arch pulled off the main road and soon turned the horses toward a barn beside a weather-beaten shotgun-style house—as familiar to Lizzie as any building at the Home. Like every other place they'd lived, the porch sagged in the front and the outhouse stank in the back.

Lizzie's mother led her inside, leaving Arch to tack the team. "It ain't much, but it does. I expect it'll do for you too." She showed Lizzie where to stow her bag, in a corner near the stove. She'd set up a bedroom of sorts—a rope cot, with a stained sheet draped across a string for privacy.

It was more than she'd had growing up—or even at the Home—but her ma only saw her disappointment, same as always. "Ain't but one bedroom. Since all you kids took off, we never needed more. Privy's in the back. Watch for black flies. We've had an issue this fall."

Black flies meant nobody had bothered to dig a new hole and move the privy or to drop stove ash in the hole. Probably both. She'd watch her backside for sure—the bites could make you sick. She'd been in high cotton the last thirteen years with indoor plumbing filling water closets hung up high. The first time she'd pulled the chain, when they left their sickroom, Docie had screamed in terror. Lizzie chuckled now to remember.

Her ma turned sharply from stirring a pot simmering on the stove. "Hope you don't think you're too good for us now. You was lucky those folks took you, but we carry on here the best we can."

"I ain't too good," Lizzie said. "I'm here to help out, like I promised." If she was fortunate, maybe she'd get the chance to show them they needn't live this way, always out to grab what they could, knocking over anyone or anything to jump ahead.

And maybe, just maybe, they'd come to see they'd hurt her too.

An apology wouldn't fix it or take away her hurt, but she hadn't come for herself. She'd come for the peril of their souls.

For supper they ate beans, likely simmered on the stove for days, a little pork butt added every few. The fire kept it from souring, and the concoction nearly seasoned itself. Her mother cooked up cornbread by browning butter in the skillet, then filling it with milk, meal, and egg, then shoving it in the cook box. Lizzie mostly remembered being hungry, but reluctantly conceded that the simple meal wasn't the worst part of her old life. Beans and cornbread at the Home had always tasted plain in comparison—unless Docie had convinced Mattie to add sugar to the cornbread before she left them for Oklahoma. Matt could never say no.

Lizzie soon became reacquainted with her ma's and Arch's habits, making herself useful where she could, even hauling and splitting wood for the stove. She'd worked hard at the Home, but she saw how soft she was now. By suppertime the second day, her palms and fingers had blistered from sweeping and digging and using an axe. She asked for cotton wool and lard to wrap them, and her mother pointed to the cupboard. She found only a tiny tuft, so she bought her own when they went to the store a few days later, then returned her coin purse to a secret compartment in her case.

Saturday, she asked whether they'd go to church in the morning.

Arch snorted and went to smoke. Her mother snorted too. "You'll know the judgment's come by my screams from hell."

Lizzie sighed.

Ma constantly walked a thin line between angry and not. All day, she sipped from a flask in a string pocket under her apron. If her snuff ran out between trips to the store, she drank extra gin from a bottle hidden in the coop—not to keep Arch from complaining. To keep him from finishing it.

Most nights, Arch still passed out before he took off his boots, often with a smoldering cheap cigar hanging from his hand. It was a miracle he never set the straw mattress on fire. Lizzie marveled she and Docie had come away alive. The cigar's aroma made her sick.

But true to her mother's word, Lizzie hadn't seen a sign of Arch's sons.

Sunday, she huddled in bed pining for her family—her *real* family. The girls would rise and don their nice dresses and march singing to the new tabernacle—huge, with white siding and a sanctuary with plenty of room for the girls, children, workers, and a thousand guests besides. A single family had donated the whole sum for building it.

Lizzie had gone lazy recently, wanting to sleep longer, bored with the sermons. Often, they went over her head, and though she carried her beloved Bible every single Sunday and every morning to breakfast, her mind had wandered while others thumbed through their scriptures so effortlessly.

A person valued something, though, once it went missing.

She sat up and pulled her Sunday dress over her chemise—the dress tight because she hadn't bothered with her corset this week unless they went to the store. Her mother had laughed her down the front steps the first day, when she'd gone to split wood in the stiff bones, her back so straight she couldn't properly bend.

"Your fancy things won't last five minutes here, missy," she'd said, but Lizzie kept at it until she got two measly chunks for the fire. The next day, she left the corset in her case. She reckoned it didn't matter much now whether she wore it.

"Take the wagon if you want," her mother said, when Lizzie

emerged from behind her curtain. "You could walk though. Church right down the road. We're a little tired."

When Lizzie had arrived, the house had reeked of filth. She couldn't make it pretty, but now it was clean and didn't stink so bad. The sheets and towels no longer stood on their own from sweat and grease, and even the windows sparkled where she'd taken vinegar to their few glass panes.

That was why her mother had sent for her. Lizzie could accept it, but she wouldn't give up on her own hope. Now that the house was in order, it was her only reason to stay. "It's all right. It's late. But will you go with me next week?" she said.

"Dammit, Elsie," Arch shouted from the porch. "I told you. We got no need for religion around here. Those sissy preachers got her brainwashed."

"Now, Arch, Lizzie's being polite is all."

It was the first time her mother had taken up for her in . . . forever.

"I really want you to go, Ma," Lizzie said. "I ain't been the same since—"

"Don't *bring* horseshit inside this house. You want to go to church, we won't stop you. But don't go meddling. We don't need nobody bossing us." Ma stroked the bulge at her hip.

Lizzie sighed. How had Mattie stood all the door-to-door visits, the handing out flyers on the streets for so long in OKC? No wonder she'd wanted a regular job. But maybe when it wasn't your own folks slamming the door in your face, it didn't sting so much.

Thank goodness the Home had taken the time to drill verses into her head persistently until she had much of the New Testament by heart to recite when she got frustrated. And days, while she worked, she sang hymns, hoping they'd catch their truth. She was no trouble to Ma and Arch now—they'd be worse off without her. But Arch spit tobacco juice where she'd just cleaned, and Ma interrupted Lizzie's singing to point out spots she'd missed.

Nights, she lay in the bed—lumpy where ropes held up the mattress and musty from old straw, even after she aired it over the line—

thinking of home, aching to hold Docie, though Docie didn't like that so much now. Aching for her babies. Even aching for Miss Hallye's nose in the air. She missed her sisters' hugs; her ma hadn't even touched her hand or shoulder.

Somehow, over thirteen years, she'd learned the meaning of family. It was not these folk.

For years, she'd imagined if her mother could just see her, straightened up and doing good works, she'd be proud. Now, she knew Ma was not fit for that, never had been—at least not since Arch broke her spirit. Maybe the few nice memories she'd had of her ma had been conjured to comfort herself.

After a month, she'd given up on church, no energy even for a solitary prayer, her defeat hitting her hard. She didn't know how long she could go on doing a servant's work for nothing.

The next Saturday, her ma brought a handbill from the store, announcing a dance at the Odd Fellows'. They'd take the wagon to town after supper, she said. "There'll be folks haven't seen you in years. Let them see how fine you turned out."

Was it true praise or words to mock her? Believing the best was a wager. But she knew helping her ma and Arch was right, and even if Ma was cruel, it didn't negate the good work she'd done.

Brother JT would say to guard her heart. And she was certain sure he'd tell her not to even *think* about going to that dance. If ever there was a place to backslide, a dance had it written all over it.

But Brother JT hadn't written to advise her. No one had, but she didn't need reminders to know what was in her heart. Besides, who would have read them to her?

She was strong now, smarter. She could mind herself. Ma and Arch said they only went to watch folks—and, she reckoned, for one more excuse to drink. In the end, they'd need someone to pile them in the wagon and lug them home, or they were liable to drive the horses into a ditch.

She'd go. This once.

CATE

Grissom, Texas
1998

I force myself to the kitchen to eat something the Sunday after prom. I keep my face and voice neutral, relaying the basics about the night to my mom, who can't wait to hear the details.

I don't talk about Seth. I'm not sure I'll ever be able to talk about Seth. Mom sighs and says she wishes I'd had more fun, but I won't regret going, one day.

I think, *If she only knew how much I will regret going—always.*

Monday, I stay home from school. Mom thinks I'm exhausted. She fusses around me all day, and when she threatens to take me to the doctor, I know I have to go back. I won't see Seth there, but the thought of seeing River is almost—*almost*—worse.

In the library, I pretend I'm busy. I skip lunch several days in a row. The day I return to the cafeteria, I slide into a crowded table with kids I don't know well. I count on River's assumptions. That I chose Seth after all. Or that I was embarrassed to hold hands or kiss in public. Or that I'd worried things were happening too quickly.

If only.

The truth is, everything is ruined. Every time I think of River, I think of that kiss, and then I think of Seth seeing us, and of his determination to prove I'd like his kiss better. Of what happened after. Of how I never expected Seth to go as far as he did until it was too late and too hard to stop him—and how I still struggle to believe it actually happened. Or how I maybe didn't fight it hard enough, or say no the right way, or at the right times.

And finally, my feeling that I never want to be touched again. Not by anyone.

Not even River.

I tell myself I can make it through graduation. Then I'll deal.

Graduation falls twenty-one days after prom. The day arrives hot and bright, and humidity bears down on the crowded stadium.

Catherine Elizabeth Sutton . . . I cross the stage to polite applause, accept my diploma, and take my seat again, thankful that's out of the way.

River's name is answered by a similar smattering of applause. I can't help looking up, at the podium, then toward the clapping. River's mother wears the hairstyle, outfit, and soft curves of a middle-aged mother, but I know she's different. She didn't take the most common path to motherhood—not for around here anyway. She's a high-ranking software engineer and the family's primary breadwinner. She's surely encouraged River to ignore the norms.

Or maybe, River is just River.

I look away. It seems obvious whom I've been studying.

My face flushes, and I try not to cry.

After the ceremony, I force smiles for photos, including some with Jess. Missing those is actually something I could regret one day. Our friendship has already cooled, mainly because we've been preoccupied with new relationships, but she's been my best friend forever. We hug and promise to call.

At River's approach, I busy myself with my family.

"Hi, Cate."

I want to turn, fall the rest of the way, collapse into River's arms. It melts me, that timbre, that tone. *It's okay. It's okay.* I want it to be, but it's not.

Instead I wear an artificial smile. "River, this is my mom and dad. Mom, Dad, this is my friend River." River flinches so quickly, nobody would catch it but me. They shake hands.

Congratulations. Thank you. So nice to meet you.

Mom's gaze lingers on River's retreating back. I think about the journal, and wonder if she's thinking of it too.

And then it's over. I don't even make excuses for ignoring party invitations. Mom knocks on my bedroom door Sunday, surprised I'm not ready for church and I say I'm staying home. It's Senior Sunday and I won't stand before the church to hear my honors and college plans read aloud. I don't want the expensive study Bible they always give, with my name embossed on the leather cover, or the personalized laundry bag either.

I don't know what I want anymore. Not those.

The following Monday, I take a test. I've woken to mild cramps and sore breasts all week. My period is due. I've counted the days repeatedly. I show the test to my mother, and she weeps. At dinner, my dad weeps too, painfully, but without a sound.

They want to know how, why. Who.

Finally, I tell them about prom night. I tell them about Seth.

My dad wants to call a meeting with the deacons immediately, and I barricade myself inside my room. My parents' arguing creeps all the way from theirs, even with both doors locked between us. Their voices are muffled, but I can discern their thoughts.

Next week, we're supposed to drive to East Texas for orientation at the tiny Christian university that offered me a substantial scholarship. But I've been thinking—not just for days or weeks, but months now—about telling my parents I prefer the public university that accepted me. I won't get much scholarship money there, but I'll be anonymous.

Big pond. Little fish. *New fish.*

Now, my decision's been made for me, more or less. Again.

I tap on their door and ask Mom to cancel our plans, and she cries new tears. She skipped college and a formal wedding—choosing a simple ceremony in a field of flowers.

And me.

She's lived her life vicariously, and I keep screwing up her second chances.

In the morning, she explains we need to meet with Pastor Lance. If I want to keep going to church, I have no choice. I shrug. I don't know if I want to keep going. I hardly care. I just want things done. Out in the open. All of it. I want a new plan, a new normal. I'm tired of waiting.

On a quiet Thursday night, we drive to the church, and Mom and Dad walk me in. I have no idea who's invited, but the face I most expect to see, the one I most dread seeing, is absent.

Seth is not there.

Pastor Lance is, and the associate pastor—Seth's dad—too. Just the five of us. Later, it becomes clear. In the conference room, Pastor Lance pats my hand and says he's sorry I have to deal with this uncomfortable situation—that we all do. He assures me the church still loves me. That God still loves me, as if the two have spoken. I nod. My tears are gone, and strangely, my doubts about God with them.

Pastor Lance asks me to tell them what happened. I don't go into much detail, beyond explaining that I was unsure what Seth's intentions were at first, that it was very confusing, that I had been taken by surprise. That I had no idea how to react.

Everyone listens quietly.

My dad asks one question. "Honey, to be clear, are you saying Seth raped you?"

The pastor takes over. "We want to be very sure of what this was. I suppose if you'd been raped, you'd know. Right, Catherine?"

I lift a shoulder. I know what it was. But what *I* did, was it enough? I'm still broken.

Seth's father says he doesn't think his son would rape a girl. He says perhaps it was a misunderstanding. He, respectfully, struggles to believe it happened at all. In fact, he says, Seth is helping the youth pastor prepare for the annual abstinence campaign. I realize in that moment, he's not even convinced Seth and I had sex, much less whether I wanted to.

Pastor Lance says we have to make decisions about how to handle things. I nod. The decisions seem simple to me.

"The one thing we know for sure is that this—these...accusations—could have serious repercussions for Seth's potential call as a minister," the pastor says, and everyone else nods.

Even I nod, again, even as I feel the trap closing on me.

The teeth of it, sharp and slow, but inevitable.

Seth's father's confusion and denial is understandable, maybe, in his situation, but Pastor Lance isn't making sense. I hear the words but can't comprehend them. I remember Seth's admission that he'd been in trouble for flirting with an eighth grader. I wonder again what his flirting looked like. I wonder why the family left. I wonder if his father even knows about that.

And now, I wonder why Seth really came home from college. Maybe he'd been in trouble there too. In retrospect, it seems suspicious.

A girl in the church became pregnant when I was younger. She had to write a formal apology to the church to be read at the end of a service. The church voted to accept it, and she was not disfellowshipped. She was not shunned. No male was named, insinuating the father was not a church boy. Church discipline is for members.

They discuss my confession now. How I'll write my letter. Who will read it.

"What about Seth?" I say.

They go silent and look toward me, as if they've forgotten I'm there, as if I've misunderstood everything up to this point. As if it's obvious. Seth will not face any consequences for his actions—at least not in the public eye. Again.

"Do you want him to *marry* you?" Seth's father asks, shaking his head slightly, as if even the idea of it is ludicrous. He's right. It is ludicrous.

"Now, Catherine," Pastor Lance says, gently, but firmly, "we have a few options here. If you'd like to stay in fellowship, naturally, we'll take your confession before the church. And based on what your father tells me, there are several variables to consider . . ." His voice tapers, and he looks toward my dad.

"We know you're seeing someone else, Cate," Dad says. "Your mom thinks it's been going on a while."

"What?" I say, but then I see my mother's lowered eyes, and I know she actually did see the journal hidden beneath my mattress, that she probably even read it. I remember her eyeing River, after graduation, watching and wondering—and distinctly denying it all at once. She hasn't told him *everything*.

For the first time in days, I'm fully aware. I've been swimming in an overly chlorinated pool, and now I burst through the water.

The sun is too bright.

"Are you certain Seth is the father?" Pastor Lance says.

I shake my head, but not in answer to his question. I see Mom's embarrassment now, the red rising from her chest to her neck to her cheeks, entire patches of knowing. *Don't tell*, the red says. *Don't* . . .

"Seth is the only person I've had sex with," I say. I look rapidly from face to face, all of them skeptical except my mom's. "I was . . . wearing the ring." Even to me, it sounds like a desperate attempt to convince them—a naïve and desperate attempt. Do they believe they mean anything at all—the abstinence campaign, the ceremony . . . the promise?

They'd meant something to me.

Pastor Lance sighs. "So much is unclear here, but can we agree, for now, that Seth should continue his plans without unnecessary drama?"

I look at Seth's father. Is he as worried about his own career as he is about his son's?

I look back at Pastor Lance, who seems to believe his own bewildering babble.

And I long to tell them that a confession from Seth might have a more profound impact on our youth than his allegedly unblemished history. Perfection is too much to live up to.

But what about me? What about my plans? I have no choice about college now—even if I still wanted one. The Christian college won't accept me pregnant and unmarried. Or if they do, I won't be allowed to live in the dorm like the other girls. I may not be able to live in a dorm at any college.

My plans, of course, are irrelevant. But what they're saying about Seth?

It's bullshit.

Now, in this room, in this conversation, I'm certain: It's not unnecessary drama.

Seth is going to get away with rape, just like he'll get away with blaming it on me.

Suddenly I no longer care what anyone thinks. And I no longer care what I've been taught since the time I was old enough to understand.

"River Wilder." I say. "That's who I was seeing. Not anymore, though. That's ruined now. But this isn't River's baby." I sense more than I see my mom shaking her head, warning me again. She knows. She wants to keep me silent.

To protect me? Or to protect her? I can't tell anymore.

"River is a girl," I say.

And I run from the church office, outside and down the street, and I run as long as I can, as fast as I can, as far as I can, until I'm drowning in sweat and my heart beats so hard it physically hurts. And then I run farther.

When I finally go home, it's late. My parents would usually be in bed, but they're waiting at the table, a sheaf of printed pages before them. I try to keep going, but my dad comes after me and pulls me, physically, to the table. "We have to talk," he says.

But I'm finished talking. I listen instead, standing at the end of the table.

I will not sit down for this.

"We want you to know that none of this changes how we feel about you. We love you. Of course we do," Dad says, looking to Mom, who nods, though her eyes are red and swollen and she struggles to make eye contact with either of us.

"But you know, too, that we can't just look the other way. This . . . relationship, it goes against what we believe. We want to be sure you aren't confused or acting out for some reason."

Of course I'm confused, I think. *Isn't everyone confused about love?*

"We'd like you to see a counselor after we figure things out."

I am astonished. And not at all.

"Pastor Lance and Barry won't say anything for now. They're allowing us privacy, given the situation. You don't have to go before the church, for either thing, until we sort it out."

What do they think they're going to sort out? I'm pregnant. I'm not married. I like a girl. I maybe love a girl. It's very simple. And undeniably complicated at once.

Especially the part where I was raped but apparently didn't fight hard enough not to be.

"In the meantime, Seth's father wants your assurance you won't say anything. He'll provide financial assistance on Seth's behalf. You can use the money however you'd like."

"How much?" I say, the first words since I came home.

"Well . . . quite a bit."

"You took it?" I see the check now, peeking out from under the pile of papers—some kind of agreement, I suppose, that Seth's father wants me to sign.

"It's not our choice. It's yours."

"They want this to go away?"

"I'm not sure that's how anyone would word it—"

"How would you word it, Dad?"

"Well, I know his son's career means a lot to him."

"Sure. And they just want this to disappear. That's what happened to girls who got pregnant in the old days, right? They just"—I make finger quotes—"went away, until the baby was not an issue anymore."

"Not all of them, honey," my mom says quietly. *True.*

Now I sit. My knees shake. "And you think this is a good idea? Should I—should *everything*—just go away?"

"Of course not, honey," Dad says. "We love you. We want to support you."

"You want to support me with counseling? To be sure I don't like girls? What if I get counseling and I still like girls? How will you support me then?"

"We'll always love you, Cate."

My mother nods, so quiet.

"Mom? If I fall in love with a girl and decide to spend my life with her, maybe even raise this baby with her, what then? Can I bring her home for Thanksgiving? For Christmas Eve? For church? How will you support me then?"

My parents sigh, together. They look at each other, at me, and say nothing.

I have one more question, for both of them. "Mom? Dad? This money—do you think they really care what I do with it, as long as the problem goes away?"

An unspoken word hangs between us now. We've been told, all our lives, as children and adults, that all sin is equal. But in practice, there's a hierarchy. And I wonder now, which sin ranks higher in the eyes of the one who wrote this check and who scripted this agreement before me—I've scanned enough to know it's buying my silence. It's hush money.

But which is the greater sin? Paying for an abortion to protect the reputation of a so-called man of God? Or being a woman who loves a woman? The answer seems clear now. Either way, I'm finished in this place.

Call me a pragmatist, but I take the money. I sign the paper. And I walk away.

The next day, with my car packed to the roof with things I'm not even sure I'll need where I'm going—because I don't know where that is, exactly—I make one last stop. River made me a CD a few weeks before prom and hid it in my backpack while I returned my lunch tray. Songs she'd written herself, though not specifying which she'd written for me. I played it again and again in my car.

I listen to it one more time while I make my last entry in the journal I've been writing since I met her. I wrap them both, the CD and journal, together in a paper bag, and then roll tape around them until the package would take hours to open without destroying the contents. I take it to an old, abandoned church we'd talked about visiting when we'd been sitting on that picnic table in the park. River had seen it one day, driving and thinking about lyrics for a tune she'd composed. We'd planned to go after school was out. After prom and graduation. She thought I would enjoy it more than any of the other places—it was for me, her "church girl."

The building is crumbling, literally falling down around the altar, and as I wander the small sanctuary, I can almost hear a choir singing old hymns, a piano, the hum of an organ played for centuries. One last altar call.

I listen to the ghosts, and eventually, cautiously, I approach the area before the altar, where the floor has opened to reveal the underside, full of webs and dirt and things that live in the dark. I leave my offering—my sacrifice—dropping it out of sight into an undefined space, together with eighteen years of faith, and eighteen years of doubt.

I leave it all behind—River, too—and drive away.

LIZZIE

Tyler, Texas
1917

The night was already dark, stars scattered across the narrow strip of sky visible above the thick pines on either side of the road, and a larger swath where the team pulled up by the Odd Fellows Lodge for the dance. She hadn't been to town since the day she'd arrived. It was no different than ever.

At eighteen, she'd been up over that saloon by the depot, waiting for Willis to return each night after she'd already been shoved down on the mattress four or five times during the day. Wondering if he'd black her eye for not earning enough for their supper, or worse, slap Docie for crying because she was hungry. She'd had to take Docie to her ma, finally, afraid Willis might go too far. Ma hadn't wanted a kid around any more than she'd wanted Lizzie in the house, no matter how sweet. But she'd agreed to keep Docie a weekend, and it turned into more, until finally, Ma brought Docie to town and deposited her in their empty room, leaving word she wouldn't keep her any longer.

Lizzie had only asked her to mind Docie one other time. That was the time she worried about most.

She didn't have the time or energy tonight for more remembering. Inside the hall, the dance was already in full swing. At least it wasn't free entry, which would keep the lowest out, and the hall manager would boot anyone who became rowdy or visibly inebriated. She hoped it wouldn't be her ma or Arch—though they were quiet drunks these days, sliding down in their chairs and snoring when they'd had enough.

Upstairs, the smoke was so thick it was hard to spot an empty table. Lizzie and her ma leaned against a wall until Arch wagged a finger from the opposite side of the room.

On their way, an older woman grabbed her mother's sleeve. "Elsie, we haven't seen you in a coon's age, darlin'. And who you got here?"

"It's my Lizzie," her ma said. "She got herself some religion, and I guess it done her good. She's finally doing us right after I worked so hard to get her back home."

The woman pushed her neck back and gawked at Lizzie, who nearly choked on her mother's lie. She'd written Lizzie once. There'd been no work to it.

"Well, I'll be. We figured you for dead by now, but good on ya. Watch out with these boys. They like you religious girls, if you know what I mean." She winked and waved them on.

Lizzie forced a smile as other women stopped them with the same kinds of comments. She was surprised they remembered her after so long. She reckoned her reputation had been even worse than she'd realized.

Arch glowered when they reached the table. "About damn time. Folks wanted the table."

"Oh, hush, Arch, you know I rarely get to jaw these days. The ladies want to see Lizzie. I want them to see she's cleaned up good."

Her mother didn't care about Lizzie's reputation—she simply wanted the townswomen to think Lizzie's transformation was her doing.

Elsie sent Arch for punch, saying she'd spice theirs up. Otherwise the lodge offered only coffee and tea, for the county was dry everywhere but saloons. Liquor flowed freely, however, flasks glinting in every prism of the cheap chandeliers. As long as folks didn't get out of hand, the lodge manager looked the other way. Arch splashed away half the contents of their cups along his return.

"Sorry, girls. Hard to carry three."

"More room for what I really want," Elsie said. She added a liberal measure of vodka to her punch, then stirred it with a finger she popped in her mouth when she finished. "Want a splash, hon?"

Lizzie pulled her cup closer. "You know I don't drink now, Ma."

"Oh, I'm teasing. I ain't got enough to share." Ma capped her flask.

It was hard to see and hard to hear, and the chaos set Lizzie's brain awhirl along with the couples dancing a waltz. Between songs, someone hollered for the Shimmy, but the music leader shouted, "The Shimmy is not permitted!" He winked, then added behind his hand, "Later, folks!"

The crowd roared. Her ma chuckled, twisting her mouth and shaking her shoulders, and Lizzie smiled. Watching her relax wasn't the worst. But after two hours and two cups of punch, Lizzie asked her ma to point out the ladies'. She was relieved to exit the rowdy room. She began to wish she'd stayed at the house.

But then she saw her reflection for the first time since she'd left the Home in the mirror over the sink. She hadn't bothered with the tiny shaving mirror at the house. Her hair had come loose in wavy tendrils around her face, and her eyes glistened from the pulsing in her head that matched the music. Her ma had insisted she rub clay tint on her lips. She had to admit she looked nearly pretty. But she also wondered if she looked cheap. She rubbed at her lips, but the color had sunk in good. It wouldn't budge.

Back at the table, her ma pushed her cup across. "Got you a fill-up while you was gone."

Children had been permitted until nine, and the drinking had accelerated once folks with kids had departed. The music picked up, and the dance floor with it. Couples turned and spun, hopped and shook, and that dance they'd clamored for made the floor quiver, bosoms shaking and twisting every which way while the men hooted and hollered. Ma said the dance had been banned as lewd in many places. Lizzie could see why.

She began to feel as if she floated above the commotion, somewhere around the ceiling. She looked at her cup, and then at her ma, whose grin showed dark gaps where teeth had been. "Can't even tell it's spiked, can ya? Vodka is the choice of proper ladies such as yourself."

Lizzie couldn't even respond. She knew she should be angry, but she felt numb, nearly as if she didn't care. But she would not drink more. She pushed away the cup.

Her mother laughed. "Loosen that rod up your back. You're too straight for your own good now, Lizzie."

A man approached, near Lizzie's age, and not terrible to look at if she was noticing. Others had come by to ask her to dance and she'd politely refused, but he'd circled two or three times already. He tilted his head. "Still won't dance with me, miss?"

"Missus," she replied.

He looked around. "I haven't seen a mister all evening." He held out his arm.

"Mister ain't been round in a decade," her ma said. "Go, girl. Take a turn. Clear skies and no sign of lightning to strike you dead tonight."

"Can't," Lizzie said. It was hard to get the words straight.

"I seen you dance all them years ago," Elsie said. "You was good." You'd have thought her mother wanted to dance herself, the way she wheedled. "Tell you what. You dance with this nice fella, and I'll go to church next week." She batted her eyelashes.

Lizzie's mouth fell open. Was this a bargain worth striking, or one with the Devil? She knew deep down Brother JT wouldn't approve. He was dead set against dancing.

But he didn't know her people. He didn't understand how tough they were to crack when they thought one way and you wanted to convince them of the other. These folks traded in deals—especially when the proceeds weighed in their favor.

It might be the only way to get her mother through the door of the church.

"All right," Lizzie said. "But only the one."

The man smiled and took her hand. As he led her to the floor, she looked back at her ma. She was laughing as if she'd pulled one over on Lizzie. But it was too late now. She'd have to hope Ma honored her word.

The man wore a decent suit of clothes and smelled clean, his breath hardly tinged with booze. He led her into the waltz, the fiddle player spinning a sweet tune, and she rose on her toes, the memory of how to follow coming as easy as the memory of her husband. He'd been a good dancer and had wooed her at a dance not so different from this.

She closed her eyes and let the music and this stranger turn her through the steps while, just for a minute, she relaxed into one of her few good memories of Willis, holding her hands, pulling her to his chest, spinning her under his arm, easily a foot taller than Lizzie, then pulling her close again, whispering how pretty she was, over and over, the first time a man had ever said so.

Her fingers trembled as warm hands grasped hers tighter, and her scalp prickled where he casually brushed it with his lips, inside a slow turn. Her leg went weak at the pressure of his elbow at her side, but she kept up, with vigor and grace she hadn't felt in an age. She leaned her cheek against the wool of his coat pocket to inhale the tobacco scent and—

Suddenly, she remembered this was not Willis, and it was not twenty years ago. It was here, and now, with a spider spinning her into the same sinister web.

She left him on the dance floor, his mouth slack as she ran off without a word. She'd nearly fallen for it, this way men flattered their way in, saying sweet things with touches that ran chills up and down your arms and spine, to get what they wanted without having to give what you needed in return.

She'd nearly fallen for it again.

Soon, Arch came back from the alley, where the older men had smoked and joshed all evening. Her ma had kept her mouth shut after Lizzie stopped mid-dance, except a scoff and a short remark—"Guess I won't be going to church after all."

In the board seat behind them, returning to the house, Lizzie wept silently. She'd not let her ma witness her tears. Her plans would never work. She saw it now, plainer than ever. This life would kill her. If not this month, another. If not this year, next.

But as they pulled into the yard, Lizzie sat up straight at the sound of a scream. It came from the house or the barn, and confused her only for that, for she'd know it anywhere.

Docie.

Lizzie was more sure of that than she was of anything.

But her Docie? Here, in this house? How could it be? Lizzie sprang from the wagon seat, shushing her ma and Arch, so she could locate the screams. They seemed surprised, but unconcerned—as if a woman screaming were commonplace, even in their home.

But they did not know the timbre of her girl's voice.

She held a hand behind her to keep them back. The screams came through the window sash, where it was missing a pane. Lizzie grasped the hatchet, its blade sunk into a chunk of wood near the doorstep, and pulled hard to release it, thankful for her newly hardened muscles. She crept onto the porch, twisted the door handle, and, with the hatchet high over her head, pushed the door open with her foot. The door was half-rotted and weighed nothing, constantly rattling in its frame and rarely latched when they were home.

In the corner, on the flimsy bedframe where she'd slept for weeks, Docie sat pushed and folded against the wall. She wore her little traveling coat, but it was skewed, buttons undone except one at the middle, with the shoulder pushed off one side. Underneath, her pretty sailor suit was torn at the neck, with her skirt hiked high, showing her stockings clear as day.

And those beefy hands, one pressing down on her knee, the other snaking between them, as if to yank down the stockings—like Docie's cry, Lizzie would know them anywhere. The sight heated Lizzie's blood to a boil in her head and ran it icy all the way through her. They belonged to a grown man now, not the twelve-year-old boy who took her down to the creek that very first time.

Her own stepbrother.

Lizzie roared. "You get off her before I kill you!"

Hugh reared back enough to turn his head, but he kept Docie pinned. "Who's that?" he said, squinting as if he didn't know her. Even two or three footfalls away, she smelled fumes wafting off him.

"Get off now," she repeated.

"Hugh, it's Lizzie," her ma said, still behind Lizzie. "Let that girl go."

That girl. She didn't know her own granddaughter.

"She was waiting in my bed, asking for it, just like Lizzie always tempted me," Hugh said.

Lizzie couldn't believe her ears. *His* bed? She grasped the hatchet tighter and higher and glanced behind her. Her ma simply shrugged. Elsie would make no apologies, not for anything. Not for this, and not for everything that had happened to Lizzie, for all those years of abuse.

"You got one more chance," Lizzie said, quiet and controlled this time, so as not to leave any doubt in the monster's mind. She would do what she said. "Get off her. Get off the bed, and leave my girl be."

He didn't. He glowered and turned away, back toward Docie, burying his face against her. In this house, it would never matter who knew, who saw, or for how long. He was free to do as he pleased. Anything was permissible.

Lizzie rushed the bed, aiming the hatchet for his leg. But as she brought her arms down, hard, Hugh suddenly reared back and swung his hands in the way. The hatchet pinned one to the footboard, and the top joints of two fingers, the ring and the tall one, flew away from the bed.

Hugh's face blanched white as Docie's blouse. For a moment there was no noise, but then he rolled away, holding his hand to his neck as blood spurted everywhere, on everything. He mewled like a treed bobcat.

Lizzie stood still. The human body was tougher than wood in places, and as hard to chop at the bone. But she knew her strength now. She'd meant to hurt him badly. Kill him if she had to.

Docie huddled, free now, but Lizzie didn't quite trust that Hugh was finished, even in his state. "Docie, baby, get off the bed." Lizzie heard her move more than saw her. "Do you see my bag, honey?"

"Yes, Mama," Docie whispered.

"Put everything in it you know is mine, then carry it outside."

"O-k-kay," Docie said, tears choking her voice now, making her sound six years old instead of sixteen.

"Arch?" Lizzie said, for she assumed the man was there, some-where she couldn't see. He huffed from the other side of the room, as if he couldn't believe she'd done it, or worse, didn't understand why. "You tend to Hugh if you want. Wrap his hand and stanch the bleed-ing if you want him to live." She shrugged. "I don't care if he does, but he's your boy."

Arch shuffled to a basket near the stove and rustled for the wool Lizzie had bought for her blisters. Hugh had stopped his mewling and lay silent in the floor, likely as not, in shock.

Or maybe the booze had deadened the pain, which nearly made her angry. She wanted him to feel it—all he'd ever done to her and nearly did to her daughter.

"Ma? You get back to the wagon to drive me and Docie to town."

"I sure will," her ma said. "Taking you right to the jail and telling them to lock you up. You can't just go and do what you did here, acting like you're the queen of innocence when we all know what you done before you went and got religion. I should've turned you in years ago."

Lizzie went cold, ogling her ma. After all that had been done to Lizzie, not just by Hugh, but by Arch, too, with her ma knowing the whole time and saying nothing, it was unfathomable that she'd throw Lizzie's own indefensible shame back at her.

But Lizzie prayed she wouldn't say more, not with Docie right here.

"Okay, Ma," she said, coming to her senses. Elsie would have said something by now if she was going to. "Take us to the jail. They helped us there once, and they'll help us again. You all ain't right in the head. They know it."

Her ma sniffed but headed for the door. She stopped to gather a bundle of papers from a drawer. "Hurry it up," Lizzie said. It felt good, in a way, to speak to her like that. Powerful. All those years, and these past weeks, she'd quivered under her, as if her ma had something on her that kept her small.

Lizzie waited another minute to be sure her brother wouldn't come after them, then carefully set the hatchet just outside the door. She wiped her face and hands on a dishrag at the dry sink. Blood splattered her skin and dress, and some of those stains would never come out. Blood set fast, rarely giving in to the washboard or even the sun. The stains would remind her, whenever she saw them, that she was not as weak or dumb as her kin had made her believe.

She walked out the door and down the path and climbed into the back of the wagon, where her daughter waited to fall into her arms.

"Go," she said. Elsie flicked the reins.

The road was darker and lonelier than it had been only an hour earlier, but Lizzie held Docie tight, and it was nearly all that mattered. She'd save her questions for later.

This, on the other hand, would be the last time she ever intentionally saw or spoke to her mother. She called up to the front of the wagon. "You said he'd left you and Arch. All this time, I've been sleeping in his bed. You knew he'd be back, didn't you, Ma?"

Elsie slapped the horse's side with a rein, as if hurrying them could save her. "He's been in the jail."

"The very one we're headed for?"

"He done some stealing from the mill. They locked him up ninety days."

"Ninety starting when?"

"Round about August."

Lizzie could count months. "Round about when you asked me to come. And you knowed—you *knew* all that time, he'd be out this month."

Elsie shrugged. "Knowed he'd be out today. They sent a note last week saying so. I knew you'd be bothered to see him, so we gone to that dance to give him time to get settled."

"What had you planned to do then? Throw me out like you done every other time you didn't need me anymore?"

"We'd of found the space. You done a good job around the house. Not likely he'll be helping now. You crippled him something good."

Lizzie snorted at the backhanded compliment. "Doing all the work you won't do, long as I didn't cause you no trouble."

"You're a good girl now, but you was starting to get that sass back," her ma said. "I reckon maybe you need to get on back to where they can control you and that mouth."

Docie, huddled into Lizzie's shoulder up until then, tilted her head back, plainly puzzled.

"I ain't never been sassy, Ma. You know that. I were nothing but a scared little girl, too cowed to stick up for myself. I never gave you trouble—none you didn't lead me to yourself. Every dark thing I done, you walked me right up to it."

Even the one Elsie hadn't spoken aloud . . . Lizzie prayed to God she wouldn't now.

Elsie laughed, low and quiet, and shook her head. Silence deepened between them until her mother dropped her chin. It was no acknowledgment, but it was the best Lizzie would get.

"I ain't scared no more," Lizzie said, "and I ain't afraid to stick up for myself, and for my daughter. I'd do anything to keep her safe. You hear that? I *didn't* learn that from you."

Elsie whipped the horse's side. "Git!" she called, her voice full of something nearly like shame. Lizzie took some satisfaction knowing her mother felt that, if not regret.

At the jail, Elsie told the sheriff what Lizzie had done to Hugh. He started to say it was good Lizzie turned herself in so he didn't have to go after her, but Lizzie interrupted. "Sir, you let my brother loose from your jail less than a day ago, and now he's attacked my daughter. He's got nobody to blame but himself."

The sheriff knew Hugh's reputation. He remembered Lizzie too. He'd locked her and Docie up when they were sent away sick from the county farm, and let the jailer's wife call Berachah all those years ago when they lay dying in his cell. She told him how she'd straightened up, then returned to help her folks—in hopes they'd straighten up too.

"I shouldn't of come," she said. "You can lock me up for what I done, but I were protecting my girl. You'd do the same."

He saw no need to fine Lizzie, much less jail her. "Let's make this simple," he said. "Elsie, you go on home, and tell Hugh next time, it'll be the state pen."

Lizzie's last goodbye could have been nothing but a measured look, for there was nothing to say, but Elsie pushed at Lizzie the papers she'd shoved in her bag. Though Lizzie only knew some of the words, she shuffled through scores of letters, from Docie, Brother JT, Sister Maggie Mae, and even one forwarded from Mattie.

"I reckoned if you knew they'd written, you'd decide to leave," Elsie said.

She might have. Instead she'd worried that nobody had thought of her at all.

Her mother had picked up the mail at the store every week while Lizzie loaded their purchases in the wagon, and never said a word. Lizzie had believed even Docie had carried on fine without her, choosing not to write because she knew Lizzie would struggle to read them. If she'd received them, maybe she would have known Docie was coming, and this night would never have happened. Angry tears soaked the letter, but not before Lizzie pulled Docie close, along with the bundle that carried love she couldn't read but that had reached her anyway.

When the door closed on her ma, the sheriff turned with a questioning glance. It was Sunday now. She reckoned they'd be frantic over Docie at the Home and might answer the telephone in desperation, in spite of the rules, but she wouldn't take chances. She didn't want to wait.

"Sir, can we use your telegraph machine? I got to let our family know my girl's safe."

She wanted to hear Docie's story, why she'd come and whom she'd told. But first she had to ask if they'd allow them back in, though she knew deep inside they would.

The sheriff transmitted her message to the Arlington telegraph office.

DOCIA BATES SAFE WITH ELIZABETH. MAY WE PLEASE RETURN?

No trains would run before morning, but no respectable hotel would receive them now. The sheriff offered the sparsely furnished room behind the desk, where he rested when he worked around the clock. He lived just up the road, and the jailer was on duty all night.

They cleaned up in a small washroom and exchanged their blood-stained garments for clean, and though Lizzie couldn't sleep, Docie dropped off quickly and deeply, her head in Lizzie's lap, her hands grasping Lizzie's. Docie was sixteen, but she was still her baby.

In the morning, the jailer greeted them with strong coffee—which Lizzie gratefully drank, though she would quickly learn to wake without its kick again as soon as she had the privilege—and milk and toast for them to share. On the tray, as well, was their answer:

COME HOME, DAUGHTERS!

On the train, Docie sobbed. "You never answered my letters, and I was afraid you weren't coming back. I was so scared. I had to come find you." Suddenly, she hung her head.

"What is it?" Lizzie said.

"I love my friends and school, but I never want to be away from you again. I love you more than anyone." She wept into Lizzie's shoulder, and though Lizzie knew one day her daughter would be her own person, it spoke to a question Lizzie had long nursed: With so many to mother Docie, did Docie need her at all?

Now she knew nobody could take her place. It humbled her. It filled her with relief.

She patted Docie's back and berated herself for putting her through this absence. "I love you more than anything, my girl. I'm the sorry one. I'm sorry for leaving you."

Docie had convinced a school friend to loan her money and left home Saturday under the pretense of visiting the same friend. She'd left a note for Ivy to find when she didn't show up for supper. She'd arrived without a firm plan for finding Lizzie. A man at the depot told her he was going her way. He was family, you see, and he'd walk her to the house. She'd hesitantly agreed. Once there, she'd dozed off, then woke to him drunk and pawing her. She begged him to leave, praying Lizzie would come soon. She'd started screaming just as they arrived.

Lizzie shushed her. Indeed, she wanted to strangle Docie for lying and coming so far alone—she was lucky Hugh had brought her to the house and not taken her somewhere else. But Docie had suffered more than enough already.

"You mustn't blame yourself," Lizzie said. "Hugh's an evil man. Everything he done is wickedness. It ain't your fault."

Before they pulled into the Arlington depot, Docie told her one last thing. "Mama?" she said. "When that man woke me up, I remembered him. I knew something bad was going to happen. I don't know where, but I'd met him before. I didn't recognize him in the light, but I was sure in the dark."

"What do you remember?" Lizzie said, her heart sinking.

Docie's face shuttered. She shook her head hard. "Just his face. That feeling."

Lizzie felt certain now: One of the times she'd left her daughter alone with her ma, Hugh had gotten to Docie. For this, she blamed herself.

She didn't tell Docie what she guessed he'd done. That was for another time. Maybe.

Instead, she kept her daughter close, even as they stepped off the train and into the arms of Sister Maggie Mae, who drove them to the Home and seemed to know Lizzie needed time before talking. Docie chattered in the back with Miss Ruth, home for her holidays. Docie had such a sure place in *this* life, she could step right back in, still a child in so many ways.

When they reached the archway over the gate, Lizzie looked up and took a whole breath.

Home again.

MEMORANDUM

DATE: January 1, 1918

TO: Mr. Albert Ferry, Printer for the Berachah Rescue Society

CC: Reverend J. T. Upchurch, Founder and Director of the Berachah Industrial Home

FROM: Mrs. Nettie Norwood, Matron of the Berachah Industrial Home

RE: Two items for next issue of *The Purity Journal*

1917 statistics:

- 24 new girls admitted
- 105 refused admittance
- 18 girls and 10 babies dismissed
- 11 babies born
- 2 deaths, one of our young ladies and one baby
- 2 young ladies married
- 39 girls and 21 babies remain

Sister Hallye has returned and would like her poem printed on the front page, along with attached photograph showing the play presented by our girls' literary society on the same subject.

The Prodigal Daughter

BY HALLYE V. TAYLOR

To the Father's home now returning
Is the prodigal weary and worn.
Is she hailed with joy and with pleasure
As she was on her first natal morn?

Oh, no! the poor prodigal daughter
Who has wandered away from her home
With no hand outstretched in fond pity
As she stands all forsaken and lone.

Ah! the man who caused her dire ruin,
And left her to bleed and to die;
Thinks not of the life he has blighted
Nor the answers, to his sins, on High.

But thanks to the Shepherd's great mercy,
That follows His sheep tho' they stray,
Has love and pardon for the prodigal
In His Home at Berachah today.

CATE

Arlington, Texas
2017

After Thanksgiving break, I wait nervously for Laurel to return to work. Her anger over my shutting her out when we returned from Fort Worth was so hot, I'm afraid she won't even show up. But Monday, she's there, as always. Her attitude is cool and polite. I tiptoe around her, closeting myself in my office when I can get away with it. I'm embarrassed by my behavior, but I have no experience in seeking out people when things get tough. I miss Laurel's quiet laughter, our little sarcastic exchanges . . . her excitement when she finds something in the Berachah collection she hasn't seen before.

At the end of the work day, I'm so sad and anxious I consider calling my therapist. I haven't seen Diana since before I moved here, when it seemed she'd done all she could to help me. I was stubborn when it came to some of the things she wanted me to try. She wanted me to journal, but all I could think about was the high school journal my mother discovered. How if a bulldozer hadn't plowed it under yet, it was still buried with River's CD under the rotten floorboards of that old church, a memorial to everything I'd left behind. That journal had been exciting at first, and then a necessity, but finally, just part of the misery I never wanted to revisit.

And my feelings for River were so entangled with everything else that had happened, I didn't even attempt to mend things with her. I didn't think she'd understand.

Now, I realized, I hadn't given her a chance to understand.

Diana thought I needed to unpack my experiences, and I did the best I could—talking. But I refused to write them down. When she released me from care, I'd convinced myself she thought I was "fixed." But looking back on our last session, I realized she simply figured she'd done all she could at that point, and that it would take something bigger to stir me into doing the hardest work. She was right.

After Laurel left that night so furious with me, I went inside my house and experienced a glut of emotions I didn't know how to navigate. Bitterness and sadness, I'm used to, but the sense that I'd finally found a meaningful relationship, and then lost it, is new again.

My feelings for Laurel fall somewhere between maternal—something I've never intended to explore again—and sisterly, as if I've found a younger sister I never knew I wanted. The rest of that weekend, I'd raged at myself, mostly, for being unable to give what she needed, but also at the world, for its double standards, its mixed messages, and the injustice of it all.

By Monday night I'm frantic. I leave a message with Diana's answering service. When my phone rings minutes later, I lunge to answer and immediately burst into tears.

"Hi, Cate," Diana says. "Not trying to be funny, but can I assume you found someone to love?"

I'm stunned into silence, but then I actually laugh through my tears. She knows me well enough that she recognizes my issue before I ever voice it—or maybe she simply knows that I'd never have called if I weren't struggling with allowing someone else in.

But she has no idea how vast this is.

I tell her what's happened. She asks me the requisite questions about my state of mind—No, I don't feel like hurting myself. No, I'm not contemplating suicide. No, I'm not feeling completely hopeless.

Then she says, "Cate, have you considered it might be time to do what we talked about?"

I'm silent.

"Tell you what," she says, "I'm penciling you in for a phone session in ten days—the first free spot I have for nonemergencies. Between now and then, I'd like you to get a journal and write. It doesn't have to be about the past. It can be about the present. It doesn't even have to be feelings. It can be whatever you'd like to write. Empty slate. See where it takes you. It's not the method I'd use for everyone, but my gut says it's right for you. The thing we are most resistant to, sometimes, is the very thing we need to do."

I sigh, but agree to her plan. I promise to call if I decide not to keep the appointment. She has no interest in returning to our old cycle. We'd just get stuck again.

I drive to the drugstore, where I pick out the plainest, least expensive spiral notebook I can find. Wide-ruled, seventy pages. Blue. At home, I gaze at the corner of my sofa, but I reject its comfort in favor of the table. And I put my pen to the page.

Where I begin takes me by surprise, but I repeat Diana's words— *Whatever comes.* My pen picks up speed, and though I pause now and then to sift through everything I've collected in my mind for so long, it surges out of me like a flood. I couldn't stop it if I tried.

MATTIE

Oklahoma City
1918

Mattie hadn't set foot inside the church in months. The boss would have given her Sunday mornings, easy, and the other maids could have used the wages, with nothing to sacrifice beyond a few extra hours of sleep and a lazy afternoon.

But the church had taken her in after her worst sin, and pushed her out for the mildest.

She had returned to the picture shows the very next week after her first time, and every time she had a day off after. Mr. Chaplin was her first love, but she enjoyed them all. She wasn't smoking or drinking or carousing, and most of the shows wouldn't have offended a child—in fact, the audiences were mainly kids. Back when Mattie arrived at the Home, women in their thirties seemed ancient. She knew kids likely thought her ancient now, at nearly thirty-seven, but because she'd never married and worked a simple job, she was still treated like a girl.

One afternoon, as she exited the theater, a church deacon passed by. She knew the rules of her membership and the consequences for breaking them. This would go from his eyes to the deaconesses' ears, and before she knew it, she'd be out.

She was old enough and mature enough to attend a movie without mortal fear for her soul—and frankly, she no longer cared, not even when the committee of three showed up on her doorstep with the accusation and evidence that violated her membership covenant.

She'd expected it, but for fifteen years, church had been her entire social life, and she hadn't expected to miss it—ironic, considering the detachment she'd always felt. When she saw the local sisters now, they still reached to hug her. She kept them at arm's length.

She wasn't bitter—just lonely, until a motherly but irreligious woman took her in.

The irony wasn't lost on her.

The hotel management changed constantly, and with each new one came new policies. Some things were better, some things were worse. She rarely pulled twelve-hour shifts anymore, but she had to pay for her breakfast. She didn't mind. She'd managed to save a little nest egg. A nickel breakfast at the grill next to the hotel wasn't going to send her to the poorhouse any more than movies or coffee would send her to hell.

Mrs. Stella worked the counter at the grill. She learned Mattie's name and greeted her each morning with a coffee—two sugars, splash of milk—a medium-hard egg, and a "Mornin', darlin'!" To Mrs. Stella, customers were family, and over time, she learned more than just Mattie's breakfast order. At some point, she invited her up to her rooms over the grill for a cup after her shift. Mattie was thrilled to have someone to chat with again. She didn't share much about her past. Mrs. Stella didn't push. Anything she did tell her, Mrs. Stella kept to herself, and Mattie began to feel her new life was just what she'd wanted—or close, anyway.

Mattie's letters to Lizzie became sporadic. Lizzie's little notes, messy as ever and nearly impossible to read unless others helped, mentioned how Docie begged to visit, but after the Tyler fiasco, she wasn't sure she'd ever let her travel again. Mattie figured Lizzie would never give Docie permission anyway. It wouldn't be because of the travels or Mattie's little pleasures, but because Lizzie feared for Mattie's soul.

Mattie hadn't been to a Homecoming or Camp Meeting since she'd left, at first because she was too busy and it was expensive to travel. Now she wondered if she'd even be welcome. If she couldn't sit with the congregation because of her membership status, she was better off staying away.

In the meantime, Mrs. Stella made a more than decent substitute. She and Mattie shared a similar sharp humor—what had always caused her trouble in the past. They laughed over the regulars at the grill, or what hotel guests expected as part of Mattie's housekeeping services—the answer being no in nearly every case.

Mrs. Stella's family had lived over the grill nearly since statehood. When the children grew up and moved on, she and her husband took in lodgers. After her husband passed unexpectedly, more lodgers filled the gap. Now four respectable older men rented her extra rooms—two in each, sharing. The rent covered her expenses, but she figured she'd miss the grill if she retired.

The apartment felt like a genuine home, with worn but comfortable furnishings and pictures on the walls. Mattie loved visiting as soon she finished her shift. She regularly helped Mama Stell—as the stout, warm woman soon asked Mattie to call her—get supper on the stove for the "boys," and then they played records on Mama Stell's tabletop Victor Victrola.

Mama Stell couldn't get enough of that. Mattie rewound the machine again and again, and Mama belted along with her favorite, Marion Harris. *"I . . . ain't got nobooooody . . . Nobody's there for meeee . . ."* Mattie swung an invisible partner around the tiny parlor, and Mama Stell laughed until she cried. Other times, Mattie read Mama Stell's beloved Zane Grey and Gene Stratton-Porter novels aloud, as Mama Stell's vision was getting cloudy.

For the first time in more than two decades, Mattie had something close to a regular home life, even if she returned to her small hotel quarters to sleep. Mama Stell depended on her more every week, with legs increasingly lame from holding water, and hands bent from the rheumatism. She couldn't make the stairs without stopping to rest every few, and she took breathers so often at the grill, customers who didn't know her—and even some who did—began to gripe. Mattie had taken to jumping up to bus a table or plate and deliver eggs. With her hotel uniform, customers didn't give it a second thought.

She wouldn't let Mama Stell share her tips. "Hush now," she'd say, as Mama tried to shove a fistful of coins in her pocket. "I eat supper upstairs at your table every night. Why would I take that?"

Mama Stell pulled her close to hug her neck, and Mattie realized how much she missed her own mother. She'd never properly grieved after her death, no time to mourn while she cooked and cleaned in service, too exhausted even to cry herself to sleep. Then Cap came along, and she was a mama herself.

When Mama Stell asked why she didn't have a fella—the one topic she wouldn't leave alone—Mattie shrugged her off.

It wasn't for lack of opportunity. "I see boys in the grill trying to catch your eye," Mama Stell said.

"You're right—they're boys," Mattie said. "I want a certain kind of man, but that kind wouldn't give me a second look."

"You're just not paying attention."

"Maybe I'm just particular."

It was true. As impatient as she'd been to pursue love and adventure when she left the Home, she'd learned that most men assumed a working girl who lived on her own with no real family around would be easy—especially if they knew her history.

Mama Stell's boys—the lodgers—were a nice enough bunch. If she encouraged any of them, she'd have a date in a minute. But when Mattie said she wanted a man, she didn't mean *that* old. Mama Stell was nearing seventy, as were some of the roomers. The youngest was fifteen years or more Mattie's senior. She had set romance aside. She was fine.

One morning, Mattie went for breakfast and work as usual. By noon she felt off. She assumed it was just a little cold, but by the time she made it to her room later, she felt awful. When she didn't show up for coffee, supper, or breakfast the next day, Mama Stell heaved herself four flights to Mattie's room to find her white-faced, shaking, and coughing like crazy.

Mattie needed someone to take care of her, but Mama Stell wasn't sure she could make the trip another time. She'd care for Mattie at her home. Mama Stell informed the hotel manager Mattie would return when she was well—a benefit of union membership, new since Mattie had started work—and two hotel employees helped her get Mattie to her apartment.

Mama Stell put her in her own bed, alternately covering her to her chin or soaking her with cool rags. She fed her warm broth from a straw when Mattie dried out from the vomiting and diarrhea. Mattie was hardly aware of Mama Stell's fussing the first day or so, but by the third day, she was coming back around, and she savored the feeling of being cared for, as if her own mother were there again. The few times she'd been sick at Sister Welch's, Mattie had hacked her way through illness alone in her narrow bed. The woman hadn't been a nurturer.

Her cough lingered—she'd been prone to wheeziness forever—but by the end of a week, she felt well enough to work a half shift. Mattie forced herself into a warm bath and then pulled on her uniform, which hung off her worse than a sack. She'd always had trouble keeping on weight, other than pregnancy, and even then at first, but this was the limit. Her hair was lackluster after rubbing the sheets all week, and her eyes were dull. Illness hit her harder the older she got, but she'd survived.

She promised Mama Stell she'd leave work as soon as she could that afternoon. Mama had given up her room all week, sleeping in her easy chair with a sheet thrown over her. Mattie felt awful keeping her from her bed, but Mama insisted she slept there half the time anyway.

By noon Mattie was exhausted, but optimistic. She'd passed the point of relapse, it seemed, and she felt mentally strong, even if her body protested.

She went up the stairs to the apartment. When she opened the door, Mama Stell was asleep in her easy chair, but her head lolled far to one side.

Mattie had seen the screaming headlines about the deadly new influenza as she made her way to work. *La Grippe*, they called it, or the Spanish flu. Soldiers overseas were dying in droves, with more fatalities from flu than combat, and it had finally hit home. The list of symptoms fit. So many cases had been reported in OKC by now, the paper issued warnings encouraging people to stay home, sick or not, and avoid public spaces. The schools had closed, and congregating in groups was prohibited until the epidemic passed.

Most terrifyingly, she'd read that it hit with no mercy and could kill overnight. She'd been lucky. But now she rushed to Mama Stell's side, who half opened her eyes, blearily smiling. "I'll be fine, darlin', just having a little rest. I'm not feeling so well."

Mattie stripped her wrinkled sheets from the bed. Mama Stell had used her best ones for Mattie. The second set was patched and nearly worn through.

She helped Mama Stell to the bedroom and spent the rest of the afternoon and all night nursing her, as Mama had done for her. She held her head when she vomited, and boiled water in the kettle to steam the room when Mama Stell struggled to breathe.

The next morning Mama Stell seemed improved. One of the lodgers had the day off, and he promised to fetch Mattie if she worsened again. On her break, Mattie ran to check on her. In the street, she froze. Two men carried a stretcher down the stairs from Mama Stell's apartment toward an ambulance at the curb, a figure huddled beneath the sheet. A third man was posting a placard in the stairwell. She saw the word in black capital letters: *QUARANTINE.*

"I live there!" she said. She *had* lived there, all last week. "What's happened?" The lodger who had promised to keep an eye on Mama Stell was nowhere to be seen. "She was better this morning!" she said to the man posting the sign. "Is she going to the hospital?"

She tried to push past him, and he held her arms. "Ma'am, you can't go up. The man who called us must stay inside until the danger passes. We're taking her away. I'm very sorry."

He gestured to the ambulance, and she read the words on the side. *City Morgue.*

Mama Stell was not worse. She was dead.

Mattie fled, afraid they'd learn she'd been the one to pass the flu.

She worried about the lodgers still at work, where they'd go tonight, and where they'd live with Mama Stell gone—and about Pat

Madigan, the lodger inside the apartment alone. She ignored the placard and carried food to the door and knocked. Pat called out. He was
well. She left food on the mat until the quarantine passed.

This time, she had time and room to mourn. She woke each
morning with her pillowslip soaked in tears she hadn't even known
she'd cried. She hadn't realized how much she'd come to love Mama
Stell, or how comforting it had been to have someone who cared for
her too.

Mama Stell's sons claimed her body and buried her without delay
next to her husband—formal funerals were a luxury now with so
many deaths in the city. Mattie chose not to impose in their time of
grief—not to mention her guilt at spreading the deadly flu to their
mother. She sent a simple sympathy note. A few weeks later, one asked
for her at work. They'd packed what they wanted from the apartment.
His mother had frequently mentioned Mattie, and he was sure she'd
want her to take anything she wanted that remained.

Mattie wandered the formerly homey space—now musty from
being closed up for weeks. The other lodgers had come for their belongings. Pat intended to leave the next day.

Mama Stell's sons had removed few of the shabby furnishings and
household goods. The pictures on the walls were out of style. They'd
taken a few personal effects—family documents and photographs—
and of course, the Victrola, but had left a few records and all the penny
novels Mama Stell had collected. Mattie began to pile those into a carton, but then her hands slowed.

The apartment had become her home. She'd saved enough to pay a
deposit and several months' rent in advance. And she was tired. Tired
of the hotel. Tired of cleaning up after guests who left rubbish strewn
about as if they had no proper upbringing, mud from their shoes on
the carpets, and hardly ever a tip.

Pat, too, seemed unsure where he'd go next.

"Would you stay if you could?" she asked.

He looked up, startled. She'd rarely spoken to him when Mama
Stell was alive.

"I could take it over," she said. "And the job at the grill, too, if they'll have me." Nearly everything had shut down while the flu gripped the city. She doubted they'd hired a replacement yet.

Pat, who'd worked as a track man for the railroad for years, was homely and rough mannered but didn't require much. He reminded Mattie of Lizzie in some ways.

"You wouldn't raise the rent on me?"

"Not if you help me fill the rooms again."

"Hard to find a place this nice even when there ain't an epidemic on. Two are still looking."

Mattie ran downstairs, fast, where Mama Stell's son was collecting his mother's final wages from the cantankerous owner. "Have you hired anyone new yet?" she said, gasping for breath.

The owner shook his head. "Flu's not good for business. Everyone's afraid to get out."

"Would you hire me?" she said. "And can I take over the apartment?"

Mr. Gaston's eyes were wary, but then they relaxed. "You're that lady always jumping up to help Mrs. Stella."

She nodded. At least he'd called her a lady. "I already know the regulars."

"Why, sure, I could use you," he said. His eyes narrowed again. "I'd have to raise the rent on the flat. I ain't raised it in years. Hated to do it to Mrs. Stella."

"How much?" she said.

"Well, she gave ten a month. I'd need at least eighteen."

"Will you take fifteen?" Mattie said.

He contemplated her shrewdly. They both knew it was fair. "Start Monday?"

"Yes. And I want a telephone," she said. "I'll pay the bill if you put it in."

A telephone might have saved Mama Stell—likely not, but Mattie would always wonder.

The owner shrugged. "All right then. You don't have kids, do you? I don't want youngsters tearing up my apartment."

"No," she said, though it always hurt and brought up conflicting emotions to say so. "I'll be taking lodgers, like Mrs. Stella." The whole neighborhood was rooming houses and hotels.

"You drive a hard bargain," Mr. Gaston said. "Make sure you get good, clean folks. Nothing under the counter, and no funny business, you hear?"

Mattie shook her head furiously. "Of course not."

He rolled his eyes. This wasn't his only building, and the area kept going down.

Mama Stell's son said, "My ma would have vouched for her. She loved her like a daughter." Mattie choked back tears to hear that Mama Stell had spoken of her so kindly.

"First, last, and fifteen for the deposit, due by five p.m. or I'll give it to someone else."

"You'll have it in thirty minutes," she said, calmly, though she fought to keep from jumping up and down or hugging the man—as grumpy as he was.

In two hours, she'd paid the rent, quit her hotel position—easy once they found out she'd had the flu—and carried her possessions to the apartment. Most still fit in the trunk she'd brought to Oklahoma eight years earlier. Pat tracked down the lodgers and proposed a dollar more per month. They agreed. Soon a new man showed up, who paid more than the old-timers.

She was at the counter early Monday, with coffee percolating and smiles. Behind it all, she grieved—especially when someone asked about Mama Stell.

"Retired."

People didn't like to hear about the flu, and Mattie didn't like to talk about it.

Before long, she was at the grill as much as the counter. Mr. Gaston recognized a good cook—each time she returned an order, she explained to the newish fry cook what he'd done wrong. As she climbed the stairs at the end of the week, she smiled. She'd always wanted to cook in a fancy hotel. Well, this was no fancy hotel, but it was her hotel, of sorts, and she spent her days cooking. Life could be worse. She felt content. On top of that, happy—more or less.

La Grippe eventually loosened its deadly claw, the city schools and theaters reopened, and within a month the armistice had finally been signed. The war was over and for the first time in years, positive headlines overshadowed the gloom.

MATTIE

Oklahoma City
1920–1921

Mattie had run her little rooming house for more than a year. Two roomers left and two more replaced them. She'd earned enough at the grill to replace the Victrola and records Mama Stell's son had taken, but she had little time or energy for picture shows now. Pat gradually took over as Mattie's sounding board, though he didn't take kindly to her calling him Old Man, as Mama Stell had done.

Her chief complaint was Mr. Gaston. She didn't know how Mama Stell had tolerated his nastiness. The customers loved Mattie's cooking, but he complained she used too much lard in the biscuits, too many peaches in the pie, too much sugar to dress up cheap coffee. "You prefer customers who complain when their coffee makes them cry?" she said. He harrumphed.

She'd often complain to Pat when he returned from his work repairing and replacing train tracks that ran through the city. He never grumbled, though she knew it was much harder work than hers. One evening, over dinner, he claimed he had a solution.

"Right," she said. "You know I can't quit."

"You can if you marry me."

Mattie shut up for a change. She gawked at his face. Was he fooling around or serious? But he wasn't a joker. She'd made so many jokes about his age, she couldn't believe he'd think she had any interest in marrying him.

"You and me get married, and I can help you more with the rent, and you can quit working for that bastard."

Mattie's incredulity turned to laughter. "Oh, Pat, honey. You're the sweetest. But you don't want to marry me." She jumped up to carry their plates to the sink. The other lodgers had already cleared out, for they ate fast and went to bed early, with jobs that had them out at the crack of dawn—and no energy for Mattie's chatter anyway. She paused to squeeze Pat's shoulder. "You *are* my favorite. But I'm not marrying you."

He pushed his chair back. From the hallway, he called gruffly, "Change your mind, the offer stands."

Mattie sat in Mama Stell's old chair, her breath suddenly stolen. She'd been short of breath more often since the flu, but this was different. Her first proposal of marriage at nearly forty, and the man was at least twenty years older, laid track for a living—not that she was a snob—and had asked her to marry him across a plate of chipped beef.

All because she needed extra money.

She felt dirty, as if Pat wanted to buy a wife. She wasn't desperate. She'd take Mr. Gaston's abuse—with no more complaining at the dinner table.

But Pat surprised her the next evening with a paper poke of daisies held shyly behind his back, and again on Sunday, when he offered to escort her to a picture show at the theater across the street. She said yes—though she insisted on buying her own ticket. When he placed his rough hand over hers in the dark, she didn't shrug it off. It was unsettlingly warm. Pleasant.

A month later, on a Friday, he proposed again, this time over a chicken dinner downtown. He said he'd marry Mattie even if she wanted to keep working for that bastard—it wasn't about the money. So she said yes.

The next afternoon, Mattie married Patrick Madigan. They rode a train north to Guthrie; Pat said the city courthouse was crowded on Saturdays.

On the application, he recorded their ages. Mattie's, forty—thirty-eight really, but she didn't correct him—and she peeked across his shoulder as he wrote sixty in the other blank. Two decades between them. Ten minutes later, two clerks witnessed the justice of the peace solemnizing their marriage.

Pat had arranged for the other lodgers to be away for the evening. The guys had shuffled off, offering their clumsy wishes when Pat announced their intent to marry.

Mattie had no time to purchase a pretty nightgown, but while Pat used the bathroom, she turned down the covers, leaving on her nicest chemise instead of wearing the old, mended one that served as her summer gown.

Pat had removed his shirt. His suspenders still held up his baggy trousers, and his undershirt showed white hair peeking out on his chest, springy and at odd angles. His arms were tanned below his elbows, with muscles more defined than one would expect from a man his age. His heavy work kept him in shape.

Mattie sat on the side of the bed, but he remained awkwardly in the middle of the floor. "You know you ain't married a spring chicken," he said. "Hope you ain't expecting much."

Mattie laughed. "Oh, Pat, it's just me. Come here. If we're going to be married, we're going to do it properly."

She was sure she was as nervous as he was. It had been nearly twenty years since she'd been with a man, and she'd tried hard to forget everything about the last time and what it had led to. She'd trusted Mama Stell with some of her history over time, but never that, and Mattie would never tell Pat—not even about Charley and Cap . . . or any of the rest—unless she had to. She'd written and sealed a letter with instructions for if she died, and she'd tell Pat where it was. But for all he knew of her, he could be deflowering an aging virgin—though she didn't think she came across as a prude, even if quiet. Now and then, they'd pass one of her old church acquaintances on the street, and she'd politely say hello. But sometimes, they caught her arm and she couldn't avoid a brief catch-up. He seemed amused that she'd been a missionary of sorts—and relieved that was over.

All she really knew of him, beyond the stability she witnessed every day, was that he'd been married before. Maybe widowed. If he was divorced, she didn't want to know any more than he'd want to hear about her buried past.

Pat sat now, and she pushed at him gently.

He rolled to the far edge. She switched off the lamp.

The fumbling that followed was unlike anything she'd expected. She'd expected haste, without much to-do. That was what her limited experience had taught her. If she'd still been a virgin, though, Pat would not have known. After he stubbornly refused to harden, he rolled away, silent. Mattie lay awake until dawn, waiting for him to stir, thinking they might try again.

He never moved.

At breakfast, he said, "Guess I'm too old after all." He glared into his coffee cup as she slid eggs onto his plate from the fry pan.

"Guess we'll have to work on it," she said. "Maybe we're just out of practice."

He shrugged and pulled the newspaper closer and turned to the sport scores. "Maybe so."

Mattie stirred cream into her coffee and swirled it around at the top of the mug.

It never really got better.

One day after work, while Mattie cleaned house, she shuffled through an envelope full of dated paperwork she found in Pat's dresser drawer. She pulled one closer—a yellowed Peoria, Pekin, and Jacksonville Railroad employee identification card with Pat's name and signature.

From 1873.

If he'd been sixty when they married in June, he would have been thirteen when it was issued. He'd mentioned working for the railroad in Illinois in his past, but thirteen seemed awfully young. She flipped over the card. It listed additional information, including his age at the time of issuance—Twenty-three years old.

If that card was correct, Pat was not a day under seventy now.

Twenty years between them suddenly expanded to thirty, and Mattie's anger like hot air. If he'd lied about his age, what else might he have been less than honest about?

After dinner, Mattie said, "How old are you, Patrick Madigan?"

He scratched his Adam's apple, his eyes rolled back as if doing the arithmetic.

"Seventy. You are seventy years old."

He didn't deny it. She thrust the identification card at him. "You wrote sixty on the wedding license."

He began drawing circles on his plate with the tines of his fork. "Figured you'd think I was too old for marrying. And you'd probably have figured right. But I did want to marry you."

She dropped her head onto her fist. Neither of them could do anything about it now, of course. But the joke was on her.

She felt lucky she had not quit the grill. She'd added up her savings, and decided she could put up with Mr. Gaston a while longer, in case Pat was not in as good of health as he appeared. Of course, Pat could die from old age before he died from failing health. But he could also live another twenty years. She'd made her bed. She would lie in it, as securely as possible.

Pat was a homebody. After his long workweeks—and at his age—Mattie guessed she couldn't blame him, but she was stir crazy. She convinced him to take the trolley to the county fair that had mounted at the edge of town.

They arrived in time for the air show, then wandered through the exhibits. Pat grumbled all afternoon, claiming he hated crowds and felt suffocated everywhere they walked. He refused to enter the vaudeville tents.

Weary of arguing, she resolved to get a snack and then board the trolley home. While she waited on the midway for roasted pecans, Pat kept his back to the wall of the exposition hall, arms across his chest, as if someone might pick his pocket if he didn't guard it. The line moved slowly, and she half worried he'd leave before she returned.

Young couples strolled past her, hand in hand, dreamy-eyed. For a minute, a person could believe romance was real. But she'd decided romance was a sham—and mostly a matter of convenience.

Suddenly, her eye was drawn by a flurry of motion. A woman stood before Pat, small and hunched and much older than Mattie. Pat's face froze in apparent shock, maybe even fear. The woman pointed at Mattie, and Mattie shrank, almost reflexively. She had nothing to be ashamed of, but this woman seemed to think so. She scowled, though her eyes sagged, more weary than anything. But then—*whack!*—she slapped Pat's cheek, leaving him reeling as if she'd knocked him off balance. She stalked away, casting a nasty glare at Mattie. Mattie was nearly at the front of the line but hurried to Pat. He was doubled over, hands on his knees and breathing hard.

She grasped his arm and straightened him up, then brushed him off, as if he had fallen. "Pat, what did that woman want? Why did she sock you?"

It seemed obvious, but she wanted to hear it from Pat.

"Guess I didn't leave things off very good. She's jealous. Forget it."

Jealous? Mattie wondered. Pat wasn't exactly a catch, even if steady in everything he did—or did not—do. If she'd known he had someone else, she would have told him to move along. But what could she do now? They were married.

They rode the trolley home in silence. Pat glanced at her now and then. Silence was not her gift, but at this point she had nothing more to say and nothing more to ask. She didn't really want to know.

Mattie stewed until she realized she'd lose her mind. It felt as if she'd be stuck with Pat forever, but she couldn't waste all the good years she had left being bitter.

At the Home, they'd taught the girls civics. The church took civic duties seriously, but Mattie had never been one to get involved in politics. The Nazarenes permitted women to preach and teach, so naturally, they thought they should have the vote, but she'd mostly looked past the suffragettes who came around the hotel and grill early on. They'd wanted Mama Stell to post placards at the counter. Mr. Gaston had put his foot down, but even without their participation, Oklahoma had passed women's suffrage in '18, right in the midst of the

Spanish Flu epidemic—and right when Mama Stell died—though the governor had kept the vote secret for weeks before it came to public notice. The national amendment was ratified around the time Mattie learned about Pat's age. In both cases, she'd been too blanketed in self-pity to care.

Labor unions had made big inroads in OKC, more each year, and the hotel and restaurant employees local of the national union was gaining a stronger foothold in the area recently. In February, the treasurer came by the grill. He invited her to their meetings, held nearly every Monday evening, with a special visit by the mayor coming up the next week. Mattie nodded and smiled, with no intention of going. She'd always paid her dues as a matter of conscience, aware the union rules had saved her skin a few times at the hotel.

But Monday, she left a stew simmering and a note: *Gone to union meeting. Serve yourselves.*

The meeting was at eight—who in a union of so many cooks and waiters could have attended if it fell at the supper hour?

Downtown, she wandered, amused at how daring she'd felt walking alone all those years ago when she'd just arrived. She could hold her own anywhere now. Who was left to fuss?

She arrived at the hall a half hour early. It was decorated for the mayor's appearance, with refreshments laid out on several tables. She spotted familiar faces with relief. Her world had shrunk since marrying Pat—down to her lodgers and regulars at the grill.

A woman she'd worked with at the hotel pulled her into a group discussing who was hiring and who was firing. Mattie had little in common with these women anymore. When the meeting began, Jeanette waved her up front to sit with them, but she shook her head. She'd leave soon. Breakfast started early at the grill.

She remembered that the young girl next to her had worked in the hotel laundry. She'd been fifteen when Mattie quit—too young to work so hard. But it was the way for many. It had been for Mattie.

"Hey, honey," she said, "what's new?"

Nora smiled and shrugged. At seventeen, she'd matured into a pretty thing, her thick, shiny hair pulled into a braided bun, her skin like china except for her hands—red and rough, the dead giveaway for a laundry girl, along with the perfume of detergent and starch.

"Still at the hotel?" Mattie lowered her voice as the press secretary ascended the podium.

"For now," Nora said. "My ma married a man with a laundry. I'll go to work for him soon. Came because I like the cookies—and getting out of the house."

Mattie couldn't argue. "Which laundry?"

"Edward's, off Robinson."

"Really?" Mama Stell had used Henry's for years, but lately the sheets came back with spots, and the towels smelled off. "Suppose they'd give me a good deal?"

The girl nodded. "Sure. Come by in a week or two. I'll tell them I know you."

They quieted for the secretary's report. The biggest news was a warrant on the treasurer. He'd left town, taking the money with him. Mattie gasped along with the rest. The man had seemed so trustworthy when he'd come by the grill.

Next, the mayor spoke. The local government was in a battle with businesses that wouldn't allow their employees to organize. He presented the union's international labor organizer, in town for the meeting, with a Kodak camera to show the city's appreciation.

Mattie intended to leave after the speeches, but the refreshments were compelling—sandwiches, cake and ice cream, prepared by someone else's hands. She hadn't eaten ice cream in a month of Sundays, and extra fat never haunted her skinny frame.

There was fruit punch, but the drinks table offered another choice: beer. She'd never had even a sip. Pat wasn't a teetotaler, but they didn't keep alcohol in the house. She couldn't live without coffee these days, but she'd never had the desire to take up drinking, even after the church took her off the membership rolls.

She glanced around, as if someone might stop her after all, and then selected a glass, balancing it alongside her sandwich and cake. She found her hotel friends again and was happy to see she wasn't the only woman with beer. Her first sip made her pucker. But after a few bites of sandwich, it improved. Better than Oklahoma water for sure. She finished the glass with her sandwich, and another washing down cake.

She felt exactly the same as always. She'd seen enough drunks to know what that looked like. As the hour passed, she relaxed in the company of other women as they laughed and passed stories of work and family.

When Mattie rose to leave, Jeanette offered to walk her. It was only a few blocks. "Don't leave on my account," Mattie said.

"Honey, you're three sheets to the wind."

Mattie had no idea what she meant. She shrugged.

"You're drunk!" Jeanette laughed. "No wonder. You were always a church girl, right? I mean, a real serious one."

Mattie didn't feel drunk. "Not anymore. And I'm fine." She covered a hiccup.

"I'd never let you go alone like this. You'd be on your face on the sidewalk."

Mattie shrugged again, still hiccupping. She could tell she was wobbly now that she was on her feet. Jeanette grabbed her elbow as they left the building. A man fell into step with them.

"That's my cousin Jim. He's a good guy. Works down Reno from the Liberty. He'll see us home."

Mattie ogled him, tilting her head around Jeanette. She winked. "Thank ya, Jimbo," she called, mimicking the mayor's jovial tone. "You're a real gent!"

Jim chuckled but kept his distance. He was a looker. And he did seem like a gentleman. He'd caught Mattie's eye a few times before and after the meeting, when he'd talked nearby with Jeanette's husband. She'd wondered why he'd looked at a woman like her, practically middle-aged and plain as fruit punch, when lots of prettier—and younger—girls had filled the hall. He could have his pick. She sighed loudly and concentrated on keeping her steps from veering too far left or right.

By the time they reached their block, the cool February air had knocked some sense into her, and her earlier boldness had passed. Thank goodness Jeanette had taken her in hand.

Jim watched from the corner until they reached Mattie's stairs. What would he think if he knew she was a married woman? She'd *winked* at him. But it wouldn't matter. She'd never show her face at the local again. The others were certainly laughing at her now.

Upstairs, she let herself inside. They'd begun locking up recently. Mama Stell had never locked the door, but Pat thought they ought to. The neighborhood was going down.

He was asleep in Mama Stell's chair—she could never bring herself to call it anything else. She'd wondered if she could stand to keep it, knowing from Pat that her surrogate mother had drawn her last breath in it. Mattie avoided it at first, but one evening, she'd collapsed in it, worn out, and it embraced her like a big hug from Mama. The chair had stayed.

Pat startled at the sound of her turning the lock behind her. She'd fumbled, her coordination off. "Who's that?" he said, his voice gruff. He struggled up from the chair, squinting. She reached to kiss his cheek, even though things were cool between them.

Pat grasped her arms and held her off. "Good God, woman, you smell like a bread factory!" Her face flushed, and she hung her head. Recognition dawned on his face. "Union local meeting, huh? You've been to the local bar, that's what." He pushed her away. "Get to bed. We'll discuss this in the morning."

Her face went hotter. He had no right to speak this way. "You may be old enough to be my father, but you will not say what I can and cannot do."

Pat leaned his face close to hers. "You're my wife. That means I can. I won't have you sneaking around and drinking—and on a *Monday.*" He scoffed.

"Because you're my husband?" Mattie allowed the words to linger between them.

He stalked to the bedroom. She slept in Mama Stell's chair. It was still warm from Pat's nap, but that wasn't what she took from it.

The next morning, he left for work without a word. Over supper, she apologized for coming home smelling of booze and assured him she'd only tried beer the first time. She acknowledged it was completely out of character. But she'd enjoyed the social setting, and intended to attend again, even if it meant the others would tease her about the night. She promised not to drink.

The next week, he observed her departure with tense shoulders and wary eyes. She knew what worried him. Not the beer.

If she made new friends, she might not need him at all.

CATE

Arlington, Texas
2017

Between writing in my notebooks—more than one now—I work, eat now and then, and sleep when I'm exhausted. When my appointment day arrives, I leave Diana a message. She calls to check in, and I tell her I can't stop. She's not surprised. "Call me when you're finished."

I keep going.

The day the semester ends, I hesitate as Laurel leaves work. I'm tempted to go after her, but I don't. I check the housing website to reassure myself the dorms are open even through the long holidays. Five whole weeks. I'm not a person she needs right now.

Not yet.

Except, after I've been off work five days, and I haven't left my apartment other than picking up microwavable food—and additional notebooks—my doorbell rings, startling me where I sit near three filled notebooks, with another half full in front of me.

I consider ignoring the bell, but there's been a spate of recent burglaries. Through the peephole, I see Laurel. Her hands are jammed inside her pockets, and she looks so nervous I worry something's wrong. I have to answer. Of course I do. I glance at my notebooks. I'm not ready to share these, not with anyone. I call, "Just a minute," then stuff them inside my work tote.

"Hi," I say, when I answer the door, cautiously. Hopefully.

"Don't say anything," she says. "Let me talk."

I nod. I wasn't planning to, though my heart races with concern.

"I shouldn't have called you a hypocrite," she said. "I'm sorry."

"Oh, honey," I say, shaking my head. "You were so right. But I'm learning. I'm trying anyway."

"Well, that's all I wanted to say." She stands there, her arms crossed over her chest, over that same old ratty T-shirt, as if she isn't sure where else to put them.

But I know what to do with them. I grab her elbows, gently, and tug. "Come in. We have things to talk about."

She starts crying before she hugs me. "I missed you."

"I missed you, too," I say, hugging her right back. "And Laurel? I'm so thankful you're more mature than I am." And just like that, our laughter overtakes our tears.

I microwave two frozen dinners. Laurel claims they taste better than what she's been eating all week. I make a mental note to ask about that later.

I tell her to prepare herself, that this story is going to take time. And I warn her it may surprise her, might even make her nervous. I'm not sure how she'll feel when I tell her about River. Will she think I'm creepy? That I have ulterior motives? A woman my age, with my history, befriending a younger one? Is that normal? I don't know. It's all new territory.

I should have known better. Laurel is a product of her generation. She has friends who have been in same-sex relationships since middle school—with many, if not most of them, certain of their orientation since they were old enough to experience first crushes. It's still not easy, she says. Parents get upset. Kids get kicked out. And few of them go to church, because churches, in general, are still bastions of judgment masquerading as refuges of grace and acceptance.

Few of her peers believe these preferences are perverted or wrong—at least not openly—or that sexual orientation is a matter of choice. Why would anyone intentionally choose to love differently, she says, knowing they could be shunned for it? And why would anyone choose the inevitable prejudice or heartache if the alternative was their natural instinct?

Eventually, I tell Laurel I have no idea if I consider myself a lesbian. I haven't let myself think about loving anyone for years, and that word, *lesbian,* somehow still sounds dirty inside my mind because that's how it was said when I was growing up—with a lowered voice, as if the word alone were contagious.

Mostly, though, I'm not sure I would have felt differently had River been a boy.

Laurel shrugs. "Maybe," she says, "you just like people. You love who you love."

Her wisdom stuns me. In the midst of my angst over how to label my own feelings, I'd never found the words to describe them so aptly. She may have hit the nail on the head. I don't know. I'm not sure it matters. Things have changed since 1999. And in many ways, they have not. Listening to this eighteen-year-old sage, though, gives me hope.

We stay up late into the night, me sharing the rest of my story, a little bit at a time. As expected, Laurel is filled with righteous indignation over what happened with Seth—and over what happened later, with the pastors and my parents. She's not surprised, though. I didn't think she would be. She's lived through a few unbelievable episodes herself.

Ultimately, I can't bring myself to tell Laurel what happened after I left Grissom. Laurel being Laurel, she doesn't ask. She knows as much as I do how deeply personal some choices can be, and how deeply heartbreaking.

By midnight, we're both exhausted. I ask if she needs to get back to the dorm. I don't want to push.

She gives me a look, and I show her to her room.

MATTIE

Oklahoma City
1921

Mattie couldn't wait for Mondays. The weeks dragged and the meetings flew. She'd eaten crow until her union acquaintances forgot her beer baptism. In retrospect, she didn't like the loss of control—not to mention, if a few light beers made her silly, no telling what she'd do fully drunk.

Nora, the little laundry girl, had switched jobs but planned to attend as long as her stepfather allowed it. Mattie lugged the sheets and towels over to Edward's. Nora pulled Mattie's bundle across and dumped it in a weighing bin. While she wrote the ticket, a man came from the back office. He squeezed Nora's shoulder. "Good job, doll. I like how many new customers we're getting since we put you to work."

Nora visibly shrank as he held on a second too long. He winked at Mattie as he swaggered away and stuck his cigar back in his mouth. She wrinkled her nose. Smoke was everywhere, but she didn't want her fresh laundry coming back stinking of cigars. She'd give Edward's a try, but so far it wasn't promising. She didn't like how he treated Nora—she could tell in a minute—and he wasn't as old as she'd pictured.

"Your stepdad lots younger than your ma?" she said.

Nora nodded, listing items under her breath. Then she looked up. Her eyes betrayed her. "What was Mama thinking? He's trouble."

Mattie sighed. "Listen, I doubt I need to tell you—you're a smart girl—but you watch out. Don't be alone with him if you can help it."

"I don't like him, but I already warned him off."

"Uh-huh," Mattie said. "Well, you know, the Liberty's just down the street. They'd hire you back if you asked nicely. And if you need anything, I'm up the stairs over Gaston's."

Nora's mouth lifted, just one side. "I'll be fine. It's my mother I'm worried about."

"Even so." Nora handed her the ticket, and Mattie patted her hand.

July's meeting at the local focused on the Labor Day parade. Heat and humidity had settled over the city like a bad attitude, and any distraction was welcome. Every year, the unions nominated women for queen of the parade. Votes purchased at the joint unions office raised money for the festivities and determined the winner. Whichever union raised the most followed the queen's float, which carried the runners-up as well. Every woman on it received a beautiful white dress, and this year, a sponsor had donated a diamond ring as grand prize.

Mattie thought Nora was so cute she'd be a shoo-in, and she mentioned it to the group. But Nora said she'd never have the guts to stump for votes—and her stepfather wouldn't approve. Mattie understood. She couldn't imagine begging for votes just to ride in the float.

Suddenly, her friends got her attention and pointed toward the front of the room.

"Mrs. Madigan? Do you accept?" the president said.

She looked at Jeanette. "What does he want?"

"Secretary Weyrich just nominated you for the float!" she said, eyes as wide as Mattie's.

"Why, I . . ." Mattie said, everything flushing worse in the heat.

What was the guy thinking? There were plenty of young, pretty women; no reason to nominate a woman her age. But then the secretary's voice captured her attention from the side of the podium. "Mrs. Mattie B. Madigan is a shining example of what organized labor can do for our citizens. She worked for years in a hotel, and now she runs a restaurant and her own small hotel. She's proven that fair labor standards—and hard work—can lift a person up." He looked straight at Mattie. "You're perfect to represent us."

They'd hardly interacted beyond a brief introduction at the first meeting she'd attended. She didn't think he'd have known her on the street. But he looked at the crowd and shouted, "She's a pretty one too! A real Irish beauty."

The women clapped and several men whistled. Mattie laughed, shaking her head. To her knowledge, she hadn't a lick of Irish except her last name—and it belonged to Pat.

"Mattie B. Madigan! The Irish Princess of the Culinary Alliance!" the president called, and Mattie's friends elbowed her onto her feet. "Do we have a second? All in favor, say aye!"

Mattie threw her hands up. She'd been overruled.

She spent the rest of the evening flustered, embarrassed, and flattered, all at the same time. After the meeting adjourned, she caught her friends whispering. One pointed at Mattie and then at the tall, slim man quietly gazing at her from a huddle at the side of the hall. It was Jim McBride, Jeanette's cousin. He'd been chaperoning them safely to the corner every single Monday, and he'd never brought up her drunken flirting. In fact, he rarely said much at all. He walked at a slight remove, hands in his pockets, while she and Jeanette chatted all the way home.

Mattie turned to Jeanette. "What's everyone whispering about? Why are you pointing at Jim?"

"We have it on good authority that my cousin threw your name in the hat and Mr. Weyrich concurred. I guess Jim's been paying attention when we walk home."

Mattie's face flamed. Indeed, the only way he'd know the details Mr. Weyrich had mentioned was by eavesdropping on her and Jeanette—or asking nosy questions around the neighborhood. To her knowledge, he'd never been inside Gaston's.

He looked over his shoulder and caught her eye. She froze, but he simply nodded with a smile—and oh, how those teeth flashed.

Walking home that evening, if Jeanette hadn't been talking a mile a minute, it would have been awkwardly silent, for Mattie was tongue-tied but desperately curious. It wasn't as if she could confront him outright. At their street corner, she spoke loudly—enough to send Jim McBride a strong message, she hoped. "My husband will certainly be surprised!"

Pat was unhappy. Mattie expected nothing less. But as a member of the local, it was her duty, she said, and she'd had nothing to do with it.

She didn't disclose her backer—and certainly not the ridiculous nickname. Mr. Weyrich dropped off an advertising placard she dutifully propped by the cash drawer. She practically dared Mr. Gaston to argue, for if nothing else, it drew extra business. Folks wanted a look at the mysterious "Irish Princess"—most likely the competition. But their money spent too.

Mr. Weyrich advised canvassing to introduce herself to waiters and cooks, maids and laundry girls on their breaks. After an excruciating start, she found a rhythm. She made light of her age and so-called Irish ancestry, playing it up with a wink, then explained that votes were for the good of the unions, to make the parade and festivities bigger and better than ever. Every penny spent at the joint unions office meant a hundred votes in her favor—and the membership enrollment cards she carried were convenient too.

The worst misery was the late-afternoon heat. Each day she conked out in Mama Stell's chair before she started supper. Pat caught her a few times. "These men aren't paying for you to sleep all afternoon and feed them leftovers, girl. Get up and make supper."

After the fair the previous fall, Mattie couldn't imagine Pat taking any interest in the parade. She dreaded convincing him to let her go unattended. She'd never expected a jealous streak from his mild manners before they married.

Naturally, someone reported Mr. McBride's hand in the nomination—one of the fellows Pat worked with was married to someone who heard about it, and so on, until it got back to him. She'd brushed it off. "I hardly know him. He walks Jeanette and me home, but rarely speaks. I was never so surprised. If it bothers you, maybe you should come and walk me home."

That lasted a week. Pat was exhausted after work. A single night waiting outside the local to walk her home had been more than enough. He told her to mind herself, and no dawdling at the corner with that man. She never dawdled and had no intention starting. But she remembered the woman at the fair. It was awfully easy to assume the worst of someone when you'd been guilty of it yourself.

One day, Nora stopped by the grill. The Liberty had refused to rehire her. Pressed for a reason, the manager said someone reported she might come looking, and he thought they ought to know she was trouble. They shouldn't even give her a reference. The description fit her stepfather's.

Nora's eyes were red and swollen. Mattie came around the counter and put her arm around the girl's thin shoulders. "What am I going to do?" Nora's voice was weary, as if she'd given up already.

"Is he bothering you?"

Nora shrugged. "He gives me looks I don't like. Mama says I'm standoffish and he just wants to be friends. He takes it out on her when I upset him, so she says to not make trouble. I thought it would be easier to go back to the hotel."

The hair on Mattie's arms stood up. Nora had been lucky—so far. Mattie hadn't taken her laundry back to Edward's after that first week. Now she felt guilty she hadn't checked in.

"You have your own room?"

"Yes."

"Keep your door locked at night, you hear? If anyone rattles it, holler, *loud*. You can always tell your mother you thought a stranger was trying to get in." Mattie shuddered to imagine the tension.

Nora's eyes filled again. "I don't know what I'll do if it gets worse. I'm afraid of what he'll do if I can't keep him out. I have nowhere to go."

"Do you have family anywhere else?"

The girl shook her head. "Mama was an only child. Everyone else is gone."

She was in the path of a storm, with ample warning to evacuate—but nowhere to go.

Mattie wished she could take the girl herself, but Pat would never agree. They'd let the rooms to men only from the start, and it had probably saved them more than a few headaches.

But Mama Stell had taken Mattie in, the minute she needed help.

And then died for it.

Mattie made Nora promise she'd find her, any time of day, if things got worse. She'd figure something out. That night, she called Lizzie. It cost her—she'd saved to buy a little camera, and had thought to do so before the parade. But it had been ages since they'd spoken, and this was more important than a camera. She'd written with news of her marriage but hadn't bothered since. Things between her and Pat were too awkward to merit updating.

Lizzie lived in the workers' cottage now, and nearly screamed when she heard Mattie's voice after the operator connected them. "You terrible girl!" she cried, laughing. "You never write anymore! What's wrong?"

"Nothing's wrong." Mattie wouldn't start with bad news. "You'll never believe this, though. . . ." She told Lizzie about the union, editing out what she knew Lizzie wouldn't approve and saving the parade news for last. Lizzie would think it was a horrible idea.

"A parade? With a band?"

"Yes, and floats and mounted police."

Lizzie didn't answer.

"I know you think it's bad for me, but don't worry. I'm having the time of my life. And Pat, well, he's not all I thought he was cracked up to be. I need something."

Lizzie sighed. "I still worry every day you're up there. I fear you'll get in over your head."

"Why don't you and Docie come? You can watch the parade—whether I'm in it or not. You can keep an eye on me."

Lizzie chuckled but sighed. "I'll never travel that far. Docie still ain't decided what she wants from life, and she's been out of school three years. She's all over the place." Docie had started two courses—a teaching certificate and a secretarial course—but quit after a few weeks both times. "I make her help out with the kids, and when she gets to be too much, the laundry girls remind her how good she has it. Anyway, she can't come up there alone. She'd probably forget to get off the train." She snorted.

Her mention of laundry reminded Mattie. "Listen," she said. "This young girl, only seventeen, and—sorry, I know this will upset you— but her stepfather is determined to have his way, and she has nowhere to go. The mother is no help. If I could, I'd take her in a heartbeat."

Lizzie's reply sounded choked. "I'll tell Nettie. But if she ain't already ruined, we ain't going to have room—makes me sick to think of it."

Before they disconnected, she said, "I do wish we could see you, and I hope you win. I'll picture you in your fancy dress, and you picture us waving at the curb."

Mattie swallowed a lump at Lizzie's encouragement, even over something she didn't quite approve. Lizzie was the best sister she'd ever had. Mattie swore she was going to make it to a Homecoming if it killed her. She needed to see them, badly.

Later that week, Mrs. Nettie sent a note. *"Dear Mattie,"* the matron wrote.

> *I send this with deepest regrets. We still lack funds for a new dormitory, and we have more requests than beds. Unfortunately, we cannot take your young friend. Please let me know if the situation escalates. She's in our prayers.*

Mattie considered all the pennies workers would pour into votes for one short day of amusements. People weren't as generous when it came to helping a girl in danger.

CATE

Arlington, Texas
2017

Laurel has no plans for Christmas Eve, but she asks if I'll attend midnight mass with her at the nearby Catholic church. I've never been inside one. When I was growing up, we had been given the distinct impression that Catholics did not practice the right theology and that they were going to hell for it.

Now I'm not sure who has the right answers. All I know is it's rarely me.

Laurel says wistfully that she always attended mass with her family, even through all their tumult. Christmas Eve won't feel the same this year.

"Are you sure you don't want to call your mom?" I say.

She looks at me. "Do you want to call *your* mom?"

Touché. I haven't spoken to my parents since the day I walked away, except once for information I needed for declaring independence for financial aid. My mother sounded horribly sad, but she didn't ask about my new life, and that was how I knew nothing had changed.

In my imagination, a Catholic Christmas Eve service is filled with mystery and incense and harmonious families singing Christmas hymns in a beautifully darkened and candlelit sanctuary. It turns out that at midnight, the lights still glare, as if to keep everyone awake. Bored teens sit alongside sleepy parents, and they recite the liturgy, rising and kneeling by rote. Some stare curiously as I try to follow. Eventually Laurel tells me to stay put. I'm distracting everyone, she whispers with a smile.

Still, I sense the camaraderie among these people crowded together to celebrate. I may never return to a church of my own, but I miss certain things—especially the sense of a family bigger than the biological definition—even though my family, by both definitions, failed me completely.

Near the end, when a handbell choir plays *"Adeste Fideles,"* the English lyrics threaten to escape my mouth. *Oh, Come, All Ye Faithful!*

My eyes prickle, and I stare at the brass lights and elaborate carvings in the ceiling. I inhale the sharp scent of the handbell gloves again, and feel them, dry and bulky between my fingers. I reach toward a stubborn tickle on my cheek and my sharp, naked nail surprises me, even as the Latin lyrics, which we learned in youth choir, come back easily . . .

Venite adoramus, venite adoramus . . .

After mass, we dash inside a coffee shop open twenty four hours a day year-round for hot chocolate to go. I remember Thanksgiving and tense up. I'm thankful Laurel had the nerve to come to my door, and I can't stand the thought of messing up again. I'm convinced I will at some point.

We've had a rare fall of snow, not enough to keep drivers off the roads, but enough to coat everything with a thick, fine dust that makes the sky and earth appear lighter than they are.

All is calm; all is bright . . .

We sit in the parking lot sipping from cardboard.

"Don't you want to find River again?"

I sigh. I haven't quite finished my story. I tell her now about seeing River at the concert—and about ignoring Angela's messages since.

I will call Angela, but not until spring. Small steps.

"I don't know if I can handle that much," I say. "Who knows what River's like now. Maybe she's in a relationship. Maybe she's married." I shrug, as if it doesn't matter.

Laurel scoffs. "I don't think she'd say what she did when she sang your song if she was."

This girl. She is too perceptive.

"I'm not telling you what to do, but if it were me . . ." Her words linger.

I start the car.

Christmas Day, I suggest a walk to the cemetery. I stayed up even after we returned from mass, continuing to write, and I'm spent. But fresh air sounds good. And I want to see the headstones again.

This time, while we're both in good spirits.

We tread cautiously through slush created by the snow that melted almost before the sun came up, reading the stones again. A tiny cat—not a kitten—comes out of nowhere, meowing plaintively, as if to say, *Hello, it's about time you got here.* She rubs against our legs, putting her nose to Laurel's when she leans close and pawing at my shoe. She's collarless and a little ragged, as if she's been outside a while. Maybe forever. But she doesn't scratch or nip when we pet her.

Laurel and I laugh at her funny face, split down the middle with a completely different pattern on each side.

"I wonder what her name is?" Laurel says.

"Maybe she's homeless," I answer. "Maybe she doesn't even have a name."

At the same time, we look at each other and our faces dawn in recognition. She may be homeless, but she has a story, like anyone or anything else.

"Dilly," Laurel says.

I nod. The first Berachah girl. It's perfect. Dilly follows us home.

MATTIE

Oklahoma City
1921

The headline was on the front page of *The Oklahoma Leader*'s late edition: "*SPIRITED CONTEST BETWEEN FOUR BLONDES FOR QUEEN OF LABOR DAY!*" Secretary Weyrich claimed the "Irish Princess of the Culinary Alliance" had sold thousands of votes already, and that the other contestants would need more than half a million votes to beat her.

He'd warned Mattie, but she still flushed from head to toe to see the headline.

Pat got huffy, just as she'd expected. He shoved away the paper he'd brought in and left her to serve supper alone. Mattie ran out to purchase two extra copies and carefully clipped the article—one to save, and one to send to Lizzie and Docie. They'd get a charge out of seeing it, even if they wouldn't come.

The next Saturday, another mention complimented her diligence in getting out to the local businesses. The article was buried on the third page, so Mattie carefully folded the paper and set it aside, hoping Pat wouldn't go looking. It was bedtime before he remembered, and he merely glanced at the headlines.

Two weeks before the parade, there was a final push, and then a huge crush at the Trades Council Hall to hear the results. In the last hour before the polls closed, the nominees and their fans canvassed the hall, soliciting last-minute votes. The room crackled.

By a landslide, Ina Mayfield, a vivacious young woman nominated by the railroad workers, won. Nobody was surprised, least of all Mattie. She didn't show even a sliver of disappointment. After all, she'd come in fourth and would still ride on the float. As a runner-up, she was expected to give a short thank-you speech, and with Mr. Weyrich's guidance, she'd written it ahead of time.

"The contest was for a shared cause," she said, reading from her notes, "and a successful campaign was all any of us hoped for. We are honored and thrilled with the outcome."

She meant it. The newspaper quoted her the next day.

From the podium, she spied Jim McBride, and he tipped his hat. Her face heated so much the audience laughed as the announcer commented on her bashful beauty. Later, Jim caught her resting against a wall, grateful the hubbub had subsided.

"What's this? A princess posing as a wallflower?"

She laughed at his silliness, but her heart raced. His gaze made her insides swoon all over the place. It was wrong, she knew—but her insides didn't follow orders well at all. During the last-minute push, she'd been flustered at the number of folks who said she had that McBride fellow to thank for their vote. Apparently, he'd been out in force on her behalf.

"Congratulations," he said now. "I hope you enjoy the parade."

"What are you after?" she said, her confusion no longer manageable.

He stood straighter, his eyes suddenly wary.

"I appreciate the nomination. It's been fun. But everyone says you were out drumming up votes for me. It seems a little . . . excessive." She paused. "Over the line."

Jim stepped back, his face coloring. He quietly said, "Mrs. Madigan, I sincerely didn't mean to make you uncomfortable. I was doing my best to help someone who seemed deserving. No offense meant. I'm truly sorry."

His words and tone were polite and kind. Not presumptuous at all. Mattie forced a smile. "None taken, then," she said. "I just wanted to be clear."

"You're clear," he said. "I know you're married. I'm not trying to interfere."

She was so flustered by then, she could hardly look him in the eye. She nodded.

But as he turned to walk away, he paused. "If you weren't married, though, clearly I'd feel differently." He doffed his hat and went to join the men from the local.

Walking her and Jeanette home, he maintained more space than usual. At their corner, he said, "Good night, Mrs. Madigan," the same as always.

After Mattie sent the clippings she'd collected, Lizzie replied:

> *Mat dear,*
>
> *Prowd to see you in news paper. Cant come, a coarse!*
> *Scared to show Docie. Shell be mad.*
>
> *Love all ways,*
> *Lizzie*

Lizzie had carefully penned it herself. Though her childish scrawl had changed little over the years, she could write longer notes now. The sweet mess only made Mattie love Lizzie more.

She wished her dearest friends could see the parade.

She wished Pat would stop being a heel.

Labor Day dawned with a slight cloud cover. A surprise—and fortunate—downpour overnight nudged the thermometer down after weeks of intolerable heat, though it was hardly enough to affect the drought. Mattie had dreaded sitting in the blazing sun for the close to two hours it would take to travel the parade route, as much as heat bothered her.

She'd been awarded fifty dollars for a dress at Kerr's, and she'd carefully selected one she thought youthful, yet appropriate for a woman nearing forty—and of the lightest, coolest fabric she could find. They'd tailored it and donated a hat, gloves, stockings, and shoes to match.

She pulled on her hose, careful to keep her toes from snagging the delicate white silk, then dropped her dress over her head. She studied her reflection in the mirror on the bureau, the largest in the apartment, and though she couldn't see her full reflection, she was pleased. She rarely took the time to look in a mirror.

The white lawn day dress fell just below her knees, with sleeves cuffed at her elbows. A sheer voile panel with tiny vertical pleats was sewn in at the yoke and neck and hung nearly to the hem. Peplum-style ruffles graced the sides and back of the skirt, and the sash, low on her hips and tied at the back, gathered it all just right. She'd never owned anything so exquisite.

Under her hat, her hair still shone, and though sometimes hard to tame, gentle curls framed her face. Her eyes sparkled and the face cream Lizzie had teased her over had apparently paid off. She glowed.

Pat would have to do up the last buttons on the back of her dress. She couldn't reach them herself. It would probably ruin the moment—for once in her life, she felt lovely.

Without warning, she envisioned Jim McBride at the curb, smiling and tipping his hat as she rode by. She shook herself. She had no reason to be thinking of Jim. He'd be marching, four units back from the queen's float. Chances were he wouldn't see her at all.

"Pat, honey," she called. "Would you help me? I can't reach my buttons."

He huffed and rose in the living room. He stopped at the door, and for a moment, she thought he might say something nice. He leaned against the door frame. "My fingers ain't any good on those buttons."

"Well, they're the only ones around, so they'll have to do." Mattie flirted with her smile. It did not come easy, but now and then she tried. He managed the buttons but ignored the smile.

He'd grudgingly agreed to accompany her to the starting point, though he wouldn't march with his local. She'd wondered if it was a show of loyalty, considering Ina Mayfield was from the railroaders. But he wasn't one for gestures and never even attended the meetings.

He'd turned down a seat in a section reserved for the families of the court. She'd been embarrassed to tell the committee she hadn't needed any tickets. Pat said he'd watch the parade begin, and then get back home—he didn't want to spend his rare weekday off in a crowd.

Downtown, Mattie drew on her white gloves, and Pat handed her up onto the float. The parade committee had festooned the platform with ribbons and flowers and outfitted it with a throne and smaller chairs made of painted wood. Twelve white horses waited under the shafts to pull the float. She'd never seen anything so elaborate—that it was partly for her seemed absurd.

A committeewoman pinned Mattie's sash, emblazoned with *Hotel and Restaurant Employees*, settled her into her chair at the foot of the queen's throne, and then demonstrated how to rest her bouquet in the crook of one arm, leaving the other hand free to wave.

Pat stood awkwardly at the side of the float until the woman moved on to the next attendant. "Guess I'll see you back at the house."

"You could come out to the lake after. It's not too late to change your mind."

He shook his head. "Not for old men like me," he said. "You watch yourself. Some fellow might get the wrong idea with you all gussied up like that. Don't stay late."

Mattie's face flushed hot, and she almost wished he hadn't come at all. Since she'd confronted him about his age, he'd taken to trying to shame her. It made her feel as if she were, once again, the girl disowned by her family all those years ago, though she'd never shared her whole history—and she wasn't even the one with former lovers tracking her down.

"I'll be home when I'm home," she said. "Don't bother waiting up." He turned away and stalked back toward the opening in the barricades, hands crammed in his pockets and his shoulders hunched to the front. He seemed half-embarrassed to be seen with her.

While the grand marshal waited for the signal to move, Mattie scanned the growing crowd for familiar faces. Suddenly, though, she noticed the committeewoman who'd arranged them whispering with another, who glanced at Mattie with a frown. Mattie supposed they were gossiping about her age—likely fifteen years more than the most mature girl on the float. She felt an odd twinge of sympathy for Pat to suddenly imagine that her maturity made her stand out. She straightened her shoulders and smiled at them both.

She'd won fair and square. She belonged as much as anyone else there.

But then the older woman waved down one of the representatives from the joint unions office and spoke close to his ear. He looked at Mattie too. Suddenly sweat trickled down the back of her neck and tickled the spot just between her shoulders. What were they saying?

They approached the side of the float where she sat close to the edge. The man cleared his throat. "Excuse me, ladies. We'll be starting a few moments late while we clear up a small matter. Sorry for the delay. Mrs. Madigan, may we have a word?"

She stared at him helplessly. She'd done nothing wrong.

The man leaned to speak privately, but she supposed the other girls were straining to hear. She shrugged and sat up straight again. "What's the problem, sir?"

"I'm sorry, ma'am, but there's been a last-minute inquiry into your suitability for representing the unions on the float. We just want to clarify something."

Were there rules for eligibility beyond active membership and current dues in each union represented? She hadn't seen anything. But the man showed her a small printed pamphlet—the rules of the parade. She supposed it outlined the costume and float contest rules. She glanced down at her dress. It was as modest as anything she'd worn in recent years—more so than any dress the younger women on the float wore today. Was it her age?

He pointed to the tiny print under the section about the queen and her attendants. She'd never noticed it. "See here, ma'am, it says the winners must be women of good character, with no known reasons for disqualification, thus."

She was unable to form a coherent response. To her knowledge, no soul in Oklahoma City knew anything of her past beyond the testimony she'd given more than a decade earlier at the mission. She'd told few details—mostly that she'd been desperate until she found a home at the Berachah.

"What's the holdup here, Mr. Hewitt?" a familiar voice asked from behind her. She knew it well enough, despite his usual quiet presence and their brief interactions.

"Why, hello, Mr. McBride. Pleasure to see you. Just private business between the committee and Mrs. Madigan. I'm sure we'll have it cleared up momentarily."

Mattie wanted nothing more than to slide off the cheap, painted chair and off the float and then to run for any dark doorway she could duck into until the parade was well on its way.

But Jim smiled up at her. "Can't imagine there'd be anything to clear up about our Irish Princess. She's an upstanding member of the Hotel and Restaurant Employees. Why, she doesn't even drink." He winked at her with his head turned just enough that Mr. Hewitt couldn't see.

"Well, Mr. McBride, we had a report that Mrs. Madigan has questionable history. That she may have been, for lack of a genteel way to put it, a lady of the evening before she came to Oklahoma."

Mattie gasped. Jim turned his head to study her but swiftly turned back to Mr. Hewitt. "That's impossible, sir. I've known her for . . . well, longer than I remember. Her reputation is as spotless as any young lady's on this float."

The other girls were staring at Mattie blatantly by now, but as Jim scanned them, along with Mr. Hewitt, several blushed.

"Mrs. Madigan, can you give us an honor oath that there's no reason you should be disqualified?"

Mattie kept her eyes steadily on Jim's as thoughts whirled in her mind. Cap's conception, even if out of wedlock, would not give her the shameful label, so was it possible her single and lowest moment had somehow been discovered? She couldn't imagine how. She'd never confessed to anyone but Lizzie how her second childbirth came to be—Brother JT had found it in his heart not even to ask. Lizzie would never tell.

Even so, would that singular act for money label her as a "lady of the evening" for all eternity? It had been one time, and technically, it had been broad daylight. "Sir, I have no idea why someone would say that," she said. "Of course I'm not . . ."

She couldn't even finish it out loud.

The crowd was restless. Teenage boys began to ball up programs and toss them into the street, jeering at the master of ceremonies, who shrugged helplessly on the podium.

"Mr. Hewitt, surely you should let the parade begin," Jim said. "Hasn't this caused enough stir—not to mention embarrassment for Mrs. Madigan?"

Mr. Hewitt nodded and stepped back with the committeewoman, who continued to look suspiciously at Mattie. Mattie felt a soft touch on her sleeve. She turned and Jim said quietly, "Put your smile back on and show them what you're made of." He began to move away from the float but then stepped close again. "Hold up a moment—turn slightly to your right."

Mattie had turned sideways in her seat to speak with Mr. Hewitt and had leaned so far forward in her embarrassment she was hardly balanced in her chair. She nodded to Jim. "Thank you."

"Not yet," he said, and carefully reached toward her back. "No worries, ladies," he called a little louder, "just a little spider. You won't want it riding along with you."

Mattie felt him pinch the fabric at the back of her dress with both hands, and then he straightened. "Just a few undone buttons," he said under his breath, and tipped his cap and walked away, leaving her with her mouth hanging open. He rushed toward the hotel and restaurant employees' unit without looking back again.

The parade began with an apology and a speech from the mayor. Mattie didn't take in a word, still reeling. She couldn't imagine who would make such an accusation—or why. She'd worked hard to get on the float—though perhaps not as hard as Jim McBride—and she tried to put it out of her mind once the other girls stopped gawking and turned their attention to the crowds.

After the master of ceremonies announced the court, their float followed the grand marshal and the police down Grand Avenue, accompanied by the first band. Waving to the crowd felt pretentious at first, but the spectators were so enthusiastic, it soon became easy—especially once the float was out of sight of the grandstand, where people had continued to gape curiously at Mattie.

Little girls jumped up and down, squealing, or perched on their daddies' shoulders to see the float. Mattie couldn't contain her smile to see how dazzled they were by the queen and her maids of honor. Nora had promised to attend, though her stepfather had refused to let her march. It was unbecoming, he'd said, and besides, she no longer worked for a hotel. Mattie scanned the crowd, and a thousand brown-haired girls in hats . . .

But then Mattie spied one so familiar she turned her head as they passed. The girl's eyes were dark, and it was obvious they were nearly black, even at a distance, in contrast with silvery blond hair. As excited as the little girls, she waved a fan and smiled so wide, her teeth flashed. She made eye contact with Mattie and clapped her hands and waved again.

Mattie tried to place where she'd seen her—maybe the grill, or perhaps one of the restaurants she'd visited for votes, but she didn't make the connection until they were half a block away.

Docie! She hadn't seen Docie in eleven years. She'd be twenty now, and the girl was exactly how Mattie had pictured her, though still so tiny.

Could it be? Had Docie and Lizzie come after all?

The young woman had stood between two men, however, with no Lizzie beside her. Mattie would have recognized Lizzie instantly, even after all this time.

She sighed. Her mind played tricks like that sometimes. She'd seen Cap in a crowd, holding the hand of a strange woman or playing in the streets with other children, sometimes still two, other times the right age. She'd wanted so badly to see a loved one cheering for her that she'd projected Docie's face onto a complete stranger. Mattie forced herself to keep smiling, forbidding the loneliness, even in this crowd, from ruining her day. By the time the float reached the final stretch, she was surprised. The experience had flown by. She would never forget it—for reasons good and bad.

A reserved trolley car conveyed the queen and her court to the fairgrounds, where they had their own private tent with drinks and refreshments and sofas at their leisure until the presentations began later. Most of the young women hurried away with their sweethearts or families. Mattie selected an iced fruit drink, content to rest. Though she spoke with her customers every day at the grill, and attended the local's meetings each week, the crush of so many strangers overwhelmed her.

But Jeanette had promised to find her, and soon the hostess reported she was outside—not just with the girls, but a whole crowd, who cheered as she emerged. They pulled her along to the stands, and for the next several hours, they watched the egg races, the potato races, the fat man's race . . . more races than she'd dreamed existed. Later, a representative from the AFL would present the diamond ring to Ina Mayfield and prizes to contest winners.

She'd agreed to wear her union sash all day, but now she wished she could remove it, even for an hour. It clung to her neck, soaked through. Cute little girls had approached her all afternoon, shyly asking her to autograph their programs, and even a few boys—though not nearly as many as the younger women drew.

Her feet practically cried out on their own. She climbed until she found a stretch of empty seats near the top of the stands. She collapsed, hoping she'd be ignored during the presentations.

As the AFL representative presented the queen's ring, Mattie sensed rather than saw someone take a nearby seat during the speech, and she glanced down the row. The profile was unmistakable. She nearly rose and fled. But when Jim McBride turned his head to smile, she found she couldn't—or wouldn't—move. He scooted until he was a mere foot away and apologetically offered her a bag of popcorn. Suddenly, she couldn't gather the steam to feel any emotion—appreciation or offense. She was finished pretending she wasn't intrigued. In so many words, he'd already promised to behave.

"I couldn't help noticing you up here alone, and I felt it was my duty, as a representative of the union, to see that you were properly escorted so as to protect your reputation," he said, his grin teasing her, at least in part. "However," he continued, "I'm certain you're equipped to handle any unwanted attention or accusations without my meager assistance."

Mattie laughed and tilted her head to study his face. Why did he still trail her when she'd made her feelings clear? Did something in her manner invite, or even solicit, his attention?

Jim, even in his banter, seemed genuinely concerned for her well-being, and his tongue-in-cheek acknowledgment that she could handle herself was both appeasing and appealing.

"Going out to Belle Isle later?" he asked. The man-made lake powered the electric plant for the trolley lines, and others had mentioned going after the festivities wound down here. There'd be a dance with a live band.

"I should get home to my husband, though I said I'd be late."

"He should have come," Jim said. "Who would sit home on a day like this?"

Mattie took a sharp breath and looked away, frantically searching the crowd for Jeanette.

But her decision came easy. She'd go to Belle Isle and leave when she was ready. Jim was correct. Pat was a spoilsport. She wanted a little fun, and he'd live with it.

"We should hurry," Jim said, "or the trolley will leave without us."

He held her elbow as they descended the steep steps.

In the open-air car, Mattie and Jim sat in a straight-across row, next to Jeanette and her husband. If Jeanette thought anything of Mattie and Jim arriving together, she did not cast even a questioning glance. In fact, Jeanette had hinted more than once that Pat was a stick-in-the-mud.

All the way to Belle Isle, Mattie asked and Jim answered. His history wasn't unlike Pat's. He came from Illinois. The railroads had brought him to Oklahoma. He'd been a track man until he learned he could make a better living managing rooming houses. It was easier on his back and legs too. He'd run a good-sized suite down West Reno from Mattie's the last few years and picked up extra money waiting tables. Jim was older, Mattie could tell, but nowhere near Pat's age. His graying temples and his skin had seen too much sun, but he was solid and strong.

Belle Isle at sunset was enchanting, with newfangled electric light strands decorating the pavilion. It was like a fairy tale, with Mattie's fancy white dress, the romantic setting, and a handsome man at her elbow. She ignored the gnawing guilt. She was with her local, enjoying the sights and music. No harm in it.

Jeanette and Travis came and went from the dance floor, only slowing to gulp lemonade—and, Mattie suspected, whatever Travis added from his hip flask.

Jeanette encouraged Jim to take Mattie for a spin, but Mattie shook her head. "I don't even know how to dance," she said. "I'd step all over his feet."

"Oh, come on," Jeanette said.

Mattie had not let Jeanette spike her lemonade, and her next decision was made in full control of her faculties, with full knowledge of what it would do to her. She thought of the dance Lizzie had gone to in Tyler, and the nightmare that followed.

But she was not Lizzie, and this was not a nightmare. She stood.

She and Jim pushed their way onto the dance floor, dodging a hundred other couples. Mattie was thankful for a simple box step, and that Jim knew exactly how to lead her. It came easily—except when she trampled his toes. He laughed.

Beyond brief instructions from him, they didn't speak. Her complete concentration was required to keep going in the right direction—and to keep her heart from pounding nearly out of her chest. When the song ended, Jim's eyes asked for another dance. They stayed. And stayed. And stayed again. After four or five numbers, many familiar from the films she used to see, she felt as comfortable dancing with him as she did mixing biscuits or stirring gravy until it thickened.

Kind of like home.

At one point, the crowd was so dense, they were as close together as she and Pat had ever been. At the same time, it seemed they danced alone. In the crush, it was as natural as breathing to rest her ear against Jim's neck—it hit right there.

She turned her face eventually, nestling her nose into the same spot, and he inhaled sharply, but let her stay. His thumb drew a slow circle against her palm. When the song ended, they continued as though the instruments still played. But then he dropped one hand from her back and unclasped the other from hers and gently nudged her away.

"I suppose that's enough dancing," he said. He guided her through the crowd, his hand at the small of her back.

He went for lemonade, and a lump threatened to close Mattie's throat. Though the musicians increased the tempo, she knew he was right.

It was enough dancing.

They ended the evening in mutual silence, neither mentioning the parade's delay. Jim lazily rested a cigarette between his tanned fingers, bringing it to his lips now and then. Mattie gazed at the lake. Moonlight shimmered against ripples stirred by a gentle breeze.

CATE

Arlington, Texas
2017

Two days after Christmas, Laurel bursts inside. "River's in Oklahoma City on New Year's Eve. You have to go!"

My chest tightens, my hands suddenly clammy. I've been stalking River's social media for days. "I can't."

Laurel's shoulders deflate where I've burst her idea.

"What about Dilly?" I say.

I own a cat now. A local vet scanned Dilly for a microchip and gave her the once-over and shots. We've watched for flyers, but the vet guessed she'd been on her own for some time—maybe not forever, but long enough. "Congrats!" she'd said. "Dilly's a beautiful dilute tortoiseshell. And she's yours."

Laurel has things all figured out. "I'll housesit while you're gone. And Cate? No more excuses."

Maybe she's right. Maybe it's time.

I'm nearly finished filling my notebooks anyway, and I want to see Oklahoma City. I want to see the places Mattie walked and worked. I need that closure, and it's a good excuse.

No matter what happens with River.

MEMORANDUM

DATE: September 5, 1921

TO: Mr. Albert Ferry, Printer for the Berachah Rescue Society

CC: Reverend J. T. Upchurch, Founder and Director of the Berachah Industrial Home

FROM: Miss Christine Collins, Assistant Matron of the Berachah Industrial Home

RE: Thoughts for next issue of *The Purity Journal*

To Berachah Girls, Wherever You Are

Dear Girls:

I was disappointed you did not attend Homecoming this year. Even many of you who live nearby were absent.

Mrs. Norwood asked in early March, "Whom do you hope to see this year?" I reminded her of every girl we've loved and the times we've shared, funny or sad, good or bad.

I thought surely we'd see Mabel or Bertha, and we'd all sing together. I hoped Joan M. would bring her famous pies. Charlotte has a new little son we still haven't met. And more than anything, I wanted to laugh again with Mattie. (Elizabeth missed her too.)

These and so many more still had not arrived by the time the benediction rang out and we adjourned for another year. We missed you so.

Remember, our upcoming Berachah Anniversary is May 20–25, 1922. Make plans to attend now!

Love,
Miss Christine

MATTIE

Oklahoma City
1921

Mattie eyed the stairs to the apartment and her feet slowed. Crossing the threshold meant leaving her enchanted day behind. It meant returning to real life, to Pat's apathy and escalating flashes of jealousy.

Jim had walked home from the trolley stop with her and Jeanette and Travis, and she glanced back now. He stood at the corner, still leaning against the signpost. The glow of his cigarette illuminated his hand as he lifted it for another goodbye. He knew she was looking.

Though he'd been as much a gentleman tonight as ever, and had done nothing more to encourage this than she had allowed, her heart was involved now. Unless she was reading him wrong, his was too.

Was this what it felt like, finally, to be in love? It was a form of infatuation, surely, but differed from the nervous excitement she'd felt around Cap's father. She'd fallen for Charley hard enough that she didn't argue—for long—when they fumbled in the hayloft behind her employer's house. Now she recognized the longings of a girl faced with the unexpected freedom that came with losing her mother.

This was something else.

She'd always acknowledged that her marriage was one of convenience, but so far, it felt more like inconvenience, for both of them. Neither of them was happy. Once again, she'd tried to soothe her grieving heart with a warm body that couldn't satisfy. When her mother died, she'd gone to Charley. With Mama Stell, it had been Pat. Lizzie's friendship had been the singular healthy choice she'd made when her grief was too intense to outrun it—both times.

And yet, there it was, her marriage. She'd solemnly committed herself to Pat in that courthouse in Guthrie, and if nothing else, she tried to be a woman of her word. She could no longer see Jim McBride, not at any time or in any context.

Mattie ascended her stairs with strong, if bitter, resolve. She'd remove her fancy dress and any thought of another life. She would be content with what she'd been given—a life of stability, even if it meant going through the motions.

As she neared the door, voices came from the other side—unfamiliar, but only in that they didn't belong here. She thrust her key into the lock, but when she attempted to open the door, it wouldn't budge. The voices cut off, and she banged on it. "What have you done to the door, Pat?"

"Aunty Mat?" a voice called softly from the other side.

Suddenly, Mattie remembered the young woman who'd caught her attention that morning. "Docia May!" she cried, practically falling into the room as the door came unlatched, with Docie dragging a dining chair away. "Docie! What on earth are you doing here? Where's your mama? Where's Pat?"

Her questions fell away as she ran to Docie and pulled her close, squeezing her petite shoulders in a hug she'd missed for eleven years. More than a decade older, but the same Docie as always. It had been her sweet girl waving after all. Docie was still tiny, barely reaching Mattie's chest, and she looked up at Mattie with shining eyes—but something else Mattie couldn't quite read.

"Aunty Mat, Pat's not here. Someone else is."

Mattie caught her breath, unable to believe Lizzie had changed her mind. Her heart thudded with delight, and she nearly had to sit in the chair Docie had used to block the door.

But when Docie tugged her into the living room, the visitor was huddled on the couch in a quilt from Mattie's bed, her hair in knots and her face streaked with tears and grime and terror. It was not Lizzie, but Nora.

Mattie rushed to squat near Nora's knees. Nora didn't speak. Mattie queried Nora with her eyes and a sick feeling in her stomach. Nora nodded, and Mattie pulled her into her arms. The girl buried her face on Mattie's shoulder and wept.

Mattie tempered the fury that threatened to erupt. She didn't want to scare Nora more. Nora needed quiet, and a sense of safety—for she *was* safe now. Mattie would not let the man hurt her again, even if she had to physically keep him away.

She patted Nora's back until she'd finally spent her tears.

"Can you tell me?" she said. "Do you want to?"

Nora leaned back against the couch and nodded. Docie had clasped and unclasped her hands, as if she didn't know what to do, how she was needed, and now she sat, balancing at the edge of Mama Stell's soft old chair.

"Edward sent my ma and little brother off to the parade today. Said he needed my help straightening the shop since we were closed." Nora paused to sob, as though she knew it sounded like a bad idea from the start. Mattie wouldn't scold her—as if a young girl had any say.

"It was fine at first, and I began to think my worry was nothing, but then . . ." She closed her eyes, and her pale face tightened as if she were experiencing it all over again.

Mattie stroked her hand. "You don't have to say any more. It's okay, honey."

"I'm not finished."

Mattie nodded. "When you're ready."

"He sent me to the storeroom to count supplies. I should have run when he came inside. I thought to, but he grabbed my sleeve. I decided to cooperate until I had a clear chance. 'What's wrong, girlie?' he said. 'You have nothing to be afraid of. I won't hurt you.' But he did . . . terribly."

Nora doubled over, as though her insides hurt even now. She probably ached physically, but more than likely, she burned so with devastation she could hardly stand it. Mattie had seen it on the faces of the girls at the Home. Some for different reasons than others. She'd seen it in the mirror. Devastation was a pain you thought would never go away, and sometimes it didn't. Sometimes you learned to live with it.

"I've got you now, honey," she said. "What happened *was not* your fault."

Nora moaned softly.

"We are going to take care of you. I'm so sorry I didn't help you enough earlier."

Mattie wanted to kick herself. Why hadn't she made another arrangement, even when the Home couldn't take Nora? Why hadn't she taken the child in, even if two of the men had to leave so Nora could have a proper room? The lost rent wouldn't have made a big dent in their budget. She'd been scared Pat would complain. She'd let another man make her most important choices.

But they all needed to do more. Folks were willing to spend buckets of money on silly parade floats and fancy dresses and places for fat men to race, for God's sake. She thought of the AFL representative, how he'd insisted the unions must work to improve conditions for every worker, whether American or in the world at large.

But what about these young girls, at the mercy of their bosses—some, from their own families—who took advantage when they had nowhere else to turn?

Who was looking out for them?

Brother JT and Sister Maggie Mae were a second line of defense, willing to take them after they'd already been destroyed. But only *after*. It was all they could afford to do. They were two people, with a small staff, and never stopped begging folks to give more.

Clearly, it was up to her—and many more besides. She'd vowed never to return to the local after tonight. But now she knew she'd attend more meetings after all, and others all over town, if they'd have her. If they could give up money for frivolous entertainment, they could dig deeper. They could raise money to help girls like Nora too. The AFL representative, she suspected, would approve.

The door rattled and Docie sprang up. She ran to press her shoulders into the chair, which she'd propped under the knob again, as if she could keep anyone out with her tiny frame.

"Let me in," a gruff voice called.

"Hold on!" Mattie hollered. She looked at Docie. "Was Nora's step-father here earlier?"

Docie nodded. "Nora pounded on the door, yelling for you. He was chasing her, shouting she couldn't run off. And that—that nobody would want her now anyway."

Mattie cringed.

"I didn't know what else to do. I let her in and tried to close the door, but he kept pushing. Finally, I said if he didn't leave, I'd . . ." Docie blushed.

"She hit him over the head with the chair," Nora said. "I thought she'd killed him at first, but he just stumbled around and then went off down the stairs. You scared us coming up."

"You hit him? With the chair?" Mattie struggled to even picture it.

Docie's face went redder. "I'm not sure what came over me, but I knocked him flat."

"Good girl, Docie," Mattie said. "Your mama taught you right."

She sighed. The pounding on the door continued. "That's only my husband. Let him in."

Pat got as far as the living room. He pulled his cap off and scratched his scalp. Mattie smelled him clear across the space. The fumes wafted as strong as if he'd bathed in booze. She suspected he'd been drinking for much of the day.

"Wha's all this?" he said, anger rolling off him along with the fumes. He was not himself—or, maybe, he was who he'd been all along. His face was dark with fury and he gazed at the girls as if he wanted to hit someone.

"Pat, it's just a girl from the union. And one from home—from my home. Come to visit."

"I know who she is," Pat said.

Docie interrupted. "He was here when I came to find you after the parade. He said to stay, because the fairgrounds were no place for any woman to go alone."

"That's true," Mattie said. "And it's lucky you were here for Nora."

Pat had done one thing right today.

"That other girl wasn't here when I left," Pat said. "We ain't running a charity."

Mattie kept her voice measured, for she heard a vague threat beneath Pat's words. "She was hurt. They'll both stay tonight."

"They will, huh? I figured your boyfriend would take up any extra space."

Mattie gasped, and Docie's head snapped up. Nora dropped hers. But Jim was not Mattie's boyfriend. And Nora didn't know how she'd spent the evening.

"Pat? Why would you say that?"

"I saw you tonight."

Docie's eyes suddenly filled with dread, and maybe guilt. "I was so worried about you, Aunty Mat," she said. "He said you'd been gone too long, and that he'd find you."

"The fairgrounds were nearly empty when I got there. Someone said the party had moved to Belle Isle." Pat hiccupped. That small movement alone made him grab for the wall.

Mattie knew by now what he'd seen. She didn't want him to say more, not in front of the girls. She cared what they thought. She'd worried about Nora this morning, before Jim McBride had distracted her. She should have come straight home from the parade and marched to the laundry to check on Nora. "Sit down, Pat," she said. "You're drunk."

"Don't tell me what to do, woman!" Pat roared, and he started toward Mattie.

She'd sat down close to Nora again, but now she stood straight up and stopped him with her glare. She wasn't scared of him. Not one bit. "I'll say what to do in this house," she said. "It's *my* house."

"I saw you whoring around with that fella. I warned him off, and he didn't listen. And you didn't listen. And I just . . . I just laid him out in the street." He puffed out his chest.

Mattie's face went cold, and she thought of Jim at the corner, still smoking his cigarette. Was there any way Pat could have physically knocked him over, as drunk as he was? Or ever?

"I was not whoring around, Pat. That's not fair. Jim's a friend. A gentleman. I've told you so many times, but you won't believe me. What have you done?"

"I know what I saw," Pat said. "You all cozied up to him, dancing, kissing his neck. That's enough for me. Not for you? Huh?"

Mattie gaped, furious he would say these things in front of the girls. And though half of what he said was untrue—she had not kissed Jim—there was enough she couldn't deny. Had Pat really hurt Jim? She didn't even know the name of the hotel he ran.

"I'm so sorry, Aunty Mat," Docie whispered. "Mama said I shouldn't come, but I wouldn't listen. I'm always making trouble. Now I've really messed up."

Her guilty tone startled Mattie into action. "Nonsense! You're a grown woman. You're smart and you do what needs to be done. If you hadn't, think what might have happened with Nora." She turned to Pat. "And you're a jealous old man. I should never have married you. I've regretted it since the day you fooled me into thinking we could have a real marriage. I've defended you long enough. You pack yourself a bag and find somewhere else to stay. This is my house, and I'm through with you."

Mattie's heart physically hurt from the force of her words. She needed to sit down, but she stood her ground. It was braver and truer than anything she'd said in her life.

Pat stared at her, shaking his head. He went into their room, and she waited, right in that spot. When he came out again with a small leather bag, she was there.

"How am I supposed to find a place to sleep?" he whined, as if he'd simply be gone for the night and she'd let him come home in the morning.

"There's a hotel on every corner in this town. You can find a room easier than you can find a penny in the street. I'll give you money if you need it." She'd continued to keep the books. He was hopeless with money and math—except for subtracting years from his age. But she gave him generous pocket money, never stingy like he was about everything else.

"Don't need nothing," he said. "But one thing you ought to know. You're right. This marriage ain't nothing. That woman at the fair? She's always hounding me. She's my wife. I ain't never divorced her." He chuckled, mirthlessly, mercilessly.

Mattie was now, without question, an adulteress. But still, she remained on her feet until he'd let himself out, clutching at the walls to stay upright, and then she sank into Mama Stell's chair.

Docie's and Nora's eyes reflected what Mattie felt—disbelief, disappointment, sorrow.

But also a strange kind of relief. They'd gone all the way to the worst places tonight and survived. They'd won, even if it looked as if they'd lost.

Now they'd begin the climb back up again.

Mattie ran a bath for Nora. Nora tested the temperature and shook her head. "Hotter," she said. "More." Finally, Mattie said she'd burn her skin to make it any hotter. She expected that was what Nora wanted, to erase all evidence of her trauma. Hot water seemed the only solution at this moment. But it would be a long time before Nora fell asleep at night without horror creeping in. Right as she began to drop off, it would jolt her awake again. Mattie knew. She'd shared that strange sisterhood of uneasy sleep with nearly all the girls at the Home.

Nora didn't want to go to the police. Mattie couldn't argue. They both knew it wouldn't do any good. Nora was a year over the age of consent at seventeen and not a victim of someone from another race. The police, who marched at the front of the parade, leading the rest of labor, disregarded most crimes against working girls unless there was a colored man involved.

Edward would say she'd seduced him, and in all likelihood, the police would take his side. Most painfully, so would Nora's mother. She had never chosen her children over Edward.

Mattie listened carefully outside the bathroom door for movement. The thought of slipping below the water, of allowing it to take her far away forever, had seemed soothing at one point in her own life. Somehow Mattie had fought through, more times than once. Nora would, too, but at first, she'd need someone to watch out for her.

Docie made up Mattie's bed with clean linens. Mattie would keep an eye on her there. When Nora finally dozed, Mattie helped Docie make up the sofa.

"You okay, honey?" Mattie asked. It was her first quiet moment with Docie.

Docie had told Lizzie late last night she was coming to Oklahoma for the parade, even if Lizzie wouldn't. Lizzie had been so worried about every little thing, for so long, that Docie finally insisted on making her own decision. Mattie ran her hand down Docie's trendy bobbed hair and imagined her journey wasn't the only thing she'd done without her mother's approval lately. She imagined Lizzie's terror, putting Docie on the train in the dark, before dawn. It would have been too late for her to warn Mattie last night, and too early this morning. She'd had to trust her daughter's intelligence and abilities.

Docie had written Mattie's address in two separate places, and figured, rightly, it wouldn't be hard to find the parade. She'd brought money in case she needed to pay for a hotel room. She'd covered all the variables. Mattie smiled, listening to Docie's assurance that she could take care of herself, and thought of all the other mothers who'd witnessed the same terrifying transformation as their daughters claimed their independence.

"Aunty Mat," Docie said. "I want to ask you something."

Mattie shrugged. Everything seemed laid bare now—practically in one day.

"When I went after that man with the chair, something happened to me, inside my brain."

Suddenly Mattie knew what Docie would ask. But was it her place to answer?

"I knew I had to help Nora, and I was terrified for both of us. I think he would have hurt me too. But when I hit him over the head, I wasn't seeing his face."

Mattie nodded.

"I saw Hugh. Mama's stepbrother."

Mattie sighed internally. Lizzie had told her that Docie had recognized the man, subconsciously really, when she fought him off in Tyler, but Lizzie had said nothing to Docie since to clarify their connection, afraid to give Docie a concrete confirmation of what she'd long suspected had happened when she'd left two-year-old Docie with her family.

"I saw other things, too, in my mind. Flashes of something . . ." Docie paused, shook her head. "Something *awful*. But it gave me strength I never had before. Enough to make sure Nora's stepfather wouldn't hurt her again—or me." She took a quick breath. "Aunty Mat, I'm almost sure my uncle did something to me like what that horrible man did to Nora, when I was just a tiny kid." Her brimming eyes asked if Mattie knew the truth—and if she did, for her to reveal it.

"Oh, baby," Mattie said. "Your mama always suspected, but she didn't want to interrogate you, or put horrible images in your mind if not. She worried it would make things worse if you knew for certain. She felt such guilt for leaving you when she couldn't care for you. She never left you again. Then you two came to the Home."

Mattie wondered if Docie would cry, or scream, or be angry with Lizzie. But she simply went silent, as if contemplating Mattie's words. It would take time to process.

Early the next morning, while Nora still slept, the operator put a call through to the Home. Lizzie had worried all night, she said, knowing something wasn't quite right. Docie assured her she was fine, then put Mattie on. After Mattie explained Nora's situation, Lizzie said, without any hesitation, "Docie will bring her. She'll have a home here as long as she needs it."

"Do you need to check with Nettie?" Mattie said. Suddenly, saying *Mrs. Nettie* seemed unwarranted. Neither she nor Lizzie were girls anymore, and it occurred to her Lizzie hadn't said it in a while.

"No. We'll care for her ourselves if we need to, but they'll take her. You know they will. Pray she ain't pregnant, but even if she is, she's safe here."

Lizzie's self-assurance startled Mattie. Where had the woman gone who asked permission for every little thing—the woman too nervous to leave the Home to see Mattie in nearly the most exciting moment of her life?

But then Mattie remembered May. And Hugh. And way back, when Lizzie had lamented for days after witnessing a pregnant colored girl turned away at the back door of the Home. Mattie had tried to help her see the light—they couldn't take a colored girl, the community would have a fit—but Lizzie kept on about it, more and more frantic, until Brother JT pressed his colleagues to fund a similar home for colored women, and Lizzie stopped being so morose. The Berachah Home for Colored Girls had opened that very year in St. Louis, and they often sent girls who needed it up on the train.

When it truly mattered, Lizzie made up her own mind and nothing could change it.

"I been thinking all night," Lizzie said now. "Docie's grown. Twenty years old. She has to start making her own choices, and I can't do much about them. Same as you and me. We made our choices and lived with them."

"I wouldn't call all of them choices," Mattie said.

"You're right. Too many was made for us. But that's why I want her to do what she needs to, nobody saying she can't, or that she has to be a certain way. All I want is a kind, sweet girl, and Mattie, she is. Nothing can change that. She always pushes right up to the edge. That's who we made her. Me. The Home. Maybe you, especially. She's independent and brave—more like you than me. Maybe she won't be scared to live a great big life."

Mattie sat with Lizzie's words for a time. They'd need to disconnect soon—this conversation would cost her another camera—but she had to warn Lizzie about Docie's epiphany, her questions, and what Mattie had told her.

Except Docie hovered close. Mattie wanted to tell Lizzie about Pat, too, and about Jim, firsthand, not leaving it up to Docie when she didn't know all the pieces. Didn't *need* to know all the pieces. "Docie, honey?" she said. "Will you check on Nora? Maybe . . . give me a minute."

Docie nodded and went to Mattie's room, quietly closing the door behind her. On her way, she dropped a kiss on Mattie's head. Mattie's heart contracted, so surprised and yet so thrilled to see how Docie still trusted her, even after all this time. Docie was still hers too.

Lizzie was surprisingly calm. She thanked Mattie for her honesty with their girl. She said she'd known it was time, a while now.

Then Mattie spoke quickly and efficiently about her relationship with Pat, what a disappointment it had been from the first. She told her how embarrassed she felt now to have been living with the man, thinking she was legally wed, while his wife still wandered the city looking for him. No wonder he'd insisted on marrying in Guthrie.

And then, cautiously, but with pleasure she couldn't hide, she explained about Jim. About how he'd been a quiet, constant presence in her life for months, never pushing his way in, all the while supporting her, knowing implicitly what she'd needed.

The way she'd felt when they walked. When they talked. When they danced.

Then she waited for Lizzie to judge her.

Lizzie was silent at first. But then she laughed, great big gales bursting up through her, and Mattie didn't even know what to think.

"You know," Lizzie said. "No telling how many women my Willis has married—likely more than Pat." She chuckled again. "Mattie, honey, you landed on your feet. You ain't married after all, and this Jim McBride, he sounds like he's your one."

Lizzie's simple logic made it perfectly plain.

"Promise me you'll give it some time," Lizzie said. "Make sure this man is what he says. If you waited this long for love, you can wait to marry him too."

Mattie walked the girls to the train station that afternoon. Nora was content to go, of course, and ready to follow the rules of the Home—the same ones, still in place after all these years. There was nothing for her in Oklahoma now besides bad memories, and she was thankful for a safe and welcoming option. She didn't seek out her mother to say goodbye.

After the train left the station, Mattie walked slowly back toward her apartment, past the building where the local met, along the same route she'd walked every Monday evening for months. As she reached the intersection where Jim waited each week to see that she and Jeanette made it safely back to their buildings, she wasn't surprised to find him. His eye was bruised, but not so dark anyone would notice it except her. He said he hadn't bothered to fight Pat. He'd let him get his punch in and go on. It hadn't mattered to anyone but Pat.

They stood at the corner between their two lives, and she told him what had transpired after he'd watched her walk away the night before—for the last time, they hoped. And then she told him her history, of her terrible losses, from Mama to Cap, and how the Home had taken her in without judgment, and then, about their subsequent and repeated grace—especially when she chose to give up her second child. That heartrending decision went completely against what he believed about mothers and children being together, but ultimately, Brother JT had understood she just couldn't do it. Even if they had their differences now, she knew she was still loved and welcomed by those who mattered most.

Hours later, Jim walked her all the way to her building, and waited at the foot of the stairs until she called out from just inside her door. She felt safe and secure, in all the ways she wanted.

Over the next few months, the two of them made a life. Jim was good with money. With the economy iffy, he suggested transforming her good-sized rooms into space for twice as many lodgers—still all men, for with Mama Stell's example, they tended to become her "boys," and Mattie's Place their harbor of good food and quiet rest.

She made enough money to render Pat's absence immaterial, and soon she gave herself the pleasure of telling Mr. Gaston to take a hike—but politely. She had no desire to move.

Mattie made good on her promise to herself. She went from local to local, organizing a fund for women left out in the cold for refusing their bosses, fired from their jobs for complying, or for becoming pregnant out of wedlock, regardless of their situations. She mentioned some details of her own story. Sometimes the union members listened politely, sometimes they jeered. But eventually, more interest in rights particular to female workers emerged—nearly always because the women supported that interest first.

Finally, in June 1923, twenty-one months after the parade, and after being granted an annulment upon confirmation that her marriage to Pat had indeed been a fraud, Mattie married Jim. Her new surname seemed appropriate. For the rest of her days, she'd be Mattie McBride.

Mattie went through her documents before they went to the courthouse and realized her papers were in messy order, replaced in haste. An old letter of reference from Brother JT was on the top, brought from Texas in case she'd ever needed to prove her time and work experience at the Home. Underneath was the pamphlet she'd pulled from the light pole in Fort Worth, telling what the Home did for erring women of any stripe—and saved because of its fateful part in her story. She pictured Pat digging through her papers at some point, seeking dirt on her as his jealousy intensified, but saving what he'd learned for the morning of the parade. She was sad, but not especially surprised to recognize that he'd been the one to tip off the committee, so petty he'd nearly ruined the entire parade.

Instead, it had turned out just right.

The wedding was small, just the bride and her bridegroom, with Jeanette and Travis for witnesses. Lizzie still wouldn't come, and Mattie didn't push. She'd see her soon enough.

For the wedding, she wore her white parade dress. She'd worn it the day she fell truly and irrevocably in love. And Mattie and Jim consummated their marriage, truly, irrevocably, and over and over again. If they practiced a little beforehand, who needed to know?

·∙⊰[PART FOUR]⊱∙·

לֹא לָכֶם לְהִלָּחֵם בָּזֹאת הִתְיַצְּבוּ עִמְדוּ וּרְאוּ אֶת־יְשׁוּעַת יְהוָה עִמָּכֶם
יְהוּדָה וִירוּשָׁלַ͏ִם אַל־תִּירְאוּ וְאַל־תֵּחַתּוּ מָחָר צְאוּ לִפְנֵיהֶם וַיהוָה עִמָּכֶם:
וּבַיּוֹם הָרְבִעִי נִקְהֲלוּ לְעֵמֶק בְּרָכָה
כִּי־שָׁם בֵּרֲכוּ אֶת־יְהוָה עַל־כֵּן קָרְאוּ אֶת־שֵׁם הַמָּקוֹם הַהוּא עֵמֶק בְּרָכָה עַד־הַיּוֹם:

*Ye shall not need to fight in this battle; set yourselves, stand
ye still, and see the salvation of the LORD with you, O Judah
and Jerusalem; fear not, nor be dismayed; tomorrow go out
against them; for the LORD is with you . . .*

*And on the fourth day they assembled themselves in the val-
ley of Beracah; for there they blessed the LORD; therefore
the name of that place was called the valley of Beracah, unto
this day.*

2 CHRONICLES 20:17, 26

CATE

Oklahoma City
2017

Oklahoma City in late December is cold and windy, though the snow that dusted the South and Midwest over Christmas is gone. I walk the entire length of the parade route, in a long loop around downtown. Some of the buildings that were along the route in 1921 remain, and I pause to read historical markers, then step back to imagine them through Mattie's eyes.

Finally, I contrast my walk around the downtown landmarks, still freezing even in my heavy jacket with a warm scarf around my neck, with how Mattie must have felt on an oppressive July day in 1933, and my eyes water.

The city tore out the trolley tracks decades ago, but they're laying new ones for modern streetcars. Soon you'll be able to travel the same area Mattie must have for more than twenty years. Humans move forward, backward, and forward again, like streetcars—depending on what drives us in the moment.

I save Mattie's block for last. Her building has been gone almost fifty years, but I want to see the spot. I walk south from where the original courthouse stood—where Mattie and Jim registered their marriage— until I reach Reno Avenue. I peer west, toward a corner where a rescue mission still stands, where Mattie must have spent much of her first years in Oklahoma. I walk east, past Myriad Gardens, with impressive modern art, water features, gorgeous things growing tall and strong, and a small ice skating rink, where children race to stay warm in the bitter wind.

I wait where Jim might have leaned against the old-fashioned light post, watching Mattie turn into her stairwell and climb until she was safely inside, and then finally, I arrive in front of the hulking concrete convention center. It looks like an alien spaceship that landed fifty years ago, swallowing up the beehive of activity that kept these blocks busy from sunrise to sunrise for nearly a century. First, as that brand-new city on the plains. Next, as an area booming with businesses below and housing above—not so different from the walkable urban areas everyone wants to create now. Finally, as the classic Skid Row of Oklahoma City, crawling with homeless people and junkies. I spy a young man behind a column, resting on a slab of cardboard until a security guard moves him along.

Tearing down buildings doesn't make the problems go away.

Right here, I think, standing on a broad sidewalk to the left of the entrance, leaning against a reproduction ornate iron post topped by a clock. Right here is where Mattie might have stood at the grill, turning eggs or bacon on the griddle. I look up and know with certainty that Mattie slept above me, though not precisely where her bed was located. I close my eyes and soak up the presence of thousands of souls who have flowed through this living river, in search of new lives, or in defense of old ones, including a woman who simply wanted to love and be loved.

All their stories resonate with me, but maybe Mattie's the most.

When I open my eyes again, the sun, just visible on the horizon, is sinking. It's time to say my goodbyes to Mattie, and hello to possibilities, old and new.

But first, I step inside a gift shop, surprisingly still open, to warm up before I leave. My eyes alight on two identical tumblers, ivory crystal-cut glass, filled with delicately scented wax. *Fleur de Sel.* Flower of salt. I pull out my phone. *A salt that crystalizes on the surface of the sea, forming intricate, flowerlike patterns that never touch the bottom of the pool.*

I turn one over. They're overpriced, but I purchase both anyway.

Mattie. Lizzie. I'll finish my notebooks by their light.

I pass several antique and junk shops on the way to my car. Their

Closed signs are all turned out, but I slow to gaze through a display window at tiny christening gowns and other vintage children's clothing. I'm drawn to a single toddler's shoe, resting on its side near two complete pairs. The leather is scuffed and the sole worn, but beyond a tiny stacked heel, the arch is nearly smooth—except for small scratches that look like they may have once been letters.

I swallow the lump in my throat.

At the Blue Door, parking is easy on the street or in the tiny lot, but it's early yet. There's nothing to see except this small building with, appropriately, blue doors. On New Year's Eve, the adjacent college campus is a ghost town. The local coffee shops are closed, and the only place lit up is Asian. Any other day, I'd grab some pad Thai, but food seems iffy just now.

Eventually, I park near those blue doors just as River should be taking the stage. I'm ready to see her—I think—this time, on purpose, with time to observe through my eyes and listen with my gut and heart. I check my name off an unattended will-call list—Laurel purchased my ticket before I even agreed to go. I slip down the side aisle and into the last row of folding chairs. The industrial space is all painted brick and concrete and exposed pipes. Music is the main thing, no loud drinkers or blaring TVs, and the sold-out audience honors the small stage just inside those doors with single-minded focus. The kind of audience River's music craves.

She plays songs I recognize from the CDs Angela purchased, dug out before I left and played on repeat in the car. She plays songs I've never heard, but they're as familiar as my own heartbeat. She plays songs I remember from twenty years ago.

I feel almost as if I should close my eyes to experience their full essence, but I can't take my eyes away. If I hadn't seen her the previous fall—or photos on her website, on her social media pages—I'd still recognize her. But I look through different eyes now.

Her jeans, frayed over suede moccasins, cling to hips that don't allude to the widening of childbirth, yet are softer than the lean angles of an adolescent. Her ivory blouse, loose, but collared and open to the third button, flows with her movements—a style I'd never pull off. I always admired that about River—her ability to wear anything with an ease I was completely missing. But I see now: Her style was already in place, even then. She's not so different now. Her golden-brown hair is pulled through a ponytail holder into a messy loop, and random strands dangle loose around her temples, her neck. A feather pendant rests against her collarbone. Otherwise, even her earlobes are free of adornment. She doesn't need jewelry. Hers is the simplest beauty I've ever witnessed, then and now.

And I may be looking through different eyes, but all I see is River.

At the end of her set, she places her guitar in its stand, and she says nearly the same thing she said that night last fall in the historic Oak Cliff house, mere blocks from where the Upchurches lived before they built the Home in Arlington.

"This is my last song. Thanks so much for coming out to listen to a simple girl and her simple tunes. I always finish with this one. I usually play, too, but tonight I'm a little shaky. A little uncertain. It's for someone I used to know, someone I always wish was around to hear it. It sounds silly, I imagine. The funny thing is, sometimes wishes come true."

River takes a breath and then looks straight into my eyes and sings the words she wrote before I even knew they were for me.

MATTIE

Oklahoma City
JULY 13, 1933

It was hot. It was so hot. Mattie knew she should take a break, try to cool off, but there was too much to be done. Friday evenings, the men with pay packets—not many these days—wanted a clean place to shower and rest for the weekend, even if they'd slept outside the rest of the week. Where she'd once had six beds, now there were twenty—ten, nothing but floor space. Thursdays, she had ten real beds to strip and double that many sheets and towels to get to the laundry and back by the next morning. The toilet and tub to scrub. Decide what to prepare for dinner—breakfast was easy, never different, but figuring how to make it stretch was a feat. Make a list and run to the market, find what she could afford to fill bellies—those who could pay, and those who couldn't too. Everyone came in exhausted and hungry. Food was their only comfort.

She'd sent Jim with a dollar to the air-conditioned theater downstairs to watch a double feature. He'd yammered and fussed, wanting her to stop working and go with him. It had been tempting, and holding hands with him in that cool, dark place—an irony, right down there while they sweltered in the rooms above—seemed like a dream. She'd said no, go on, there was too much to do. She was younger. Stronger. He'd had trouble lately with his heart beating out of rhythm. So he went on. And she got to work.

But it was just so hot.

By the time she lugged the linens to Henry's, then climbed the stairs again, it was over a hundred degrees. The radio said the temperature would keep climbing all afternoon—find shade, drink water, generally keep cool if you had any way at all. She laughed. As if.

To be honest, she and Jim were both a sight. She'd been coughing and sputtering all morning. Nothing would budge in her lungs. Lately, she'd had more and more of that. She couldn't catch a good breath. The doctor at the County couldn't tell her anything different to do, just kept giving her the same advice, which didn't help at all. And her stomach was killing her, though she'd gone through nearly a full bottle of BiSoDol salts in the last several days. In fact, she needed to mix a glass, but she'd been too busy to slow down just yet.

The last time she remembered being this hot—even hotter than that first parade she'd watched, followed by her first picture show— was the summer after she arrived at the Home. She'd been out in the field, her and Lizzie and a few others, picking cotton they'd worked so hard to plant and keep alive. That summer had been brutal for several reasons. But she didn't recall feeling this weak. Somehow, that sun beating on her, making sweat ooze from her pores like thick, salty tears, gave her relief from the grief she'd carried so many months. She'd welcomed the pain, as if it cleansed what she'd been unable to release before.

But not this pain. The heat and the pain were too much. After she mixed her salts with tepid water from the tap—it wasn't even a pleasure to drink the stuff right now, like drinking dirty bathwater—she sat at the kitchen table to make her market list. She sipped, hoping it would ease the place under her ribs that never ceased aching these days, bloated while the rest of her wasted away. She could never eat enough to feel full, but what she ate made her hurt more.

No surprise, what with the plain and simple stress of living. The economy was so bad, the papers screamed with the news of folks living in the most horrifying conditions anyone had seen in America. Mattie thanked her stars she and Jim had a roof over their heads, even if she couldn't predict how long they'd hang on to it. All Jim's careful saving had dwindled the last few years, and if they couldn't keep the business, how would they pay for the roof? The only reason they paid the full rent now was being on the relief—the same reason most of the men could pay for a room some nights.

So many were alcoholics. Selling liquor and alcohol had been illegal since statehood—but that didn't mean you couldn't get it. You could call a bootlegger and have it in five minutes, but raids were common—especially in this part of town. Mattie didn't allow alcohol in the apartment. A sweet shop had opened on the other side of her stairs from the grill, with patrons not strictly in the market for candy. Maybe not even for liquor. Bottle-shaped bags came out the door, but the owner sold girlie magazines, too, and who knew what else? Just being upstairs made her nervous these days. The vice squad could swoop in any time, tumble a place, then book folks on charges of running a disorderly house.

Her house was not disorderly. As long as they kept things straight, they'd be okay. But every time she saw the girls who worked in the candy store, she worried for them.

She pressed against the soft spot again. Sometimes pressure eased it for a spell.

The movement reminded her of Cap, and how when his stomach hurt so bad, sometimes the only thing she could do was push that same spot, rubbing back and forth, up and down, singing him the little song that soothed him a minute or two.

"Hush, little baby, don't say a word," she sang now, quietly.

It brought pain and peace all at once.

She'd been singing it to him off and on the day he died. Walking from the trolley to the Home, she kept telling him to hold on, sure someone could produce a miracle for her baby boy.

And when Lizzie found her and stepped off the porch for the first time since they'd brought her and Docie in, and she helped Mattie stand and took her to Sister Susie, Lizzie, too, had been sure. They'd saved her and Docie, hadn't they, nursing them back from the threshold of death to health so well they were nearly ready to participate in the life of the Home?

If they could do that, Lizzie had believed, they could surely help a little boy with a bellyache and a cough.

"Suffer the children to come unto me," Mattie remembered thinking, gazing at the portrait of Jesus on the wall as Sister Susie helped her undress and put on a borrowed nightdress.

Lizzie had held Cap in those moments, over to the side in that little rocking chair, and for that Mattie had been thankful. She'd had no idea Lizzie had only just recovered, but in retrospect, it hadn't mattered. What had mattered was Lizzie's knack for comforting babies, and Cap had relaxed in her arms, gazing up at her honest brown eyes as if he trusted her to keep him safe while his mama was occupied, and as if that mutual focus somehow drew the pain from his emaciated body into hers. Mattie knew, when she witnessed Lizzie's glistening tear fall upon Cap's cheek, tenderly anointing it, that the woman understood.

When Lizzie lifted her from where she'd collapsed on the lawn, she'd been grateful, but when Lizzie held Mattie's dying boy, it forged something between Mattie and Lizzie that the years apart had never been able to break.

Mattie raised her head from the table where she'd rested it a minute. She'd drifted in a dream of sorts, thinking about that day. She struggled to get her bearings—to recognize the water and grease-stained paper on the walls of her tiny kitchen, worse behind the stove where she'd boiled countless pots of beans and cabbage or anything cheap the last several years—bacon, when Lady Luck smiled. Mattie wondered that she'd ever dreamed of being a fancy hotel cook.

But this was her hotel. This was what she cooked.

Never let it be said that a man left her home hungry, she thought, and smiled. That was what they could put on her headstone when she died. She'd tell Jim later, and he'd get a charge out of it. She could still make him laugh.

They laughed every day.

She pulled up from the chair, grasping the grooved metal table edge with fingers and palms too dry for such heat. They should be wet and sticky with sweat. Instead they burned like fire. She shuffled to peer through into the bedrooms. The beds seemed different, stripped of wrinkled linens and worn blankets and the never-ending parade of men looking for a simple place to sleep, stinking of alcohol and rotting teeth, some worse, in clothing rarely laundered.

She blinked. Haze floated through the windows, which they kept open to try to get a breeze. The house faced the wrong direction for fresh air; mostly it was just the stench of the packing plants down the road that wafted inside.

But now . . . now, she catches it, just the hint of it . . .

And now, the beds are covered in pure white linens and the light from the window is clear. She's at the Home again, and she's so tired. She just needs a rest. She walks toward her bed, on the end, just down from Lizzie and Docie, and pauses to listen for the clamor in the distance. The dinner bell calling them to table. A child laughing on the lawn. A fallen girl singing the chorus of a hymn, in harmony with the creak of garments threaded through the wringer.

> *Grace, grace, God's grace, grace that will pardon and cleanse*
> *within . . .*
> *Grace, grace, God's grace, grace that is greater than all our sin . . .*

Lying on top of the soft bed, not bothering with covers—she's plenty warm on a nice day like this—she hums along, smiles at those roses on the walls, on the ceiling, because the girls need reminders of beauty, even when they've seen nothing but ashes.

Peace be with you. And also with you.

She turns her head, and her breath catches. She can't get a breath. But she's not afraid. At the door, she sees him, walking toward her, one arm outstretched, his yellow blanket under the other, just where she'd tucked it the day they took him away.

She sits up to meet him, leaning, tumbling, falling with him into a heap on the floor, and she clings to her Cap, making up for all the lost time and all the lost embraces.

I'm here, love, I'm here.

They rest. They're Home.

LIZZIE

Arlington, Texas
JULY 14, 1933

Lizzie was on her knees when the call came. They fetched her from the tiny stone chapel built in Brother JT's and Sister Maggie Mae's honor, said a man was on the line for her, waiting. She didn't have to guess. Mattie had said years earlier if anything ever happened, Jim had the number for the workers' cottage.

"Lizzie?" he said, and her heart sank.

She knew, before he even told her, maybe because of his tone, or maybe, as happened so many times before, because she had a sense of sorts.

Some would say it came from the Devil.

She would say that wasn't necessarily so.

She just knew, like twins knew, when something wasn't right with the people she loved. And she knew this time. It was why she'd gone to the chapel. Something had felt off this morning, and as was her habit, she went down to pray.

"What's happened?" she said. No *Hello*.

"It's Mattie . . ." Jim's voice faded, and Lizzie heard it catch, as if he'd choked on a sob.

"She's gone?"

"Yes."

Lizzie drew a big breath and released it in a sigh. "When?"

"It was the heat. She wouldn't listen to me. I knew she was sick, and she insisted she had to work. It was over a hundred degrees, and she wouldn't let me help. And now she's gone."

Jim went quiet again, though she could hear him gulping, swallowing, trying to be manly about his tears. She could just see Mattie, so stubborn, same as always, insisting that Jim take it easy, being a decade older and not so spritely anymore—even with her own bad health. Mattie had feared losing him after waiting so long to find him. Now, he'd lost her instead.

"She told me if anything ever happened, I was to let you know first," Jim said. "That you'd know what to do."

"Yes, you done the right thing. Me and Mattie, we had promises between us."

"She's at the city morgue. The ambulance came, but there was nothing to be done. She was already gone. It happened so fast, Lizzie, and when I found her, she was—"

"Stop, Jim, I can't . . . I don't want to hear it just now."

"It was terrible," Jim said. "Terrible."

"Please."

"I'm sorry." He exhaled.

"You'll need to bring her back here."

"What?" Confusion and maybe disbelief altered Jim's voice.

"She wanted to be buried here. I'll let the Upchurches know. There won't be any issue. But you'll have to get her to us."

Jim didn't respond at first. Lizzie reckoned he turned the situation over in his mind. "I have no money," he said, finally. "We're on the relief. Most of the men can't even afford the nightly rate for a pallet on the floor, and Mattie, of course, you know she won't—wouldn't—ever turn someone away. They always ask if they can stay on credit, and, of course, she lets them. We've got no cash. I assumed we'd bury her here. I knew she wanted you to know so you could come, though I'm not planning on a big service. We know a lot of people, but not so many we'd consider friends. And, you know . . . she hasn't been to church in years."

Of course she knew, but to hear Jim confirm it again made her heart hurt.

"Jim," she said. "She wanted to be buried here. Even though she done things they didn't like, both before and after she left, and even after she stopped going to church. This ain't nothing to do with her spiritual condition. It were a promise we talked about long before she met you, right about the time she went up there. More than twenty years ago."

"Maybe she changed her mind—"

Lizzie interrupted. "No, she hadn't changed her mind. You got to hear me on this. If you can't afford it, we'll pitch in. We'll figure it out. We have to."

Jim promised to call back that evening. Lizzie would take it to the Upchurches and determine how they'd get Mattie home.

First, though, she went to her room in the workers' cottage and sat before her desk, a little secondhand one Docie had bought and helped her paint so there'd be a place she could keep practicing her lettering, even if it was for her eyes alone. She clutched her pen and pulled her tablet toward her. *Dear Mattie,* she wrote . . .

Lizzie paused, her hand already cramped. She'd never write the whole thing today, or any day. It was too long. Too messy.

So she laid her pen on the blotter and rested her chin in her hands. She closed her eyes and talked to Mattie inside her head, just like she talked to God now, certain she would hear . . .

> *Though I done my best to be a good friend and sister, you never believed I could understand exactly the pain you went through after you come to the Home, or that biting pain you felt at seeing me with Docie, or that hollow ache when you held her . . .*

Mattie had always said Lizzie couldn't know how closed-in life felt for her. Like as if she didn't go off and try something new, she'd lose her mind dwelling on things too close to ignore.

But the truth was, Mattie never knew everything Lizzie had lost. Lizzie had tried her best to forget, and now and again, she woke and realized she'd gone a day and night without remembering, but those times were weeks and sometimes months between. If Mattie had known, she'd have asked how Lizzie carried on without losing her mind, or why she wouldn't want to forget more often. The second truth was, Lizzie had done what she had to. If it meant staying there all those years to be sure Docie was safe and fed and loved, so be it.

Even now, she regretted going off that time to try to help her people see the light—even if the Good Book said to—seeing as they'd tried to get her right back in the worst of places. She shuddered to think if Docie hadn't come after her—and if they'd convinced Lizzie she was worthless again. Brother JT and Sister Maggie Mae would have cared for Docie like their own, for Lizzie would never have taken her into that life, but her girl would have forever wondered why her own mother left her for good, just as Lizzie had spent a lifetime pondering how her mother turned her out again and again, caring less than if she'd been a mangy dog at the door.

But staying at the Home so long wasn't the first time she'd made a choice for Docie.

She'd *told* Mattie she was bad luck.

She'd held Cap, and he died.

Those puppies? Lizzie was sure she'd killed the runt, only trying to help.

Bea in the nursery? She'd rocked her one day, and Beatrice died from grippe the next.

Lizzie knew now it wasn't bad luck, of course, but just the way things happened. She'd held and cared for so many others over the years, her chances were always good to be where she was most needed.

Mattie had thought God was punishing her, taking Cap.

But if she were right, Lizzie would have been struck down long ago.

They both had their secrets. She should have told Mattie, but they never talked about the babies. Mattie never let her cross that line, not about Cap and not about Ruth, the baby she gave away. Lizzie had a line, too, but she never breathed a word of it, not even to Docie.

She couldn't bear it. She knew Mattie couldn't either.

Lizzie had birthed Docie in Indian Territory—Oklahoma now—going up in a covered wagon with her Ma and Hugh, who wanted to try for free land, only stopping to bed down at night. That kind of birth might have done some other woman in, but Lizzie was young and strong, even for all her shame.

Docie was a strong little thing too. Lizzie didn't know how she'd have survived otherwise—not from her own precautions. Docie fought from the moment she came, maybe before, when she curled in Lizzie's womb, for Lizzie never took care even when she realized she was expecting. She hadn't the energy. She knew her time was coming but no notion how to tell it from bellyache or weary bones. The first pains nearly knocked her flat. She screamed for her mother from the rear of the wagon. Her ma had gone to bank the fire, with Arch already asleep on his bedroll under the wagon.

Ma shushed Lizzie as she came rushing back and hardly helped her swing up to the wagon bed. Ma believed Lizzie could only blame herself. Willis had shown up enough that nobody else ever questioned if he was the daddy of the baby in Lizzie's belly, but Ma picked out the details after he ran off, of every man who'd used her.

Lizzie was the guilty one. Ma always believed it.

Ma said to stop her bellowing. The land grants were by lottery that time, but they didn't trust the Sooners. They had to travel sunup to sundown to register in time. If Lizzie didn't want Arch leaving her beside the trail, she was to keep quiet.

Lizzie didn't for a minute think her ma was lying, not that time. Lizzie was little more than a nuisance now that she was old enough to keep Arch off her. She'd been shocked they let her ride along, but Ma said she'd be another set of hands to cook or drive the team.

Lizzie gritted her teeth and bit her lips raw when each wave hit. She'd have done her Injun granny proud the way she sweated and grunted through labor, so quiet after that first holler she'd surprised Arch the next morning, sitting by the fire with a squalling little bundle.

She was lucky Docie came in a few hours, healthy and about to bust a lung with her wailing once she woke to cry for mother's milk.

Lizzie did her best to feed her, ignorant as she was—and with a ma less interested in her granddaughter than her daughter. Docie did the rest, her little mouth grabbing Lizzie's teat even as they slept off the birth.

The wagon rolled up to the Territory and it was hot as damnation on the plains, with Lizzie's lips so parched she feared her baby wouldn't survive. But Docie had proved to be the stronger of the two, determined to make her own way even when it wasn't strictly wise.

Lizzie had named her after a lady who gave her advice about birthing. Her wagon had trailed theirs until a broken wheel took them out while Arch repaired it. She and Lizzie walked a bit, near enough to feel safe from the Injuns, but distant enough for quiet talks. Her name was the prettiest Lizzie had ever heard, and she asked her to spell it out on an old bill of sale. *Theodocia*. But that was an awfully big name for a tiny baby whose mother couldn't write the letters. Her husband called her Docia. Lizzie had thought it would do fine for her scrap of baby girl. And May seemed pretty for a middle name.

Docia May Bates.

At least Willis gave her a last name.

They made it to the land office to register in good time. While they waited, Lizzie's folks dropped her at her youngest stepbrother's place, which he'd won in the earlier run—probably by cheating, though he'd generally treated Lizzie better than the rest.

Ma and Arch lost out on the lottery but didn't claim Lizzie on their way back to Texas. Her stepbrother's wife seemed to think she was some kind of threat. They'd be stuck with two extra mouths to feed. Maybe he'd told her how his brother and father had done her when she was younger, and she thought Lizzie had brought it on herself too. Or maybe she'd wanted to keep her husband from Lizzie's wickedness. Either way, she couldn't be shut of Lizzie fast enough.

So they put her out.

Lizzie and Docie wandered, staying first with a widow lady who said Lizzie could help her for their keep. But Lizzie was slow on her feet, with a baby to suckle. The woman didn't seem sorry to send them on. Before, Lizzie had always been in the company of family or acquaintances. She'd always had a place to lay her head, at least. Now she had a baby to shelter too. Her desperation that first night was new.

She found a deserted sawmill and thought to hide with her baby until sunup. But a man surprised them inside. He said he'd get a room in town in exchange for something to warm him.

Lizzie didn't blink, though it was the first time after Docie's birth, and she was not quite healed. He paid no mind—and said he'd keep them longer too. She could do for the baby during the day and keep him company by night. Docie rarely fussed, snug in a nest of rags in the little trunk Lizzie carried. As long as it wasn't too often, she could rise from the pallet where she slept with the man and see to her.

Joe wanted to go west. He left his wagon in town and they rode his horse to an Injun settlement. They stayed going on five months, through the worst of winter, warm and fed. The squaws welcomed Lizzie and the baby, teaching her curing and easy beading.

When they left, they went west to the mountains. They squatted half a year in an abandoned miner's hut, living on what Joe trapped or shot and what Lizzie grew from seeds from trading skins. Docie was more than a year old by then, and getting into things. Lizzie feared she'd fall down the old mine shaft.

At harvest time, they returned to the valley to pick cotton. Lizzie carried Docie in a sling on her back. She was seventeen and hunched over like an old woman.

After the cotton, Joe said they should head home. He came from a town not far from where her ma and Arch always lived, so she went.

Joe sold the horse for meal and supplies and to pay his brother-in-law to get a team for the wagon. He used Lizzie to pay for their keep in a section camp in the woods, and promised it was just the once. Four or five nights, he held on to Docie while the railroad men kept at Lizzie. Then his brother-in-law returned, and the horses pulled them to East Texas.

At home, Joe had a wife, a grown daughter, and a son barely older than Docie. The wife was no more surprised to see Lizzie than Lizzie was to see her. With her husband gone most of a year, she likely reckoned he'd been up to something, but Joe promised Lizzie would earn her keep.

He didn't sleep with Lizzie right out like he'd done before, but he didn't hide his noise when he came to her. The wife's corner stayed quiet. Lizzie tried not to be in the way, though Docie played with Joe's son. Once the wife figured out Docie wasn't Joe's, she was inclined to be civil, pretending Lizzie was household help. If she heard Joe's noise at night, she didn't say.

Three months on, Lizzie realized she was expecting again—she'd weaned Docie except for night, when she needed her quiet, but the blood hadn't come in two months. She kept it secret until it was impossible to ignore the bump, even when she tied her apron high.

Joe didn't say anything at first. But one day Lizzie was sweeping, and he said it was past time for them to move along. He gave her a dollar to get to her aunt's in Longview, not far away.

That began the true test of Lizzie's will to keep her babies alive.

Her aunt kept them a while, until Willis showed up out of nowhere and said he wanted her back. He took her girl, too, though he knew she wasn't his flesh and blood.

If Lizzie had stayed with her aunt, things might have been fine. She would have put them up as long as Lizzie pulled her weight. But she trusted that man again. Willis took them to a room over the saloon in Tyler. Her husband said she'd earn their keep by living in sin with the saloonkeeper or anyone he found in the daytime while Willis did odd jobs. He said if she did not do what the saloonkeeper wanted, he'd kill her and Docie too.

Lizzie believed him after how he roughed her up when he'd had a few drinks.

Her time came near and the saloonkeeper pushed Willis to pay cash for the room. Willis said he'd take them to her ma. Instead, he took them to a logger camp and told her to live in sin with the workers to get money. For the first time, Lizzie refused, though she feared he'd beat her.

Instead, he ran off and left them there.

Lizzie carried Docie, dragging their trunk, until they wandered into a section camp. A man said he'd drive them—if she did what she'd refused to do for her husband earlier. The man was more honorable than most. The next day, he took them to her aunt's as he'd promised.

Her aunt wouldn't take them again, so they took the train to the nearest station to her ma and Arch's, outside Tyler, where they waited on a ride. A man said he'd take them for free, though she had money from her aunt. He took them into the woods, and when darkness fell, he took them to an old boxcar. He lived in sin with Lizzie all night, and they nearly froze with no covers. The next morning, he dropped them within a mile of her ma's, but claimed he'd leave the trunk at the station. Of course, Lizzie didn't see that again.

Ma gave them a corner, better than living in sin just to eat or sleep with a baby coming.

After a week, she birthed a baby boy. He was pale and never had anything but a thin cry, and within a few days he took on a gray, waxy look, as if he weren't a real baby but a doll made of painted leather. He scarcely moved his little arms or legs or even his mouth.

Lizzie shivered that last night, pulling both babies as close as she could, Docie burrowing into her and crying to eat, their pallet far from the fire and her stomach empty but for bits of bread and gruel. Lizzie couldn't feed them both. She looked down at her baby boy and knew she needed to make him eat. But he would hardly take her teat.

And this was her third truth: She let Docie suck all she wanted.

She watched her boy's chest rise and fall until it stopped. When her ma got her up to help with the bedding she'd stained with her labor, she saw he was dead. She took him, and Lizzie tried her best to remember his features. In her mind, he still looked like that pale baby doll, still as stone.

Lizzie had no way to record the facts of either of her babies. Docie grew to know hers and had her records. But her little boy had nobody to keep track of his birth or death, and she was too weak to follow where her ma took him.

She didn't know where her ma buried him, or if she buried him at all. The day after Lizzie lost her boy, her mother drove them away and said to never come back.

Lizzie wondered, had she made the right choice?

When they came for her and Docie in the jail, she thought about him.

When they said everyone was worth saving, she thought about him.

She knew a guilt she'd never felt before, and she knew something new: She had to always try. But then, when she took Docie back Home, after she tried so hard with her ma again, she remembered the biggest truth. She'd learned it again and again.

Everyone might be worth saving, but not everyone can be saved.

Lizzie lifted her damp face the day Mattie died, recalling her mother's betrayals—each a knot in a long, impossibly tangled string. She took up her pen again and with her own hand carefully recorded what she hadn't before, not because she couldn't, but because it had seemed it wouldn't matter to anyone at all. She wanted it to matter. And she knew whom to tell.

> *Dearest Mattie,*
>
> *I gave my boy a name. You are the first to know it.*
> *His name was Benjamin Thomas Bates.*
> *And I will miss you.*
>
> *Love all ways,*
> *Lizzie*

LIZZIE

Arlington, Texas
JULY 25, 1933

Eleven days later, Lizzie glanced in the dresser mirror before she went downstairs, straightening her collar and fluffing her hair and wiping the smudges from her glasses, which she couldn't seem to keep clean—especially when she'd been crying. How could she hope to smile this time when the photographer posed them on the lawn? A bittersweet Homecoming day lay ahead, for Lizzie would stand without Mattie again. It was the day Mattie had longed for, and Lizzie's promise to fulfill. But, Lizzie wondered, how could she bear to see it carried out?

The day after the news came, Miss Hallye—now just plain Hallye to Lizzie—found her in front of the prints Sister Maggie Mae had framed for the parlor. Each showed versions of the Home girls, looking so much the same, yet entirely different. The variations might have been less obvious if one didn't know the stories behind their expressions.

Hallye had put a light arm around Lizzie's shoulder—the first time Lizzie ever recalled the woman touching her, except for the dark night in the cemetery long ago. They'd looked at the photographs together. Hallye quietly told Lizzie she'd saved her small salary until she could afford three plots near her mother's in Oak Cliff. She'd purchased three markers, for herself, her brother, and her sister, each engraved with their names and birthdates, waiting for the inevitability of time. She'd wanted to ensure that her final resting place was with her family.

After her first time out at her sister's farm, the Upchurches insisted she move into their home, taking the bedroom vacated by Alla Mae when she married, and she'd been there ever since. Fifteen years on, she still wondered if it was mainly so they could keep an eye on her.

In her opinion, there was a line to being part of a family when they weren't yours to begin with, she said. Sometimes the line was moved. Sometimes you moved it.

After her break with reality—and who wouldn't have broken under that pressure?—people tiptoed around her even more. But she'd grown accustomed to it. She'd come to realize being broken had one of two results: death, whether physical or metaphorical, or becoming stronger where you'd fractured.

She and Lizzie had both healed strong, in her opinion.

Two years ago, Mattie had finally turned up for a Homecoming, bringing her youngest sister's girl, who'd run wild ever since the sister died. The girl was in the sort of trouble they were accustomed to at the Home. Despite their abandonment of her and their long estrangement, Mattie's family had tracked her down, sure she'd know how to handle it. They were right. She'd known the Home would care for the niece she hardly knew, just as they'd cared for Mattie three decades earlier.

The day Mattie arrived with her, the photographer was making a current photograph of the girls—from the newest to the women who'd made the Home their own for years. Brother JT hoped to inspire their existing sponsors and newer readers of the *Journal* to dig deeper for funds desperately needed to carry on the work.

That photograph showed younger women, some glowing with pride and babies on their hips. It showed older women like Lizzie and Ivy Bernard, still putting foot after foot in daily service, years of experience and hard-earned wisdom plain in their expressions. It showed the children, many of whom Lizzie or Ivy had rocked and soothed while their mothers worked. In some cases, they'd been left at the Home, with mothers unable to save themselves but determined to give their children a better chance. The kids sat in clusters on the lawn, most with bright smiles and emerging confidence.

Docie was grown, trying to navigate a world that seemed, in ways, easier than the one that dragged Lizzie nearly to damnation before she washed up on the shores of Berachah, with Docie barely clinging to her fingers. That history had saddled Docie with quirks and problems that never quite healed—just as Lizzie had her own permanent reminders—and a fragile innocence that seemed implausible in light of it all. Lizzie had nudged Docie from the nest, finally, a few years before, but whenever she returned, it was as if she'd never quite left, a funny little bird who loved to make them laugh, but all the while, a sorrow beat in her soul that kept her from truly soaring.

In the photo, Lizzie grinned up at Docie, who stood on the wide porch railing, leaning daringly away from the edge with a smirk. It seemed Docie had no fear that day, or ever really—as long as she was at Home with her mother. Everyone loved Docie. Few could bear to correct her. Maybe it was a mistake, but her innocence was irresistible. Lizzie worried it would be the ruin of her eventually.

Or maybe she'd be fine.

It took convincing, but Mattie had stood close to Lizzie in that one, their final picture together. It felt right, though she'd been gone more than two decades, living a life not entirely approved by the Upchurches, or even Lizzie at times.

Maybe things had turned out differently than anyone had hoped—even Mattie herself—but she'd made her way. And she'd known to bring her niece when the girl had stumbled. Mattie might not have believed in everything the Home proclaimed, but she believed in what they did.

Now, two years later, the Home was struggling even more. In the Depression's vicious grip, everyone pretended to ignore the proverbial writing on the wall but quietly wondered how long the Home could stay afloat, and what they'd do when it sank. Their futures—all of them—had a murky horizon. The Upchurches wouldn't let them down, near-term. Nobody would go without a home, earthly or eternal, as long as Brother JT breathed. But keeping that vow for nearly thirty years had been tough. A rougher season lay ahead, no doubt, and their new lives might not be as cloistered or soft.

Still, they'd gather today for one more photograph. They'd post-poned the thirty-year celebration in May while Brother JT traveled. They suspected he thought it might be the last. The timing had turned out for the best, for Mattie was here again, though the circumstances were unexpected. Maybe, had they had the Homecoming in late spring, as always, she would have come. And maybe someone would have seen the signs.

But *maybe* was a treacherous word. In retrospect, it never did Mattie any good.

Docie whispered at Lizzie's door now. Lizzie walked outside, where her family, the biggest she knew, had collected to see Mattie reunited with her first and greatest love. Little Cap had waited in the burying ground under the faithful protection of an oak tree for nearly three decades, the tree growing tall and strong while he remained eternally two years old.

Lizzie would do this for Mattie. And for herself. She would do it for Cap Dewey Corder and for Benjamin Thomas Bates. She would never see her own baby boy's grave, but she would see that another mother— her dearest friend, her confidante, the sister of her heart—would rest next to her little son, exactly as Lizzie had promised when Mattie set off to find a life beyond the grounds that embraced him until she returned. She'd stayed away while she walked the earth, but she'd come home to him now.

Two stones would cradle the narrow box that cradled Mattie herself. An oversized rose granite memorial, commissioned by Mattie's husband Jim, and paid for by years of Lizzie's hard work at the Bera-chah Home, would read:

Mattie B. McBride, 1881–1933
Wife of J. F. McBride
Cap Dewey, 1902–1904

And nestled close, that other little one. It had been there twenty-nine years, with only one word engraved on its weather-beaten surface: *CAP.*

Lizzie stepped into line with the other girls, including Docie, the daughter she'd shared with her friend as best she could, and they carried Mattie. Covered by the promises of Lizzie, the Home, and the man who'd loved her, unfailingly and without judgment, Mattie was on her way to meet Cap there, beneath the sheltering trees of Berachah.

CATE

Arlington, Texas
APRIL 2018

I close the last of the notebooks I've been filling with words for months, writing and rewriting, page after page of the story I've pieced together of Lizzie and Docie, Mattie and her first and last true loves, and even Miss Hallye, with her hopeful, hapless stumbling, and maybe her very real secrets. Who will ever know?

Laurel knows I've been working on it—after she saw me lug the notebooks to my car when I left for Oklahoma City, she asked what they were, and I said I'd tell her soon. When I returned, I shared my therapist's advice and how the story had poured out of me, though I'd slowed as it came to an end.

What percentage of my version is accurate, I'll never know. I simply know I needed answers, on a real and metaphorical level, and if I could only find certain ones by answering them myself, by filling in the blanks around what I'd gleaned from the collection, from digging through decades of censuses and archived newspapers, and from hours of other research, online and in person, it was what I had to do. My only regret is, after all that, I've never found a single photo of Mattie—or at least, not one I knew was her. I'll never stop studying the photos for hints.

As I read through the whole thing again over the last few days, I was surprised how well the story flowed—how true it rang. Perhaps enough is correct that the spirit of what I've had to imagine suffices. Perhaps, eventually, I'll learn things that will contradict what I've merely guessed. In a way, it would be good to know. In another, I hope not. I'm satisfied.

Laurel will read it, and River, too, if they choose to. Perhaps it will help each of them know me more, over nearly two decades: my dreams, my nightmares, my frustrations, my fears, my nearly irresistible tendency to run, and finally, my decision—with their help—to face it all head-on and try to make it right again.

My own particular and unique version of making good.

The night at the Blue Door, after River greeted the rest of her fans, selling and signing her music from a little vintage suitcase while I waited over to the side, she came and stood before me, nearly close enough to touch, but holding back a fraction, as if she didn't know whether I would bolt if she came any closer. She'd watched me slip into the venue, almost sure it was me from the moment I'd entered, but certain by the time she sang the last song.

"No pressure," she'd said, smiling, "but would you like to get a drink and catch up?"

She imagined we had a lot to cover, twenty years on.

The sound guy had directed us to a pub open New Year's Eve, not as rowdy as other places, just off West Reno in Bricktown. I assured him I knew exactly where it was, and River followed me after she loaded out. She travels light, with a minimum of equipment.

Over craft beer and cider, we worked backward. It was easier to reacquaint over the new. She works in Austin as a software engineer—genetic after all—but travels often, playing venues like the Blue Door. Her music isn't really a way to make a living, she said, but it's a way to make a life. I told her about my library, where I mesh my love of history with a paying job, too—due, in part, to her influence.

She's been in relationships, some more serious than others, but only one ever hit her hard enough that she's never stopped grieving. "I haven't given up on it just yet," she said, looking straight into my eyes, and the hair on my scalp and neck tingled, but not from fear. From relief.

She wanted to know what happened, naturally, and why I'd abandoned our fledgling relationship without warning. She admitted her hurt and anger, but ultimately, she said, she knew that if I'd left, there had been a reason.

She'd known something was different when she detected my distance at school, but it was more obvious the day she met my parents—the ring missing from my finger. She'd assumed Seth and I had more in common than I'd believed, but it had surprised her anyway. But Seth stayed in town and married within a few years—River had seen the two in a restaurant when she was home for the holidays. She'd dared to hope then, but my car was never in front of my house, and I never called. She'd decided it wasn't about him, but about her.

I swallowed guilt, and said I was so very sorry—it had never been about her at all, but about my belief that everything was ruined beyond repair. Mostly me.

I told her about the night I was broken, and how broken I was for years, until the last year had necessitated critical healing. About Laurel, and the collection we'd bonded around—a community absorbed back into its habitat now, except for the little cemetery that still guards the remains of those with nowhere else to lie in repose.

"To think," River had said, "all this time, you've been exploring places and people who disappeared, and all I've been doing is writing computer code and playing my silly songs."

"It's true," I replied. "You really started something."

I wasn't sure I could talk about what I'd left out when I talked to Laurel, too—what I decided to do after the meeting with the pastors and my parents, after I took the money and walked away. I made a nonnegotiable choice the day I wrote that final entry in that leather journal. I wrote why I had to go away, and why I never intended to speak that history aloud.

Then I wrapped it up tight and left it at a broken altar, and I ran.

River said, "It doesn't matter. It was your decision to make then, whatever happened."

She didn't need to know, unless I wanted to tell. "We all have our things," she said. "This one's yours."

I'll tell her one day, I think. I'm not running anymore, unless it's

to relieve stress and feel the wind on my face. I run because I love to—
and I always end up back home.

As the dust settled around this history, River pushed her glass
away and reached across the table and placed her hand over mine.
I struggled to leave it there, under its warmth, with those rhythm-
callused fingertips against my wrist, the ones I'd kissed so long ago.

It wasn't that I was embarrassed or ashamed. It was that I knew I'd
never leave if I didn't break the bond right then, before I was too far
gone. But I also knew it already:

I'd been too far gone forever.

She had a gig the next night in Tulsa, and more over the next week,
and then she'd head back to Austin for work. She asked if, when it was
convenient for both of us, she could see me again.

We've spent the last three months much the way we spent those
three months in 1998—on the phone late at night, talking about nearly
everything, with the added convenience of texting and email. Every
few weeks, we meet somewhere in between. We stick to places where
the buildings and people are very much alive. And we haven't been
stopped by the cops for breaking and entering a single time.

This Sunday evening, she'll play and sing for a tiny congregation
of believers and skeptics who meet in a Fort Worth pub. She'd already
surprised me, telling me she'd recently become involved in a faith
community in Austin that accepts her exactly as she is, arms open
wide. Our many conversations about church had made her curious,
and made her search until she found one that would welcome both of
us, if and when the time ever came.

But I haven't decided yet if I can bear to accompany her Sunday,
even to see her play.

Today, though, she's coming to Arlington for the first time, and I'll
introduce her to Laurel, and to our sweet cat, Dilly, who fusses over
both of us like a tiny, obsessed matron.

After Christmas break, when I got out of my own head, I finally put
the pieces together. Laurel, in those same three shirts, with the overstuffed backpack and questionable personal hygiene, was as homeless
as Dilly. She'd been living in her car, or sleeping in the main library

under the guise of studying, too embarrassed to admit her financial aid wouldn't cover housing. Showering at the gym. Staying in the teen shelter when she was desperate for warmth. Sometimes, she admitted, she'd even slept in the Berachah cemetery.

I remembered the first time I'd seen her there so early in the morning, lying under the jagged tree. I also remembered telling her that so many secrets hide in plain view, waiting for someone to notice them. I was guilty of not looking for that one.

I spoke with the housing director, and Laurel finally has the dorm room I've assumed she was living in all along. She stays with me whenever she wants to.

I recently told Laurel to think about something: I'd like to legally adopt her. She's an adult, and she gets to make her own decisions, but I know she's going to need mothering for a long time yet. People might think it strange, but sometimes we need to make things official. If she says no, it's okay—I'll feel exactly the same. By choice, she's my one chance to be a mother.

Recently, my own mother contacted me. A simple note to my work email, easy enough to find online, saying she has many regrets and would like to talk, if I'm willing. She said it doesn't matter to her now what my life looks like—or whom I love, and that she makes her own decisions these days.

I remember when they called River's full name at graduation.

River Grace Wilder . . .

My mother's head swung up, her eyes full of fear, but strangely, no surprise.

My heart broke again, thinking of all the wasted years between us. I'm not sure we can make up for them.

Today, I have promises to keep. The first is just for me. I'm going to have one last good cry in the cemetery over my girls from the Home, for all their hopes and heartbreaks and miracles, now peacefully buried in the past. Then I'll walk into this glorious spring evening and enjoy it with my two favorite people in the living and breathing world.

My family. My Home.

Our story is there. It waits to be written.

The Berachah Industrial Home in Arlington, Texas, was dedicated May 14, 1903, by Reverend James Toney and Maggie Mae Upchurch, and closed January 1, 1935. Alla Mae Upchurch and her husband, the Reverend Frank Wiese, reopened it as an orphanage shortly afterward but were unable to sustain it financially long-term. The orphanage closed in 1942, ending nearly a half century of work at the location with rescued women and children. The Upchurches retired to Oak Cliff, where J. T. died in 1950 and Maggie Mae in 1963.

Approximately three thousand erring and outcast girls, more often than not with their babies or children, passed through the home, some only as long as it took to find new footing, while others stayed for years.

Mattie B. McBride, who inspired the character of Mattie, died tragically in the midst of a record heat wave in Oklahoma City on July 12 or 13, 1933, and is buried next to her son in the Berachah Home cemetery, with a stone dedicated to both of them by her husband, J. F. McBride. According to *The Purity Journal*, "Cap" Dewey Corder died shortly after they arrived in 1904. I took authorial liberty in imagining them both suffering from cystic fibrosis before the disease was formally identified—Cap with the severe form from birth, Mattie with the milder form that didn't affect her until much later in life. The real cause of Cap's death is unknown to me.

Maudie Elizabeth Bates, together with her daughter, Docia May Bates, who inspired the characters of Lizzie and Docie, lived at the Berachah Home for years. In spite of copious amounts of research,

I've never learned what happened to either after their last appearance in the records, around 1926, but I'd like to think they both found a happy ending. According to the theology of the Nazarene Holiness Church, Elizabeth Bates could have remarried in 1940 at nearly sixty years of age, when her husband died. He married her and deserted her when she was fourteen. He married at least three more times. The account near the end of this novel of Elizabeth Bates's earlier years and death of her son are a paraphrase of her own testimony from *The Purity Journal* with some details fictionalized.

Hattie/Hattye V. Saylor, who inspired the character of Hallie/Hallye V. Taylor, never married and retired after years of faithful service to the Berachah Home. She died in 1963, though her headstone in the Oak Cliff cemetery lists no year of death. The stone with no name in the Berachah cemetery is real, and local legend says she chipped her name away to avoid embarrassing rumors. Legend also hints at an affair, but I have no personal knowledge of one.

Real women and children who lived at the home inspired many minor characters. Maggie Mae Upchurch discovered the real May living in a burned-out carriage in Dallas and brought her to the home shortly after Elizabeth Bates arrived. The story of May's return after running way is imagined. The Refuge Cottage was real, created in the old barn for rehabilitating the hardest cases, and was Elizabeth Bates's vision. Before renovation, it was where she went to pray.

After changing hands several times, the land where the Berachah Industrial Home was located was purchased by the nearby University of Texas at Arlington. The lone reminders of the home's campus, which ultimately had around fourteen buildings, are the foundation of the small chapel and the cemetery, sometimes called the "Lost Cemetery of Infants," though several adults are buried there as well as babies and children. The cemetery was protected as a Texas historical site on March 7, 1981. Majestic trees still inhabit the surrounding park.

Cate's character came from my imagination. Some of her experiences, however, reflect those of women and girls I have known, through parenting and foster parenting as well as witnessing the underbelly of church politics as a pastor's daughter, former minister's wife, and lay-person. The reputation of the church has often taken precedence over the well-being of an innocent child or adult—most often, but not always, female. Like any human organization, religious institutions can be safe havens in some instances, and the opposite in others.

The Purity Journal was a real publication of the Berachah Home, originally called *The Berachah Bulletin*, then *The Purity Journal*, and eventually *The Purity Crusader*, all now in the public domain. I used *The Purity Journal* throughout the novel for clarity. Notes appearing as "Memorandums" in this novel are either paraphrased or fictitious, with two exceptions, reprinted from the journals: "The Prodigal Daughter," a poem by Hattye V. Saylor, and the set of thoughts from J. T. Upchurch in the April 15, 1905, Memorandum, compiled from several issues. My tremendous appreciation goes to the University of Texas at Arlington's Special Collections department, which maintains the Berachah Home Collection. This remarkable area is much as I've described in the story, with dedicated employees passionate about preserving the history they touch every day. A master's thesis by Cody Shane Davis entitled *Historical Archaeology At The Berachah Rescue Home: A Holistic Approach And Analysis Of An Industrial Homestead In Arlington, Texas* was extremely helpful in identifying some of the topography and physical characteristics of the Berachah campus.

While I remained true to the history of the Home and its inhabitants wherever possible, utilizing primary and secondary sources, including interviews with family and friends of the Home, they, as well as the other locales and historic time periods and events in this novel, are used fictitiously, with broad editorial license. Any errors in facts or references are mine alone.

"In conclusion, friends, let us look over the field, hear
the heartbroken cries of the lost girls of the land,
remember time is short, eternity is long . . ."

—J. T. UPCHURCH

ACKNOWLEDGMENTS

A host of publishing professionals deserve my gratitude for ushering this novel to publication. Wonder agent Elisabeth Weed has my deepest appreciation for patiently waiting as I set eight unfinished stories aside as "not quite right" before learning of a tiny cemetery in Arlington, Texas. She recognized I'd finally struck a vein of gold, and helped me mine it. Thanks also to Hallie Schaefer for keeping The Book Group in line, and Jenny Meier and Jody Hotchkiss for continuing to shop foreign and film rights. You've all made so many of my dreams come true.

Hilary Rubin Teeman, my incredibly smart editor, first at St. Martin's Press and now at Crown, pushed me to make this the best story it could be—and gave me the space to do it. What new world will we visit next? Editorial assistant Jillian Buckley completed my author questionnaire with my vague input while I was in a medically induced haze after herniating a disc while finishing the first draft (Sit up straight, friends!). She keeps the wheels turning. I may never meet my copyeditor, proofreader, typesetter, cover designer, or production editor, but these fine folks, as well as the publicists and marketing teams who will deliver this project into the hands of all the right people—thank you. To Crown Publishing at large, especially Molly Stern and Annsley Rosner Slawsky, thank you for giving me a new publishing home and another chance to work with Hilary.

My former publicist at St. Martin's Press, Katie Bassell, deserves unlimited kudos for driving much of the success of my first novel, *Calling Me Home*, affording me the opportunity to sell another book, even if she can't come with me to Crown. (Oh, come on, SMP, loan her out, please!) Katie, you're a champion and a friend.

Carolyn Smitherman has my eternal gratitude for sharing an article on Facebook about Arlington's "Most Haunted Places," where I first read about the Berachah Home (though I'll never believe the cemetery is haunted, but instead, graced by the presence of so many sweet souls). Local authors Tui Snider, Evelyn Barker, and Leah Worcester published several informative pieces that jump-started my research.

Our dear friend John Lobley graciously allowed me to ask many questions about cystic fibrosis, a horrible disease still in need of a cure. His son Sam, a talented writer and musician, lived valiantly until May 10, 2019, a week before his graduation from Tufts University, summa cum laude and Phi Beta Kappa.

Chloe Gropper is responsible for one of the best lines in this novel, which stood out for me the first time I heard it, as related to me by my friend and fellow author Amy Sue Nathan. It sums up, generally, what this book is all about.

Countless readers have sent emails and messages—and even real letters!—telling me about their experiences reading *Calling Me Home* and hassling me to finish another book until I finally did. Thank you for your enthusiasm and grace and for sharing your own stories. I want to especially thank Kristy "Bee" Barrett, Tonni Callan, Susan Peterson, and author Barbara Davis, four book evangelists who never stop telling the world about *Calling Me Home*. Librarians, booksellers, and book club members, you have kept me in business long enough to provide a built-in audience for my new book. Thanks, and please keep being amazing.

My sweet cousin and a voracious reader, Ann Lacy Ellison, in her excitement at finding it online, was the first to post the cover for *Home for Erring and Outcast Girls* on social media. I asked her to take it down because I wasn't quite ready to share. This is to my great regret in retrospect, as she would have enjoyed the responses so much. She was suddenly taken from her family and her vast world of author and reader friends on October 1, 2018, after a fast and furious battle with cancer. I wish, more than anything, she could have read this book. I will miss having the greatest cheerleader of all.

My critique partner, Joan Mora, has read as many versions of this story as my agent and editor, with patience, enthusiasm, and wisdom. Others have read all or parts of the manuscript—Emilie Boggs, Gail Clark, Margaret Dilloway, Heather Hood, Susan Ishmael, Jerrie Oliver, and Seré Prince Halverson. Each helped me navigate a difficult story to tell.

Heather Hood, who assisted me with research for this book from the beginning, was as taken with it as I was. She searched out details before I realized I needed them, visited the cemetery more than was strictly necessary, and loves the characters as fiercely as I do. We have a history of erring and being cast out together, experiences that have only strengthened our twenty-five-year relationship as foster mother and daughter, sisters of the heart, and friends. Even if you still don't love Miss Hallye as much as I do, how could I have done it alone?

My husband, Todd Kibler, listens endlessly to my rambling brainstorms and eureka moments and keeps the home fires burning while managing his own busy career. To all of my precious children and grandchildren and my extended family, thanks for putting up with my weird ways. Some members of our diverse clan may struggle with the story, but I know they'll always love me, for our family is built on acceptance and unconditional love. You guys are the best family ever, full stop.

University of Texas at Arlington Special Collections, *The Nazarene Archives*, Newspapers.com, the *Oklahoma Leader* archives, *The Arlington Journal* archives, and so many other resources, including hundreds of professional and amateur photographers, genealogists, and historians who have posted photos, family trees, and other helpful information online, made researching this novel easier and quite fun. The rabbit holes are real.

Those who labored and sacrificed to found and run the Berachah Industrial Home—the Upchurches, their children, the many workers and donors—are mostly gone, but I wish I could meet and thank them. I appreciate the Reverend Kay Lancaster, an Upchurch great-granddaughter, for letting me interview her about her knowledge of the Home and her family lore. I regret that I never managed to visit with her mother, Dorthy Nelle Upchurch Betts, before she was gone.

Most of all, here's to the Erring and Outcast Girls—all of you, past and present—who have persisted in the face of unimaginable adversity and fought for truth, grace, and acceptance. And here's to those who "fell," but couldn't rise again.

If not for these women, there would be no story.

ABOUT THE AUTHOR

Julie Kibler is the bestselling author of *Calling Me Home*, which was an Indie Next List Great Read, a Target Club Pick, and a *Ladies' Home Journal* Book Club Pick and has been published in fifteen languages. She has a bachelor's degree in English and journalism and a master's degree in library science. She lives with her family, including four rescued dogs and cats, in Texas.